BY CHIGOZIE OBIOMA
The Road to the Country
An Orchestra of Minorities
The Fishermen

The ROAD *to the* COUNTRY

The ROAD to the COUNTRY

A Novel

CHIGOZIE OBIOMA

HOGARTH
LONDON NEW YORK

The Road to the Country is a work of fiction. All incidents and dialogue, and all characters with the exception of some well-known historical figures, are products of the author's imagination and are not to be construed as real. Where real-life historical persons appear, the situations, incidents, and dialogues concerning those persons are entirely fictional and are not intended to depict actual events or to change the entirely fictional nature of the work. In all other respects, any resemblance to persons living or dead is entirely coincidental.

Copyright © 2024 by Chigozie Obioma

All rights reserved.

Published in the United States by Hogarth, an imprint of Random House, a division of Penguin Random House LLC, New York.

HOGARTH is a trademark of the Random House Group Limited, and the H colophon is a trademark of Penguin Random House LLC.

Map by David Lindroth Inc.

Library of Congress Cataloging-in-Publication Data
Names: Obioma, Chigozie
Title: The road to the country: a novel / Chigozie Obioma.
Description: First edition. | New York: Hogarth, 2024.
Identifiers: LCCN 2023036244 (print) | LCCN 2023036245 (ebook) | ISBN 9780593596975 (hardcover; acid-free paper) | ISBN 9780593596999 (ebook)
Subjects: LCSH: Nigeria—History—Civil War, 1967–1970—Fiction. | LCGFT: Bildungsromans. | War fiction. | Novels.
Classification: LCC PR9387.9.O2756 R63 2024 (print) | LCC PR9387.9.O2756 (ebook) | DDC 823/.914—dc23/eng/20231206
LC record available at lccn.loc.gov/2023036244
LC ebook record available at lccn.loc.gov/2023036245

International edition ISBN 9780593733820

Printed in the United States of America on acid-free paper

randomhousebooks.com

Book design by Diane Hobbing

To Adamma, who first called me "Daadi"
and to the memory of all who perished during the war

The story of a war can only be fully and truly told by both the living and the dead.
          —*Igbo proverb*

It is not easy to speak about Biafra—it was like the end of the world, of civilization. Half of the population was starving, dying, and most were too weak to even care about sheltering from the war going on around them. Writers and journalists who were there, like Kurt Vonnegut, would tell you that this war was of such scale that more small weapons were used within the borders of this small country than in the Second World War! . . . If World War I produced new diseases like trench foot, this war gave us new diseases like kwashiorkor and cancrum oris. The war was the reason the French doctors who were here formed Doctors Without Borders.
          —*Anonymous*

We can only tell the story of Biafra as if it did not happen, as a speculation or riddle, or something that may yet happen—maybe as a vision, as fiction, or a prophetic warning.
      —*Sergeant Isaiah Nwankwo,*
   Biafran 39th Battalion, January 1970

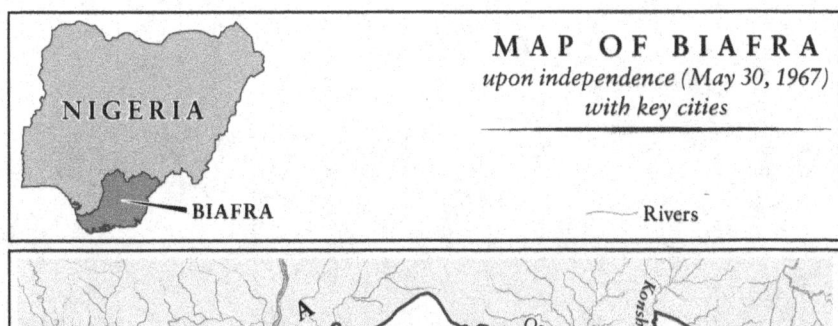

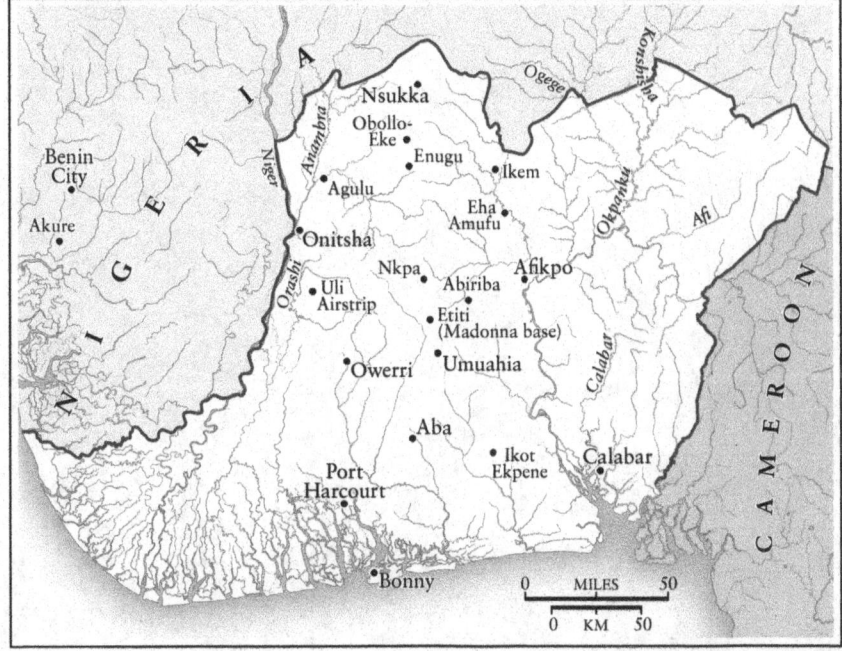

Cast of Characters

The following are the names of the people whom the Seer, Igbala Oludamisi, encountered in his eight-hour vision which stretched into the early hours of March 19, 1947:

1947—AKURE
Igbala Oludamisi, also called "the Seer"
Tayo Oludamisi (his wife)

1967—AKURE
Adekunle "Kunle" Aromire (the unborn man, subject of vision)
Tunde Aromire (his brother)
Dunni (their mother)
Gbenga (their father)
Uncle Idowu (Adekunle's uncle)
Nkechi Agbani (friend)

1967—BIAFRA 51ST BRIGADE, 1ST BATTALION
Felix, also called Prof (comrade)
Bube-Orji, also called Bube (comrade)
Ndidi Agulefo, also called Fada (comrade)
Ekpeyong, also called De Young (comrade)
Major Patrick Amadi (Battalion Commander, 1st Battalion)
Brigadier Alexander Madiebo (General Officer Commanding, 51st Brigade)
Captain Irunna (Commander, D Company, 1st Battalion)

1968—BIAFRA 4TH COMMANDO DIVISION

Agnes Azuka, also called Agi (comrade)
Rolf Steiner (General Officer Commanding)
James Odumodu, also called Inamin (comrade)
Taffy Williams (battalion commander)
Lieutenant Layla (officer, Special Commando Platoon)
Sergeant Agbam (translator for Steiner)
Captain Emeka (second in command)
Sergeant Wilson (platoon commander)

1968—BIAFRA

Chinedu Agbani (Nkechi's brother)
Ngozika Agbani (Nkechi's sister)

1969—BIAFRA 12TH DIVISION, 61ST BRIGADE

Colonel Joseph Okeke (brigade commander)

1969—NIGERIAN RECAPTURED TERRITORY OF IKOT EKPENE

Mobolaji Igbafe (soldier, Nigerian 3rd Marine Commando Division; Kunle's primary school friend)

Part 1

The BIRTH *of the* STAR

The road to the hills is tenuous in the dark. When approached in daylight, it presents itself as a straight path. At night it acquires a mystic character, appearing sinuous and much farther. But once the Seer crosses the small creek, the road becomes more distinct, glowing under the eye of the moon as if patiently waiting for him. The trees at the foot of the hills are thin and short, but their leaves—like those of all old trees—bear in them a provincial history of the universe. And now, having reached the summit of the hill, he stands in triumph. The star he has been following for much of the night has dissolved into a mosaic of colors—a bright purplish mass ringed with scattered archipelagoes of yellow and crimson. He stands under the fugitive colors of its light, teetering on the verge of tears.

The Seer unrolls the raffia mat first, then sets down the things he has brought: a silver bowl, a water-filled demijohn, an amulet of stringed cowries and snake teeth. With the weight of dreams bearing down on him, he empties the demijohn into the bowl. The water stirs, bubbles up, and settles, its dark surface creased with spots of bluish starlight. He feels an anxious thrill in his body, for he knows that he is inching closer to that moment when Ifa's vision will begin and he will bear witness to the future of the child about to be born. The Seer has done this ritual only twice before: once under the supervision of his master a decade ago, in 1937, and three years later by himself. He has come to these hills bearing the dignity of a transgressive, knowing that he seeks this vision in part to redeem himself. Since the death of his beloved wife, his life has been stripped of its purpose by grief, so that all he wants now is to someday understand what happened to her.

He clasps the amulet between his fingers and looks up at the horizon as it constricts, folding into the center where the prominent star he'd come to observe stands radiant. The star combusts in a spasm of light and falls, tracing down like a flaming spear. It comes to rest just above the hill, over the Seer's head, drowning him and the bowl in its bluish light. The Seer gasps, for he knows the meaning of this: the person whose star falls out of the sky and rises back up will be among the rarest of mankind, an *abami eda:* one who will die and return to life.

"Baba, are you seeing this?" the Seer says, pointing to the sky as if his master, dead now two years, can see it. For so long, he's been wanting to experience this galactic miracle his master had often spoken about, to bear witness to the vision of a life that will defy death. After twenty-five years of practicing astral divinations, he has beheld it.

The Seer throws the amulet into the bowl. The water bubbles, calms, the ripples spreading in a widening gyre. The Seer begins to hear voices—first distant and indistinct, as if worlds unknown and familiar are bleeding into one another from different times and planes of existence. Colors flash in his eyes as voices erupt, fade out, and rise again out of the chaos. All the while, he mutters incantations. Around him, the night thickens. Drawn by the strange light of the bowl, insects mob him, and bats flit about the surrounding trees.

The first images of the vision are grainy—like something seen through wet glass. But slowly it clears, and there appears the figure of a man in a room with a yellow bulb hanging from the ceiling by two colored wires. He is young, dark-complected, with a boyish face. The man is looking out the window of the room.

As if he has slid from the old universe into the vision's new, future one, the Seer finds that he can see the same things as the unborn man in the vision. He gazes through the unborn man's eyes for a moment, transfixed, awash in the light of this yet uncreated world.

1.

For the first time in nearly an hour, Kunle rises from the cane chair and looks at his wristwatch, then at the small bush outside. The rain, which had started shortly before he sat to write, has stopped now. On the soft earth closer to the window, a small bird totters, a writhing red worm clasped in its beak. He feels again the presence, the unusual sense of something, a thing alive yet invisible, watching him. He glances up, then around. But there is no one.

He begins to go through the "story" he has just written. At once he is surprised by how many of the details about the accident have remained in his mind, even after all these years. It was only this morning that he'd walked into the auditorium near the Law Building and heard a lecturer speak about writing to free oneself. He'd rushed home, picked up a pen and the notebook. And now, pieces of his childhood—blown in from remote corners of the past—are gathered in these few sheets of foolscap paper.

As he rereads, the details rise before his eyes in vivid colors: Nkechi, standing beside him, nine years old just like him. She wears on her face the beauty of youth; her hair is permed and ribboned, and her skin shiny with cream.

"Darling, let us send Tunde outside, oh?" she says, leaning into his left ear. "Let him not disturb us."

"Oh, okay," he says.

Nkechi whispers something else to him, and abruptly he turns towards the door as Tunde, only six, comes in swinging. Tunde tells them he wants stew, and rice, and goat meat. Kunle listens to his brother's chatter with half his mind as Nkechi steps closer, cups her hand around his ear, and says, "Darling, send him away—o? Mmhuu . . . Send him away so that he will not disturb us again."

Kunle leads his brother out of the kitchen to the yard, partly grassy, partly dirt. He picks up a small green football from the dirt and kicks it over the fence.

"It is a goal! It is a goal!" Tunde yells and runs out of the compound after the ball.

Kunle hurries back into the house and locks the door. He is clasping his hands around Nkechi in embrace when they hear Tunde's scream.

This moment was hard for Kunle to write—four lines on the foolscap sheet here were erased and rewritten, in some places twice over. But what he allowed himself to put down in the end is that he is confused, dazed. He runs in the direction of the scream and meets instead a small crowd of people. Tunde is lying on the ground beside an Oldsmobile whose fender has been damaged, doors flung wide open, and from whose rear a whiff of smoke is rising. Tunde's face is covered in blood, his hands thrown apart. "Tunde! Tunde!" Kunle cries, rushing forward towards his brother. He finds himself being pulled back by stronger hands as he kicks and flails, crying his brother's name.

Kunle puts the book down presently and rises as if new blood has been pumped into his body, stirring every limb with its fresh, hot life. What should he do with this writing? For a long while he stands there with these thoughts, until he hears a knock on the door. He looks about at his room and then, quickly, he dumps the half-eaten bowl of garri into the bucket under the table and tosses a dirty shirt behind the bed, leaving only a library book on the bed.

Uncle Idowu's belligerent voice follows the persistent knocking: "Kunle, have you gone deaf?"

At once, Kunle fumbles with the lock, opens the door.

"Alagba?" Uncle Idowu says. "What is the problem?"

"Am sorry, sa. I was asleep. I was—"

"Eheh—by this time?" Uncle Idowu says, closing the door and gazing at the clothes hanging on a blue rope along the wall.

"I'm sorry, sa."

Uncle Idowu sits on the sofa, his protruding belly looking like a big round ball.

"I don't even know if . . . What are you doing?"

"I want to go and buy you mineral, Uncle," Kunle says, glancing up from tying his shoelaces.

"No, no, sit down, Kunle. I am not here to drink Fanta or Seven Up. Your father sent me to give you a message."

Kunle sits on the bed, facing his uncle in the full glare of the evening sun.

"You have heard that there is war in Eastern Region, abi?"

Kunle shakes his head. "I've been—"

Uncle Idowu's eyes go wide. "What? You have not heard?"

Ashamed of his answer, Kunle only mutters "No" under his breath. His transistor radio has been out of batteries for a long time. But now it becomes clear to him that there were signs he simply missed: the first was of two boys in his class who simply disappeared—Igbo twin boys. Both were outspoken and raised several issues during the course on Nigerian history. Since the middle of the last semester, both have disappeared. And only two weeks ago, on his way to the hall to take his Law of Contract exam, he saw students protesting outside the vice chancellor's office, holding up banners that said things like NO WAR! ONE NIGERIA! END TRIBALISM!

"Kunle, do you know the meaning of this?" Sitting forward, Uncle Idowu pushes the sleeve of his agbada from his elbow back to his shoulder. "There is a war happening in your country and you don't know? Just imagine that!"

"I am sorry, sa."

"Turn a new leaf, eh—turn a new leaf, young man," Uncle Idowu says, reverting to English, the language he speaks when angry or tense.

"I have told you this isolation is not good, eh? You are a young man, nitori Olorun!"

"Yes, sa."

"Ehen, Ojukwu and his rebels have declared war . . . Anyway, that one is their problem. I am here because of your brother. That boy has vanished like a mist."

"Eh?" Kunle says, turning with the hurried shock of a snakebite.

"Oh, yes! Your father sent me telegram and told me. Somebody—his friend, a girl. Imagine small boy like him following woman into a war zone. A boy who cannot walk . . . who sits only in wheelchair?" Uncle Idowu sighs. "Children nowadays, eh! Can you imagine? . . . Sha, you have to go to Akure as matter of urgency—first thing tomorrow morning."

Kunle nods.

"After all, school have finished for this term, abi?"

"Yes, sa—since last Friday, sa," Kunle says and casts his eyes down again.

"You see? Almost three days since school finish and you are still here, eh? Don't you have family?"

"Not-thin, sa . . . I was . . . I—"

He does not lift his eyes to look at his uncle, knowing that he cannot admit that for the past week, he's been thinking of going home. But every time he made up his mind to go, he would recall the accident—Tunde being carried away, bloodied—and it would bring the fear of encountering his brother, of being faced with the reality of what he did. Instead, in the past few months, he's been writing letters home every two weeks—to Tunde. He did all his talking in the letters, usually about small things (the books he'd read, the history of English common law), but always, he ended each note with a plea—that Tunde forgive him. And each time he mailed a letter home, he felt relieved. But soon he'd become doubtful of the letter's efficacy, and it was this feeling more than anything else that kept him away from Akure.

Uncle Idowu hands him two one-pound notes. "That's your transport money, eh? Make sure you go tomorrow."

Kunle stands behind the door after Uncle Idowu leaves, pained by the fact that his uncle is right: he is living a hermitic, selfish life. For the last few days, he has been gathering up bits and pieces of his past like a mole, filling the room with images of his brother before the accident: the times they slept together on the same bed, when they played kantas with bottle caps or drew sketches of each other on the wall of their shared room, or sang with their mother. One of these memories stood out: the moment in '58, two years after the accident, when he overheard his mother say to his father that the accident had happened because Kunle was cursed: "It is a curse, surely . . . I have always known since the prophet came here on the day he was born. If not, then explain it to me how this evil would befall his own brother?"

For many years since that night, Kunle has lived within himself, carving his own small roads. He has no friends and has avoided—as if by some inner protestation—anything that could bring him close to anyone. He hadn't thought of this as a problem until the morning after the military coup in July the previous year, when he rode his bicycle into the streets, oblivious of the coup and the attendant curfew. A convoy of soldiers immediately shouted at him to stop, and in fear, he keeled over and the bicycle slid from him, its wheels spinning. They searched him thoroughly and confirmed that he was indeed a nineteen-year-old, first-year student at the university and not one of the coup plotters. From that morning onwards, he began trying to mend his life—visiting Uncle Idowu every two weeks and becoming friends with a girl in his class. But he soon found her talkative and overbearing. And when she asked him one evening if he'd ever had sex, he withdrew.

Now Kunle lies on his bed, staring at the yellow bulb at the center of the room. When he was a child, he often stared at lights until spectral worlds emerged from them and led him into wild landscapes of the imagination. He tries to imagine how his crippled brother could possibly survive a war, but he finds instead an increasing sense of unease, which keeps him awake for much of the night.

He leaves at first light with his belongings in his briefcase, treading with the rhythm of a thing severed from its anchor. He finds a crowd of Igbo people gathered at the motor park like refugees, some carrying a strange multicolored flag. At once, the feeling of something fundamental having changed in the world takes hold in him. It floats and eddies along the expanse of the five-hour bus journey to Akure, but once he steps through the gate of his parents' compound, the feeling settles. The gravity of what has happened is clear on his parents' faces. He has not been home in thirteen months—since he started university in May '66.

His mother looks older, patches of gray hair at the edges of her weakening braids and wrinkles around her eyes. She embraces him. His father—once a strict, commanding figure—now appears thin, his face full of hair. Small sands of sleep are nestled in both ends of his bloodshot eyes. He speaks with a tremble in his voice, as though he were not the same man who'd often wielded the whip. Like the accident, Tunde's disappearance happened so suddenly—as if the trouble had walked in on them in broad daylight with noiseless, black feet, and wreaked its wrath before anyone could stir.

2.

When he has washed himself and settled back on the couch, it strikes Kunle that he must find out more about what is happening—this "war." First, he notices that there are more photos on the sitting room wall: ones of Tunde's christening; Tunde in a red bow tie and suit at his two-year-old birthday; one in which all four of them pose with Father Christmas in December '54; one of Tunde in his wheelchair. Kunle turns away from the last photo, reminded of the day it was shot: in '65, only two years ago. Nkechi had insisted that her family take Tunde with them on a journey to their hometown for Easter. On the day they left, Tunde had dressed in a sweater and bell-bottom trousers. He looked the happiest Kunle had ever seen him since the accident. As he was about to be carried into the car, he turned to his parents and said, "I love you, Maami, Paami." And, glancing reluctantly in Kunle's direction, he said, "And you, Egbonmi."

"Do you think Tunde is in serious danger?"

"Eh—ewu? Do you ask a rat trapped in a cat's den if he is in danger? He is in the baba of dangers! I am not saying this with a small tongue. You have not been listening to news?"

His father says "news" in English, his voice tinged with quiet anger.

"No, Paami . . . Ehm, we have been writing exams, and I was reading."

His father groans, and begins to rub his hairy shins. "It did not begin yesterday. Our elders say what dies flatly on the ground remains more visible than what hangs on a hill. I have been following this crisis—from its morning till now."

His mother appears with a plate of boiled yams and sets it on the table between the sofas.

"As a matter of fact, we can say it began in fifty-three—yes," his father continues once his mother returns to the kitchen. There is a rise in his voice, which Kunle can tell comes from the excitement of being asked to showcase his knowledge, something he loved doing when they were children, staying up late to teach Tunde and him about everything from math to history. At such times, their father diluted his Yoruba with a smattering of English.

"That year, there was a riot, because northerners did not want independence to happen in fifty-six, but southerners said it must happen . . . Remember, it was the following year that Agbani and his family came to Akure—from, ehm, Kano."

Kunle remembers clearly: it was the first time he saw Nkechi, as she stepped out of the lorry that had brought her family from the north. Her skin was as fair as ripe pawpaw, and her hair was bound into an ordered braid. Perhaps to impress him, the girl had somersaulted right outside the Aromire front porch. Kunle knew at once that he wanted to be friends with her. For weeks, they drew together on their school slates, exhausting sticks of chalk. They nudged butterflies from roses and frangipanis, chasing them around. Their friendship soon blossomed in those days, to a degree that many years after Kunle stopped talking to her, he still feels her absence.

"After that riot, everything changed. Then . . . in fact, wait, I am coming back." His father returns with three recent issues of the *Daily Times,* all from the current year, 1967. He thumps them down on the seat beside Kunle and says, "In fact, everything is here."

Kunle's eyes skip across the headlines: "FORCE WON'T BE USED ON

SECESSIONISTS SAYS EJOOR," "FIGHTING BEGINS," "'I CAN'T CONTINUE TO GO ON MY KNEES'—GOWON WARNS OJUKWU."

He picks up the July 8 paper and begins reading, swatting insects away from the pages, answering questions from his mother halfheartedly, so that by the time he closes the last of the papers, darkness has fallen. His legs have grown stiff from sitting for hours. He rises once they come alive again, opens the door of Tunde's room, and stands looking at the fraction of the side wall illuminated by a splinter of light from the neighbor's backyard. There was a period before the accident when he and Tunde played the game of who could draw the other the best. In various sketches, Tunde made Kunle thinner or smaller each time, and he, in reprisal, drew Tunde with big eyes or without legs. For days, despite their mother railing about how they were defacing the wall, they'd drawn all over it, stretching as high as their small arms could reach.

One looking at Kunle from above can tell what he has learned about the war now. All night, the events take shape in his head. First, there was the bloody chaos of 1953 in Kano, in which southerners, especially Igbos, were killed and their properties destroyed. By nightfall, hundreds were dead. Next, a group of mostly Igbo officers killed many of the top politicians in the country one night in '66. The following morning, the nation (except Kunle) woke up to the realization that a decapitation of top government officials of the Nigerian state, most of whom were northerners, had occurred. Northerners flocked to the streets, ambushing and killing easterners everywhere—at schools, marketplaces, churches, train stations. In the following months, the mass killings of easterners had progressively built up to a pogrom, culminating in the July murder of the new head of state, General Aguiyi-Ironsi, an Igbo man.

THE BLUISH LIGHT of dawn is falling through the jalousies when Kunle wakes in the morning. Tense voices on Radio Kaduna are leaping into the air from his father's transistor radio. He lifts the curtain, props his back against the wall, and begins reading, half-listening to the radio. The door bursts open, and his mother appears in the sharp train of bright light with a cup of Ovaltine.

"Ka'aro, my son. It is Sunday. Hope you still go to church?"

He hesitates. "Yes," he says.

"Ehen . . . because God is all we have now. Gbenga, your father, is getting ready. Let us go and pray for your younger brother."

She sits across from him at the dining table on the other side of the parlor.

"Is your studies going well?" his mother says almost too loudly.

He hesitates. "Umm, Maami, it is doing well."

"Ope oh! Ehen, my son will be a lawyer?" She raises both hands to heavens, the bread knife in one, with crumbs of buttered bread on its serrated blade.

He sips from the cup and murmurs, "Ese, Maami."

He is surprised to find the church half empty. Usually, by this time, it would be full, teeming with so many people that the ushers would have to arrange the benches outside. Again and again, he glances at the rows towards the far end where Nkechi, her sister, and their mother often sat every Sunday, as if he can summon them out of thin air. From the lectern, the pastor's Ibibio-accented English is followed by the Yoruba interpreter's rendition:

"Look around you."

"Ewo awon ti o wa legbe yin."

"See how empty our congregation has become."

"E wo o bi ijo wa se di ahoro."

"Amen?"

"Amin?"

"Satan has risen among our people . . . he has set his camp among our leaders. Hallelujah! We are now divided. We say we were brothers . . . But now we are fighting our own brothers . . . Some of you here, the few of us southeasterners who haven't returned, are afraid . . . but you belong here . . . Nigeria is for all of us!"

The pastor's words—full of rage and sorrow—weave themselves into Kunle's mind, so that even during the drive back home, seated in the back of his father's Opel Kadett, he continues to contemplate them. They accentuate the fact of the war, this dangerous thing into which Tunde has been thrown and from which he must be rescued. He looks out the window at the long footbridge crowded with market people, the big UTC building under construction, the workers climbing up and down ladders, covered in white dust, like lepers. It has always seemed to him that the world was full of things; that even in one's loneliest moments, there was often a crowd. But the things one loved remained invisible, hidden amongst the multitudes he did not love.

He feels this even more now as they approach their house and he gazes intently through the window of Omoge, the modern hair salon where Nkechi's mother worked, at the women seated under the bonnet dryers. There is no sight of Nkechi's mother or any of her sisters. Again he wonders, what will happen if Tunde dies in the Eastern Region? Would it not be because of him?

He realizes that his mother has been speaking to him.

"Kunle," she repeats.

"Es-ma, sorry, ma."

"You still don't talk? Even though you are now in university, you still have not started talking."

"I . . . I talk, Maami."

She shakes her head. "How many words have you said since you came back? I count them on the fingers of my hand."

He turns away. He was once a garrulous talker who participated in spelling competitions and acted in school dramas. But after Tunde was taken to the hospital, Kunle had returned to the house in terror. For the next three days, he lay under the bed in his room, afraid that his father would punish him. For three days, he spoke to no one, beyond answering panicked questions from his parents. His mind circled universes of events, and contemplated fate, shame, fear, love, death, hatred, anger, revenge—all that man could experience. The days acquired a palpable darkness, and together they became the night of his life.

"I am thinking of how . . . how we can bring Tunde back," he says as his father drives towards the house.

His mother turns quickly to face him, a sheet of light on her face. "Eh-eh?"

"Yes, Maami, that's why I did not hear you at first. I am thinking of going to the post office to send him a letter so he can come back."

"Ah, omo mi! Shey e, wa she orire!" She dabs her eyes with the hem of her wrappa. "God bless you!"

Back in his room, he picks up the newspapers and is reading about the ongoing war between Israel and Syria when he hears his mother's shrilling scream. He finds her lying facedown on the kitchen floor, sobbing. Blood patterns the floor, creases the wrappa around her waist, and covers her finger. In the heart-pounding panic, Kunle's father rushes past him out the doorway and returns with cotton wool.

In the evening light, the sight of his mother's blood, the acid smell of some liquid gel, and the low mumbling of "Tunde, why have you done this to me?" stir in him an untamed sorrow.

"Go to the toilet, bring iodine! Quick!" his father cries.

Quickly, he rushes out the door. In the old chest, still lined with used medicines, he finds a black, empty bottle of iodine.

"Paami, no iodine!" he calls.

"Ah, what is there?"

He looks at a plastic bottle, turns it around. "Dettol! Only Dettol!"

"Bring it!"

They sit his mother down afterwards, the bandaged finger held above her head. Quietly she sobs, making her quiet plea for Tunde to return, to take away this misery. His father, now dressed in a familiar shirt and suspenders, asks that Kunle go with him to the pharmacy to buy iodine and cotton wool. They take the footpath behind Nkechi's house, past the dry stump of the big pawpaw tree that had been struck by lightning and is drying from the roots. The pigs are gathered near a waterhole, filling the air with low grunts and a dizzying smell. In years past, Kunle used to chase them with Nkechi's brothers—Chinedu and Nnamdi—and Tunde. They'd throw stones at the pigs to hear their screams, which often sounded like those of babies in grievous pain.

The air is damp, the edge of the horizon to the north reddening. His father's shadow extends up the path, his trailing behind. They have gone a few blocks when Kunle feels a rush of wind in his chest, against his heart. They are close to the colonial-style bungalow where Igbala, the Seer, lives. "This is why I told Idowu to tell you to come. She can't . . . she can't endure this *problem*. I know Dunni. She is no longer herself—"

His father stops to answer the greetings of a woman from the neighborhood who genuflects, a child strapped to her back by a wrappa.

"As I was saying, you can see it for yourself. When did your mother ever cut herself with a knife?"

Kunle does not answer, for he knows the question is a balloon in the air, to be caught again by his father.

"I can't remember at all. But just . . . just . . ." His father stops in front of the Seer's house, where a big boulder sits, half-concealing the house behind it. The sun, now a reddish blot in the far corner of the sky, illuminates the edge of his father's pitted and hollow face. His father meets his eyes, shakes his head, and walks on.

"That man who lives there," his father says with sudden fervor, "you remember him?"

"Es sa, eh, mo ranti."

"He said he predicted this war—many years ago." His father snaps his fingers a few times. "Oh, I remember now. It was nineteen sixty! *Independence* time. He came out and announced it in public. He predicted that Nigeria would divide. Oh, yes! He said, 'There will be war.' Can you believe it?"

They are now at the front of the pharmacy, behind a line of people standing on the small wooden bridge over the drainage pit that separates the pharmacy from the road. Shaking his head, his father repeats, "Can you believe it?"

For the rest of the evening, Kunle's mind is ruffled with many questions. He's been interested in the Seer ever since he overheard his mother admit that the man had visited on the day he was born with a message, but they had turned him away. Everything else he knows about the Seer has come from a boy in their church to whose father the Seer had made a damning prediction. The boy had said that to understand the Seer's ancient practice of divining the future through the stars, all one needed to do was to read the biblical story of the Magi who traced the star of Christ at his birth. After this boy's revelation, Kunle began plotting to visit the Seer's house and hear the vision himself, but he could not bring himself to do it for fear of what he would learn. One afternoon when he was sixteen, he let himself circle the boulder outside the house, pass a rowdy flock of chickens picking at grain scattered on haystacks, and walk up to the stone porch, where an old woman sat, naked to the waist, picking her teeth with a chewing stick. He greeted the woman by flattening himself on the ground in prostration, saying, "E ku asan, ma."

"Come closer—come closer and speak louder so I can hear you," the woman said. "Closer, yes . . . ehen, that is enough. Speak now—what do you want?"

"I want to see the prophet," he said.

"Eh . . . want . . . prophet?"

"I—want—to—see—the Seer!"

"Ah—I hear now, I hear . . . you want to see Baba. Who are you?"

"Adekunle Aromire! Ade-kun-le Aro-mi-re! When I was born, he saw a vision about me—"

"Baabaa!" she shouted. "E ma bo oh!"

When the Seer appeared at the door, wearing only a loincloth, Kunle felt an urge to run. But he stood there as the Seer came close, peering into his eyes, smelling of native concoctions—agbo, palm wine, dudu-osun.

"Is it you, Abami Eda?" the Seer said, blinking. "I have been looking for you for so long."

The Seer touched the side of Kunle's head, patting the tangled, uncombed hair, and said, "It has not yet happened." The Seer stood in front of Kunle, muttering incantations in a singsong voice—"Ifa, the spotless amongst all; pure white is your color. Langi-langi is the footwalk of the grasshopper. . . ." It was this: the familiarity of the Seer's voice and words stirred up fear in Kunle and caused him to turn at that moment, stumble past the flock of chickens, and run out of the yard. And he left without asking his questions, carrying instead a bag of new ones: Had the Seer truly seen his future? Could anyone see the future? Why had the Seer referred to him as one who defies death?

The house is quiet that evening, so his thoughts feel loud—like a band of tensed men in a shouting match. His father has treated his mother's finger with iodine, plastered it, and led her to their bedroom. Kunle drops the newspapers in the closet. Because of the things he now knows, he's resolved to turn his attention to the plan that is taking shape in his mind: to save his parents from this misery and, in so doing, redeem himself in their eyes. For over the years, he's come to sense, by some secret law of the soul, that he will someday be called upon to atone for his sin. All night, he turns the dice of possibilities about in his mind: How might he bring his brother back home? He stares at the still splash of light from the neighbor's porch resting on the window of his room, the dice spinning through the night. Then, just as he starts drifting to sleep, it suddenly becomes clear what he must do.

HE GOES TO the motor park early the following morning and tries to get a vehicle to take him to the Eastern Region. In the heat, between ululating voices and shouting drivers, he finds none. Two conductors loading a Greyhound bus for Lokoja tell him that the only way is to be smuggled, and this is risky. "E risky ga-an," one of the men says. "Person fit arrest or even sef, person fit die if you no be expert."

By the time it is noon, the idea has been beaten with many sticks and now lies paralyzed. He shelters under a towering tree, birds wailing through the cacophony of the park, wondering what he might do next. A wagon drives up the rutted dirt road, bearing the inscription P & T SERVICES HQR, LAGOS on its side. As he's watching the wagon, it occurs to him that the post office might have a directory of everyone in the Eastern Region. Perhaps he can find the Agbanis' address and send them a telegram.

An hour later, he is gazing at the familiar sculpture of an envelope outside the post office, an old building that—with its patterned bricks and stone porch—wears its colonial history like an ill-fitting mask. The last time he was here, a big Union Jack still hung from its front porch. They had come from church, and as they'd entered, five-year-old Tunde had stopped to stare at the life-size mural of the young queen of England, the thin white woman with a small delicate hat, waving with gloved hands. Tunde had pointed at the mural and said, in a loud voice, "Maami, when I grow up, I want to marry her." The hall had broken into a rush of laughter from the people waiting in line. An elderly British man had said, "Yes, young sir. And you, sir, will become the first Negro king of England!"

Now, as Kunle stands on the same spot, the initial idea that brought him here is darkened by the fumes of new thoughts. He rushes in the direction of the loading lorries and asks who is in charge. Can they smuggle him to the east? The manager, wiping his face with a wet handkerchief, regards him with strained bemusement. The man, clearly seeing this as a fool's errand, has little patience: "Twenty-five pounds. No addishan, no suprashan."

"Okay, sa," he says.

The man turns and regards him again, rubs his soot-stained fingers across his face.

"Four in the morning—four sharp!"

Kunle nods.

Four o'clock, like something he's anticipated for ages, arrives too quickly. He has barely slept, but he is at the post office at the set time with the money and a few clothes in a nylon bag.

"So, you have come?" the driver says in English, looking around as if to make sure no one lurking in the darkness has seen Kunle. His words are stitched together with thin, floating threads. "Do you have the money?"

"Complete, sa."

He stretches the money towards the driver. The man steps back and looks around again.

"Aburo, listen to me. Don't risk your life like this." The driver shakes his head. "Listen—you're too young."

One of the man's assistants turns off a battery torch, and now Kunle can barely see the driver.

"Aburo, I tell my wife yesta-day night because I can't sleep. She said it is bad to allow you to risk your life because of money . . . your blood for my head. War is happening, and even me, with government ID card, I am still afraid—"

"Sa, I know—"

"The soldiers can do anything."

"But I—"

"Go home or look for somebody else."

The driver mounts the lorry and, starting the engine, puts his head out the window and shouts, "Maybe go and join Red Cross . . . near Owode. Maybe they can help you!" The lorry lunges into the road, gravel grinding under its tires, and vanishes. Kunle stands for a moment, gazing after the lorry, then up at the horizon, where the pink hue of dawn is beginning to appear. Then, with the slow necessity of one burdened with a secret promise, he turns in the direction the man pointed towards, mouthing the words so he will not forget: Red Cross, Red Cross . . . Red Cross.

The Seer has been ecstatic at the miracle only Ifa can concoct: the miracle of a past not yet formed, but that is unfolding before the bright eye of the present. However, something in the last few sequences of events unsteadies him. He has seen the unborn man, Kunle, and his father stop in front of what is unmistakably his house, although he cannot recognize it yet. The Seer remembers that his master had spoken about wanting to make the place a sanctuary by having a boulder on which he could sit and divine the stars rather than making the twenty-minute trek to the hills on arthritic legs. Will he fulfill his master's wish?

The Seer is bothered, too, by the version of himself he's just witnessed—his badly wrinkled face lined with gray hair and his young, newly married second wife looking so old, shriveled and deaf. The loud burp of an engine coming from the vision throws him into a shudder. Rising from the bowl is a flurry of human voices. He realizes that the vision has continued, but he struggles to unfasten his mind from the unbelievable specter of his aged face.

He bends over the bowl again, but a thought like an insect bite props him upright. What had the young man's father said? That he, Igbala Oludamisi, would betray Ifa and reveal this vision to others for whom it is not intended? The Seer shakes his head.

"Impossible," he says. "I cannot disobey Ifa—lai-lai, my maker cannot beat a thorn into the palm of his own hand."

But wait—does he doubt Ifa? Does he think some things here won't come true if Ifa is revealing them as a definitive vision of the future? At this he shakes his head and pleads, "No, no! I can never doubt Ifa! Ifa is all, everything—life itself."

The Seer is sweating, his heart thumping. What is it that he has come to witness that has the power to destroy his loyalty to Ifa? Should he stop now? In fear, he raises his eyes, but the star is almost fully obscured by a darkening patch of clouds. The bowl is quiet, covered with a sheet of impenetrable darkness. The Seer feels a quickening in his heartbeat—has he pricked the indignation of his divine master? Is Ifa taking away the vision because he has expressed doubt when he has seen only a few years of the unborn man's childhood?

He lifts his hands and cries, "Ifa, Historian of the Unconscious, forgive my intransigence! Let me back into your fold. Let the smoke before the valley be swallowed by Olodumare's air. Let . . ."

A sharp rattle from the bowl forces him to open his eyes to see the man seated in a vehicle whose door has just closed. He knows that Ifa's vision, once it begins, continues unhindered, and that with each moment of break, it is he, the Seer, who misses parts of the story.

He lifts his eyes and sees that the star has returned—glowing, surrounded by a bluish halo whose light sits on the surface of Ifa's still water. Reassured, the Seer settles himself. The vision, he realizes, is still far from over.

3.

As THE RED CROSS station wagon races out of the city, Kunle feels relief. The man sitting beside him in the middle row, blind in one eye, is perhaps the age of his father, while the man in the backseat seems to be in his thirties. The reverend sister in the passenger seat is much younger. Kunle has been a member of this small group for only a week. Yesterday he helped load up the Red Cross wagon with supplies for the Eastern Region. Now, as the wagon increases its speed and air rushes in, he cranks the window up.

He gazes out, the smell of medicine thick in the air and the gentle sound of small bottles rattling filling his ears. As if nudged, the one-eyed man begins an account of the previous week's mission to a place called Garkem, on the border of the Eastern Region. But Kunle's mind keeps returning to Tunde, imagining what it feels like to live with Nkechi's family in a place where there is fighting. Is Tunde thinking of home, of their parents, of him?

He sees that they are approaching a checkpoint, slowing down to join a queue of vehicles. Between the vehicles are soldiers in leaf-green uniforms and black helmets. On the roadside, where the earth has turned red, two other soldiers sit on a bench under an awning.

"Everybody listen!" the reverend sister says. "Please listen very well.

When we get to that checkpoint, please, please, in the name of God—don't say anything. Okay?"

"Yes, Sister," the rest of them say.

"Many of them are drunk," the sister says. "Some have been at the war front and their friends have been killed. They are angry . . ." She crosses herself as a soldier wielding a rifle comes towards the station wagon. "They are angry and . . . they can do and undo."

As the procession of vehicles moves forward, someone shouts, "Moof!" The soldier points his gun at the car in front of them, whose boot is half open and held down by strong cords fastened to its underside.

Kunle's fear stirs a fever in his gut as the soldier with the rifle gestures to the Red Cross driver to wind down the window. The soldier bends to gaze into the wagon.

"Red Cross, eh?"

"Yes, sa," the driver says with a crack in his voice. "We are on a mission to Enugu, sa."

The soldier nods. "Enugu, hmmm. All of you, ba?"

"Yes, sa!"

The soldier, his rifle hanging over his shoulder, walks around the car, stopping to examine the cloth banner bound over the bonnet, bearing the Red Cross symbol. The soldier motions the driver to move forward, and he accelerates slowly between the two wooden barricades placed as speed breakers. Once the wagon enters the highway again, it feels like a dead weight has rolled away from Kunle's flattened heart, and he gasps, waiting for his heart to come alive again.

The fear returns the moment they approach the next checkpoint, but it gradually slackens over the next few, where the soldiers allow them to pass more quickly. The sun is high, and now they stop behind a Mercedes-Benz lorry filled with sacks of food. On both sides of the road sit military jeeps with mounted guns. On the shoulder of the road, a family is being searched by soldiers, their belongings scattered about. One of them is an Indian man with a red dot on his forehead; he is speaking in muffled tones to one of the soldiers, oranges from a ruptured basket lying about, many of them mashed into the asphalt.

"We're close to Onitsha," the sister says. "There will be more checkpoints now. More serious ones. They—"

A soldier holding a cowhide whip shouts, "Windows down! Windows down!"

"Everybody wai down—wai down!" the sister says. "Quick, biko."

Hot air rushes into the wagon, carrying the smell of dry grass and orange pulp.

"Out, out—everybody!" The soldier brandishing a whip is screaming now, banging on the body of the car, speaking Hausa. "Damburoba, ever'body out!"

Kunle takes out the piece of paper on which he'd scribbled the address of the Agbanis in the Eastern Region and stuffs it in his shoe, beneath the sole of his foot. He rushes out with the rest of the passengers, and they stand on the shoulder. Nearby, half-lying in the bush, is the body of a man, his torso hidden in the grass. The body has left ribbony patterns on the dirt, as though it's been dragged into the bush, the dirt spotted with blood. Kunle feels his legs hold him up more rigidly than he's ever stood in his life. The soldier who stopped them returns and asks, "Wetin una carry?"

"Clothes, food, medicine, sa," the driver says. While he is speaking, the soldier climbs into the station wagon. "If you . . . if you look, you will see, sa."

"Books," the one-eyed man, whose name Kunle can't recall, adds, motioning forward, then, as if warned not to, stepping back.

The soldier searches the crates and boxes packed behind the seats, bends to look under a seat, raising one leg, the skin of an orange stuck to the sole of his boot. The team members stand still, seemingly united in a fear that, like a mysterious and unknowable thing, measures itself against all that is known and obvious. "No weapon for Ajukun rebels, kwo?"

"No, Officer," the sister says. "We are Red Cross."

As if he has not heard the sister, the soldier probes the one-eyed man, who answers all the questions and shows the soldier his ID card. Next, the soldier wipes the sweat off his forehead with the back of his hand and points at Kunle.

"Aboki, you ma na Red Cross?"

"Yes, sa. I joined to help, sa," Kunle says.

"Why? Which kain help?"

"Em—because of the news, sa. I always volunteer in orphanage, sa . . ." He fears that the officer's eyes on him means that he is not believed, and adds, "I want to help, sa!"

The soldier frisks him. "You be which tribe?"

"Yoruba, sa—from Akure."

The soldier nods, purses his lips, then turns. Relieved, Kunle peeks at his wristwatch—at the long arm moving steadily. Since his days of hiding under the bed after Tunde's accident, wristwatches have become his escape. In the three days under the bed, his wristwatch had come to life, and he had begun to look at its face as if it were the face of a secret friend.

When the soldier orders them to proceed, Kunle says "Thank you" like the others, but he can feel his heart intruding upon his words, tripping them.

"You see the dead body?" the one-eyed man says once the soldier is out of earshot. "They suspect that man was going to join Biafra army—Igbo man."

"You people have seen nothing," says the other man. "They kill somebody on highway? Huhmm. Go to Garkem or Nsukki—"

"Nsukka," the driver says.

"Yes, sorry, Nsu-kka—go there. They have the big university, and you will see war. Houses have burned. Dead bodies everywhere. Everywhere. Even in daylight like this, you will be hearing army firing. In fact, this is why I was happy sister did not take us there again."

And in disturbing detail, the man tells of seeing the dead, of explosions, as if narrating the plot of a matinee. It is hard to listen, since Kunle has come this far in this quest to finally, after these many years, do something of so great a consequence that it would compensate for what he did and cause his brother to forgive him. The narrative, coupled with the sight of the soldiers, the rifles, bubbles up into a frightening steam within him. If this much trouble is happening in the Eastern Region, then Tunde must be truly in danger. He hopes the wagon will get there as soon as possible and that by morning he will have brought his brother to the safety of the Red Cross.

He feels uneasy and nauseous. He winds down the window. They have come upon a traffic jam, and the line of vehicles in front seems to be floating in water, a ripple running over the mirage. The station wagon stirs to life and dashes into it.

FOR THE REST of the ride, he sits lightly, with half of him present and the other half scattered over landscapes of his past, imagining how his parents must have reacted after discovering the note he'd written on the back of an old telegram and left on the dining table. They must have said that this was good, noble. His mother must have cried—this time for joy at the hope that Tunde would be brought back. After all, she had expressed the desire to go find Tunde herself, saying to his father that it was a shame she had grown up in Akure and had no relatives except distant ones still residing in the East. The sister's voice rattles him—"In the name of the Father, and of the Son, and of the Holy Ghost . . . Mother of God, pray for us now and at the hour of our death." He looks out the window and sees, a few meters away, the cantilevers of a great bridge and, on the side, the marshy brush submerged in water.

They have arrived in the Eastern Region. He wipes the face of his wristwatch and puts his hands on his forehead as jubilation erupts from the cars parked at this checkpoint, instead of the fright that had marked the last ones. People are waving out of their windows. One of the vehicles is an open-backed Isuzu lorry with a group of people standing in its back, singing Igbo songs. Someone among them is waving the strange flag he saw at the motor park in Lagos. The soldiers at this checkpoint look different: dressed in olive-green uniforms and helmets fitted with foliage. They appear cheerful. One of them, with a whistle between his lips, raises his fist in the air as the people cheer and cry, "Hail Biafra, the Land of Freedom!"

Kunle gazes at anything he can see—tin roofs with tires on them, bougainvillea flowers lilting in the breeze. The one-eyed man points at a green sign on the shoulder of the road and says, "Una see the signboard?"

The evening sun's glow is on the signboard, and Kunle cannot make out its lettering.

"River Niger!" the one-eyed man says.

The station wagon inches forward a few meters, and the large metal barricade almost two kilometers from the bridge comes into sight. The road is wider, and on its shoulders, more soldiers in the same olive-green uniforms stand within stalls of sandbags. The bridge is grander than Carter Bridge, which, in January, Uncle Idowu had driven him across on the way to Lagos Island. Uncle Idowu had mentioned the Niger bridge during that trip, saying it was a big achievement and a sign that if the new countries were ruled by their own people, there would be no heights the countries could not attain. Beyond the cantilevers are tight black ropes that seem like protective barriers for pedestrians.

They enter the new country with the sun setting in the vast, open sky. Even though his mood has been brightened by the drastic change of atmosphere, Kunle searches for any sign of the war, but he can see nothing save the usual movement of people, hawkers and traders thronging cars, and the traffic of lorries and wagons. Kunle digs out the address from inside his shoe and puts it back in his pocket. The driver pulls through the gate of a white, two-story building, and the group cheers.

An elderly man in a half-buttoned brown shirt and knickers waits in front of the building. A dim fluorescent bulb lights up the inscription above the front door: OPI HEALTH CENTER. The man shakes the hand of each one of them and then helps them carry the supplies into the clinic—large luggage full of drips, crates of syringes, sacks of hospital gowns, boxes of books, crates of glucose and canned milk and vials of pills, aprons, and a polythene bag full of gloves—through a brightly lit reception hall on whose walls hang portraits of two men, one of whom is Lieutenant Colonel Ojukwu.

People are seated on benches in the reception area; among them are men on crutches, one of them missing a leg, his stump covered by a white bandage. The sight of these wounded men gives Kunle the sign of war he's been dreading. He pauses in a storage room and looks out the window, up at the outcroppings behind the hospital, to a stand of banana trees. When he returns to the hallway to bring in a box of syringes, the elderly man reaches out to shake his hand again. The overhead bulb twitches and goes off. From the darkness, the elderly man's voice rises: "Welcome, welcome oh . . . welcome to Biafra!"

4.

It is dark when Kunle wakes. He is in a room with the rest of the men, everyone sleeping on bamboo mats. He fell asleep with his mind still caught like a kite between the branches of the last events, and now the image of the dead body in the bush returns to him. He wonders, has Tunde seen federal soldiers with battle weapons everywhere? Does he know how dangerous the Eastern Region has become? And do Nkechi and her family feel safer within this new country they call "Biafra"? Perhaps if he can get to Tunde and the Agbani family and tell them what he's seen, he might be able to convince them to return to Akure.

He raises the curtain a bit and sees on his wristwatch that it is a little after four. Through the window he glimpses the station wagon in the moonlight, spattered with mud and wearing the marks of long travel. He must leave at once so he can return on time to travel back home with the team. The reverend sister had mentioned that they would rest one day and return to Akure early the third day.

He finds his shoes near the door and looks quickly in the left foot. The paper is there, softened by damp and reeking of footsweat, but still legible. He reaches for his Red Cross jacket. He empties the bag containing some of the files, a leather bag with a strap he can wear across his chest, onto the floor. From the kitchen countertop, he takes the remains of sliced bread and a bottle of Lucozade, and puts these in the bag. He pauses at the front porch of the clinic, which is littered with wingless moths, waiting for the light to turn off. A sudden doubt sparks in him like a small flame, illuminating the image of the angry soldiers at the checkpoint. As if called upon by a voice to which he must harken, Kunle hastens through the gate and into the town, running till the clinic is long behind him.

When he stops, the predawn dark has been moistened and he is wet with dew and sweat. He leans against a tree, and at once its black branches heave and birds leap into the air, their sudden calls long and throbbing. He steps away, panting. He is supposed to be heading for a motor park to find a ride that can take him first to the city of Umuahia, then to a place called Nkpa, where Nkechi's father's family house is located. The old man who welcomed them the previous night had told him that the motor park was seven kilometers from the clinic, in the center of Enugu city. But it is dark, and in this unfamiliar terrain, he does not know where he is going. He cannot read any of the billboards without light. Now he worries that he may have been heading in the wrong direction or even passed the place. He stops, the road spread out on either side of him, empty and ominous.

It is a while before he hears a vehicle approaching from the opposite direction. He steps back into the road, waving and calling at the Volkswagen, which is occupied by a lone driver. It slows, and in stopping, it covers Kunle in a glow of white light.

"Help me, sa. Help . . . me," Kunle says, panting.

"What?"

He labors to speak, puts his hand to his chest, points to the road, then at himself. "Re— Red . . . Cross."

"Oh," says the man, bespectacled and dressed in a milk-white doctor's coat.

"Going to em . . . the motor park, sa . . . I want to go to Umuahia."

"Mo-tor park—motor park by this time? You mean, Ogbete market park?"

"Yas-sa . . . for first bus."

The driver tilts his head backwards, as if to find more space to look at him, and sweeps the light from his torch over the entirety of Kunle's frame. The man puts the torch away, shakes his head.

"Am not going that way. It is far. Far . . . inside-inside main town." The man's lips purse, his face contemplative. "Mmhuu, you know this is close to Opi? Just go that way and stop, eh? When morning come, maybe you will find somebody who is going inside town . . . I am a doctor, heading now to Okpaku urgently."

Kunle goes in the direction the man has pointed with a sense of one journeying into a strange, ornery world. As he walks, he recalls in disorienting bites the letters he wrote to his brother, the last contentious argument the Igbo twins in his class had had before their disappearance, his mother's lamentations. A flash of light comes from behind him, fades, and rises again, washing over the road. Two open-backed lorries and a pickup wagon approach him, filled with soldiers standing and holding on to the rails. Kunle remains on the roadside, his legs limp and unsteady. One of the lorries stops, and Kunle raises his hands.

Someone shouts, "Mister-man, stop! Don't moof!"

He sees, above the frame of light, the barrel of a rifle. He falls backwards and, picking himself up, runs into the bush.

HE RUNS FOR some time through a forest so dark he cannot see anything except the outlines of trees and bushes. Something catches his legs, and he tumbles into the grass. There is a rustling in the bush, a rattling of wings, attended by the accipitral cries of birds. He looks in the direction from which he has come for a long time, until it becomes certain that he is no longer being chased by the armed soldiers. He rises, dusts the leaves and dirt off his clothing, and sits on a fallen trunk fruiting with wild mushrooms. Although he cannot see by the dim light of dawn, he knows it is nearly five. He's been out of the clinic for over an hour, and pent-up questions crowd his mind: What will happen when the team wakes up and sees he is gone? Should he have told them what he wanted to do? What if they do not allow him to return? And the soldiers—would they have arrested him or killed him if he'd waited? His bowels grumble with a new surge of anxiety. He slaps his neck and, looking at his palm in the fresh light of day, sees dark blood and the mashed body of some insect.

He cannot recall falling asleep, but presently the morning has brightened. The doctor had pointed him in the direction of the motor park, but he lost his way when he fled from the soldiers. And now it is hard to know which way would lead to it. Kunle drinks some of the Lucozade and heads back the way he came, wading beneath the slanting branches of wild trees, swatting at twigs and tangled creepers, kicking lianas out of his way. All morning, birds range freely through the trees, whistling and cooing above, with the incessant susurration of insects below. Sometimes the foliage is so thick and tangled that there is no path.

He reaches a clearing filled with dead and rotting trees, and there he stops and listens to the indistinct sound that has been slowly reaching him. There is so much wind here, but the sound returns, clearer: the *ta-ta-ta* rattle of gunfire. "Oluwa mi oh!" he cries. He turns left, scales a dead trunk, hesitates. Where is it coming from? How might he avoid it? He jumps off the trunk and steps forward, but after a few meters the rattle of fireworks or gunfire sounds so close that he trips. He lies there on the wet grass, a ruffled wisp of a stem rocking slowly over his head. He can feel a sharp, needling pain. He hitches up one leg of his trousers to find a sheet of skin opened like the flap of a miniature envelope and examines the cut. Desperate to stanch the bleeding, he pours the Lucozade on it and screams.

Later, he moves in the opposite direction, walking and running for what must be another two kilometers before it occurs to him that he is lost again. He glances at his watch, shakes his head. The hope of reaching Nkechi's village before nightfall now clings to the lower rungs of his mind with oiled hands. A sharp sound to the right forces him to look up at the tall trees, and there: small monkeys hanging from the branches like figures out of a childhood dream. One plunks down into the grass, curls its hand about its coal-black face and lets out a cry. Kunle turns and flees.

At last, he throws himself against the buttress of a giant tree as if emptied of life. His hands are chapped and covered with pricks, his trousers stained with fragments of grass and thorns. He can now see his folly. He should not have come here. Why did he think that because he had the address of Nkechi's village it would be easy to simply board a bus and go there? Why did he not understand that because of the war, he could not travel safely within the region?

He realizes, with sudden certainty, that he let his guilt—which had grayed his life like a wet cloth, despite his having tried many times in years past to atone—control him. Only four years ago, he mounted a ladder and threw himself off it, hoping to fracture his spine and suffer the same fate as his brother. But he was too afraid to fall on his back and landed instead on his two legs.

He comes upon a plain, scant of trees, with strange, sporadic clumps of vegetation spreading up the hill, the earthen smell thick in the air. He wants to take a sip of the drink, but now there is no bag. He looks about him in the grass, down the path dented by his footsteps. It must have fallen when he fled from the monkeys, which means that he's lost his documents. What will he do if he is accosted by any authority? Where is the Red Cross certificate to present to them? He stands there, drained of all motivation, small drops of rain falling on him.

He stops at a point where the vegetation turns into a tangled network of wild banana trees, the smell of something decaying and dead seeping out from among the leaves. At his approach, unseen birds lift from the trees. To his left, the forest floor yields to a pit hewn by erosion where a dead pool has formed, covered with moss and leaves, with more detritus gathered at its edges. The buzzing of flies here is loud and revolting. He spits and holds his wrist to his nose. When he returns his eyes to the pool, something is scissoring through the mat of moss and dead leaves. The surface clears, revealing translucent waters; then the engorged skin of some being, black and rotten, appears, a crowd of worms in the split-open gut. A few paces down, the face of a human corpse spawns to the surface, its head reduced to a skull wearing only a twig of bristling hair, gently lolling.

"Oluwa mi oh!" he cries and flees, running blindly, wondering what happened to the corpse. Had the man been killed or did he drown? Now, his muscles straining, he becomes certain he has just heard human voices. He stops, and though his throat is parched and his voice is hazy, he cries, "Somebody there?" Feet crash through the grass and soon there are raised machetes, rifles, and the heads of people. He thinks he must run, but his heart lurches—what if he gets lost again and night falls on him here?

"Hands up, don't move!" a voice shouts.

Kunle turns swiftly. Before him, over the brush, the barrel of a rifle is pointing at him. He wants to clutch at his chest to steady his heartbeat but, compelled, he raises his hands instead.

Two men, one of them carrying a long gun, with painted faces and bodies covered with foliage, as if some strange plants are growing on their clothes, jump out, brandishing machetes. One of the painted men whistles with his fingers clenched between his lips, and another half dozen people, some of them women, rush out of hiding. He waves to a man carrying a large, old, and sooty aluminum pot. The man stamps his feet, raises his hand in salute, and shouts, "Shun, sa!"

"Search this man!" the man with the gun says.

The fellow drops his pot on the grass and motions for Kunle to come forward.

"I say stand hiah!" The man points at his toes, sticking out of his sandals.

"I am Red Cross—Red Cross member, sa."

"Sharrap!"

One man says something in a language that he knows—from having heard his mother speak it—is Igbo. The man notices the look of incomprehension on his face and shakes his head. For a moment Kunle wants to speak, but he finds he cannot.

"Are you deaf?" the commander says, and with a quick movement, he strikes Kunle on the face. Kunle twists away and falls, feels the snapping of something in his mouth and a stab of pain. His blood glitters on the grass, and he knows, from the sudden freedom between his gums, that a tooth has fallen out.

Someone shouts, "Up!" and quickly, he makes to rise.

"Sorry, sa," he says. "I am Red Cross from Akure. Western Region, sa . . . I come last night."

"Oh, oh," the man says and repeats something in Igbo. "So, what are you doing hiah, eh? Red Cross—you come dey waka inside bush, inside Biafraland!"

"All clear, sa!" the searcher says, stepping away from him.

More painted faces come forward. One of the men who wears foliage on his head raises his fist and addresses him in long sentences, Kunle's ears picking up only the intermittent English words—"surrender," "enemy," "sector." The group of people cheer, and a tall man waves a poled Biafran flag again and again, the rising sun folding in and out of the cloth.

"We are members of the militia for the People's Republic of Biafra," the commander says to Kunle, shouldering a rifle.

The troops cry in unison, "Yaa!"

"You, man, you are from enemy country! The general of the people's army commands us to arrest you for illegal trespass into the Republic of Biafra."

Kunle feels an aloofness, as if his body—with his arms clasped by these strange men—has lost its life. It is this body that the men drag through a wild forest of bamboo and lianas into a village, singing. The village is a gathering of huts and brick buildings whose intricate patterns and markings remind him of his mother's village. His family had visited only once, for the burial of her grandmother, the last close relative of his mother who had not moved to Akure or Lagos. It had been a long, tortuous journey by bus to Otukpo, then by train to Enugu, and then another bus to Ovim, Tunde throwing up repeatedly until they arrived, in the dead of the night.

The militiamen bring him into a hut whose thatched roof has been reinforced by fresh palm fronds, and on whose porch soldiers in uniforms stand watch behind sandbags. Three officers in identical olive-green uniforms are hunching over a piece of paper spread out on a table, each with pistols in pouches attached to their belts.

"Shun, Officers, I salute! Commander of the People's Militia here, Commander Chimaroke, sa!" the militiaman says.

The officers turn.

"Sa, our members of civil defense caught this impostor in Biafraland—inside the bush, twenty-five kilometers from Obollo-Afor. He was going to enemy side."

Kunle feels the eyes of the officers on him, and he wonders what he looks like under the light of the yellow bulb—shattered as he is, with a broken tooth.

"Gentleman, is this true?" asks one of the officers, who wears round tortoiseshell glasses.

"I . . . am a Red Cross volunteer," Kunle says. He fingers what remains of his shirt, pushing up a torn and curled flap where the badge had been. He holds it up and says, "Red Cross from Akure, sa—true to God. I came to help because my brother is here."

The officer shakes his head and dismisses the leader of the militia, who takes a practiced step, salutes, and begins to leave.

"Wait, Chima!" the officer calls. "Are your men seeing anything around Obollo-Afor today?"

"Yes, sa . . . Enemy concentration, but no movement."

For a while after the militiaman leaves, no one says anything to Kunle, nor looks at him. One watching from above can see that he is panicked: What would they do to him? Would he be shot, thrown in prison? He lifts the flap of cloth at the knee where his trousers are torn. The wound has darkened. As he often does when in trouble, he wonders if the Seer has seen this. Was he destined to be killed for the mere crime of wanting to bring his brother home? Occasionally, there is noise from some road he cannot see—the sound of a vehicle or some machinery. For quite a while, the officers talk in English about the map on the table. They speak of bridges, forest, erosion, natural barriers, barricades, armor, their voices leaping and eager, laced with a strange mix of toughness and fear. And just as it seems they are concluding their meeting, Kunle feels as though something has nipped his heart, worrying it. While the meeting had lasted, he'd felt somewhat safe.

Now a storm of ideas and pleas rush into him as the officers rise in an abrupt movement that feels rehearsed, stand apart, and curve their hands in salute. They shake hands and two walk out, leaving the bespectacled officer who had spoken to the militiaman. The officer, tall and broad-shouldered, carries himself with a tilting poise—as if bearing an invisible weight on his back. He wears a green Fidel Castro cap, which casts a shadow over his face as he speaks.

"What is your name, young man?" the officer says without turning.

"Ermmm, sa . . . Kunle—Adekunle Aromire."

The officer raises his tortoiseshell glasses, stares at him, and slowly puts them back over his eyes. "Mmhu, so, a westerner, eh?"

"Yes, sa. But my mother is Igbo."

There is a twitch in the officer's eyes now, and he seems to search Kunle intently, tracing a slow and steady gaze over his face and body. Kunle holds himself still, wanting no sound to escape. But his stomach rumbles, releases a series of bellows loud enough for the officer to hear. The officer removes his glasses, rubs the corners of his eyes, and says, "Mhuu—Igbo . . . From where?"

"Ovim, sa."

"Hmm, so you came to help us?"

"Yes, sa," he says. Because he thinks the major has not heard him, he says it again.

The officer rises and his frame again strikes in Kunle a swift pang. He watches the major's hands, rubbing each other. "I am Major Amadi, and with my colleagues you just saw, we are fighting for our lives. If you want to help us, we don't need just food. We need brave men like you whose mother is one of us and, therefore, who is one of us. We need men like you . . . we need weapons." The officer removes his cap, rubs at the crease it has formed on his forehead, and sets it back on his head.

The major starts to speak again, but the bulb erupts with gaseous sounds, dims, makes a prolonged twitching sound, and goes out. In the dark, Major Amadi lifts a pencil and dangles it between his fingers. "If we are to follow our rules, you will be imprisoned, then shot for trespassing in Biafraland . . . Yes, you came to help us, but you left your group and started traveling without permission in the country. You see?"

Kunle feels his body throbbing. He kneels, his hands trembling, "Please, sa, I—"

"No, no, no—no! You're a brave man. Stand up!"

Surprised by the major's praise, Kunle feels his fear loosen its grip. He rises and wipes his mouth with the back of his hand. The major passes him a half cup of water, and in haste Kunle gulps it.

"You are brave Igbo on your mother's side," Major Amadi says, taking back the tin cup. "In fact, you made a trip knowing we are at war. You come . . . one of us . . . to help." The major coughs and spits into a handkerchief. A woman arrives with a candle, and the major watches as she drips a seal of wax and stands it on the table.

"You will help us," the major says, gently now.

"Yes, sa. But, sa, if you let me go, I promise I will go back to my parents and never come back here again. Never, sa, please. Please."

Major Amadi folds his arms around himself, and for a moment he seems to muster a quiet laugh. "It is too late for that," he says, his voice taking on a tinge of tempered anger. Kunle steps back at his approach, but Major Amadi simply places a hand on Kunle's chest and says, "Breathe in."

Kunle lets himself suck in air.

"Out!"

He releases the breath.

"Turn your back!" Then: "Squat down and raise your hands!" And: "Turn again and press your hands on the floor, lift your legs!" As Kunle, panting, feels his strength begin to fail, the major shouts, "Last one: stand on your toes!"

Kunle staggers, almost losing his balance as the strain in his calves grows. Major Amadi nods, a glow on his face.

"Good—good . . . oh, good. Now—raise your hand and repeat after me: I pledge to Biafra, my country—"

"I . . . I . . ." He looks up at Major Amadi, his lips wobbling. "I pledge to Biafra, my country."

"To be faithful, loyal to the Biafran revolution and the nation—"

Kunle repeats each phrase after the major:

"To defend the land against all aggression through land, air, and sea—"

"To fight as part of the Biafran Armed Forces with all my strength—"

"Knowing that the cost of desertion will be with my life—"

"So help me God."

Kunle closes his eyes through the oath-taking, and when he opens them, the room is darker, as if night has fallen more deeply in that short time.

For a moment, Major Amadi faces the window, as if steeped in contemplation, so that when he speaks again it feels sudden, unexpected. "You have sworn to support our revolution—to help Biafra. With your life. To abandon this will result in death."

"Yes, sa!" Kunle finds himself responding for the umpteenth time.

Major Amadi falls silent, nodding slowly for some time. When he speaks again, his voice is softer: "And, lest I forget, you cannot bear that name here. From now on, you are Peter, you hear?"

"Yes, sa!"

"Peter . . . em, maybe Nwaigbo . . . since you're our son. Peter Nwaigbo."

"Yes, sa!"

The sounds of the night insects fill the room now, as if invited. Beyond that there is only the grinding hiss of the candle, irritated by a moth dying in its fluttering flame. Major Amadi's words feel sudden, trenchant: "Congratulations, then. You are one of us!"

THE SEER HAS been lost in the unfolding vision of the unborn man's life. What he is seeing is difficult to believe from where he stands—twenty years away. Many things about the vision surprise him. For one, it is hard to believe that colonialism will end, when just two years ago the British issued a new constitution. A great darkness fills the bowl now and he can see nothing save the star cast in silhouette. He knows from past experiences that this is an intermission, and that when Ifa wants to take a seer further into a person's future, he blanks out the terrain of events and curtains off swaths of time with sheets of luminous darkness.

The Seer waits, chanting the mighty names of Olodumare, Ifa, and all the pantheon of deities. He must use this time to keep himself from sleeping. As he rises, he recalls—almost as if it were a vision—the night he first met his dead wife, Tayo. He'd seen her standing at a bus stop alone in the dark and felt an almost desperate need to pick her up and take her wherever she wanted to go. Once she got into his car, he launched into a litany of questions: Did she not know it was dangerous at this time of night in Lagos? Was she not afraid of kidnappers? He'd spoken for a long time before he realized he had been scolding this beautiful young woman. Yet she said nothing. He asked her name, and she said simply, "Tayo." Her unbroken taciturnity even in the face of his generosity and his interrogations stunned him. He marked the number of the apartment complex he dropped her off at, as if bequeathed with a great treasure sealed in a box whose key she alone had, and which he was eager to unlock. He returned the following night.

The intermission is taking so long the Seer is worried. Has he done something wrong? He has stuck to the rules so far and has not uttered a word that the unborn man, far away in that world across time's mystical bridge, could hear. He picks up the spotless white shawl he brought with him and drapes it over his shoulders, whispering, "Ifa, the spotless among all; pure white is your color. Langi-langi is the foot-walk of the grasshopper. I have stepped behind the spirits of time, shukuloja-shukuloja—Ifa, I seek you."

In the wake of his supplications, the Seer feels as if a vital light has been turned on. Yet when he opens his eyes and gazes into the bowl, darkness remains and there is no sound. He wonders what he must do. In times like this, he has often wished that his master was still alive. He raises his amulet again but stops in a shudder. A sudden circle of light has broken out of the bowl, and he can see a long convoy of men two kilometers long, traveling like a train of ants on the side of a road. The young man, Kunle, is among them. Like the others, he is naked to the waist, swinging his arms and legs in rhythm, singing.

5.

Kunle marches and sings for the first time in the four days since he came to the training camp. Major Amadi, having conscripted him into this strange army, had sent him here in a car. He arrived knowing that his desire to atone for his brother's injury, when cast against the mirror of his present circumstances, felt like a grievous mistake. From that night onwards, his desires—even of making some contact with his brother—have become humble and plain-clothed, while his fears wear opulent garments. So he has become preoccupied only with the thought of how to save himself from heading into the war. For days, he's tilled the earth in vain, but this morning, an idea came to him with forceful clarity. And all day, he participated in the marching and maneuvering drills with a lifted mood. At the blast of the gun announcing what must be the last drill of the day, he runs, thinking of softer years when he used to race around the yard with Tunde and Nkechi's brothers, Chinedu and Nnamdi, shooting toy guns. It was so long ago that he's forgotten how the body can exhaust its own strength. And now, after reaching the pole indicating the end of the five-kilometer race, he drops onto the grass beside two of his comrades, panting.

Although he was told once he got here that there were nearly seven hundred men at the camp, he's come to know two men in D Company well. He met one of them, Felix, in the dormitory that same night. Disarmed by the raw force of events, he'd lain down to sleep on the yellow mattress with no sheets, trying to make sense of his world, which had been sundered in a single day. He was almost thrown into a shudder when he heard a voice say, "Welcome." Turning, he noticed for the first time that a man was sitting on the bed to his left, a transistor radio raised to his ear. Felix was about his height but clearly much older—perhaps thirty. His head was balding, rendering his forehead more prominent. He bore some resemblance to Chinedu, Nkechi's brother.

That night, Kunle tossed and turned in bed, in part because of the brightness—the moonlight shining through the windowless frame. And each time he opened his eyes, he saw Felix with the radio beside his ear, watching him. At some point, Kunle let his grief and frustration rip, a deep wail issuing from within him. Felix handed him a handkerchief and whispered that he should go to sleep. And when he woke the following morning, Felix was sitting facing him, scribbling something in a small jotter. Once Felix saw Kunle open his eyes, he began reading something from the jotter in his hand: "One by one we arrive, fallen angels . . . our agonies speaking with distinct voices . . . in languages beyond these plains."

Kunle sat up. Outside, a whistle was blowing, and before he could speak, Felix pulled him into the field to begin the day's drills. That evening, Felix told him that what he'd read was a poem inspired by Kunle's first night. He was a poet who had been working in Lokoja before the war and had only relocated from the north three months earlier. Felix related how he'd joined the Biafran army: he'd been on his way to give a message to his father, who worked as an engineer for a motor company just outside Enugu city. As he passed the railway, he encountered a commotion and stopped, only to witness the aftermath of a pogrom of easterners in the north. Together with the teeming crowd, Felix watched as the bodies of wounded and murdered easterners were unloaded from the train. One was the mangled body of a woman; there were only bloody stumps where her breasts had been cut off. Between pauses forced by the spectacle of new bodies being removed from the train, he found a man in bloodied rags recounting how, in the northern city of Jos, they'd survived by hiding behind a big bag when the train carrying easterners was stormed by armed youths, who'd maimed the other refugees with cutlasses and knives. A chilling outcry from the crowd interrupted the man, and, turning, Felix saw why: a headless corpse. Felix turned away and went straight to enlist into the Biafran army.

Felix narrated his experience with a singular earnestness and passion that moved Kunle. He could see in the way Felix quoted passages from books in between his own stories a love for books and storytelling. Felix's story sowed in Kunle deep seeds of pity for Felix and for the easterners. These past four days, Kunle has trained by Felix's side. Though he found himself drawn to Felix, he still felt awkward, as if friendship was a language his soul had long forgotten. But last night, after days of dwelling on restless thoughts, he arrived at a plan, and since then he's begun trying to distance himself from everyone—including Felix. There was no need to form strong relationships, since he would soon be gone.

Now, his fingers sinking into the soft, wet grass, Kunle glances up at Felix.

"Pe-ter," Felix says, wiping the sweat off his face with one finger.

"I am tired," Kunle says.

Felix nods. For a moment they stare at the clearing twice the size of a football field, which at this time of day smells of cut grass. Huts with thatched roofs sit at the northern end of the clearing, and to the east are brick buildings, formerly part of a school but now used for the Biafran army's training camp, their zinc roofs overlaid with layers of palm fronds for camouflage. The men in the distance are seated in groups in the center of the field, around several long poles on which ladders have been constructed. An officer is shouting instructions to a group near the huts, his voice heavy in the heat. Felix taps Kunle. "Come, come! Major is calling our company."

He does not hesitate: this sergeant major punishes recruits at the least provocation. They find the rest of the men of D Company seated in a long line on the ground, singing a song that, he recalls, the militiamen who arrested him had sung: "We are Biafrans, fighting for our nation . . . in the name of Jesus, we shall conquer." Afterwards, as the sergeant major takes away four men who had failed the trainings for dismissal, the company's soldiers begin to chatter among themselves. Felix gets caught up in discussions about the four, one of them a fifty-year-old man whom army doctors had found to have severe high blood pressure. Kunle gets up and moves away; he sits a few meters from the group, trying to keep his distance and maintain his sense of not belonging here and to consider the unfolding situation. Should he purposefully fail the tests? What happens if he does? Would he be sent on his way to find Tunde, or to rejoin the Red Cross? He asks Felix what would happen to one who failed.

"They take them straight to militia!" Felix says, too loudly. "Once you identify yourself as soldier and take our oath, you must serve in the army somehow."

"Oh," Kunle says, nods.

Two other men begin weighing in, but he lets his mind float to the last idea he'd come up with: he will try to telephone the clinic directly and beg the reverend sister to intervene on his behalf. The sister is compassionate, and if she knew he was a high-flying student whose term would soon resume, she would plead for him to be released from the army. All he needs to do is find a way to reach her and then plead his case in the strongest way possible.

Bube-Orji, the other man he has come to know, taps him on the shoulder and stoops beside him. Kunle wants to protest, but there is something about Bube-Orji's face that restrains him. Bube-Orji has a skin condition that causes white patches to appear on his body—vitiligo. The patches on his face look like the skin of a cut before it bleeds. The spots of white skin around his mouth that often give him an expression of warmth and cordiality. It was he who, days before, had spoken freely about having sex with his girlfriend. The girl, a nineteen-year-old virgin at the time, had been caught by her raging parents, who'd insisted she was too young for him and he, a poor man, was unworthy of her. Wounded by the split, he'd seen the war as a chance to redeem himself.

"I'm hungry oh," Bube-Orji says.

Kunle wants to say that he too is hungry, but he merely nods. Each of these four days, they've gone to bed by ten P.M. and risen at five A.M. Before the training each morning, the quartermaster whistled and the recruits filled the school hall—a big building at the center of the campus, north of the clearing. They ate boiled yams with palm oil, small balls of akara, or, sometimes, oily rice. These were smaller portions than he'd ever had, and they often ate quickly; by daybreak, they'd used up the food's energy and felt empty again from running, jumping over barriers on the obstacle courses, and scaling walls while whistling officers chased after them. The next meal came in the evening, after the training: smoked fish, boiled eggs, or yams.

"Na only God know when we go eat again," Bube-Orji says, looking up, the squint slightly wrinkling his face.

The sergeant major returns, blowing his whistle, and orders A Company, the group at the far end of the clearing, to "Incline!" At once, the group of men rush up the crudely constructed ladders. Kunle sits with his eyes closed, wishing for some respite, for even now the ache in his body is too much to bear. "D Company!" Kunle and the other men run forward. Kunle mounts a hanging ladder, suspended from the horizontal bar of a pole. It swings unsteadily under his grip as he struggles to pull himself up. He hears cries with his new name in it: "Go, Peter! Peter!" He climbs down, then races into the pillbox five meters away.

Later, when they retire to the camp rooms, he lies in bed, wondering what is happening to Tunde. Is there fighting near him? Does he think of returning home, and even if he does, being crippled, how would he do so without some help? So disturbed is Kunle that he barely hears the men speaking. The past four nights, after supper, the recruits told stories of joining the Biafran army, most of them speaking in English because of the recruits from other ethnic groups. One man, from Katsina, saw his entire family killed; he was spared only because he hid in a tree in the backyard. Another man returned from traveling to find his brother's head on a pike. The man speaking now is much older than most of them—in his early forties, perhaps. A pastor, he had been shot in the back during the bloody night in Kano and left for dead. He and two members had managed to crawl through a secret back door before the mob razed his church, killing most of the churchgoers, including the pastor's wife and his two sons. Like many others, this man is fighting not just for his family, but because he knows what would happen to them if the northerners came here.

These stories fill Kunle with anguish, as though the things the men describe have happened to him too. In the wake of the pastor's speech, a fragile silence descends, occupied by the sound of crickets. As they all wait for another recruit to begin, he wonders what his story would be, were he asked to tell it. How could he say that in a stroke of poor reasoning, he embarked on a journey into a war? How could he explain that he has not been himself since '56, that much of him has been ruptured by guilt, which has led him here with the hopes of bringing his brother home? He is relieved when a man begins telling about leaving Lagos to come here.

He rises the following morning at twenty minutes to five, before the first whistle. The night had been filled with thoughts of his mother. In the letter he left for them, he wrote that he would be back within three days. Red Cross missions were often that quick. But a whole week has now passed. He washes his face at the water drum outside the dormitory, swats bits of chewing stick around his mouth to clean his teeth, and runs to the sergeant major's lodge, a bungalow that was abandoned at the outbreak of war by its previous occupants, most of its furniture still intact, with a modern, standing television set.

Once the sergeant major's batman lets Kunle in through the door, he tells the sergeant major, with his eyes cast down, how he came to Biafra. "It is not my war, sa," he says, struggling to contain his voice. "I did not come to join like my comrades. Please . . ."

For several minutes, the sergeant major does not speak, and the silence begins to make Kunle question his own words. So in haste, he adds: "Sa, I love Biafra and will fight, sa. I . . . jus' saying that I am very worried about my mother and father—sa."

The sergeant major's silence remains, and from somewhere in the house a female voice begins singing a tune. The sergeant major seems caught by the tune—*but if the price is death for all we hold dear, then let us die without a shred of fear*. When the voice is drowned out by the rushing of some tap, the sergeant major finally says, in a hoarse voice, "So, what do you want now? You already swear our oath. You are a Biafra soldier, not a Red Cross member again."

"I just want to tell them, sa . . . that I am here. In case they are looking for me."

The sergeant major nods towards the telephone set, "Do it quick."

For nearly five minutes Kunle holds the green rotary telephone receiver to his ear, his eyes fixed on its rotary dial, afraid that he might not reach the center. He shudders when he hears a woman's loud, commanding voice say, "Hello? Hello—Opi Health Center."

Kunle breathes in, steadies his hand, looks up at the sergeant major, who is watching him. "I am . . . I was a member of the team that came in July—from Akure."

"Mem-ber? Who—"

"My name is—"

"Ehen, your name is?"

Again he glances up at the sergeant major, afraid to say his true name. "My . . . eh? I am the member who left Opi Health Center."

"Oh-oh—the boy Sista Rose were looking for?"

"Yes, ma."

"Jesus! Where did you go? Why—"

"Am sorry, ma. Am really sorry—"

The woman on the line seems to detach from the phone now, talking with someone in the background in Igbo.

"Madam?"

The woman comes back on the line. "Look, Sista is very, very angry. In fact, you have been dismissed . . ." He tries to speak, but the woman does not seem to hear him. "They look for you and look for you—eh, Chineke! Everywhere—they *looked* for you."

"I—"

"They even went to Biafra Radio, BiafraTV—"

"Am—I am . . . ma?"

"Yes, yes, go ahead."

"Am at Udi camp. They arrested me, and I joined. Please tell Sister Rosemary that. Am going, please."

The phone buzzes with the sound of a car starting. There is a noise in the background, the car starting and someone shouting something. The woman whispers to someone in Igbo, and Kunle waits, his hope resting on a thread. Then her voice returns, calmer than it had been before. "Look, my friend, I understand," she says. "I will tell Sista, and if she wants, she will do something. If not, good luck."

He puts down the receiver, salutes the sergeant major. For days he waits, his mind hung on the tip of a pole he cannot reach, thinking only about what he'd said and how he'd said it. He'd pleaded his case; but would it help him? The drills intensify as the days pass, and the men are constantly dripping with sweat, their muscles tensed and aching. Twice, they march the five kilometers up into a nearby village and back, real and demo rifles balanced in their left hands. With the increased intensity come injuries—on the way back from one march, a man faints. That same day, a pump-action rifle misfires, barely missing one of the sergeants. The officers become increasingly prickly, screaming constantly, their voices a continuous echo in his head.

Nightly, Kunle sits at the margins of the gatherings, waiting. Three days after the call, B Company is sent off to the front, leaving his group as next in line. In a day, two, three, a week, two weeks—no one knows when—his group will be deployed. The realization is a wound somewhere inside him that feels raw and bloody. Each day, it deepens, expanding, filling him with bitterness.

Upon waking on the sixth day after the call, it strikes him that the reverend sister may have resolved not to help and he will head to the front, and of his future, there will be no telling. As the sun drops in its intensity and shadows lengthen over the training field, they go out to the practice range, this time with Lee-Enfield rifles. He holds his rifle with hands that would not close their grip, sweat breaking out on the back of his neck, while his comrades, among them Felix and Bube-Orji, wave their guns and beam. For three days his platoon has carried wooden demo guns—sticks carved into the shape of a rifle. And now he thinks only that the wooden rifle felt heavier than the real one he is holding.

They crawl on their bellies through wet grass and tangled vines for two hundred meters while the noncommissioned officers shoot over their heads at a wooden board. Twice he feels the force of bullets as they whip past his head, striking the pole and resolving into frightening sparks of fire. Moments after he reaches the end line, trailing behind Bube-Orji and Felix, a sharp cry rises from the midst of the others still behind him. The officers, blowing whistles, race towards the pole, where a man hit in the head by a ricocheting bullet lies writhing in the grass. The training ends at once, and after the body has been carried out, the soldiers return to the dormitories.

All that night as he lies in bed, trying to sleep, the stricken face of the dying man and the skeletal face of the corpse in the pool stare at him from some unknown space. How might one be safe here amid such death and sorrow? How can anyone survive the front if during training there is so much danger? His one hope was the benevolent sister, but it is now six days since he made the call. At the end of the hall, Felix and Bube-Orji sit, listening to Radio Biafra on Felix's transistor. Kunle looks out the window at the empty field in the glare of the moonlight and it seems that the spirit of the dead man is moving there.

THE FINAL DAYS of their training are sullen, Kunle's despair acquiring the brute fecundity of poison. On the day before they leave, Major Amadi arrives at dawn, as if summoned out of Kunle's inmost wishes. For the length of time the major addresses the recruits, Kunle totters between poles of courage (to go up to Major Amadi and plead for his release) and the fear (of Amadi's reaction to such a request). He cannot muster the courage, and instead, he watches Major Amadi get into his command car, a dark Peugeot 404, and disappear up the road that winds away from the school.

While his comrades, energized by Major Amadi's speech, sing songs of war, Kunle sits by himself, aware with paralyzing certainty that there is no way out of his circumstance. The wish to escape Biafra lies in him like a fallen monument. What he must do, he realizes, is find a way to let Tunde know what is happening; that he is in Biafra. If he goes to the front and is killed, his brother must find a way to return and be with their parents. One of them must survive. He asks Felix for a piece of paper, and he carries this in his pocket through the morning drill in which they march through roadways, wielding demo rifles, singing. They are on the long highway towards Emene when one of the officers blows a whistle and shouts, "Atte-shon!" All the men stop and stamp their bare feet on the blacktop.

"Peter Nwaigbo—Recruit badge number B wan thirty wan, hop high!"

It is he. "Here, sa!" he shouts, and there is an instant ache in his gut.

The sergeant points to a vehicle waiting on the other side of the road. "Go with him to camp immediately."

Kunle is flustered, but there is no time to settle his thoughts, for near the entrance to the school camp, the Red Cross station wagon is waiting. The reverend sister is sitting in the passenger seat with the windows rolled down. She looks thinner than he remembered, her fair-complexioned face weather-beaten, dotted with pimples. She steps out of the wagon, whispers to the driver to wait. She crosses herself.

"Sister, Sister—am very sorry." He tries to speak through his winded voice. "I . . . wan . . . wanted to see." He bends over, claps his belly with his right hand till the air rustling inside has steadied, and says, "Sister, I wanted to see my brother quickly and come back . . . I wanted to quickly . . . am sorry . . . sorry, Sister."

He finds that he is crying, and he drops his gaze to his legs, to his bare feet, covered with grass and dirt, mobbed by flies.

"Is okay. It is done." He can feel the hesitation in her voice. "You have joined the army—"

"Please, Sister—please." He kneels, looks about to check if any of the commanders or his friends can see him. He knows that this is the moment, that this is the time when he must seize his life back. He must find a way to persuade her.

"I have not even finished school," he pleads, wiping his eyes with the back of his hand. "I am a student . . . University of Lagos, Sister."

There is a shadow on the sister's face, for she closes her eyes now. His heart pushing its limit, he says, almost with a shout, "Sister, please, I am Yoruba. I am not even from this place."

She shakes her head, turns to look at a man calling a name in the far end of the field. There is a leap in Kunle's gut when she turns back to him, as if he has swallowed something without knowing it.

"Sister, Sister, my mother," he says urgently. "She will kill herself. Please, pl—"

"You have joined," she says, her face darkening. "We have gone to Enugu garrison. Look, before coming here we went to talk to Major Amadi himself yesterday. But they refused. We have seen helele because of you."

"Ah . . . Oluwa mi oh!"

"Look, I want to tell you—to tell you . . . there is nothing I can do now."

He cannot bear to raise his eyes, but he sees the sister's feet move backwards, hears keys rattling. His body trembles with a desperate surge.

"Can you tell them—my parents, please . . . I . . . please, Sister." He crawls forward on his knees, his hands clasped in supplication.

"Stand up, stand up," the sister cries, stepping back. She turns, signals the driver. "Bring paper and write down his parents' address."

She shrugs, crosses him. "May God be with you."

6.

For the three days since his company completed the training, he's stood at the margins of everything, his spirit wandering the roads out of Biafra in search of a way out. He'd risen in the dead of the previous night, walked to the porch, and surveyed the land: to the west of the school, only the silhouette of the forest; to the east, a checkpoint manned by armed men; to the north, oil drums and an old lorry. He'd wondered: If he plunged into the bush, how far could he go? Would he get lost in the forest again and be arrested by some Biafran military police or run into federal soldiers and be shot? What would Major Amadi do, seeing that he'd attempted to break his oath—set him up for death? This thought had pushed him back into the room, broken.

But this morning, the old door of escape clanged shut when buses arrived to take them to the front. They do not leave because the storm that began before dawn has continued. They have waited in the assembly hall with their belongings all day and now it is almost four p.m. He sits at the outermost end of the hall, near a pile of broken desks, chairs, and blackboards.

"Peter!" a familiar voice calls, and opening his eyes, he finds Bube-Orji settling onto the bench beside him, Felix close behind.

Since the reverend sister's visit and his own subsequent despair, Kunle has felt that he has no choice but to reestablish friendship with his comrades as much as possible and no longer seek solitude. So much is unknown and worth fearing here that he has realized that his well-being depends on this camaraderie.

"I am thinking," he says, facing his friends. "Do you know where Nkpa town is?"

"Nkpa . . . ah, Nkpa," Bube-Orji says, tapping his head. "I have heard of the place."

"Is it the one near Uzuakoli?" Felix says.

"I don't know," Kunle says, looking now at Felix, whose fair complexion is starting to dim after all these days of standing in the sun. Pimples have sprouted all over his face, one just below his lower lip.

"It is near Uzuakoli, after Ovim," Felix says.

"Oh—oh yaa oh, I remember!" Bube-Orji shouts, tapping his fingers multiple times. "It is after Umuahia, you drive down maybe another forty kilometers."

"Bube-Orji is correct," Felix says. "But, Peter, why do you want to know?"

He nods, frames a smile. "Well, because my brother is there."

Felix takes Kunle's hand and, turning it so he can see the time, whistles. Felix sets down his goatskin bag and brings out his transistor radio.

"That radio," Bube-Orji says as Felix stretches its antenna up, "is like his god."

"Egwagieziokwu, I hear your gossip." Felix shakes his head as clear voices begin to emerge from under the smatter of static. He's said many times that he loves listening to the four and seven P.M. program on Radio Biafra called *Talk After the News*. "It is for you, Peter, that I want to play the thing, sef. You will—"

"What is that thing he keeps saying, 'Igbangi ekiku'?"

His friends laugh, Bube-Orji rocking as if in the throes of fever.

"Say it again, please oh, biko, say," Bube-Orji says, nudging Kunle's arm.

But Kunle, afraid that someone will question the validity of his claim to be Igbo, hesitates.

"Shh," Felix says, "the program is starting."

Felix raises the volume, and at once Kunle recognizes the moving song: it is the same song the female voice at the sergeant major's quarters had sung. When it is over, a male with a soft voice who announces himself as "Emeka Okeke" reads the news. The man speaks of tributes pouring in for an officer named Major Chukwuma Nzeogwu who had been killed in action while fighting for Biafra; there is a new oil well being drilled off the coast of Warri that holds promise for the young nation; Colonel Ojukwu is going to address the nation the following day to announce this breakthrough. The rain outside is starting to ebb, and now the hall is quiet, save for the voice on the radio. Another voice breaks out, and the room thunders with a shout of "Okokon Ndem!"

"Good evening the great, auspicious, undefeatable, extraordinary people of Biafra!"

The men in the room shout, "Yaa!"

"Hail Biafra, Land of freedom! Land of the rising sun, comrades in arms, brave men and women . . . the hope of the black race. I am glad to announce to you that the thespian cowardly acts of the vandals is bared to the world like a script from Shakespeare. They scattered helter-skelter before our boys, and Obollo-Eke was defended against the evil army of the Hausa-Fulani and their Chadian and Soviet and Egyptian mercenaries. Nde Biafra kwenu! Abasi do! All hail the commander of the venerable Fourteenth Battalion, GOC Alexander Madiebo and Major Patrick Amadi . . ."

The officers enter the hall screaming, and quickly, as recruits rouse to attention and Felix turns off the radio, Kunle realizes that—like a ball kicked down a bold field—his entry into the war will not be stopped. From large woven sacks, they pick olive-green uniforms of the Biafran army. The two dozen helmets are gone even before Kunle and his friends can make it to the sacks, but Felix is among the few who pick up Fidel Castro caps. There are boots to go around, but most are used military boots from the USSR army, imported from a dealer in Yugoslavia, Felix says. Kunle finds a fit—a black boot that looks as if made of rubber, with hard pebbles in the patterns of its undersole.

Felix puts on his uniform in no time, as if already used to wearing a military uniform. As Kunle struggles to snap all the many buttons into place, Felix helps him fold his collar. Stitched to the top of both sleeves are rectangular badges with a black background and the image of a rising sun. Beneath the badge of the right sleeve is a white cloth with the designation LI. He thinks he has finished with the buttons, but Felix, smiling, points to his shoulders, where two straps lie.

"What is this, sef?" Kunle says.

"Shoulder pads," Felix says, buttoning up the left strap for Kunle. "This is where the rank insignia will be added if you are promoted in future."

"Ah, I see."

Felix slaps his shoulder. "Just don't die before then!"

There are four hundred of them, and once they are seated in the three identical buses bearing the inscription EJIKEONYE TRANSPORT LTD, Bube-Orji leans against Kunle and whispers something in Igbo that he does not understand, but he nods anyway. The convoy passes a continuous stream of commuters traveling on the side of the road, some on or towing bicycles, most on foot. A group of elderly women and men are seated under the shade of a big, dirty umbrella. Among them, his eyes catch a young woman, fair in complexion; she wears a calico scarf on her hair. He thinks quickly of Nkechi. In the years since the accident, his feelings towards her have become amphibious: at times swimming gaily in a warm pool of admiration, and in the next moment thrashing on the banks of resentment. He'd resented her for revealing to both their parents the full extent of what had happened that day, including the naughty game they'd been playing. Her parents punished her, and for months she would not speak to him. And in those times, he'd felt her absence so deeply, he'd developed a wasting, obsessive curiosity about her. And even when, years later, he'd settled fully into the habit of seclusion, she lurked behind the door of his desire.

They arrive at a field with a long column of soldiers and trucks painted in the green colors of the Biafran army, all covered in foliage. The men break into a song that is now familiar to Kunle, and he joins them, singing with a longing that scares him: "If our generation does not go to war—who will go?" "War! If our age group does not go—who then will go?" "Young men, the time has come." "War! If our age group do not go—who then will go?" "Young men of Biafra, the time has come!"

Major Amadi stands on the hood of his command car and waves his truncheon until the singing stops. The major wears a Castro cap and a long-sleeved, khaki camouflage shirt, hitched at his elbows.

"Privates of D Company, First Battalion, Fifty-first Brigade!" Major Amadi says. "Brothers, brave men of Biafra. Survivors of hatred and pogrom. You all know why we are fighting. If you don't, just look at our flag. The red symbolizes the blood of innocent Biafran civilians massacred in cold blood in northern Nigeria. Pregnant women butchered in broad daylight like fowls!" The major's eyes are fiery now, his voice rising in accelerated rage. "We wear their blood! The black signifies our collective mourning—for our brothers and sisters, our mothers and fathers, our children and grandchildren. The green stands for prosperity. We shall win!"

A muffled roar runs through the lines of men.

"And last but not the least, the rising sun stands for new birth. We are fighting, brothers, for the greatest black nation ever seen!"

He orders the men to march single file towards a tent made of bamboo sticks and roofed with hessian mats.

"Private Nwaigbo!" Major Amadi calls as the men begin dispersing. Kunle, feeling a sting in his heart, nearly falls.

"Yes-sa!"

"Step aside."

Kunle steps out of the line, his hand curved to the edge of his face in salute as the others march in the direction of the tent.

"At ease!"

Kunle relaxes from the salute position, and the major says, "How are you?"

"I . . . I . . . sa . . ." he says, then falls silent. "Fine, sa!"

Major Amadi raises his eyes to the sky as if suddenly interested in the small band of pipits revolving in a distant thermal, then casts them down and shakes his head.

"Look, my friend, you must understand that you're not being punished. No. You are one of us . . . Yes, from your mother. There are many people all over the world who want to fight for us right now. That is why even some white people have joined us. Because everybody is seeing with their korokoro eyes what we are going through. But you . . . you are already here."

Kunle looks up at Major Amadi. "Yes-sa."

"Besides, you took an oath, a soldier's oath. This is standard all over the world."

He nods. "Yes-sa!"

"So, I don't want to hear anything from you again. Other than that you're doing your duty, that you are fighting bravely."

"Yes-sa!"

"You know what it means if you desert the army." A dangerous shadow crosses the major's face. "But if you fight—and we win this war, then . . . maybe you can go back home."

"Yes-sa!" Kunle cries.

Even though the words have been said in a softer voice, the major's eyes convey a passionate finality.

"Good, my friend." The major squeezes his shoulder bone, and nods. "You will be fine."

One watching him from above can tell that as Kunle stands there gazing at Major Amadi's receding silhouette, he realizes that his last effort to avoid fighting in this war has failed. He wonders now if, while at the training camp, he had taken off down the road, where would it have led? He turns to where his comrades stand—they are all armed with rifles now, and Felix is raising one in his direction, beckoning. He feels again the sense of being trapped in a burning house.

HE WAKES IN the middle of the night in the open field among his friends, who lie on the naked grass, their heads pillowed on their arms. The only sounds he can hear are the men's snoring and the whistling of crickets, yet he feels that something invisible and inexplicable is gathering itself around him. From when he was a boy, he's often heard strange words spoken by a voice that seems to originate behind him, often with the word "Ifa" in it. Usually when he feels this presence, he wanders into deep tunnels of wonder about who it might be. But this night, with a gun in his hand and only a few hours between him and the battlefront, he lifts up his eyes and says in a voice as low as possible, "Help me! Whoever you are . . . please, please save me."

His mind is hanging onto this presence when at first light the company marches between ridges of abandoned farmland, the darkness lifting off the face of the horizon with every step. C Company is ahead, followed by two noncommissioned officers with submachine guns. Both companies are to provide flank support for the advance of the rest of the 1st Battalion. He is in the front row beside Felix, Bube-Orji, two other men from their company, and the company commander, Captain Irunna. Behind them is a line of men who have no rifles; they bear machetes, baskets loaded with hoes and stones, and beer bottles. Ahead is a signal platoon, made up mostly of men in civilian clothing, riding bicycles. Thoughts come to Kunle as he walks, orchestrated by the beat of his footsteps: What must be happening at the university now that the new semester is only a few days away? Has the reverend sister been to their house in Akure yet? It's been more than a week since he gave her the address. If she has gone, then perhaps they have sent a response—or have his parents died? What of Tunde—

For a moment he feels himself on the verge of vertigo—he falls to the ground and clutches a blade of grass. He opens his eyes, slaps his ears. There is dust in his eyes, and a film over his vision. Everywhere, voices are screaming, and from somewhere close, he hears the rattle of gunfire. The march has been disrupted, he can see, and the forward line is scattered about the field, the air thick with dust. The commanding officers are yelling orders, and the world seems momentarily thrown into a fit. He blinks many times and sees now that the face staring into his, attached to a man kneeling over him, is Felix's.

"Idi okay?"

"Yes!" Kunle cries.

He rises, but he is afraid to walk. What had knocked him over a moment before had been the precipitance of the explosion and how it had shaken the ground.

"What happened?" he says, to himself mostly, but Felix points in the direction of the broken regimental line. "Peter, we must join back!"

Kunle rises, dusts off his blackened hands, his heart sounding so loud in his chest. He runs alongside the other men with his throat tensed, a transient sickness rising first in his stomach then his mouth, dissipating into an indiscernible region of his body.

"Artillery," Felix says, pulling Kunle forward by the shoulder. "They say the vandals have reach Ikem—only fifteen kilometers from here."

Kunle begins to speak but stops so they can hear the orders being shouted by the commanding officers. Then he asks, "Where are we?"

"Here?" Felix says, blinking. There is dust on his face and a blade of grass in his hair.

"Eha Amufu," a man answers from behind.

They turn to see one of the four surviving corporals from what is left of D Company; he is now the company's second in command. The man, stout and with a broad forehead, wields a light machine gun and has a black bandanna around his neck. "They are bombing us again. It is mortar, high-caliber. That is what killed almost all of us."

The corporal bounds forward to the shoulder of the road, swatting aside a clump of elephant grass. Felix, Bube-Orji, and Kunle follow, coughing rapidly. He tells of how they'd been misled due to lack of communication with the rear company and ended up in the open, strafed by federal bombers so much that, of ninety-six men, only four were left.

The corporal ends his story as they reach the rear of the Biafran front line, where a cloth hung between two poles jammed into the earth bears the inscription FIRST AID POST. Everywhere, uma leaves stained with food are strewn over the grass, as well as papers, pieces of clothing, sticks, hats, bloodied shoes. There are vehicles loaded with the wounded—one man's face split open, another bleeding through a fresh bandage, a third man stripped naked to the waist, the exit hole prominent on his back. On the edge of the open field, more wounded lie on a dozen grain sacks and raffia mats in different shades of affliction—one, with a black wound on his chest, lies still, as if dead, green flies congregating on the wound. The face of a man with a stump where an arm had been is blue, but he is blinking still. Other sacks are stained with blood, and some of the men on them are dead, half-covered with banana leaves.

They step aside to make way for a black van, its roof piled with fresh foliage. At once, men with white sleeve patches embossed with a red cross jump down from it and start loading more wounded into the van. Kunle stands there, feeling a sudden, manic compulsion to break loose and run up the flank, into the bush and towards home.

They resume their march under strict instructions not to scatter except under fire. Kunle follows the man in front of him, flinching at every sound. A kilometer from the first aid post, they are ordered to pause near a tactical command post—a tarpaulin tent camouflaged with foliage—where officers are seated, hunched over a table, crates of ammunition beside them. A few meters from here a group of soldiers are lying or sitting on the grass, their rifles in their hands. These men are covered in sweat and mud, and their uniforms are in varying states of disrepair. A few of them wear helmets, even pith helmets, and one has a black bandanna around his head. At the sight of the new replacements, a cheer erupts among the seated men. Kunle swallows again and feels an urgent thirst.

They reach a field cut by a long ditch that trails in curving arcs for kilometers, disappearing into the bush. In the trenches, men sit behind sandbags and rough log walls, guns positioned through the slits, their eyes focused on the distance beyond the clearing.

"A-tteen-shon!" the company commander, Captain Irunna, shouts. And the men stop. The captain, a dark-hued man who resembles one of Tunde's former physiotherapists, observes the company, mopping his brow with the back of his hand. He has a moustache that angles down both sides of his mouth, throbbing when he speaks and forming a spectacle which, in another time, Kunle would have found funny, but that now gives the captain an angry look.

"Stand fast!" Captain Irunna shouts so loudly that his rope-held glasses slide down his nose. The men stamp their feet to a standstill, dust floating into the air.

Kunle, feeling as though something is biting him within, snapping at every hidden organ, turns away from his friends to look at the men in the trenches, then throws his glance back to the dying men being taken to the first aid post. For weeks he's tried, hoped, and struggled against the might of the world to prevent this, but here, at last, he has come to it: the front.

Part 2

The PROMINENT STAR STABILIZES

THE SEER IS struck by the unborn man's situation: the sad image of a man who must fight in a war against his will. It seems that the unborn man, Kunle, has been pushed to the wall and has given in. The Seer reckons that he himself was once in this position, when he made the decision many years ago. He was then a businessman in Lagos, recently in love and living a quiet life, when the visions of his wife lying dead surrounded by a small mob began to plague his sleep. In the dream-vision, there was always a wrecked blue car with a damaged fender.

On the day Tayo died, the vision—which had recurred at least seven times—had been especially vivid. He woke to find that his wife had gone to work. He was still processing what he'd seen when a neighbor arrived at his door, screaming. Before he could open it, he knew. He would find that the repeated vision had been an unheeded warning confirmed by the sight itself: his beloved, having been pulled out of the ruined taxi, lay with her head mangled, nearly unrecognizable. From then on, just as Kunle had done with his brother's accident, the Seer consumed himself with the guilt of her death and resolved that he would seek out the source of these visions and devote his life to divining and interpreting them.

The prominent star is now radiant, brightening much of the horizon. The Seer wants to sing to Ifa, but he remembers that just moments before, Kunle had thought of the "strange voice" he often heard. The Seer knows that the wall between him and the unborn man is hymen thin. If he speaks or makes any sound, the man could hear it, and the Seer would be interfering with the course of events. Ifa forbids it, and this is why one is supposed to go as far as possible from human habitation, atop a hill preferably, to access Ifa's sacred bowl.

With his eyes closed, the Seer whispers chants praising Ifa: "Historian of the Unconscious, the white vulture who casts its shadows across Orunmila's skies."

He drapes the white shawl over his shoulders, and when he looks in the bowl again, what he sees is a sun shining so brightly that his face is awash in its light, shining two decades from the future.

7.

THEY ARE SITTING in a line, shoulder to shoulder outside a trench, the sun directly above them. Kunle's body aches. The night before he'd slept in the open, savaged by mosquitoes, his uniform offering no protection. The three men Kunle now calls friends—Felix, Bube-Orji, and a third man, whose name begins with "Chi," but the rest of which is hard for him to pronounce—are seated beside him. The night before last, they'd slept huddled together in a small part of a trench, body to body like rabbits. Now Kunle has an urge to share a thought with Felix alone, but the latter is scribbling in his jotter. Kunle still does not understand how his comrades share details about their lives with strangers so freely—even personal stories about sex with their girlfriends. But now Kunle, too, has developed this strange desire to reveal every thought, and he is beginning to understand why they do this: First, they do it to check their own disintegrating minds against the stability of others', to be sure they are not the only ones falling apart. Second, perhaps the men question the point of keeping secrets when tomorrow, or even tonight, they could be dead. So they give everything—their dreams, stories about their intimate relationships. Even when they fall silent, Kunle feels their presence intensely, like he's never felt anyone's before.

There is a strange noise, and the men reach for their rifles and point left, right, up, down until it becomes clear that it is a Biafran helicopter with the Biafran coat of arms painted on its doors. As it makes its descent, it fills the air with a whorl of dust and dirt. An officer steps out of the copter, moves quickly towards the field, followed by the other officers. Captain Irunna, the legs of his trousers darkened by water, rushes to meet the men, two apparently senior officers. Kunle recognizes one officer as one of the men who was in the hut with Major Amadi when he took the oath. Bube-Orji identifies the man as Brigadier Madiebo, the new general officer commanding the 53rd Brigade and 51st Brigade, which includes the 1st and 14th Battalions. The man wears a red field cap, carries a truncheon, and often holds his hands clasped behind his back.

Kunle watches the officers' deliberations with anxiety, images of the rotten corpse in the green pool, the wounded on the field, all floating about in his head. And after the brigadier leaves in his command Mercedes, the captain reads out the brigadier's orders: A and B Companies of the 1st Battalion are to advance towards the outskirts of Ikem from the direction of Eha Amufu, where another brigade is engaging the enemy, and provide rear support. Ikem is only fifteen kilometers away, and the enemy, having arrived there two nights before, has by now taken almost full control of the town. To set off the march, the officers distribute ten rounds of ammunition to each soldier carrying a CETME or Madsen rifle. There is food: meager pieces of boiled yams and corned beef shared among the men. They drink from two buckets of water, each man cupping his hands to his mouth.

While they eat, a black infantry support vehicle arrives. Its wheels have the trimmings of a mammy wagon, but its elongated metal body resembles a reconstructed tractor. It has a slit big enough for eyesight that spans across the front and the sides. It makes an indescribable grating noise—like a great mass of steel and metal being dragged across a smooth surface. Painted on both sides are the colors of the Biafran flag and the rising sun emblem. Captain Irunna, wiping palm oil from his moustache with the back of his hand, announces that the truck's name is Genocide, and at once the soldiers mass behind the vehicle, shouting, "Genocide! Genocide!" Felix puts his hands around Kunle's neck and they both jump in rhythm to the chant.

"We are the lucky ones," Captain Irunna says after he and his second in command have managed to calm them. "This is the first time Biafra is using an armored car in this war. And we are the first to have it!"

The soldiers cheer, "Biafra or death! Biafra or death!"

Captain Irunna, waiting for them to quiet down, removes his glasses and wipes them with his shirttail. His uniform is a deeper green, with camouflage patches all over it.

"And," Captain Irunna says next, "do you know that this was made in Biafra? Yes, an armored vehicle manufactured here by Biafran Research and Production—in black Africa!"

Again, the men exclaim.

"It is time!" the captain shouts, his voice slower now. "Prepare weapons!"

Kunle lifts his rifle and immediately feels the half-consumed food slouching in his stomach.

Singing, they march in two columns behind the vehicle. In the first two rows of each column, men with rifles, and in the rear, men without guns but who bear ammunition boxes on their heads. The road to Ikem is empty, strewn with grass and dirt and some belongings dropped by fleeing refugees—clothes, papers, plates, a bucket, a broken radio, raffia mats—and broken trees. A lone brick house with a zinc roof stands in a clearing to the left, the top of its wall cracked and singed. Coils of dead electrical wires slant lengthwise over the house across both sides of the road, over the blackened forms of dead bodies.

Their march is slow—the armored vehicle pauses every twenty minutes or so. After a few kilometers, it stops for a longer while, smoke rising from it. The singing gives way to murmurs. They are on a motor road that cuts through thick forests on both sides, kilometers on end covered with vegetation. They start again but are stopped by a loud thud against the armored vehicle's front. Screams fill the air, and through the smoke, Kunle sees two men on the right flank fall, one of their helmets rolling off into the bush.

"What—what?" Kunle says.

He blinks, coughs—where are his friends? The men have scattered behind fallen logs, lying on their bellies on both sides of the road. A few, including the colonel, crouch behind the vehicle, their rifles at the ready. Kunle rolls beside a tall, lanky man from his company. They lie near an anthill, his rifle resting on a dead pineapple plant. The man is speaking when another volley of bullets hits the vehicle continuously, like a rattle of chains, sending off red sparks and filling the air with the smell of burning metal.

"Return fire! Return fire!" Captain Irunna cries, and at once their position erupts with a frightening clatter of returning fire and used cartridges ejecting from the guns. He falls and cowers beneath clumps of grass, covering his ears with his hands. Something lands beside him to the left, and, screaming, he drops his rifle and crawls backwards into the side of a man who shoves him.

He turns. Felix's face is raw and dark as he growls, "Stop it!" Kunle sees then, as if his eyes have just been unsealed from a blindfold, smoke rising from the barrel of the rifle in Felix's hands. Felix points again, and now Kunle sees in the bush, a thousand meters away, the turret of an enemy vehicle wending its way through a cluster of small trees, infantry on both sides of it, their helmets gleaming in the sun. Felix shakes a fist at him and cries over the collective thunder: "Shoot them!"

The rattle from Felix's rifle shakes him, but Kunle lets his finger press the trigger of his gun with hasty force. As if kicked in the gut, he falls backwards. When he opens his eyes, smoke is rising from the barrel of his rifle. There is dust in his eyes, and in his ears a cruel clamor of battle noise. But he remains crouched in the grass, gazing at his trembling hands. At once the air is thick, and the sound like a rip in the fabric of the universe. An arm lodges a grip on his shoulder and a voice, husky yet low, cries into his ears, "Peter, you shot one! . . . Well done, you finish am!"

The man is lying beside him so their drenched shirts touch, but he cannot raise his head to see the face; bullets are whizzing over him. He sways to the other side, and there a man is lying in the grass, dead, blood pouring in slanting curves out of a hole in his neck. Kunle recoils at the sight and presses himself deeper into the grass.

He is shocked to hear Bube-Orji shouting, "Well done, Peter!" He turns, and there is Bube-Orji. Felix, who only a moment ago had been beside him, is nowhere to be seen, nor is the tall man who first announced his action. Is it true? Has he killed a man? He lifts his eyes away from his hands, up towards the smoking distance in search of the man he has shot, of some confirmation of what he's done.

Rapid gunfire forces him to plunk down again. He feels a sharp pain, and looking down, he sees two splotches of blood on the left leg of his dirtied trousers. When was he wounded? And by what? Captain Irunna shouts from the direction of the armored vehicle. Kunle rises but is thrown back again by an explosion, which shakes the ground and knocks him against Bube-Orji's side. He pulls himself up and sits against the root of a tree, convinced that something has hit him. For a long moment he closes his eyes, then opens them to find that nothing has pierced his chest, though it feels like something is weaving upward along the frame of it. A soldier, knocked down by one of the ricocheting bullets, is dragging himself towards the bush, his blood staining the road and drawing a wet, sinuous red line through the grass. A few meters further in the direction of the enemy, there is a burning field from which a line of crackling fire has broken off and is now eating through the open field, filling it with moving streams of smoke.

For another half an hour they wade between the trees at the blare of whistles and the shout of "Moof," "Fire," and "Fall back." It seems impossible to move forward when one's head can be split open by a shot, like what happened to the man two meters from him. But somehow, they do—coughing, weeping, screaming, smoke uncoiling between the trees, fires breaking out in branches and racing through the grass. At last, they reach a pile of dead and wounded federal soldiers and, to the rear of the singed field, Biafran soldiers gathered, singing and waving their rifles in the air.

It is hard at first to believe that it has ended. Kunle follows Bube-Orji to the road, where his comrades are turning the enemy dead over, stripping them of their rifles, money, helmets. On the edge of the grass, a Biafran man lies, wriggling his legs and moving his head in a dying fit, spitting blood. Another man, his eye hanging outside its socket, a blob of rich, bloody matter and uncoupled nerves, is screaming, "I can't see!" Kunle looks away, tightening his fists to fight the shock, loosening them only when they arrive at a deserted village where smoke is still rising from bombed houses. In the center of the market, a singed Land Rover lies, burning from the inside. Bube-Orji, who has been chewing a lobe of kola nut to stave off his hunger, points to the left, and, turning, Kunle sees Felix approaching. Felix looks different—his face and uniform are covered in fragments of leaves and dirt, and his lower lip has swollen into a pulp. Felix hugs Kunle and shakes him violently, shouting, "We won!"

Unclutched from Felix, Kunle feels vertigo coming on, like he's climbed down from some height too quickly.

"How are you? How are you, Peter?" Bube-Orji asks.

"I don't know," Kunle says.

Felix looks at Kunle, then at his own stained trousers. "Nwanne, egwagieziokwu, we will win this war." Felix shakes his fist. "True to God, we will win—see how they ran, eh, because of just one vehicle."

Kunle feels the wound in his leg, his skin torn by a sharp twig. He wants to sit down, relieve his bowels, eat, and sleep, all at once. But the urge to empty his bowels seizes him and he rushes off.

He covers the fly-mobbed mess with leaves and walks out of the forest with the sore consciousness of one dazed. Once back in the streets, he is surprised by the destruction. Everything has happened quickly, as if time in war possesses a different, hyperactive character. The ground everywhere is filled with dead bodies, craters, blood, fire. It all feels like a mystery written in some dark, indiscernible language.

BARELY HALF AN hour after the fighting ends, two soldiers from A Company are killed when they step on unexploded ordnance in a brick house now in flames, black smoke rising from it. Captain Irunna orders that everyone in D Company gather in a township stadium at the center of the town, a section of its plastic seats burned and the awning caved in upon the seats. An iron sheet from its roofing is rattling in the wind, and black birds hover over the field against the backdrop of the dying sun. Kunle sits in the grass of the football field, along with Felix, Bube-Orji, and the tall man from their company. The man, who is swarthy, with a broad forehead and a permanent, soft smile, had said his name was Ekpeyong.

They are supposed to sleep here, in the open stadium, but it is too noisy, and the frequent traffic of refugees coming out from hiding in the bushes does not allow them to rest. One of the groups is persistent; federal troops have harassed them and killed some of their kinsmen. They tell stories of massacre by the federal troops, who forced them to chant "I support one Nigeria!" or be shot. As the troops retreated towards Ikem, they abducted some of the women, and one of them was the fourteen-year-old daughter of a man who keeps wailing, begging the soldiers to pursue the enemy and rescue his daughter, till Captain Irunna orders that he be dragged away to the safety of Eha Amufu.

D Company's second in command, the corporal with a nickname in Igbo that means "rifle," decides to go into town and find a suitable place to sleep. Some of the company, including Kunle and his three friends, follow behind the corporal, who carries a long, dry stick into the town, their path forged by the burning end of the stick, red sparks dropping from it and dying out in the gloom. The night is so dark the corporal's torch is barely able to illuminate it, and they step on bodies, broken rifles. Bube-Orji kicks something dark that rolls away in the dark with the ringing sound of a tin can. Its strange echo hammers quick pins of dread into Kunle and sends the bats perched on the overhead electrical lines to flight, dozens of them vanishing into the distant gloom. But it is clear that the town has been heavily damaged. As they wade among rubble, Ndidi says that this is why they call the federal troops "vandals." They can see by the light of the torch that on almost every inch of wall still standing, federal troops have stitched posters, mostly of Nigeria's president, Yakubu Gowon, pointing a warning finger above the inscription TO KEEP NIGERIA ONE IS A TASK THAT MUST BE DONE. At last they find a house, half of which has been damaged into a pile of rubble, but its living room is still mostly intact. Inside, crumpled mats, rugs, and possessions are scattered about the floor. They spread the mats on the floor and lie all in one straight line except Felix, moonlight shining through the open window. The moonlight rests on a poster with an oversize multiplication table hanging on the wall, cast in bluish light.

There was one like that at their primary school the year before the accident. Once, Kunle brought lunch to his brother, who was then in form one, and found Tunde standing under the poster, his hands protecting himself as four boys from form three jeered at and kicked him. Even these many years later, Kunle still cannot tell what possessed him as he rushed into the classroom. What he remembers often is the sound of one of the boys hitting the wall, the bloodied face of another, and holding the head of one between his knees while the boy yelled. Kunle was punished, and his father had to come to the school the following morning. But on the way home after the meeting with the headmistress, his father had said to him, "Kunle, listen, I liked what you did. You protected your brother. That is a good thing."

Felix sits by the window and turns the radio's dial so he can get a better signal, stretching its antenna up. The signal is starting to come in when Felix rises quickly, as if engaged in a sudden scuffle with an unseen assailant, and strikes a match. At once the room is illuminated by yellow light. From the rubble that's the other half of the house, something leaps out, slithers to the ground, and, like dark oil decanted from an invisible bottle, flows in a twisting, devilish line out the door, hissing as it goes. It is all so quick, but they have all jumped to their feet and panicked. And now they burst out laughing, their laughter mixed with relief and panic, as if they had gone momentarily mad.

The men begin discussing Biafra's advance into the midwestern city of Benin and how, just when the troops had driven unopposed to Ore, a town less than three hours from Lagos, they had pulled back.

"Saboteurs!" Felix says, his voice angry. "They full everywhere, even army HQ. But . . . How can . . . I just can't understand how Igbo man would want his own very people to fail. I can't understand!"

In the darkness, Felix's face twists as if coated with something deformed.

"It was . . ." the corporal says, coughing and swallowing. He has unwrapped the red bandanna from around his head, and he looks bald and much older. "It was bound to fail from the beginning."

"Eh-eh?"

"Yes—yes," the corporal says, nodding. "Ask youah sef this question. Why did His Excellency bring Yoruba man to command the operation?"

Bube-Orji whistles through his teeth, shakes his head, and asks, "How can His Excellency think it can be successful? How, biko gwa mu?"

They fall silent, the corporal coughing for a while.

"His Excellency must buy weapons wherever he can find them," Felix says. "Look at the vandals, they are fear-fear people. Before anything even happen, they have run!"

"Amem!" Ekpeyong cries. "I swear, I would have fired those Hausa people from A to Zed if I have bullet."

"They just have weapons, simple . . ." The corporal's words die into a loud yawn. "Just that: because Wilson is giving Gowon all the weapons they want. If not, our army will finish them."

In the silence afterwards, Kunle cannot pull his mind away from the story of this Yoruba officer who has betrayed Biafra. Did his comrades know that he was not actually Peter Nwaigbo, an Igbo who could not speak Igbo only because he'd grown up in Yorubaland, but that he was, in fact, Yoruba? But also—why is this mayhem being unleashed on the Igbos? Nkechi and her family had always been kind to him and his brother and family. He'd never thought ill of them. How is it that even Yoruba people were now joining the massacre of the Igbos?

Kunle opens his eyes and sees only the red knob of the radio's antenna and the silhouette of Felix's figure propped against the wall, hears him muttering to himself now that the others have gone quiet. He tries again to sleep, but he cannot keep away the thoughts—of school, of the disco house his uncle had taken him to on Victoria Island, of Nkechi and the *Encyclopaedia Britannica* she used to read with him, even of the Seer—from leaping continuously into his mind. Yet at the end of each thought the images from the war creep in, and all night he struggles, like a man trying to climb a slippery hill, to think of anything but the front.

8.

Light from eye-sized bullet holes rests on his face when he wakes. He recalls at once that the newscaster on Radio Biafra last night had given the date as Monday, August 14, which means that today is Tuesday, August 15. He has been in the Eastern Region for one month, and a new term began yesterday at the University of Lagos. Questions cascade into his head: Has registration for the term closed? What will happen to his academic status, to his apartment? To whom should he explain this exigent need to return to Lagos? The thought brings him such an intense revulsion that he almost screams.

His mind is heavy, like the trees around him, which are gray with rainwater. The hems of their trousers are damp from the wet grass, which shimmers in the morning light, carrying a dewy verdancy. It rained just before dawn, and now the clay earth bears an ancient smell—as of the earth in its beginnings. All over the village, rivulets of water are coursing through small ravines and grooves, ferrying debris. Some men from B Company encircle a metal drum, washing their faces and mouths. Behind them, civilians gather around a hearth outside a hut. In a ditch across the dirt road, a supply truck is stuck, and soldiers are trying to push it to get it started. There is a damaged house to the south, collapsed into a pile of stones and wood and domestic effects—a lamp, a bed frame, the singed arm of a wooden chair, shaking under the weight of the morning breeze. The corpse of one of the soldiers killed by the ordnance lies among the rubble, only his feet sticking out.

When they begin marching again, their boots gather clumps of mud from the moistened earth and they drag their feet through the ruts, swaying their hands, almost in comic dances. Some of the men fall in the slick mud, Captain Irunna among them. The captain sways, his hands floating as he dances in a hunched posture, and then tumbles down. Kunle and his comrades laugh and Ekpeyong helps up the captain, who curses and spits in blighted rage. They find a grassy path and the men walk in a narrow line until the captain orders a stop. The men cut up and cover the road with banana leaves before they continue the march.

The damaged Genocide, its top blown off, leads the way. For a while, a cheering crowd of civilians from the surrounding bushes follows, trailed by the supply wagon. One watching from above can see that Kunle feels the need to stay close to Felix, Ekpeyong, Bube-Orji, and the men from his training camp. He joins in singing the English-language song one of them started and at once he forgets that he is afraid. He realizes that this is why the men often sing with veins bursting in their faces and taut muscles in their necks: *"We are Biafrans, fighting for our nation, in the name of Jesus, we shall conquer!"*

Four kilometers outside the next town, whose name he cannot retain, they arrive at a junction where a mass of people with shovels are repairing a road damaged by a high-caliber bomb. Near the junction sits a hotel, smashed in by the bomb, still smoking. Its blue gate has melted into a crushed wreck of metal, still connected at the hinges, squeaking in the morning wind. On a tree, half of which is charred and half still darkly green, dead ash is falling, and on the topmost branch, vultures sit, gazing into the ruins. A dead Biafran soldier lies by the destroyed building. Rain has washed the man's face clean and someone has removed his shoes, and on the yellow sole of his foot, a black caterpillar is crawling. There had been a Biafran observation post a few meters from here—a roofless cage nestled on the treetop and manned by two observers, who have been killed. One of them hangs upside down from a blasted opening in the post, his head and hands suspended in the air. At the sight, Kunle feels a movement in his groin and drops of urine slide down his leg. He looks about to see if anyone has noticed; then he rushes off, unzips his pants, and lets loose into the bush.

From a damaged house, the regimental signalman emerges, covered in mud and soot, shouting that the enemy's salient is in the direction they are heading. He is waving frantically, redirecting them to where C Company has dug trenches and set up a defensive line. The men are starting to move when a soldier falls, blood pouring from where his eyes had been. Another, a man of D Company nicknamed Goliath, sprawls, screaming. The rest scamper behind Genocide. The vehicle is still turning when bullets begin hitting it again, the whine louder now and closer. Men fall, the sergeant commanding C Company among them, a film of smoke rising from the bloody hole in his chest as the sergeant screams continuously. For long, the world to Kunle is smoke and noise, something poisoned and vandalized. It feels as though there is fire in his eyes, thorns in his heart, and toxins in his lungs. He is coughing, gasping, as he makes his way through a road that for several meters is obscured by black smoke—for Genocide is engulfed in flames.

THE SHELLING THAT follows is relentless—a barrage of explosions and convulsions. Huddled beside Ekpeyong, Felix, Bube-Orji, and others from his company, Kunle struggles not to panic. At first it seems as though they are protected in this trench, four or five feet deep and wide, with parapets emplaced with sandbags and tree trunks. But with each blast, he shakes and pulls himself closer to the trench wall embankment, below the sandbags. The field rages with shells, mortar rounds. Although they land hundreds of meters away, there is hell in the terrible whistling as they fly past, and a tragic resonance in the shrapnel cutting into flesh, bursting sandbags, and killing men. He can sometimes catch a glimpse of a tangerine glow as the shells pass.

And in the far right corner of the trench, a man who perhaps has tried to leave falls back into it, screaming. Shrapnel has lodged in a deadly pocket of the man's flesh. For what must be an hour or so, the man's wailing is a cruel repudiation of a world turned upon itself. It sets fire to Kunle's soul and, perhaps, the souls of all who hear it, but no one is willing to risk taking the man out of the protection of the trench to the first aid post at the rear. At some point, one of the men makes a dash for the dying man, but Bube-Orji and another man hold him down through many scuffles, until the dying man's voice weakens and then fades away.

Now, after four hours of shelling, the front has gone quiet. It is a strange sort of silence, in which the world acquires a sudden verdant clarity. All of Kunle's senses have become heightened, and he can see, through his dusty eyelids, the worms writhing along the trench wall, the clay sparkling in the sun. He can smell his own urine, the sweat and stale breath of his comrades. And he can hear things clearly, too—the deep gurgle of the men's breathing and the rumbling of their guts, Bube-Orji's chewing of a lobe of kola nut. He wipes the surface of his wristwatch—it is almost eleven A.M.

Felix, who is wedged between Bube-Orji and Ekpeyong, breaks the silence. This morning he was happy after hearing on the radio about some Biafran unit's victory in the northern sector, near Onitsha. Now he curses, badly wanting a chance to engage the enemy again. He is given to quick shifts towards a sunnier mood, as though he carries with him a bottle full of oil that with every defeat empties, then with every victory fills up again.

Bube-Orji is bathed in the sand of split-open sandbags, and his eyelids are yellow. He says something in Igbo, but Felix does not respond, and it occurs to Kunle that he is talking to himself. Perhaps, like Kunle, Bube-Orji is thinking about the images that will not leave him—maybe the horrible face of the man with the blown-out eyes, or of the one who died in the trench without help. He cannot tell why he wants badly to know, but he asks anyway. Bube-Orji, wearing what looks like a pained smile on his face, says, "I was just saying, it is like we come to stand in front of one mirror, you know? The mirror is this war. . . .

It'av shown us different pictures of ourselves that we did not know existed." All the while, the front has been tormented with shattering noise, every sound imbued with ringing terror. But now, so firm is the silence that when a man down the line farts, it is so loud those who have stood up or climbed out of the trench rush back to position. The front line breaks into a roar of laughter.

News comes down through Captain Irunna's radio that the reason for the pause is that a Biafran attack helicopter has destroyed one of the enemy's artillery batteries, and the trench line—for as long as it stretches—erupts in wild jubilation. Kunle does not join in the singing, swatting at the persistent flies attracted to the muddy and urine-soaked trenches. The helicopter appears, flying low between the trees, blowing dirt and leaves and papers into the air. The men chant, "Hail Biafra!" and even the man beside him, who has kept to himself, mumbling quiet prayers with a rosary clasped between his hands, shouts. During the shelling, everything stood still—everyone lying where they were—but now everything has come alive again: everywhere, porters and medical corpsmen begin carting away the injured and the dead. Soldiers are passing around jugs and buckets of water, and they climb out of the trenches and wander into the surrounding bushes to relieve themselves. Kunle rushes out, too, untying the belt of his trousers long before he reaches his spot.

When he returns, the men are emptying a wooden box filled with ammunition. Captain Irunna walks up and down the winding trench line, making a head count of the troops of D Company. His bandanna is wet around his neck, and as he counts, voices rise from his walkie-talkie, shouting between the static: *Storm Wan, alpha . . . Roger, roger . . . HQ Chineke time, order halt! . . . Distress, distress, air force command here . . . Captain Oleka speaking from . . .*

"Naiti-four," the captain says, pointing at Kunle with the tip of a pen, and then, gesturing behind Kunle, "naiti-five, naiti-six . . ."

When it seems he is satisfied, Captain Irunna sets his second in command to keep watch and disappears towards the rear. The corporal mounts the embankment and orders rest at once, and in the reprieve Kunle closes his eyes to stem the fever in his head, and for a while he feels the pull of home, smells the sharp tang of his mother's Sunday cooking.

A pitched cry rises from the front, and he shudders awake. Through the moving form of dust, he sees the Biafran helicopter racing away, a stream of flame-colored smoke chasing it. Something drops from its open door. It is a man—curved first, two hands extended, as if he's diving into a pool. The dark figure flips, dangling in the air like an upturned scissors, hands waving, then spread-eagled, then clasped together as he makes an awkward somersault, until he drops out of sight. The wounded helicopter follows a short distance after, shedding white smoke as it falls.

The specter of the man's death muffles the men into silence. The corporal sits on the embankment of the part of the trench where Kunle and his friends are and leans against a stump, shaking his head. His long-sleeved shirt is hitched above his elbows, revealing the traces of an old burn. He begins telling the men about the Battle of Nsukka, where he'd first fought. A shell had killed four men in a trench of eight and left the other four completely unscathed. He'd seen one of the dead propped against the torn parapet, the rocket still smoking in his belly. "I have never seen something like that in the history of my life," the corporal says, his eyes glinting, his voice halting like that of Uncle Idowu. "Never. My eyes became sick. God. It was really rea—"

One watching Kunle from above would at first be confused, knowing only that there has been a thunderous bang and now his head and hands are covered with dirt and mud. Pain stings his right eye, and a weight presses his back into the ground. Kunle hitches himself forward, crawling on his hands and knees. Turning, he sees that the weight is the corporal, whose body is lifeless, the legs still shuddering from the deadly shock.

"Oluwa mi oh!" he cries, hurling the corporal's bloody legs from him. He tries to crawl away, but finds that this part of the trench has caved in and he has been buried under it. He attempts to free himself, but he cannot move an inch. The gun hole has closed, the trench wall is torn, and half his legs are covered in sand. He shakes his head to loosen the sand in his ears, and now he can hear the faint and nervous music of gunfire as it seeps through the ground. To the left, he sees Felix seated with fingers in his ears, a long, dark, sinuous line running along his sleeve from shoulder to wrist. Another explosion tilts Kunle forward, and in the distance some fifty meters away he sees a fountain of earth lift, limbs and bodies and foliage gesturing within it like austere acrobats.

Faintly, he hears Captain Irunna shouting an order to evacuate the trenches. Dazed, spitting out mud and blood, Kunle cannot move his lower half. He squirms, tries to muster a reluctant force through his body. Shouting, he picks up his rifle and crawls for a few meters over bodies of the slain, his hands covered in the blood of the dead. At last, he hauls himself up the breastwork and runs after his friends into the bush.

HE CROUCHES BY Ekpeyong, and at once the tall man hands him an almost empty canteen. He drinks, shaking the last drops into his mouth. From the bush they hear renewed shelling and see black smoke curl over the trees. Captain Irunna is whistling, shouting: "Take firing position!" Kunle crouches in the grass, shivering from a strange fever. Between the trees he can see the sun shining through the branches and the overstory. He can hear grasshoppers alighting on plants, and the distant rumble of enemy armored vehicles—what Felix and the others described as "Saladins" and "Ferrets" supplied by the British government. He kneels beside Ekpeyong, who seems collected despite a film of blood over his right eye. Ekpeyong's rifle is poised in a firing position in the direction of the expected enemy.

"Dem don dey come," Ekpeyong whispers in a voice so husky Kunle can barely hear it.

"What?" he asks.

"Vandals. You no hear am?" Ekpeyong points.

Now Kunle hears the distant chants of the enemy. The earth seems to come alive, as if all the dead since the beginning of mankind have begun a sudden march. His gaze falls to his boot, where clumps of earth are slowly sliding down with each tremor of the wheels of the approaching vehicles. He thinks of the Seer—why had the Seer called him an *abami eda*? Will he survive the assault when it comes? Even if he does, will he survive this war? Upon the empty road, the armored vehicles appear, their shadows moving between the trees as shouts from the direction of the vehicles rise like something imagined: "Ooshebee! Heh! Ooshebee! Heh! . . . Morale high! Heh!"

Earlier in the morning a few recruits carried crates of ammunition around for the soldiers, rounds for Mausers, CETMEs, Lee-Enfields, and others. Now Kunle checks the chamber of his rifle; there are only seven rounds out of twenty. He glances back, looking for the men with the ammunition boxes.

Something whistles loudly, and almost at once he feels the draft of something fast and quick hurtling overhead into the forest, tearing through the broad, dark leaves of the overstory in sparkles of firelight. And a few meters behind Kunle, a tree ignites. The forest is aglow with a strange, unearthly light. The tree falls, forming a long, straight depression in the sea of grass, and from under it two legs are kicking. From that direction, sharp screams arise. First, he glimpses only a mirage, then—as if torn from some other specter—he sees the digits of a man's hands framed in the yellow flame.

Kunle turns back to see the faint outline of the federal soldiers advancing. He crawls quickly, beneath thick animated foliage, past two dead Biafran soldiers in the thick bush. Voices are shouting from everywhere—Captain Irunna's, Ekpeyong's. "Peter—fall back!" a familiar voice cries. Something hits the barrel of his rifle, giving off a loud, metallic whine. He wants to cry. Again he hears his name. The bush rustles. In front of him, Ekpeyong crouches, shouting, "Come—come!" He runs, objects flying past him, hitting the grass and trees with heavy thuds, clouds of black smoke massing behind him.

With gunfire and shells raging around them, Kunle and Ekpeyong enter a ruined village, jump through the large maw-shaped shell hole in the wall of a textile store as a federal bomber flies overhead, bombing Biafran positions. Black smoke springs up a few meters to his left, as if a pipe has broken, and moves like a mob of clouds over the reddening sun. Kunle mounts the shaky steps created by brick rubble, steps over the back of a mangled corpse. Little urns of fire are scattered around. They skirt the burning bush all the way to the motor road. The blacktop is strewn with metal scraps from Genocide, shrapnel, bodies, spent cartridges, and dirt. Here, there is a unit of Biafran soldiers retreating, most of them in battered uniforms, wounded. He glances back, then at his bleeding hands, and he recalls the name the Seer had called him.

His head swooning and his vision blurred, he and Ekpeyong reach the rear, where one of the command lorries is parked. Everywhere, men sweating, fatigued, and bloodied stand or sit, trying to get water or be taken away for treatment. From a mat beside one of the medical corpsmen with the water jugs, a voice calls weakly to him and, turning, he sees that it is a member of their company who had commented at the training camp that Kunle had the face of a teenager.

The man lies there, shrapnel lodged in his neck, the left side of his uniform soaked with dark arterial blood. He is blinking, thick blood coursing from his neck like the mealy saliva of a stricken beast. The wounded man struggles to speak as he is carried onto the bed of a lorry loaded with the bodies of a dozen dead or wounded men. As the lorry drives away, rocking as it encounters the ruts in the road, the bodies of the dead or wounded men, propped in seated positions against the sides of the lorry, bounce against the metal railing, and the seated man seems to sway as if engaged in a quiet dance. Kunle, turning, finds that he has begun to weep.

W<small>HEN THE SEER</small> heard the federal vehicles arriving, he stiffened and felt a tightening in his throat as he struggled to stifle a gasp. Though the unborn man exists only in the vision, in a yet-uncreated time, Kunle can feel the weight of the Seer's gaze and can hear him. It is one of Ifa's great wonders: that he can scale the boundaries of time and the limits of existence to communicate with someone far into the future. The Seer restrained himself as he watched the carnage, young men being killed in a theater of war before his eyes. At one point, he'd wondered if this was going to be the moment when the man dies. But Kunle had escaped unhurt, a bullet merely grazing the barrel of his rifle. The Seer had once witnessed, with his beloved, Tayo, a brutal fight at an open market near Agege motor park, during which a man stabbed his assailant in the head. The undimming youth of the memory, how he can recall every part of it in vivid detail, still surprises him. But now here he is watching men fall, be incinerated, get blown up.

Now that Kunle has left the front line, the Seer rises from the raffia mat. He shakes his head again, for this part of the vision is difficult for him to stomach. He is conflicted: he wants desperately to witness the death and resurrection of this man; at the same time, half his heart is warmed by the desire for every one of these people, many of whom are not yet born, to survive.

A rush of wings nearby startles the Seer; turning, he sees a white bird rising quickly towards the stand of trees. The Seer's heart quivers. The bird, whatever it is, must have been drawn to the light from the bowl. He looks down, and for a moment the water of Ifa roils; then a strange crease appears on its surface. The Seer waits impatiently to see Kunle again, the man who has just jumped over the pit of death, carrying the full jar of his life with him intact. And without meaning to, the name escapes the Seer's own lips: "Abami Eda."

9.

It is the sixth day at the front, and already he has drunk his fill of the war's raw water. For five days they've fought, fallen back upon contact with enemy infantry, and dug new defensive positions, which the enemy then shelled. A few days ago, they held the pockets of villages and towns outside Ikem. By yesterday evening, they were left only a long, winding highway flanked by outcroppings and small hills just outside Eha Amufu. The wounded and the dead pile up in the rear and lie on the roadsides. Today the troops are massed along the eastern bank of the Eha Amufu River, flanking B Company's positions south of the river.

The bombardment today speaks a violent language that reverberates through the long house of a person's life, cracking its walls in many places. The men are broken by it—like the man who, by the third day, could not stop screaming that he had a headache: "Isi na awa mu o! Isi na awa mu o!" And who, in an act of sudden insanity, ran out of the trench. Hours later, Felix described seeing the man's legs floating in the air. It is to make the soldiers acclimate to the milieu that they are no longer allowed to sleep outside the trench. The previous night, Kunle slept while leaning his head on the shoulder of the rosary-praying man, Ndidi. An officer from the 14th Battalion stood on an open-roofed command jeep, shouting over the megaphone that no one was to leave except to relieve themselves in the nearby bush: "If anyone attempts to leave the battlefield, you will be court-martialed. I repeat, you will be court-martialed."

Usually, the night is calm, and they've become used to sleeping here on the battlefield, to the quietness of it, save for the chirping of insects and toads, and the occasional rumble of vehicles porting away the dead or bringing armor and supplies, or men breaking into wails or conversations or prayers or singing. Kunle has also become accustomed to the sounds of the dead who lie in the no-man's-land outside the salient. Through the night there are the noises of bellies bursting, of gaseous emissions from the corpses, of urine-like hissing. Sometimes it is rats or mice interacting with the bodies.

But this night is different: Kunle wakes to drifting rain and deranged cries. The night comes alive with the rattle of gunfire and the orange sparkles of moving fire. It is hard to believe that the enemy has launched an unusual night attack. Everywhere, men are screaming, wailing, and an unseen officer is shouting, "Return fire!" Kunle hurls himself in the direction opposite from where he'd heard the incoming shots. There are—for some twenty minutes—relentless bursts; then silence falls. The assault has ended, but he can no longer sleep. In the morning, on the scarred road just outside the trenches, in black, wet ruts lay four dead federal soldiers, a caterpillar crawling on the neck of one of them. Another is farther away, the mud paved with his blood, half-seated against a mound of earth, his helmet tilted over the side of his dead face, and on it an inscription: IGBO KILLER.

It is the shock of the previous night's attack, coupled with this morning's seven-hour shelling, and now Kunle feels that he, too, is broken. But for much of the time, he sits thinking of how a few days ago, just as he reached the first aid post at the rear, he heard a strange sound that only he could have heard. It was the long beating of wings followed by two words in a voice much like the Seer's whisper: "Abami Eda." It had felt real, but when he'd looked around, he'd seen no bird or anyone close by who might have said those words.

He is thinking about the voice when, later, as they engage the federal troops from the open road, Ekpeyong is shot. At once Ekpeyong sinks down, grinding his teeth, blinking. Kunle crawls towards Ekpeyong, makes to touch him, but is shocked by the quality of the dark red blood that has quickly soaked Ekpeyong's uniform. It appears redder than any blood he's ever seen. He looks up and Captain Irunna, crouched behind a tree on the shoulder of the road, shouts, "Up, carry him to first aid!"

At first, Kunle thinks Captain Irunna mad—they are under unremitting fire from federal positions in the woods only two hundred meters away, and enemy vehicles are visible even from this spot. But when the officer shouts again, cocking his pistol, Kunle reaches down to the weeping man. He hefts him up, his heart pounding, and runs with Ekpeyong.

It is a surprise to him when they near the first aid post. At once, they are among other wounded and porters from the 1st and 14th Battalions, heading in the same direction. When two men take Ekpeyong from him, someone hands him a canteen, and the water, drunk quickly, settles in his gut like a turd. One man who is being helped by two other soldiers has his left leg severed at the knee, the limb hanging by a thin stick of bloodied bone. They step into a puddle, panting, and two men rush forward to help Ekpeyong out of the muddy water.

Relieved, Kunle kicks off his shoes, carries them in his hands, and runs on with the shoes dripping like punctured bags of water.

"They are coming! Moof! Moof! Fall back!" he hears, the report of gunfire closer—less than two kilometers away.

Kunle hears his name and, turning, finds Ndidi closing up behind him. Together they chase after the retreating mass in the direction of Eha Amufu, Ndidi intoning the Hail Mary. They watch an open-backed lorry pass on the potholed dirt road; it bears mostly the dead, bodies piled upon bodies, their bare feet swerving like waving hands. One of the wounded calls out to the vehicle for a medic, but the driver merely shakes his head, pointing towards the rear. For more than two kilometers, a small crowd of civilians hobbles alongside this sullen mass of damaged troops. At last, as if nature itself has ambushed them, they stop at the bank of the Eha Amufu River. The bridge across it was destroyed by saboteurs that morning, and now it is merely piles of iron bars prostrating themselves into the water. On the near end, a throng has gathered around a large canoe, where two officers with sticks and a man in white coveralls with a Red Cross badge on his sleeve are screening passengers so that only the wounded can board. Kunle and Ndidi rush Ekpeyong towards the canoe.

A few of the soldiers slink into the water, their rifles raised above their heads, their quick shapes slurring through the mud-brown water; they emerge on the other side looking thinner, grayed, shivering. The boat returns and is again crowded with women and the wounded. The last of the 14th Battalion arrives, and the soldiers throw themselves into the river, shouting that the enemy is less than a kilometer away.

Though he cannot swim, Kunle flings himself into the water without thinking. He at once feels water in his mouth, eyes, ears, nose. He cannot see—showers of colored light sink into the soft fabric of his eyes. He lets out a hurried cry, flails his hands in revolt. A rush of water swims up his shoulders and threatens to topple him. Another man, with a bloodied back, falls headlong against him, and Kunle feels a hand tug at his trousers. The man beneath him is screaming, and for a while Kunle's face is choking in the water. He pulls himself away, beating his arms against the surface. He feels something give way, and is released. Swiftly, he pushes through the traffic of drenched people.

He is hefted out by mostly plainclothes men waiting on the other side. He stands on the soft bank, gasping for so long that at first he does not notice that the men who rescued him are pointing at his waist, speaking in Igbo and laughing. He looks down and sees that his pants have been ripped. Now approaching the shore is the man who'd grabbed him for flotation, the ripped piece still clutched in his fist, gray and dripping. He places his hands to cover his crotch and sits quickly on the shore.

Soon most of the Biafran troops have been evacuated from the other side of the Eha Amufu River. The commanding officers set the mammy wagon with the dead and supplies ablaze. The fire is loud and murmuring, its reflection cast upon the surface of the river. The officers walking or swimming away from the site of danger pass through the ring of the fire. A great sudden silence descends upon the people on the safe side of the river, for now they wait to see what will happen to the half dozen wounded men lying on stretchers with no way of crossing. Kunle can hear the voice of one of them; he is sitting up on his stretcher, gesturing and shouting something in Igbo. Another crawls slowly up to the edge of the water and slides neatly into it like a spear. The current, flowing more quickly with the force of the evening wind, drafts the man downward. A gasp ripples through the people on the shore, and for a while Kunle waits, swatting the flies congregating around his face. The man's hands appear, and through a sudden clear stretch downstream, Kunle sees his legs kicking as if he were cycling. The man's hands sink, plop up again, his head swaying to unloop itself of the water. Kunle turns away. When he looks again, the man's clothing is floating like a small raft over the water.

Half a dozen federal soldiers arrive, helmeted and garbed in foliage. One of them shoots in the direction of the escaped Biafrans, but his bullets do not reach them. Then the soldier aims at the wounded men still left on the shore, the reports ringing out. In vain the Biafran soldiers shout, curse. The general commander of the 14th Battalion orders an evacuation. They rise, hundreds of men, marching away from Eha Amufu. On their faces Kunle can see the sordid realization: that after six days of heavy fighting, they have lost both Ikem and Eha Amufu. And for a long time they tread along the road in silent bitterness, guided only by the moonlight, as if uttering a word about what has happened will provoke the agony of a future yet unknown.

10.

For four days Kunle lay numbly on a hessian mat in a room in Enugu, Biafra's capital city, with most of the soldiers lying on their uniforms spread on the bare floor. During these four days, each time there was some quiet in the hall, vivid images of the front crawled like worms out of the dead eyes of the past and into his head, filling him with sizzling dread. Every day, bitter and rattled, he shuttled between thoughts of escape and plans to go in search of his brother. On the morning after they arrived here, he asked Bube-Orji again about the Umuahia area, and the man assured him, as Felix had done before, that there was still no fighting there. And he reckoned that if his brother was safe, then he might endanger Tunde further by taking him away from where he was. Resolving that it was best that he return home by himself, he now thinks of calling the Opi Health Center again. For days he struggles to find a way to reach the clinic.

His friends, too, are sullen and sorrowful, dwelling on the recent battles, in which hundreds have died. They also lost most of their possessions; these things were burned in one of the mammy wagons that could not make it across the river. Felix lost his transistor radio in the water; Ndidi lost a prayer book. Kunle lost the paper on which he'd scribbled Nkechi's address, and for the first two days, his wristwatch stopped working. He opened its rusting silver back, took out the battery, and sunned it by the windowpane of the hall in which they're living. When he put it back, the long hand began moving again.

The loss of the northern towns has caused a reorganization of the Biafran military strategy. Daily, through radio, hearsay, copies of publications such as *Biafran Sun* or *The Leopard*, news of other sectors of the war floated in, and by the end of the first week, it became clear that the Biafran advance in the Mid-Western Region—which Felix and others had been following—had completely stalled and the Biafran troops had been routed. The men were flustered by the news. They knew the federal soldiers were not better fighters than the Biafran soldiers, but only had the equipment to better prosecute a war. And a Biafran army unit that had seen little resistance had bungled what could have been a decisive victory.

The first day of the following week, the quartermaster comes from army headquarters, and they gather at the center of the school's compound. In the center of the field stands the statue of a schoolboy dressed in white short sleeves and blue shorts, cradling books in his hands, and on the stone pedestal beneath, the inscription IMMACULATE HIGH SCHOOL, ENUGU. The quartermaster distributes several items to each of the nearly four hundred troops: two small leather pouches, one ammo holder, new uniforms fashioned by tailors in Enugu and across Biafra. On the belts, a third of the men have a rubber or metal canteen. That night, after a dinner of boiled yams and palm oil, Kunle pulls Felix out of earshot of the others and asks how he might telephone his parents. Felix, stroking his growing beard, smiles.

"It is as if you can read my mind."

"Eh?"

"I have been trying to get a pass and go home and see my family, since they are not far from here—trekking distance," Felix says. "I want to take my father's old radio also—he has two. I also want to see them in case Enugu falls and they leave. But captain say they can only give one-hour permission because of the situation."

"It is true," Kunle says.

Felix drops his eyes to reflect, the nits around his fair but darkening face visible now. "Egwagieziokwu, I know from where we can send them a telegram. Cita . . . Press—you know it?"

Kunle shakes his head.

"Oh, Citadel Press, owned by Christopher Okigbo. Wait, let me go and collect pass."

Kunle nods.

"I am sure they will give me, since my place is not far. They don't want anybody to jus' run away—many have run." He twists his head so that his neck muscles make a sound. "On the way to Enugu, MP catch many, up to sixteen from our brigade, and major ordered them straight to tribunal."

Kunle becomes conscious of Felix's eyes on his face now, regarding him closely.

"You know what will happen?"

He shakes his head.

"Firing squad," Felix says urgently. Then, twisting his mouth into a smile, he places his hand on Kunle's shoulder, as if to calm him. "I will ask in the morning, for Bube too, and pray they allow us go."

In the morning they leave with Bube-Orji, who whistles and hums a tune as he chews kola nuts. They stop first at the school's gate and salute the privates manning the gate. Rising above their guard post is a large Biafran flag, waving softly in the late morning air. Outside the gate, a steel pylon stretches fifteen or so feet into the sky; on top of it is some strange electronic equipment, with a wire running into the shack below the pylon. The instrument is covered, perhaps for protection from rain and sun, by a tin roof.

"What is that?" Kunle says.

"Siren?" Felix spits in the gutter by the roadside. "They are bombing us now from the sky, too—everywhere. I don't know what we did to this people. Why—why the hatred? Why, eh? If you see how they kill us—you even hear them in camp, eh?"

Kunle nods.

"It is terrebul—really terrebul!" Bube-Orji says. He spits green saliva into the grass.

They walk on the long paved road, past roadside hawkers and military policemen on Honda bikes, who wade through the crowds of vehicles. Kunle can see that the city is modern—as developed as Lagos beyond Carter Bridge. It seems largely untouched by the war. They pass a Mobil petrol station with a long queue of expensive cars—an American Thunderbird, Opel Kadetts, a Ford truck, a Morris Minor. The cars are being served by women in blue aprons over milk-white habits. He is surprised to find that all the traffic wardens in Enugu city are also women—all dressed neatly in blue uniforms and prism-shaped hats. The one at the roundabout where they stop waves at them to cross, her gloved hands putting a complete stop to some dozen cars on both sides of the road. A young boy crossing beside them runs up and shouts, "My daadi is soldier too!"

Felix points out the names of the streets to Kunle and Bube-Orji: Zik Avenue, Bank Road. A few blocks later, they arrive in front of a two-story building a few meters from a record store, from which vinyl music is blaring. Felix is speaking, but his voice is drowned out by a man selling ice cream from a cooler set on the back of a bicycle, ringing a bell as he passes and shouting, "Fresh ice cream! Made in Biafra, sweet as honey!"

At once, Bube-Orji begins making slurping sounds with his mouth. Felix, shaking his head and saying, "You're always hungry," waves the ice-cream man down.

"Is it really made in Biafra?" Felix says, laughing.

"I swear to God, Officer. I swear this is real Biafra ice cream." The man raises the ice cream, tied in thin, clear nylon bags, water dripping from them.

Felix hands the man some money. The man lifts the notes, peers closely at them, and shakes his head.

"You no get new money?"

"What happen?"

"New money wey come two weeks ago? Gowon don change money, oh. We no dey collect this one again."

Felix glances at Kunle as the man puts the ice cream back in the cooler.

"I sorry, Officers—we no dey collect this money again."

"What money?" Kunle says, but the man merely shakes his head, mounts his bicycle, and rides off, ringing his bell and shouting, "Fresh ice cream . . ."

"I don't even know," Felix says, taut tendons appearing along his neck. "And, egwagieziokwu, not even De Young has mentioned this. They hate our people so much they changed even money . . . common money! So we can die of hunger."

Again, Kunle nods. He wants to say something but finds only an inchoate understanding of the circumstances. They are now in front of a building on whose lintel is the inscription CITADEL PRESS. They step into the hallway and read a typed notice on a board pinned to the wall. Kunle peers over Felix's shoulder, his eyes resting first on the badge of the rising sun on the sleeve of his friend's shirt.

"It's about how to submit yuah work to the press," Felix says.

Bube-Orji tells them he will wait outside, and before anyone can say anything, he is breaking a lobe of kola nut from its skin. Felix and Kunle climb the stairs, past a motorcycle parked inside, beneath the stairs. The building smells like the insides of a new book. A ceiling fan swirls slowly, gently flapping the parted green curtains. There is a desk and chair; on the desk sits a big typewriter and a telephone. Above it is a framed photo of Colonel Ojukwu; the caption beneath the photo says, GENERAL OF THE PEOPLE'S ARMY. Beside it are three small wall clocks with the names of three different cities: Enugu, London, and New York. On a small stool sits a stack of books, all with the same green cover. There has been the clicking of a typewriter, but it stops now. A woman emerges from a room labeled PRINTING ROOM.

"Salute, Officers," she says.

"Ah, sister. Good afternoon oh."

"Yes, can I help you?"

Felix smiles. "No, ehm, we just want to see the place. We come from Obollo-Afor sector."

"Okay, sa. We have been open since June." She moves towards a desk, and stands behind it. "We have even published our first book. See there?"

Felix draws closer, glimpses the cover, and nods. "This is beautiful. When next I come, I will buy one."

They hear a number of clicks, as of one dialing a telephone, and a soft male voice begins speaking from one of the offices. With the wild smile still on his face, Felix points to the other room, on whose door is inscribed MAJOR CHRISTOPHER OKIGBO, ASSISTANT CHIEF PUBLISHING OFFICER.

"Ah, Oga Okigbo is not here. He is at front line—Nsukka. But the main oga is there. He is busy right now—maybe come after three o'clock if you want to see him."

"No—no problem," Felix says. "We just wanted to check and see the place. I am a poet too."

"Ah, maybe we will publish you."

"Ehen, ma, please I beg—my friend want to send telegram to Akure."

"Oh, Nigeria?"

They nod. The woman shakes her head. "They have cut it. You can't message anybody there from Biafra again."

"Ah," Felix says, turning to Kunle.

For a moment, Kunle stands in silence, with the rising feeling of being trapped, of every single door slamming in his face. He cannot telegraph his parents; he cannot reach Tunde; he cannot call the Opi Health Center to see if the reverend sister has gone to their house.

Later, they find Bube-Orji sitting on an old stone at the foot of a tree, his head bobbing as he chews. As they walk back, Felix recites a poem by a poet he calls "Jelan." Bube-Orji and Kunle listen, Bube-Orji moaning and mumbling at each striking line.

Felix's voice is starting to crescendo when Bube-Orji begins making uncertain, near-comical gestures, like one whose body parts are smarting at intervals—now clutching his chest, now his groin, now the seat of his pants. "What, Bube?" Kunle says, but Bube-Orji merely glances at him as if he's spoken an incomprehensible language. They are on a wide street, bungalow houses lining both sides of the road. Bube-Orji runs towards a small bush, a refuse dump mildly smoking near it. He sprints very quickly, but they both follow, scaling a rusting lorry tire on the ground. At last, they catch up with him; he is hidden behind a large-trunked tree, his trousers stripped to his ankles, dancing madly as he swats at his groin and buttocks, picking something out of his pubic hair. Kunle and Felix laugh as Bube-Orji prostrates himself and clutches at his belly. Felix slumps to the ground, half-sitting and rocking with laughter. Bube-Orji did not notice that the stone on which he sat earlier was surrounded by soldier ants. About half a dozen climbed into his clothes and trousers, stinging him everywhere.

Once Bube-Orji has made sure that there are no more of the red ants in his clothes, they continue on, then turn after a few blocks and stop outside a house with a low fence. Felix smiles as a girl who looks like him, her hair in tight plaits and her breasts swinging in a see-through T-shirt, rushes up to them. She was putting laundry on a line when she saw them.

"Boda! Boda!" she shouts as she jumps on her brother, and he catches her in a full embrace. She is saying something, but Felix, shaking his head, says, "Please, biko, speak English. Not all Biafrans are Igbo, you know?"

The girl nods and tells her brother that the shirt she is wearing was gifted to her by His Excellency during the Biafran independence celebrations. She speaks English laced with Igbo. She reminds Kunle of Nkechi. The resemblance is present in the way she gesticulates as she speaks, curling her hands, pointing, and weaving empty patterns through the air. There is also an edge in her voice, resembling the soft-sounding whisper of "Mmhuu" that often followed Nkechi's words. *You are vexing me, mmhuu? Don't be sad o, mmhuu?* While Felix's sister speaks, Kunle sees in her painted fingers the first day Nkechi painted her fingers in the sitting room of his house, the strong smell of Cutex filling the room.

Felix's sister brings ogbono soup and pounded yam in a big plate and bowl, genuflecting. The three men wash their hands and eat quickly from the same bowl, Bube-Orji licking his fingers with such abandon that Kunle fights to stop himself from laughing. They can barely listen to Felix's sister's account of all that has been happening in the city since independence. Felix's mother, very fair-complexioned like her son, is perhaps a few years younger than Kunle's own mother. She is filled with words: the state of civilians in Biafra, how a cup of salt that used to cost just one shilling coin is now two pence, the anguish of mothers whose sons are dying on the field. She is talking about the actions of the saboteurs when she jerks and falls. Kunle, too, has been thrown to the vinyl floor, a pain in his left leg. Beside him are the broken bits of the plates that have been dashed against the wall, as if a petulant child hurled them in a rage. Felix's sister is on the ground, holding on to her brother's legs, her trembling voice intoning, "Faa abia go! Faa abia go!"

Felix is visibly angry. He rises, lifts his sister, and reaches for his mother, who is retying her wrappa, which has come loose, around her waist.

"Nwanne, did you guys hear that?" Felix says, turning to Bube-Orji and Kunle.

Blinking and rising to his feet, Kunle nods. It sounded even more devastating than the artillery shells and mortar rounds.

"Chineke'm!" Bube-Orji cries, making a teeth-gnashing sound. "What did they drop like that on the city? Eh, on civilians? I mean—can you imagine? Innocent women and children—"

Kunle throws himself down again, covering his head with his hands, muttering, "Jisos, Jisos" to himself. He feels more afraid here than at the front. Here in a house, there is no escape. A bomb could hit a house and the house itself could kill its occupants. This event gives the stories the men have told of the pogrom in the north a tragic realism. The rage he feels possesses him now fully, as though a new version of himself has been made. It strikes him now that the cause he's been unwillingly roped into may actually be a good one. Perhaps instead of attaining the redemption he sought for so long in righting the wrong he once did, he could achieve it on a larger scale if he helped fight to save this people.

Once the ground stops shaking, they hear cries of anguish from the surrounding neighborhood. People are running in every direction, jumping out of their cars and taking shelter in small buildings with bunkers. A bicycle lies on the side of the road, and from somewhere beyond the block of buildings, black smoke is rising. They head in that direction and a few blocks away find a bakery on fire. A few people are trying to pull a man from the rubble, but just as they are about to free him, a slice of the side wall comes crashing down. Wails of "Chineke-eh!" shoot out from the crowd like something out of a dark tale. The man they have been trying to rescue lies flat, only his hands stretched out through the slabs of bricks and wood, his fist still clenched. Blood flows from beneath the rubble in two threads like twin snakes.

They pull out a teenage girl covered in white dust that gives the dark red blood on her white lips a strange glow. Her left thigh has been torn open, and with each movement, she lets out a bloodcurdling scream. They are pulling another man out of the rubble when Bube-Orji bends towards Kunle's ear and asks him what time it is. When he raises his wrist so Bube-Orji can see his watch, Bube-Orji whispers in a panicked voice that their time is up.

After Felix picks up the new radio from his house, they return to the camp to find their comrades stamping their feet around a bonfire, cheering, "Kerenke obi!" Kunle joins the men in singing, aware of a certain élan in his spirit. Moved by the indiscriminate bombing and with nowhere else to go, he feels bound to these men now, despite having been brought here against his will. It occurs to him that if he were given the chance to leave, he would not immediately jump into the Red Cross wagon to go home. He would ask himself if he wanted to be away from these men—from Felix and Bube-Orji, and Ekpeyong, leaving them to face every trying day alone. As the flames sparkle and light up the faces of his friends, he sees that it is possible that he would choose to stay.

11.

It is Kunle's suggestion that they visit Ekpeyong before heading back to the front. The four of them, dressed in their uniforms—except for Ndidi, who wears a body-tight white T-shirt with the image of Pope Paul VI on it and a rosary around his neck—wait at the gate while Bube-Orji secures the permission. By noon, they are in front of this place that looks like no hospital Kunle ever saw before the war: there are two long poles holding a white flag with a red cross on it, and on the top of the slanted roof, a big, painted red cross visible to the pilots of the federal bombers. At the sight of the banner, Kunle's heart stirs as if he's stumbled upon the door of longed-for salvation. He runs to the spot, under two densely leaved trees where cars are parked. He soon realizes this is a different Red Cross wagon and there is no Sister Rosemary. He returns to his friends, who have puzzled looks on their faces.

"Sorry," he mumbles. "I thought I saw someone I know."

The clerk at the desk asks them to write their names in a foolscap logbook lined with red ink and filled with names. Then they pass through the long hallway to Ward B, for the newly wounded, the antiseptic smell of Izal disinfectant thick in the room. The room is wide open, two white curtains parted to fill it with daylight. They move slowly between the beds, where men of various shapes lie, swathed in bandages or in shawls. For such a crowded place, it is oddly quiet, with only the sound of two white ceiling fans rattling above, and the soft clink of needles in tin medical bowls, and the scraping of a man spooning something out of a tin plate. A young man is sleeping quietly while a nurse with gloved hands cleans the open wound on his leg, putting bloodied cotton wool and surgical needles on the tray beside the bed. Kunle's eyes meet those of another man, whose back is propped against the wall as he drinks from a cup; there is a great mass of bandages around the man's lean torso. Even though the man has no clothes, he wears a steel helmet dented on the side, the straps clasped around his jaw. A nurse, her white cap tilted to the side of her head, rushes in and waves at them to leave. Explaining that they cannot go into the ward, she leads them to a waiting room.

Ekpeyong appears, naked to the waist, a swollen, impregnated plaster of Paris covering the entry and exit points of the bullet. At the sight of him, they break out in muffled shouts of "De Young!" Ekpeyong smiles, his face beaming. His voice is full, more alive now, and seems eager to fill every silence, to slap the words of the others flat so he can erect his own. Yes, he heard about the withdrawal; yes, he heard about the bombings. He adds quickly before anyone else can speak that they have been assured that there will be no attacks on hospitals.

"Ah, mba, I don't trust vandals," Felix says.

"Ah, yes—yes!" Ekpeyong says quickly.

"You know?" Bube-Orji says quietly, his eyes cast up. "I keep remembering Corporal Egbe . . . all of the dead bodies."

Ekpeyong mumbles something, and a shade falls over his face.

"I don't jus' know—I don't know why all this 'av to happen, eh? Why must we keep dying . . . like this?" Bube-Orji, eyes still cast up, shakes his head. "Maybe . . . maybe life is jus' a necessary evil."

"You speak truth, nwanne!" Felix says, smiling. "Out, out, brief candle! Life's but a walking shadow, a lonely . . . sorry! . . . a poor player who struts and frets his hour on the stage."

"You know, this war humbles all of us," says Ndidi, who has been nodding all along, his voice just above a whisper. "Before the war, we always want this or that; we always have big dreams, big ambitions.

But now our needs have become so small, and our dreams have vanished. What is the hope we have? Just that we survive . . . that's it."

"You speak true!" Felix says, nodding.

"Yes . . . or for the war to end. That's it." Ndidi rubs his hands together in a gesture of completeness.

For a brief time no one speaks, and then they hear a bang and the hospital walls shake. They rush to the window. Somewhere around the hospital, a siren is blaring, and outside a man stands waving a large Red Cross flag. Kunle and his friends cannot not see the bomber. Its din is far, and at last they hear it no longer. When they sit again, Ekpeyong assures them that the federal forces would not attack the hospital because there are foreigners here—Irish, British, Americans, like the nurse, many of them from the Red Cross and other organizations. But so vivid and recent is what they witnessed in Enugu only a few days before that none reply or seem to believe this. In the silence, a midge flying about becomes prominent. It hops on Ekpeyong's bandaged wound, which is coated with gentian violet, and flits up to Felix's skin bag. Bube-Orji, rising as if on cue, snaps the midge between his hands with a loud clap. The men cheer, and Bube-Orji laughs, his face lighting up as if the vitiligo spots were filled with light. Felix, to keep Ekpeyong entertained, narrates Bube-Orji's ordeal with the army ants in a quieter voice meant for only the group of friends. This time, it is Ekpeyong whose ringing laughter causes Kunle to worry that they are being too loud. He and Ndidi say, "Shh!" Ndidi still has his finger over both lips when they hear from the ward next door a man wailing, calling for his mother.

"Is over now, gentlemen," a male voice, foreign, says, jerking his thumb sideward.

It is a bearded white man in a Hawaiian shirt who stands a few paces from them, rubbing his hands together, nodding towards Ekpeyong. Ndidi insists that first they must pray—and quickly, he intones the Hail Mary, crosses Ekpeyong, and hands him a small paper from the new prayer book he now carries, which he claims is from the Vatican, blessed by Pope Paul VI himself. It is a palm-sized white sheet with the simple image of a parenthesized cross at its center.

"A brave soul," Felix says once the four of them are out of the hospital.

Kunle nods.

"He wants to return to fight badly. Even though, you know ... his brother is fighting for Nigeria."

"Jesus Christ!" Bube-Orji says.

"Ooo-yes!" Felix lowers his voice. "He doesn't tell everybody. But his brother, and many of his kinsmen—Ibibio people—are supporting Gowon. His brother is in Second Division, fighting against us."

"Kai, this is truly sad," Bube-Orji says. "Imagine if it is even his brother that shoot him?"

"Yes!" Felix says. "But, you know eh ... egwagieziokwu, in this war fair is foul, and foul is fair."

"Yes, Prof. It is true." Bube-Orji's voice is wet now, for he has thrown a splinter of kola nut into his mouth.

But the thought does not leave Kunle's mind: Only a few weeks ago, a country was one and these people were neighbors. Today, they are killing each other, and even among the same family, brother is fighting against brother. And the world, like an injured bug, lies on its back, unable to turn itself over again.

Bube-Orji whistles and directs the other men's gaze to the field outside the hospital. About half a dozen wounded men—all of them with one leg amputated or heavily bandaged, most on crutches—are playing football. At the goalposts, men with two legs intact stand as goalies, one of them a mere teenager with a bandage around his head. A few people sit watching on the sidelines, including two nurses, their hair neatly permed, their gowns sparkling white in the dying sun. Kunle studies the men curiously, as he'd done with the wounded at the front, their sight causing in him a sudden eruption of fear: Could what happened to these men happen to him too?

They stop to let an old mammy wagon, carrying in its open back oil drums full of petrol, drive past, into the hospital grounds; its side bears the inscription BIAFRAN RESEARCH AND PRODUCTION. Then they walk between long, moss-covered walls hedging an empty piece of land outside the hospital. Kunle is thinking about Bube-Orji's words about the necessary "evil" of life when, from some unseen corner, four boys shoot out onto the dirt road, barefoot, chasing a kite whose thread has leapt out of the hand of one of them and is now curving into a sinuous hump in the air, the polythene making a waving noise. "Uncle, help us!" they cry, two of them touching Kunle. He grabs the thread and hands it to one of the boys. "Thank uh! Thank uh!" another boy shouts as they walk on. "Daalu . . . I want to be a soldier too when I am big!"

THE FOLLOWING MORNING is so dark that Kunle can barely read the time on his watch when the whistle and bugle sound. He washes and cleans his mouth with a half-pressed toothpaste tube passed around, rubbing the paste on two fingers and running the fingers over his teeth and gums and tongue. They board three Greyhound buses, several open-roofed Land Rovers and jeeps, and a mammy wagon and head into the empty streets in a mild, drizzling rain. Kunle is starting to fall asleep when panicked shouts erupt. Bube-Orji whistles through his teeth, and Felix taps Kunle on the shoulder. He sees through the window the football field outside the hospital and the body of one of the disabled soldiers, still wearing the white T-shirt from the previous day, hanging now from one of the goalposts, his body swinging lightly. The rope with which the man hung himself has pulled his head to the side, thrusting out his tongue. Rain is dripping from the shimmering figure, running down the vacant space in his hitched-up trousers where his left leg had once been.

Kunle looks at it until he can see it no more, for the sight is a spectacle from which no one, even against his will, can turn away. Ndidi, fiddling with his rosary, keeps staring in that direction, long after the wagon has passed. In the world in which Biafra now exists, this is life. There is nothing either he or this man can do about it. This is how it will be for him and for all the soldiers in this war. They have seen much, and they will see yet more. They must learn to withstand what they have seen, to adapt. If it shocks you, then it can haunt you; if it haunts you, it can damage you. A soldier who is already hurt by his own mind, how can he stand a chance against a vicious and well-equipped enemy? How can such a soldier withstand the sight of the machine guns or the tanks?

They arrive at the new brigade headquarters, a village only twelve kilometers from Eha Amufu, to find a crowd cheering them from the roadside, many holding small Biafran flags, chanting, "Hail Biafra, Land of Freedom!" Under a makeshift tent roofed with thatch and covered with camouflage foliage—tall palm frond and banana leaves—are two Biafran Red Devil armored vehicles and wheelbarrows full of CETME and Madsen rifles with slings, towards which the men plunge like a pack of chickens rushing a corncob. The vehicles look like Genocide but with stronger plating and machine gun turrets.

The men, who earlier were imploring Colonel Ojukwu to give them guns and armor to go into war, now sing the leader's praise with mad fervor, Felix translating for Kunle as he dances, raising his rifle in the face of the rising sun: "Thank you, Ojukwu, thank you!" Again Felix shouts, "I shall join with the army as my peers." The song is in Igbo, but at each dip into adagio, Felix tips his head towards Kunle and says, "Hang my good CETME around my neck . . . wear my good helmet on my head." Again the men burst into euphoric shouts. Felix, lost in the moment, throws his fists in the air. "Thank you, Ojukwu, thank you!"

A THIN JOY remains in Kunle when they ride out the following morning, before it's light. The front at Eha Amufu, when they reach it, is familiar, yet strange. Kunle feels as though he has entered the landscape of one of his most unpleasant dreams. It is a field freshly cleared of trees, their stumps left everywhere, the smell of fresh-cut grass in the damp air. On a lone tree, to the left of the trench stacked with rain-soaked sandbags, the corpse of a headless snake hangs, dripping with water. A multitude of voices are shouting. He takes in, with a slow, reluctant joy, the evidence of the nearly three weeks of planning to recapture the town. The defensive line is stacked using anti-tank barricades created with tree trunks, sandbags, and the wrecked carcasses of vehicles. The trenches look safer, with extended parapets lined with stacks of sandbags. This is the conscientious work of the Biafran militia, who'd worked under the cover of darkness.

Captain Irunna, wearing sunglasses, is waiting for them at a makeshift command post outside a thick barrier of bush. He and other commanders from the 53rd Brigade are poring over maps. When he steps out of the meeting to inspect his troops, he reeks of fuel, and the tips of his fingers are blackened with soot. He offers the company two big wicker baskets of food. The men eat quickly, wolfing down the food—rice in stew wrapped in banana leaves. Kunle licks his fingers afterwards, thinking of how, at the battlefront, food became a luxury, an afterthought given only to sustain them. Just the day before, at the camp in Enugu city, they had goat meat—the first meat he'd had since he joined the Biafran army. Kunle looks out at the singed fields, at the tree stumps blackened by fire, and a thought comes to him with a rush: What will happen to his parents if he is killed? From nowhere, he feels a sudden force pulling him away from his resolve to stick with his comrades.

That first day, they score unexpected victories: a Biafran gun shoots down an enemy fighter-bomber and shells federal positions with the newly supplied Biafran artillery. The bomber drops a bucket explosive somewhere near the front, and immediately the single anti-aircraft gun fires a few bursts at the plane, its sound like a storm trapped in a tin drum. The bomber begins to fly in circles like a blind bird, hovering over the front. It rallies on the updraft, scarring the latticed face of the sky with long lines of white contrails. Slowly black smoke begins to ooze from its wings. In a flash, it is falling, transforming into a burning thing like the tip of a matchstick.

Perhaps surprised by this unexpected Biafran firepower, the federal forces pull out of the center of Eha Amufu and move beyond a market to a safer position. The reprieve has come, a time of rest. Except that they know the enemy will return in the morning. For Kunle, light has become the enemy, a signalman to the foe prepared to kill them at any cost. He wonders what this new pattern of living will mean for him after the war. To become accustomed to darkness, to fear daylight and resent the sun?

The anti-aircraft gun is destroyed early the following morning, and the shelling is more ruthless than before. Before the engagement, Captain Irunna informed them that Biafran Directorate of Military Intelligence provided information that the federal army brought in through Onitsha 106mm recoilless rifles and high-grade mortars. They feel the impact at once: a mortar shell bursts through the reinforced trench line, killing eight men. Rain falls and blood pools in the grooves and flows down the line. But they remain in the trenches, hungry, drinking rainwater with their hands cupped together. Kunle's shoes are soaked, and he smells of blood and mud. And in the misery, the longing for home returns. So great is the suffering, so terrible the reverberations of concussions through the vein of the earth, that it feels, in the second night, as if something in Kunle has been killed. And what remains is a thing strange and unfamiliar.

The next four days are the same: they stay stiff in their trenches, their bodies becoming attuned to the sound of an incoming mortar round, like a storm of cold air rushing through a tunnel. Each man's body is alert, almost certain a shell will burst through the parapet and sandbags and kill it. Most of the shells land far away, but the few that land close destroy. Near noon, a concussion knocks Kunle against the trench wall, and in a split second, he is bathed in sand. In the aftermath of this rain, the sand in the bags becomes like stones.

After a while, Kunle opens his eyes, surprised that he's fallen asleep. He glances at his watch—it has been five hours since the barrage began. Soaked in the urine of other men, he lets his own out and watches the yellow line run along the trench floor like a snake, curving between the ruts, soaking through the trousers of his comrades. A man curses the parents of the person who peed. Kunle wears a face of indifference and laughs inwardly. Many years ago, he used to wet his bed and always had to carry it out to dry in the sun. Now the war has made him a child again. All the men here—they cry constantly, leave snot smeared on their faces, wet and shit themselves. Many men shit right next to others in the trench under bombardment. Who would risk standing? A man from B Company told Felix a few days ago about how a shell-shocked man vomited on the face of another soldier, and that soldier, driven mad by another man's retch on his face, rose to leave the trench to clean himself, only to be immediately knocked back into it by a shell, dead. Thus, in the trenches and forests of Biafra, there is no shame.

THE SUN HAS travelled away from their position and now illuminates a distant field. Looking about, Kunle can see that the trench has thinned, only about half the men remaining, two of them looking at him. He has moved into the interior of the embankment, bathed in the sand of the split-open sandbags. On the parapet, all morning, the body of a private killed at the start of the bombardment was tossed about by the shells until it was swallowed up in the rubble. Only five hours, but the devastation is great. Twenty-four men of the battalion are dead, one of them lying a few meters from Kunle, disemboweled by a shell. A dugout by the edge of the bush, farther back, has been damaged, forming now a mound of mud, clothes, and timber, along with stretched-out hands and feet and disembodied parts. Who knows how many there are in the rubble? A large fragment of one of the exploded mortar shells stands in a blasted hole a few meters away. Outside, at the top of the trench from which Kunle emerges, a man crouches on the ground, vomiting, a hand on his stomach. Everywhere, soldiers, shell-shocked and wounded, sit wailing or speaking to unseen persons. And a group of men stumble across the smoking craters and wounded earth like weary somnambulists, their bodies shattered, falling and rising, pointing and trembling.

Much of the battalion is destroyed, save D Company. Captain Irunna looks tortured yet relieved. He sips from a black bottle of the strong gin the Igbo soldiers call "kai-kai" and orders that D Company must now take up a flanking position near the lip of a dense forest a kilometer away. At once, Kunle and his comrades rush forward, wet leaves clinging to their boots and uniforms, and to the Castro hat

Ekpeyong wears over his new duck-hunter camouflage uniform. He was discharged from the hospital only two days before and still walks with a slight limp, but he'd insisted on being sent back to the front, rather than visiting his family in Calabar, which is now in federal hands. Kunle and his friends make an effort to stay close to Ekpeyong during this combat, and Ndidi has given all four of them—Bube-Orji, Felix, Ekpeyong, and Kunle—one of the papers with the drawing of a parenthesized cross for protection. Kunle lies in the brush beside Ekpeyong, their rifles poised in firing position, facing the field of jungle from which the enemy infantry is expected to emerge. A few meters to his left, there is an A Company machine gun unit, the gun mounted on a tripod, the gunner wearing a long bandolier.

As they wait, the world recedes again, in a quiet march, like a thing on wheels being slowly pushed to the back of a stage. Kunle chambers four more rounds and places the barrel through the gunhole. He can feel the pressure of his heartbeat in his arms, and in the faces of his comrades he sees terror of an indescribable kind. When the captain shouts, "Fayah!" the enemy infantrymen are already in the bush, accreting on all sides. At once, the front erupts in a thundering hail of gunfire.

When his ammunition is used up, he wants to run to the rear to get more, but the air is filled with bullets and a chorus of metallic objects flying in either direction. He lies down with the rifle in his hand. Soon Captain Irunna is shouting, "Retreat! Fall back! Retreat!" From beside him, Ekpeyong, Ndidi, and Bube-Orji lift off. He makes to follow, trips. He catches sight of Ekpeyong in a flash, and when he looks again, Ekpeyong has fallen in the brush, a few meters from him, the others much farther away. Kunle rises, dashes madly in the direction where Ekpeyong now lies.

There is a cry, followed by a burst of machine gun fire from behind. Kunle falls into the scrub and lies still, his heart pounding against the raw earth. Smoke curls through the wild grass and cocoyam plants, filling the air with the smell of burning. From somewhere nearby, Bube-Orji whistles, and his voice rises in chants of "De Young, De Young!" Kunle crawls forward and sees Ekpeyong seated with his back against a tree stump, his hand on his chest where a bleeding hole has sprung open, blood sliding out like a frenzied mass of dark worms between his fingers. Ekpeyong's face appears suddenly ashen. Shouts come from the enemy position, and the bush rattles again with the feet of fleeing men. Ndidi leaps away. Bube-Orji, after pulling briefly at Ekpeyong's arm, follows.

"De Young, let's run!" Kunle says, crawling closer. "Please."

Ekpeyong lifts himself through his trembling, strains to form some fumbling words, but returns to the ground as if deciding on the cusp of speech to remain discreet.

"De Young!" Kunle cries. Raising his head again, he sees green helmets appearing, some covered with foliage. He flees with half his body prostrate, darting behind trees as shots ring out behind him. And when he reaches the place where the rest of the company has retreated to—back beyond the trenches manned by the 14th Battalion, halfway on the road between Eha Amufu and another town—he is weeping. He cannot shake off the feeling that had Ekpeyong not risen in the very moment the sniper shot came, it could have been he who would be lying there in no-man's-land, shot through the lungs—dead. In the distance, above where black smoke is rising, birds are congregating on a thermal over the flames, their form silhouetted, imperceptible in the dying light. The queasy surge in his belly returns, and in haste, he makes towards the nearest bush.

12.

THE NEW LANCE corporal chevron on Kunle's shoulder is the only bright spot in the days following the second defeat at Eha Amufu. The sun shines on his face and those of his three friends while the crowd of soldiers on the parade ground applaud. One watching him from above can see that Kunle is surprised to find himself in this position. Four days ago, after the retreat, he was lying on a broad banana leaf, trying to sleep, when Ndidi, whom they'd begun to call "Fada," roused the three of them and said he wanted to bring Ekpeyong's body out of no-man's-land.

"Fada, how—but-tu how can we go there, eh?" Bube-Orji whispered, yawning.

"I don't care—we must go," Ndidi said, in the lowest voice he could muster. "He must not lie there like that, ifu go? Look—look at what he did for us, for Biafra. Mba—no, my conscience will not let me just keep quiet like that."

For a moment, no one stirred. Ndidi sighing, rose, loaded his rifle with the two single cartridges left in his ammo pouch. Felix thought him mad, and Ndidi hesitated but remained resolute: "The book of Proverbs, tiree, verse twenty-seven: 'It is a sin not to do good when it is in thine power to do so.'"

They would not let Ndidi go alone. So, though Kunle was tired and his head was aching, he, Felix, and Bube-Orji followed. Felix borrowed a torchlight from the militiamen and a stretcher, which Bube-Orji carried. With fear like a slug in his bones, Kunle turned at every step, glancing wildly as the torchlight washed the field with its dim yet concentrated beam. He was surprised at how close the spot was—only four hundred meters from the Biafran defensive position. It was, as Felix whispered, a no-man's-land.

The dead lay there in a quiet mass: bodies curled into themselves, the dark ink of their fatal injuries upon their uniforms. A soldier lay with his torso bowed over the torn branch of a tree as if hugging it, his back soaked in blood. Beside his body lay that of a young man with a handsome face whose eyes were open and whose lips were turned up as if smiling. The torchlight leapt to a field farther away, and black wings flitted from some unseen place in the dark. Felix gasped, and for a moment they stood staring at a severed arm whose fingers were curled in an invitational gesture. They heard a wild, piercing cry, like that of an infant. Felix swung the torchlight in obvious terror and the light rested on a squirrel-sized animal perched on the leg of a dead man, its ball-sized eyes. The animal cried again, leapt up the giant tree nearby, and disappeared into the black branches. Terrified by the cry of the creature, Kunle had tripped over a body. Ndidi propped him up, whispering, "Don't worry . . . don't worry—it is jus' a bushbaby."

They found Ekpeyong seated against the tree stump as they had left him, his head bowed to his chest, his rifle on his lap. In his back pocket, the letter from Biafra's vice president, Brigadier General Philip Effiong, thanking him for his bravery (which in part had spurred him to come back despite not being fully well), was sticking out. Beside him was another man from their company, Jonas Mmereghini, a kind man with a scar on his jaw who'd greeted everyone with the simple word "Olia." Jonas was resting on Ekpeyong's left arm, the right still clutching his rifle. Save for the blackened tips of their fingers, they both possessed the terrible beauty of the freshly dead. The friends placed the two bodies on the stretcher and carried the dead weight at a steady jog, hurrying back to safety as fast as they could manage.

Now Kunle feels the eruption of an unfamiliar emotion as the man he'd first known as Major Amadi, now a lieutenant colonel, calls his name. Here is the man who consigned his life to this hell. Yet the man shakes his hand and announces that he is now "Lance Corporal Peter Nwaigbo." As the crowd of soldiers cheer, Lieutenant Colonel Amadi, who now wears a peak cap and whose shoulders bear stitched insignias of an eagle and a star, whispers, "Now you are really one of us."

"Yes-sa!" he shouts and salutes.

Kunle's new uniform bears the simple chevron of a corporal on the shoulders, beneath the badge of the rising sun and the 51st Brigade's marking: LI. When he returns to the crowd of men, he is clasped in embrace after embrace. In the hands of each man, he feels joy and a sense of belonging. The last time he was celebrated this way, he recalls, was a year before the accident, when he won the debate competition in the primary school. His parents were at the school to watch him receive his prize, as was Nkechi, who sat in the front, cheering, a red flower in her hair.

Lieutenant Colonel Amadi announces afterwards, in his usual high-pitched voice, that it is the end of the five-day rest. They are headed for the imminent and all-important battle of defending Enugu, the capital city, from falling and the new republic from immediate collapse. The dread of this, in the past few days, crept into some of the men and unsettled them. Two days after they came to this camp, bad news of the Biafran war effort in other sectors trickled in: Nsukka had fallen, and the University of Biafra had become a federal army garrison. When, near noon the following day, someone announced that Port Harcourt had been captured, a B Company rifleman stepped out into the open sports field and shot himself through the head.

The enemy, Lieutenant Colonel Amadi says now, is only twenty kilometers outside Enugu, confronting a depleted 14th Battalion, the 51st Brigade's other battalion. The 1st Battalion, which he commands, is to mount a new defensive line off the Milliken Hills, whose rocky terrain will offer a defensive advantage.

At the announcement, Kunle feels his spirit fall to the ground. But his comrades cheer at the end of Amadi's speech. To boost morale, Amadi gives them gin from Fernando Po. Kunle joins in drinking—his first alcohol ever. He tries to force his face to stay smooth, not to express the sour and bitter taste of this thing sliding warmly down his throat. And later, when he rests that night, feeling a roiling in his stomach, he has a dream of being alone on the battlefield where they found Ekpeyong. Kunle has no torch, but the moon is aglow with a deep, fiendish light. He is in search of his brother. He turns about among the crowd of the dead, past a man whose belly is torn open, a dark hole where his gut once was, past the severed arm whose fingers are curled as if in an invitational gesture. He is shouting, "Tunde! Tunde!" when he sees a hand stretched in the distance and hears a voice much like his brother's calling, "Egbonmi! Egbonmi!" Waking, he hears the bugle sounding.

THEY RIDE IN a convoy through the city and stop in front of a place that, by morning light, Felix immediately points out as the former premier's lodge. Lieutenant Colonel Amadi and his aides step down and, taking salutes from the guards standing on the front lawn, go into the building, now known as the State House. While the troops wait, Kunle gazes with intensity at the big Biafran flag above the lawn, drenched and wrapped around the pole, which itself has been darkened by the rain. Lieutenant Colonel Amadi returns a few minutes later with rolls of papers and two men, at whose sight the soldiers cheer. Blue-uniformed guards, armed with automatic rifles, move to flank the first figure, who is unmistakably Colonel Ojukwu. He sports a thick beard that forms a semicircle around his face and is dressed in a uniform much like theirs but with a green belt fastened to his waist. He wears a peaked cap, which, as he stands beside Amadi, who has on his usual Castro cap and tortoiseshell glasses, gives him an outsized dignified appearance.

Lieutenant Colonel Amadi, standing with his chest out, raises his hand in salute. Colonel Ojukwu nods, waves to the convoy, and goes back towards the building, leaving the other officer. The leader walks a few steps under the overhang of the front porch, then stops, waves as the convoy begins singing his praise.

"So, that is the people leading us," Ndidi says, his voice low but concentrated, so that Kunle and Felix can hear him above the loud singing and the din of the vehicles' engines as they get back on the road. "Your leaders—that is Emeka Ojukwu and Philip Effiong. No wonder Biafra is falling. In fact . . . we have fallen into deep mud and everything will soon end—it fit even be tomorrow, sef, once they take Enugu."

Felix shakes his head. Ndidi has been criticizing the Biafran effort since the loss of Eha Amufu, and each time, Felix has retorted with optimism. It has become almost like a game between the two, to push each other's perspective on the war to the limit.

"Fada, I no gree with you at all—at all, *cha-cha*," Felix says, clicking his tongue a few times.

"Okay, be there believing—"

"No matter what you say, I still believe we shall win." Felix seems to want to say more, for his mouth remains open, but it also seems there is now a hole in his thoughts, filled with the sad realization that Ndidi might be right. Felix looks at Ndidi with a fumbling expression, for he knows that things are going badly—city after city, town after town is falling to the enemy. And there are saboteurs everywhere and moles in the army, fighting Biafra from within. Felix can see that the enemy possesses too much firepower, which no amount of Biafran will or zeal can overcome. So, in a downcast voice, he says, "Well . . . see, I jus' don't like discouragement. What else can we do? Sit down and die?"

"Nobody said that!" Ndidi's voice is tense.

"Ehen, don't discourage me. Don't forget, I am a poet. I live a hopeful life!" Felix pauses, then, in the affected voice that often signals that the words are not his own but from a book, he begins: "The miserable have no other medicine but hope."

"Amen!" Bube-Orji says, clasping his hands together and nodding.

They fall silent as rain begins to drizzle, and the men seated in the back of the mammy wagons are soaked, hugging themselves. The rainstorm occludes the sun and simulates a gentle night in the daytime, so that by the time the combined forces of the 51st Brigade arrive at the foot of the Milliken Hills, it is almost dark. The hike up the hill is tortuous and slow, but after nearly an hour, they reach the top and plunk down, winded and gasping. Kunle feels at once a desperate restlessness—as though a vicious thing asleep has awakened and will soon unleash itself. The militiaman who carries the large water cask on his back yields to their prodding, and Felix, Ndidi, and Kunle fill their canteens. Kunle takes a few sips and is flushed again with life. An idea lights up among the ruins of other thoughts: Should he write a letter to his brother and give it to Lieutenant Colonel Amadi to send to Tunde? Wouldn't Amadi, who likes him now for his valor, help him? Kunle hands the canteen to Bube-Orji, who has been standing there, limp and flustered, like a thing from which too much blood has been drawn. He no longer has kola nuts to chew and looks increasingly pensive and pale, as if the vitiligo scarring has increased and filled more portions of his face.

Kunle gazes at the scenic view of Enugu city: a thousand flags flying all over it. From this height, the world for kilometers on end seems like an archipelago of houses and forests. The sky spreads above the city, a shadow of whitened blue, lit from within by an invisible sun. As if a fog has cleared in his mind, he remembers the last time he mounted a hill. It was in '62, during a tense few days after multiple medical diagnoses had pronounced Tunde permanently crippled, due to the severe injury to his spine. Their parents turned to the fledgling blind prophet by the name of Obadare, who had been healing incurable illnesses. They carried Tunde to the top of the hill where the sick waiting for healing sat, but after the two-day crusade, Tunde remained the same.

How can a person sleep when their mind is thicketed in terrible fear of losing everything they love? Kunle is groggy but, wiping the murk off the surface of his wristwatch, he sees that it is now twelve past five in the morning, and Captain Irunna's radio has come alive with frantic voices. A signal post two kilometers behind enemy lines has sent word down that enemy armor and heavy vehicles are starting to move in three directions: towards Emene Road, Ninth Mile, and the Milliken Hills.

There is panic—Ndidi prays with his rosary in one hand and a stone in the other; Felix writes frantically in his mud-stained jotter, constantly wiping his sweating palms on his trousers; Bube-Orji, out of kola nuts, chews a stick. Kunle dwells on the strange experience he had the previous night. He'd been falling asleep and, opening his eyes, thought he saw, in the distance, a man seated on top of a hill swaddled in white clothes, staring into some source of light. Kunle looked around and saw only his comrades in the dark. What was this? Had he dreamed it? The Seer comes to his mind at once. The boy at their church in Akure who knew the Seer's story told him that the man often went up a hill to see his visions. In the past, the boy said, the Seer had had repeated dreams of his wife dying in a car accident, but even on the day it happened, he'd dismissed it. Hours later, it had happened. The Seer was almost driven crazy by guilt for having ignored the repeated warnings of his wife's death as mere dreams. He left his job at a British company in Lagos, traveled to India, and became a seer.

They have waited for hours, sweating in the heat of the sun, so the first explosion comes as a shock. It is thundering—so loud that at once Kunle feels a movement pressing down in his gut. Captain Irunna removes his sunglasses, rubs his forehead. And his radio comes alive again: *"Moses Group one—two—fire! Roger!"* . . . *"Batman coming . . . Over?"* . . . *"Roger!"*

One of Lieutenant Colonel Amadi's batmen arrives with news that the federal infantry, led by artillery batteries, is approaching the northern axis of the Milliken Hills. The S Brigade, Ojukwu's special brigade, has pulled back to defend the Awkunanaw Boys' High School and the northern entrance to Enugu. Amadi believes that the federal troops will try to push through the hills into the Iva Valley coal mine sometime soon. So, all the troops defending the city must take their positions. The batman is panting, breathless, and his gesticulations and slurred speech convey a familiar yet recessed fear.

A camouflaged lorry brings food and water. Kunle does not eat. Something occupies his gut that he has not put there. He listens to the lorry rumbling away, thinking of the Seer, when one of the men shouts, "They are coming!" For a while, they wait, for no one can raise his head and they cannot see anything. Kunle recalls an experience from his childhood when, like now, it seemed that time itself had halted. He and Tunde were standing with their father on the side of the street to see a group of animal charmers. One of the charmers told everyone to prepare themselves, and a wave of excitement surged through the crowd. "Remember, nobody move. Okay?" their father said to Tunde and him. They both mumbled, "Yes." The charmers pulled the tarp off the van and the lion roared. It flew in a leftward direction, where the crowd melted away, and was reeled back by the chain around its neck. It fell to its side kicking, a hell of dust. The crowd on their side scattered, a man falling into an open sewer. His father, somewhat calmer now, pointed as Tunde began to cry, saying, "You see—lion!"

Kunle shudders at Captain Irunna's order to prepare weapons, and now, over the hills some five or so kilometers away, they can see the approaching column of federal infantry led by two battle tanks, a jeep mounted with a machine gun, four carriages towing recoilless rifles, and various infantry vehicles. Kunle watches the effect of this amount of heavy armor on his lightly armed comrades. It is, he reckons, the type of fear that lives in the eyes, which he has sometimes seen as they've marched into battle when the whites of the eyes of some of the men disappeared completely, as if turned backwards, leaving only an oasis of blackness. And suddenly, without a clue of how it happened, he is standing by the commanding officer of A Company, a lieutenant. The lieutenant, speaking as if to himself, says, "May God save us."

There is something in the lieutenant's words, a dark power that lifts Kunle like the hollow wind that moves a kite when the world turns into a cloud of orange dust filled with the smell of sulfur and singed flesh. He cannot see or breathe. The pain in his head is numbing, a raging infirmity of the nerves. He thinks that he can see Felix and Lieutenant Okoye, but the colors swirling around them do not seem real. It is as if they are moving about the creased surface of some oily water. He blinks rapidly.

His vision clearer now, he sees that he is being carried away in the bed of a wagon with other wounded people. There is wind in his face, but as the wagon winds down the incline, he sees in the distance men falling four hundred feet from the top of the hills among fragments of rocks and debris. He looks about him, cries, "Felix! Ndidi! Bube!" But there are only bloodied bodies, folded into themselves. None of them is his friend. For long he gazes, until the hills are gone from sight and the explosions distant. He feels thirsty now—"You have water, sa?" he asks the man seated by his side.

"What?" the man says.

"Water—you fit gi-me water?"

"Eh?" the man says again, and Kunle sees that where the man's left ear had been is just a bloodied network of swollen veins and dark matter. Kunle jerks back. He realizes that he is surrounded by wounded and dead men waiting to be evacuated. To his left is a dead man with one of his hands gone, leaving a bloodied stump of flesh—which is the source of the flies raging about. He lifts his voice and begins to shout, "Help me! Take me out of here! Please, take me home!"

IT BECOMES CLEAR to Kunle the following day that he has not been taken home, but two days pass before he understands where they are or what has happened: the new British artillery has devastated the 1st Battalion's defenses, and in just one day, Milliken Hills was lost, with Captain Irunna cut in two by the first shell and Kunle wounded on the head and arm by shrapnel. The retreat was hasty and chaotic, soldiers sitting on the roof and clinging to the open door of the lone bus that had been sent to take them back to Enugu garrison.

Earlier this morning, Kunle asked the man in the bed next to him where they were, and the man—who'd been blinded in one eye—explained that they were at Queen's College, a girls-only secondary school that had been filled with girls only three weeks before. With a leer, the man said that the girls had left behind some important relics—pieces of wrappa, half shimmies, and even crumpled panties under the beds.

He is in a clinic or shelter for the wounded, away from his comrades. And he has been keeping to himself, fastening his eyes only on the fluorescent bulb just above him, which, like a soft, yielding door, leads him back into the past. As he is revisiting the day in '55 when Tunde drew him as a dinosaur, suddenly he hears Bube-Orji's voice in a corner of the room: "See am there!" He glances up and there are Bube-Orji, Ndidi, and Felix, looking like men rescued from some muddy pit, smelling like smoke and filth. Felix's green beret is brownish, and his face is spotted with so many pimples his skin appears almost dark. Ndidi, who is dressed in his faded pope T-shirt, which has developed a hole in its back, looks five years older than he was a few days ago. Bube-Orji seems sick, thinner, his Adam's apple sticking out like a boil. Kunle wants to laugh at them, only they start laughing at him instead. Bube-Orji, jerking like one intoxicated, tries to speak, but his words get swallowed again and again in a hungry fit of laughter.

"Ku . . . k . . . aghahahaha."

"Egwagieziokwu, I am thinking what he reminds me of o," Felix manages at last.

"It is easy," says Ndidi, who now is dabbing his eyes with a handkerchief. "Arab man!"

Again Bube-Orji rocks and begins to gasp from exhaustion.

"Tu," Bube-Orji struggles to say. "He loo . . . he look like . . . Tu . . . Tuareg man!"

Felix claps, and they all laugh harder.

"From now on, we must call him Tuareg or Ottoman Dan Fodio," Felix says.

Kunle raises his hand to his head and lets out a gasp. He had not noticed, but now he feels the thing wrapped around his head like a turban. He thought the only wound he had was on the arm, where there are stitches. But now he reckons that the headaches he's been having have been caused by a wound to his head.

At this realization, his friends become pensive. Felix tells Kunle what happened, about Captain Irunna's death and that of one of the other men they knew from the training camp. They are quiet for only a moment and at once begin to speak about the ongoing assault on Enugu—the new mine invented in Biafra, which the S Brigade has unleashed to slow the federal advance. Kunle listens, bothered by how quickly he and his comrades seem to forget serious things. There is in this war an urgency about the present that is all-consuming and leaves no room for reflection. The next thing beckons, tugs at you with inviolable hands, until what was only yesterday a great cause of sorrow is relegated today into silence. And even when they speak in the aftermath of a tragic event, a crowd of unsaid things seems to limn behind their words. No one, for instance, has spoken about Ekpeyong's death besides Ndidi, who, in a moment of mild insanity, shouted, "Peace be unto you, De Young!" Then he crossed himself. No one replied, as it was hard to tell if Ndidi was praying or not. And the words danced in the air for a while, then faded out, like Ekpeyong himself.

As if to answer Kunle's thoughts, Ndidi, making a sign of the cross, says, "May God rest Captain's soul and souls of all the departed—amen."

"Amen!" Bube-Orji says, unusually loudly. "But-tu, Fada, you—"

The explosions that interrupt the speech are so loud that Kunle is shocked out of his skull. For a stretched-out moment, no one speaks, for they can tell that this was not the sound of a bucket explosive dropped from a plane, but of artillery. They can also discern the larger message: that the entire Biafran defense infrastructure at Milliken Hills and outside the city limits, which includes the army of civilians armed with machetes and stones, has crumbled.

Kunle rushes out of the room and gazes limply in the direction of the explosions. The air is thick and humid, and beyond the low fence surrounding the school, they can see that the city is in flux. A large number of cars and caravans of fleeing people fill the streets and roadways, their heads loaded with goods, basins of clothes, naked bedsprings, chairs, pots, everyone moving in the same direction. The soldiers gather at the fence, shouting back and forth with the people outside it. The military police at the gate won't let anyone leave without an order. As Kunle and his friends wait, a flash of hope, like a strange fecund plant, begins fruiting across his mind's burning fields. Perhaps if this is the end, he will be able to go home at last. But as soon as this thought rests its feet, a shared fear among the soldiers awakens every bit of nerve in his body. If Biafra loses, a massacre awaits—a continuation of the pogrom that has driven these men to take up arms. And now that he is one of them and wears their uniform, he too will be killed. The capital is being surrounded by nearly fifty thousand men of the federal 1st Division, the men against whom they have been fighting for weeks and who have shelled them with unrelenting brutality. They will spare no one.

Near noon, Lieutenant Okoye, the commander of A Company, orders evacuation. But to where? The lieutenant does not say. Instead, he disappears in his command jeep. While the rowdy soldiers are asking, another explosion rips through the air. Kunle lands on the ground, near a mango tree by the outbuildings and latrines. A branch of the tree snaps and falls, with a blow, to the ground. The gathering scatters and empties out into the small area of bush outside as the silver-colored bombers hover still, whirring furiously through the low sky. One of the bombers comes so low that they can see the painted green eye just beneath the plane's wings, the Nigerian flag on its tail, and the face of the bespectacled white man piloting it.

"Mercenary! White mercenary!" Felix shouts.

The next blast sends a whiff of dust through the air and Kunle coughs, a cruel pain lodged in the side of his head. From some distance, an anti-tank rocket whistles into the sky, but the bombers evade it. People are shouting that a building in the school—the one Kunle had been in just before his friends arrived—has been hit and that six soldiers, all of them convalescing men, have been killed. The building is engulfed in fire, and men are attempting to quench it with plastic pitchers and buckets of water. The bitter, crackling sound mixes with the frantic shouting of panicked men. A figure steps out of the fire, his body from head to foot framed in it. The smell of burning flesh fills the air. Men step forward, douse him in water, retreat from him as he staggers about. He falls, kicking his legs, screams issuing from the very core of his being.

In the wake of the soldier's death, it is quiet again. Kunle and his friends go to find food in the abandoned houses at the teachers' compound. Felix puts Kunle's right arm across his shoulders and helps him walk to the different buildings until they find one recently vacated. He waits in the sitting room, seated on the floor, squinting from the ache in his head. At last, his friends return from scouring the house, bearing a pair of rain boots, a tin of Quaker oats, a photo of a white woman and her mixed-race son labeled "Rosina with Ezenwa, 1965," and a book Bube-Orji tosses at him as if he knows Kunle loved it as a child: *The Queen Primer, Part I*. He remembers now, in a quick dash of images, Nkechi lying beside him on the mat on the front porch weeks before the accident, asking him to recite one of the stories about a man cutting a wooden log with a saw. With a slight stammer, struggling with the rhythm of the words, he'd read, *Saw, jaw, draw, straw,* while she lay there laughing.

A distant clamor shakes the ground, and quickly they leave the house and run through the open gate into the great, teeming crowd of people, who are mostly bearing their belongings on their heads and moving towards Onitsha. They march behind women tired and limping. An old woman walking with a stick clutches a rooster to her chest, and beside her, an elderly man is borne on the back of a young man. A few paces to the left are two sick men in thin hospital gowns, one of them dragging along a drip pole still connected to his veins. Along the side of the road, wounded soldiers—covered in mud and blood, their clothes torn and ripped—trudge alongside lorries loaded to the brim, crawling between the seething masses of walkers. Kunle and his friends chew the raw oats. What is left, Ndidi hands to a man and his teenage daughter. As the sun sets and the road winds uphill, the small crowd swells and insects hover above them. Behind them, the city lies lower and now appears like the front: shells are dropping without cease. Twice, a bomber races with quick menace over the exodus, throwing the people into a pandemonium. The armed soldiers shoot at it with eager fury. As night falls, it disappears.

They go on in the growing darkness, fringed by pockets of light from many hurricane lanterns, battery-powered torches, and the headlights of a lone car wending its way through the crowd. To an eye viewing them from above, they appear like a throng of hundreds of flames marching among thousands of human silhouettes, whose voices rise in unison with the quick, penetrating force of quiet sorrow as they sing: "Dibe, dibe . . ." Felix translates the lyrics of the song to Kunle as the crowd sings, and Kunle feels tears on the sides of his nose. His friend, wounded by the song, keeps translating as if every dip in the melody, every step into an adagio, further afflicts him. "Endure, endure, endure. It is better to be patient. It is better to be patient. He whom bad things have happened to . . . Endure! Endure! Endure! It is better—better to be patient!"

With the great mass of people now evacuated from the city, Kunle feels a calm as if a thing that had been on the top of a hill has now come down. There is a strain in his neck from the hours of constantly gazing into the sky in search of bombers. They have come to a stop, and now the only things visible from Enugu are the lines of black smoke rising into the horizon. The city is reduced to an altered stipple of undamaged buildings. Felix stands staring at it, shaking his head. "E-Enugu has fallen," he says, pointing to the distant smoke. A smile creeps up his face, and he says in a wounded voice, "It is over."

The sight of so many people, including the despondent and the sick, fleeing is more shocking to the Seer than anything he has witnessed so far this night. But his mind dwells on the dream in which the unborn man saw him. This phenomenon, of being able to access the dream state in a vision, has always surprised him above all else. The Ifa bowl experience alone is a mystical wonder in which the past becomes the future, the future becomes the present, and the present becomes the past. But the dream state is neither the past, nor the present, nor the future. It is an expression of the subconscious that transcends time.

Elated and forgetting that the unborn man can hear, the Seer raises his hands to the heavenlies and begins to sing an oriki to Ifa and the pantheon of deities eternally assembled at the lodgments of Ifa's hills. For what feels to him a long time, he is lost in the enchantments. When he gets hold of himself, it is too late. The unborn man must have heard it and wondered where the voice only he can hear has come from. The Seer beats himself: he must not speak. It is dangerous and can cause the person whose visions are being revealed to him to develop mental illness from frequently hearing unknown voices. Troubled, the Seer brings himself to look in the bowl, and the darkening surface signals the quick passage of time as the changing lights of the flipping scenes cast glows of differing hues upon his face.

He rises, groaning softly. He has been holding his urine, but he is beginning to feel pain in his abdomen. He steps away from Ifa's bowl, removes the leaf clenched between his teeth, and loosens the ropes of his kembe. The pants slide, and he lets the urine run down the edge of the hill. The night has grown very quiet. The star is stagnant, a shaved brightness on its face. His master has often told him that the Ifa bowl experience is of such spiritual and transcendent import that even its physical demands are paid for by the soul rather than the body of the seer.

Once he sits again, he catches the familiar voices of the unborn man, Kunle, and his friends. And then Kunle's face appears in the bowl, slightly changed from what he last saw.

13.

IT'S BEEN TWO months without action. Kunle and his comrades arrived here thinking the war was over, with Enugu lost. But a few days later, it became clear that the Biafran resistance would continue. Locally made mines and anti-tank barricades had led to so many losses that the federal 1st Division, exhausted from long fighting, did not advance farther after the capture. Most of the Biafran 1st Battalion arrived here—eight hundred soldiers, at this cement factory in a place called Nkalagu, thirty-five kilometers from Enugu. With their weapons confiscated and the brigade disbanded, they have remained here for two months, waiting. Food comes twice a day, but no one is allowed to leave. Daily, they received news of the rounding up of the nearly three thousand troops who had deserted at the battle of Enugu, and of the federal massacre of those who had surrendered. In the second week here, rumors started to cycle through the camp that the 51st Brigade might be reorganized to help prevent the imminent invasion of Onitsha, but nothing happened.

In this time, James Odumodu, a lance corporal from C Company, wound his way into their clique. He'd grown up in America and had been caught up in the war while on a visit for the burial of his sister, killed in the north. From time to time, the military police allowed family members to visit the soldiers, and James's mother visited frequently. Once she brought fried chicken and the men exploded in applause and frenzy, everyone jostling for a slice of the oily meat. Another time, James's mother gave him an unusual shirt, which he wore when no officers were around. Of strong build, James aspired to play cricket, which he called "baseball," and rugby, which he called "football." The shirt was a white-striped V-neck with SENATORS printed across the front when buttoned up and the number 35 on the back. It was Bube-Orji who first befriended him for the food, and when, days later, Felix's father visited with a jerrican of palm wine, James joined in.

Within a week of their stay, Kunle lost interest in the endless chatter his friends engaged in, and the desire to return home or go find Tunde was rekindled. He plotted, and in the third week, he scaled a broken part of the fence at midnight in an attempt to flee. At once, a searchlight raced after him; it moved over him, lying flat on the other side of the fence. The MP, shouting, "Onye no ya?" and cocking his rifle, ran in Kunle's direction but skidded to a stop only a few meters away from where he lay, hidden in the brush. Kunle pushed the MP headlong into the bush, and jumped back over the fence. The MP swung after him, shouting, "Stop!," but he'd reached the porch of the hall where they were camped and climbed back in through a window, seen only by Felix and Bube-Orji, in between whom he'd lain. The MPs would storm the factory hostel demanding to know who it was, but no one would say, despite the punishment of fifty push-ups for everyone. For several nights afterward, Kunle did not sleep, afraid that he would be found out, and sad for the trouble he'd caused his friends. He settled from then on into reading the books he'd stolen from the library of the school near the factory. He read one of those books, *Jane Eyre,* so many times over that some of the lines stuck in his head.

Now he is reading, and so lost in the book that he does not hear the clamor around him. Eventually he looks out the window, where soldiers are rushing to the parade ground. It is the last week of November, and so far, no one except the regimental sergeant majors has addressed them. But Lieutenant Colonel Amadi, looking paler and sniffing constantly, announces that the Biafran army—under the command of Brigadier Alexander Madiebo—is being reorganized to face the enemy better in the future and that the men will be reassigned to new units in the next few days. The men break into a jubilant song. In the meantime, Amadi says, some of them will have to join other units. He calls forth all seventeen sergeants and lance corporals, one of whom is a woman, and asks them to stand aside.

When the speech is done, Kunle and his friends mount the bed of the mammy wagon and stand in a huddle. It is starting to move slowly when one of Amadi's batmen rushes after it, waving an envelope and shouting, "Corporal Peter Nwaigbo!" Trembling, Kunle reaches down and takes the envelope. The letter is yellowed and stained—like something sent long ago. Its edges are frayed, and its top is ripped. But on its front, his father's handwriting is clear: *To My Son*. He turns it about in his hands, his friends crowding around him, wondering who brought it. There are no stamps—perhaps the reverend sister? Kunle says it is from his father and puts it in the front pocket of his shirt, but he cannot stop thinking about it, what sadness it must contain. He is so fixated on the letter, on the thought of home and of the mission that had brought him here, that he does not engage with his friends through the three-hour drive.

It is a surprise when Felix announces that they have reached the Biafran unit at Agwu they were being sent to join. Felix taps Ndidi, who has been fiddling with the plastic effigy of the crucified Jesus Christ at the end of his rosary.

"Fada, we don reach."

Ndidi opens an eye, looks up, and sighs. Kunle laughs and shakes his head at Felix, who is passing his hand lightly over the face of a sleeping man.

"Prof—leave'm be, Prof. The good man's in tha presence of tha angels, na'amin?" the man, James, says in his American accent, calling Felix by the nickname Bube-Orji coined because of Felix's fixation with poetry. Felix had protested, saying, "I'm a poet, not a professor," but the name has stuck.

"Egwagieziokwu, he is in the third heaven!" Felix says, grinning.

Everyone laughs, save the female soldier who was picked alongside the six other lance corporals from the former 14th Battalion. Kunle had seen her a few weeks before, near the damaged water tank at the factory, with a red bandanna around her low-cut hair. He'd found himself staring at her, at the beauty that, despite her dirt-stained uniform, stuck out most visibly. She'd been gazing into the distance with unusual focus. He'd walked past her, finding his movements growing tense. Later that evening, he heard his comrades talking about her with the others in the long hall where they bivouacked, one man from A Company vowing to woo her. Now she is one of their small group—a corporal. She looks sterner, the bandanna wrapped around her wrist. On her side is a goatskin bag, slung across her body. Kunle has heard that there were two women with the battalion, one of whom died at Ikem.

Since the first time he saw her, there has been something about her appearance that has endeared her to him—the way she stood looking, as if, like him, she could see and hear what no one else could. Now their eyes meet momentarily, and again it feels intense, as if she is searching for something on his face. Kunle tries to imagine this woman in the trenches, under a barrage of mortar shells—during which one's soul seems to die a temporary death—when someone taps him on the shoulder. Felix has craned his head towards him and is saying, "Ho—how are you, Corporal?"

"Fine, Prof," he says.

"Mhmm—"

Kunle nods, looks down. "I am just hungry."

"See this nigga," James says. "You lucky we not in the fucking front."

"Chai, Peter," Bube-Orji says, laughing. "Even James, Mister 'Inamin,' is shelenke you!"

"I mean, nigga, for real? Na'amin?" James says.

Kunle nods. He came to know James in the two months at Nkalagu and got used to his antics. He casts his eyes sideward and finds the female soldier looking straight at him. He turns away—too quickly, a throb in his chest. He thinks at once of his youthful looks, of the missing tooth on the upper left side of his mouth, of the nervous ways he is acting—like a child caught in an act of mischief. He is relieved when the wagon stops at the assembly ground of a school turned into a military barracks, where three officers, two of whom are white, stand waiting.

"You see, sleepyhead," Felix says to Ndidi, a tinge of joy in his voice. "You see, it is not over."

Ndidi shrugs. "Prof, let us see, first. All I know is, we Biafrans . . . we are running on wooden legs. On crutches."

"See, we have foreigners coming here from everywhere. Now the world is listening. They are seeing us." Felix unslings his empty rifle, on its rope, over his shoulder and climbs down, and once they all are on the ground, he says, "We will win this war—you get me?"

Ndidi laughs, shakes his head. His face bears on it a rich sense of muffled joy, like a man who outside the war would have been happy, but who now wears an almost permanent expression of seriousness. He has a broad forehead, the marked feature of most Igbos, and speaks with a slow, measured tone, especially when arguing with Felix. Kunle listens to the banter with discomfort, thinking he should speak lest the woman think him shy. So before Ndidi can respond, he says quickly, "I believe you, Prof. Biafra will win this war."

"Oh-ho!" Felix cries. "You see . . . even Peter has faith! Listen, His Excellency has promised to bring more expert fighters from everywhere—France-oh, Germany-oh, Italy-oh, even America—black Americans, two of them are even in Forten Battalion. They come all the way from America to help us. One of them is Dick Tiger's friend. Even sef—"

An officer calls, "Attention!" They fall silent and all stamp their feet, bring their heels together, and lift their chests. "Hand salute!" the officer cries, and they curve their hands in salute. At last, the officer who yelled the orders, a major, comes up and walks through the line, stopping momentarily to stare into each corporal's face. Standing before him, Kunle recognizes him as the officer who, in the moment they first sighted the federal convoy on Milliken Hills, said, "May God save us."

The officer orders, "At ease!" and introduces himself as Major Okoye; he now commands the 14th Battalion. He is tall and lanky, with a truncheon whose end is dented as if it's been struck too many times against a hard surface. The officer gives a speech, to which Kunle barely listens. He is hungry and sleepy.

The officer gestures to one of the white men and says, "I now deliver you to your new commander, Captain Ruf Stana."

The white captain, smoking and squinting in the sun, walks towards the soldiers, who all again stand at attention. He seems to be into his forties, with a thin, pointy nose and deep creases in his forehead. He is tall, with a deep forehead that reflects the beginnings of balding. He is long-limbed and broad-shouldered, and his face is wrinkled at the edges close to his eyes. Under the shade of the green beret he wears, which has the strange insignia of a dragon holding a sword stitched to it, his face looks deeply angry. He is dressed in a military uniform that looks different from the others—a duck-hunter camouflage. When Okoye said his name, the captain's eyes lit up and his mouth folded into a smile. As he walks past the men, he drops the butt of his cigarette and grinds it into the soft earth.

"Coco, Rolf Steiner," the white captain says.

"Okay-okay, my friend. Ro-lf," Major Okoye says, laughing.

"Merci!" the captain says, clapping.

Major Okoye leaves, walking with a group of men up towards the nearby village. Captain Steiner poses for some time in salute; he steps forward, then sideways, and for a moment, his face is obscured by the sun. He is silent, as if in search of what to say. Then, suddenly, he cries, "For-ma-si-on!"

"Line up formation!" the Igbo officer cries. "Commander ask you to line up!"

Kunle turns to see where the lady is standing, and almost jumps—it is no longer Felix standing by his left side but the lady, a tense look on her face. There is a faint scar on the side of her face above her ear.

"Merci," Steiner says. He introduces the two officers: the other white officer is Sergeant Wilson, from England. Thick-armed and stout, Wilson is dressed similarly to Steiner but wears a black beret, like the bearded Igbo officer beside him. Steiner introduces the Igbo officer as Sergeant Agbam, his interpreter.

Captain Steiner inspects them, stepping from soldier to soldier, looking into the faces of everyone as if to register them in his mind.

"Thank you for volunteering your service to your country, Biafra," Steiner says, through the interpreter. He continues, smoking a fresh cigarette, and pinching the crook of his nose while waiting for his words to be translated. He says he heard about Biafra while in his country, France. Before that, he was a soldier fighting in Algeria. He left the French army for a few years, got married to a woman he loved, but was "bored" and wanted "positive" adventure, to do something good for humanity. One day while meeting with his old legionnaire friends, he was introduced to two Igbo doctors, who convinced him to come to Biafra and join the cause.

The translation is greeted with renewed joy. Captain Steiner continues: He wants them to be legionnaires. He wants them to fight not like the other Biafran units. No trenches, just tactical maneuvers: "Attack and surprise." Steiner himself says it in a way that sounds comical, like a child grappling with its first word: "I saying, Attack und supris!"

The soldiers burst into applause.

"Yes, we say this is the new Biafra Taarti-two Brigade," Sergeant Agbam shouts. "We will be special force . . . We will be true legionnaires . . . Like in Europe, commandos . . . We will fight until the last man—without fear . . . As far as I am your commander . . . We will win this war . . . So welcome, Biafra legionnaires!"

LIKE HIS FRIENDS, Kunle feels somewhat relieved to be joining a unit commanded by a veteran soldier who has fought in European wars, but he cannot, even now, understand the joy and elation in his comrades, save Ndidi. After Steiner and the officers led them to a classroom and left, Felix and James danced, and even the woman mustered a quiet laugh. At every turn after they were taken out of the hellish front, these men always wanted to go back. After returning to the front, Ekpeyong, for instance, told stories of wounds he'd witnessed at the hospital—of the officer from whose body more than forty pieces of shrapnel had been picked out, leaving him stitched up from head to foot. Yet despite witnessing these traumas, Ekpeyong had begged the nurses to let him return to the front. During the two-month-long wait at the cement factory, nearly all of them were pained to be out of the fighting and unable to stop the federal advance. Only yesterday, before Colonel Amadi arrived, several of them threatened to break into the weapons storage unit. They sang angry songs, imploring Ojukwu to give them weapons so often that the Igbo phrases had become etched in Kunle's brain—Ojukwu *nye* (give) *anyi* (us) *egbe* (guns). They craved the front as if unconcerned about their parents, wives, or children. James, who has two children and a wife back in America, seemed to care only about "fucking up dem goddammed basterds!" Even worse, they seemed free of past sins for which they must reckon and to be totally empty of dreams.

Now they are seated on long benches, gifted with new rifles and uniforms. Kunle watches the lady, who is seated directly opposite them, handle her gun. She rises slowly and hangs the rifle on her back by its sling, so that the strap folds into the parting between her breasts. He realizes, as if by epiphany, that this was why he liked Nkechi as a child: seeing her somersault, do what he could not do. He'd found her manifestation of superior bodily strength appealing. In those first few days, Nkechi often mocked him and even her brother, Chinedu, because neither of them could do a back flip like her. He felt a similar thing when he saw the lady soldier on the mammy wagon to Agwu, eager to return to the front. And here she was arousing even more reverence in him by how she was handling the rifle. Even though he's fired rifles many times and been in battles, his hands still tremble when he touches them. But this woman here seems to hold hers with so much ease. He wants to speak to her but does not know how to do it. He is grateful when Ndidi says, "Sista, good afternoon o," standing in front of her.

"Good afternoon," she says.

"My name is Ndidi Agulefo. I am from Aguleri. These good-for-nothing people call me Fada."

Ndidi shakes her hand.

"Agnes . . . from Abiriba." Her voice is solemn, almost as if she is speaking from a distance.

The men fell quiet once Ndidi began speaking to her, and now they cheer—everyone in the room seeming to focus on her. Someone says something in Igbo with the word "Abiriba" in it, and the woman's face lights up. She nods and responds in Igbo. There is an exchange, the woman's soft voice answering each time to cheers. Because Kunle does not understand what they are saying, his mind floats and lands quickly, with the agility of a butterfly, on his brother, then leaps onto the letter in his pocket. How sad his parents must be now. His mother—how is she living? He feels a shudder and looks up to find Bube-Orji's hand on his shoulder and the woman's eyes fixed on him, with slight bemusement on her face.

"Ah, please let us speak English," Bube-Orji says. "Sorry—our friend here doesn't speak Igbo. He grew up in Yorubaland—Akure. He only hears *mgbati-mgbati*."

Kunle finds himself flushing with shame as the men laugh. Unsure of what to do, he nods and feigns laughter. He is worried about what Agnes must think of him being mocked.

"My name is Ebubechukwu Orji—I'm from Ogbaku." Bube-Orji throws a wave in a semicircle. "They call me 'Bube-Orji' or 'Bube-Ọjị' because I always chew ọjị when hungry." He turns to Kunle. "And, oho, *ọjị* means 'kola nut' in Igbo."

They all laugh, Kunle finding himself laughing too.

"What is your name?" the lady says now, looking straight at Kunle.

"Emm . . . me? Ku— Oh, sorry, Peter." His heart beats louder. "My name is Peter Waingbo."

Again, they all laugh, the lady joining in.

"You see, abi?" Bube-Orji says. "He no fit even pronounce his name."

Kunle is grateful that Bube-Orji has interrupted the conversation and that no one noticed that his real name had almost slipped out. Ndidi is beginning to speak when Steiner and Agbam return to the classroom. They all stand at attention. Steiner explains that the new expectations for the commandos are for them to strike behind enemy lines. For this, they need to form a special forces unit commanded by Steiner himself, reporting directly to the head of state.

"Lady corporal," Agbam translates. "Fall out and choose eight men from this room."

Kunle feels his pulse rise, and it is a surprise when she steps out and, without hesitation, points at him.

"Fall out!" Agbam shouts, and Kunle steps aside, beside Agnes, his legs shaking. She points to Felix, then James. She points to four corporals from her former 14th Battalion, and then her finger lands on Bube-Orji.

They follow Steiner to an office, where he immediately sits behind a desk with a green telephone and smokes for a long time, as if oblivious to the presence of the nine soldiers and his interpreter, tilting the ash from the burning cigarette into a cup of half-drunk coffee. Kunle's eyes pass around the room, up the glass cabinet beside Steiner's seat; it is filled with old folders. On one shelf there are plaques and cheap trophies, on one of which is inscribed 2ND PLACE, BRITISH PROTECTORATE SCHOOL DEBATES COMPETITION 1958. A typewriter sits on a small table. Steiner's figure is framed by a poster on the wall behind him of Joe Louis hitting a man whose face is turned as he ducks. Under the caption, someone has crossed out the names and replaced them with BIAFRA VS. NAGERIA.

Again Kunle wonders if his comrades, visibly happy, have heard Steiner's charge. Have they considered the scale of the danger that awaits them? He desperately wants to reach his parents, to see his brother again—if only just once more.

Steiner thrusts his hands in the air with a suddenness that unsettles Kunle and shouts something in French.

"Commander says—" Agbam begins, but Steiner stops him and

adds a few more sentences, his fingers floating with the strange rhythm of his words.

"He say this unit will be nothing like elsewhere in Biafra army ... You will implement and teach his war philosophies and sacred laws of fighting war to others ... I already have another twelve—Wilson and me (Agbam) and ten officers from the Hilltop Academy of cadets. Now salute First Commando Platoon!"

Two elderly women walk into the room, carrying a big steaming pot, followed by some children with nylon bags full of plastic plates and spoons. Again the men cheer, and Bube-Orji, whistling and rubbing his hands together, says, "Ah, glory be to God! Food!"

As Kunle eats, it strikes him that the letter might be the evidence that, in fact, the sister reached his parents, and like a sudden illness, he can no longer resist opening it. He steps out to the front porch of the building, where a lone yellow bulb hangs, mobbed by moths and flying termites. He tries to open it but his hands tremble as all the wrongs he's ever done against his parents come toppling onto him from some unseen height. He puts the letter back in his pocket and follows behind an open-roofed Land Rover driving slowly up the field towards the school's admin building, used as the officers' mess. Its taillights are dim, but they illuminate the faces of his friends.

IT IS CLEAR from the start that the new brigade is different from the 51st Brigade. For the first week, rather than fighting, they set about building an infrastructure of warfare. With nearly all of Biafra's frontier cities and towns fallen and the country effectively encircled, engineers at Biafra's Research and Production directorate, as well as Steiner himself, have devised a new plan to bridge the Biafran army's deficiencies by building mines. All day, Kunle and his comrades work on the mines, following a prototype Steiner has drawn; they use wood and nails to form square boxes, in which the explosives are stored. Locals from around Agwu bring what they can: logs, bags of nails, wires, metal, and whatever can be gotten from nearby stores or factories. Then they stitch torch batteries and detonators to earthen pots of explosives in which holes have been drilled and cover them with beeswax. Kunle feels a strange kind of joy while carrying out the new challenge. The Special Commando Platoon camp, instead of being a camp of drills and endless battle plans, becomes a factory.

At the end of each workday, they return to the residence halls with strained muscles and blackened hands, smelling of gunpowder, ammonium, and sweat. The labor takes away their anxiety about the deadly actions Steiner described in his welcome address. Kunle is further relieved by his increasing closeness with Agnes. It seems, by the end of the week, that he looks for her, tries to get as close to her as possible, and that he is drawn to listen every time she speaks, as if with every word she forces a pause to his thoughts. It becomes clear, too, that she is no different from the other soldiers: she wears the same uniform as them (a duck-hunter camouflage with a chevron on the shoulder, beneath the rising-sun badge); she desires a clique and comradeship. Yet each time she speaks she seems detached, often as if speaking through a veil. Even now, the sixth night here, there is hesitation in her voice as she describes an aerial attack against her former unit at Eha Alumona, in which two federal bombers swooped in on a lone injured soldier trying to get to the first aid post and destroyed him. She seems to speak English sparingly, with a thick Igbo accent that is, however, clear.

Supper arrives—a generous meal of eba and dried stockfish in loose ogbono soup, about which the men speak now. It is the best meal Kunle has had since the one at Felix's house. He feels, as it settles in him, happier and safe here. Yet he cannot reconcile why at the same time he feels a strong sense of dejection. This is the pattern of his mind in Biafra. Before he joined the military his feelings were more delineated, but here his emotions twist into each other like vines. One moment he is happy, and then a sadness cycles into his day on invisible wheels and detonates itself. He realizes now that it is the food that has made him sad—had he not come here in search of Tunde, he would be back in school, eating his mother's food, or at the restaurant near his apartment.

His comrades have been speaking for so long—everyone except him. So when Agnes rises from the bench and taps him, he replies with a shudder.

"Come escort me, biko," she whispers.

He follows her, his friends making funny faces at him. She chose him first for Steiner's special platoon, and from that first night, he's become her escort to the toilet and bath. Here, there are outbuildings where the students of the school now departed used to bathe. And opposite them, pit latrines with waist-high doors. He's become used to the smell of the front and of his friends, who were always dirty and strong-smelling. But she has been washing herself almost nightly. Once most of the soldiers have gone to bed, she would tap him awake, and he'd follow her to the back of the bath stalls, where she always had a bucket of water waiting. He'd hold her canteen, shoulder bag, and ammunition pouch while she bathed. He has often wondered why she carries the bag and what it contains, but usually his mind is too occupied with thoughts of her naked body and the rising closeness between them.

Usually she says nothing—perhaps because it is often deep in the night—except to thank him. But one night, under the glare of the moonlight, she wants to speak.

"Peter, where is your mother's village?"

Her voice is so low, yet it causes him to shudder, for he did not realize that his eyes had closed again. He blurts out an "Eh?" She repeats her question.

"Ovim," he says.

"Eh—Onye Ovim?"

He says yes, turns back. Her eyes meet his. He feels afraid—has he done something wrong? She is naked. The bucket squeaks now, followed by splashes of water. The smell of Imperial Leather soap fills the air. He fights the urge to look back, and he is relieved when he doesn't. He can tell that she is drying herself; the croaking of toads and the chirping of crickets is louder now.

"How old are you, Peter?" she says suddenly.

He hesitates, feeling again that wrecking nervousness. "Twenty-five."

She does not speak, and in fear he turns and sees her standing there, dressed only in black underpants, staring at him. He can make out the silhouette of her breasts, and the curve of her waist. Leaves crush under her feet as she reaches for the things he holds and drops them slowly on the ground, away from the reach of the bathwater, which has spread over the dirt. He watches her dress slowly, his body warming and his organ swelling. He's never had sex before but has kissed Nkechi a few times. The desire to kiss Nkechi and the thrill it gave him were overpowering. But after the accident, the desire became a black snake—shy yet venomous—that crept unwanted into his soul at various times, and each time, he clobbered it to death. So, for a long time, the desire for sex had lived outside the province of his thoughts, until earlier this year, when he found an American magazine at the university library. He ripped the delightfully shocking photos of bare-chested women out and put them inside his ledger book. For several days he touched himself, moaning. By the third day, with his exams approaching and finding the pinkish clip of the vaginas and breasts all he could think of, he pitched the pages into the trash heap outside his apartment. He watches now as Agnes covers her breasts with the black brassiere, feeling an intense sadness as sharp as pain.

Later, as they walk back, she says, almost too quietly, "That is not your age. What is—"

"Twenty-five," he says quickly. "I am twenty-five this year."

She shakes her head, stops, and faces him. "Please let this be the first 'n' last time you lie to me—okay?"

In shame, he says yes. What is it about his face, his looks, that makes him appear so young to everyone? Ekpeyong sometimes called him "Peter-boy," and there is among his comrades a certain awareness that he is much younger than the rest.

"I don't know why," she says, "but my spirit make me trust you . . . I don't know why. This is why I ask you to help me every time . . . You understand?"

"Yes."

"Good night."

Her voice seems to come from a time long past, back when his mother would come into his room to ensure that he and his brother were asleep and, in her sweet, somber voice, whisper, *Good night, my husbands.* His mother's whisper was soothing, as if her words found a different path into his heart and Tunde's. It did not matter how angry or sad they had been, the degree of their stubbornness, or if they had been punished prior to bedtime; they always fell under her spell. He follows Agnes back towards the big hall they've been told to sleep in, as she shifts her rifle from her shoulder into her hand.

14.

At the moment they are gathered—all 180 commandos—at the assembly field, their silhouettes spread across the field like a pool of dark heads. The bugle woke them quite early, but Kunle wasn't able to tell the time because he lost his wristwatch at Milliken Hills. He is struggling to unfasten the image of Agnes's naked body from his mind as he listens to Steiner address the crowd. Steiner speaks mangled English, with a looseness to his voice. He has just been promoted to the rank of major and now wears an eagle on his sleeves. Kunle can barely make out Steiner's words—his mind is fixed on what could have been if he'd been man enough and tried to touch her. Would it have led to somewhere deeper, more fulfilling? He reckons that it would have, and this softens the fear he's harbored about returning to the front.

His thoughts remain fixated as the Special Commando Platoon rides in three Land Rovers towards Obeagu in a predawn darkness so thick that the bright yellow glow of the headlights seems to carve a new path through the forest as they go. The officers—Steiner, Sergeant Wilson, and Sergeant Agbam—sit with Agnes in the first Land Rover, a commando flag and a Biafran flag attached to its hood. Kunle and his friends, except for James, who has come down with a fever, sit in the last one, the vehicle filled with mines, mats, pickaxes, hoes, and boxes of ammunition. It is rare that his friends are quiet, but no one speaks. For a long while they drive up a hilly path flanked on both sides by rocks and outcroppings. Loose breeze careens intermittently into the Land Rovers, creating an eerie, loud echo like the clashing of subterranean forces, all the way to the edge of Obeagu. It is here, Steiner announces, that a unit of the federal 1st Division's infantrymen and cannoneers are to pass the next day, on their way to a counterattack.

They set out at once, digging three holes in the road, seventy meters apart, and planting three large boxes of mines. They work efficiently, and just before six A.M., they pitch camp in the thick of the bush adjoining the road, on mats spread out over flattened grass. Kunle, his muscles strained, sits gazing around at the great nothingness, a wild imagination fruiting in his head of some snake or an animal like the bushbaby in no-man's-land striking in the dark. They have brought a hurricane lamp, but Agbam winds it down so dim that it covers only a small fraction of the place. And Steiner, who's been smoking Marlboro after Marlboro, is now seated with his back against a tree. By the yellow light, Steiner's white face looks shadowed and mysterious, like one who's eaten bad fruit.

"All of you, tell me, s'il vous plaît . . ." He lets out another whiff of smoke, rubs the top of his nose with the back of his hand. "Oui, tell me . . . why you—every—fightin'?"

The men murmur. One of the lieutenants lies on his side on the mat, swatting moths from his face. Felix raises his hand.

"Oui, monsieur," Steiner says.

"Thank, sa," Felix begins, in a voice that carries the same energy and bitterness as it had when he'd told the story at the training camp. Even as Felix tells it again, Kunle can visualize the frightening sight of the train-maimed passengers and can hear their helpless cries. Then Bube-Orji narrates his own story, followed by one of the lieutenants and Ndidi. As Kunle listens to each of his comrades' stories, it occurs to him that they are all wrong in their understanding of the cause of the war. This war has not merely grown out of the dark desires of evil men who had set upon their Igbo neighbors in the north, killing and wreaking destruction. Instead, it seems the war sprouted out of the natural soil of society and has been growing for many thousands of years in the old blood of mankind itself. If it had not been the north, perhaps it would have been someone else starting the fighting, or even Nigeria against other countries. War, he thinks, is something inherent in mankind: to strike another for a cause, no matter what the cause might be.

A moth, big and ugly, with a wing pattern that makes it look as if it is covered with eyes, perches on Kunle's legs. He swats it away with a quick wave, and the group breaks into laughter.

"Monsieur," Steiner says, pointing at Kunle.

"Sa, me?" he says, though he knows Steiner means him, for all have spoken save him and Agnes. When the major nods, Kunle lets his gaze linger on the blinking traces of fireflies spread over the brush, thinking that this is the time for him to say all that he's never said to anyone before. He bares his heart, as he described in the story he wrote the day his uncle called, and when he describes the accident, a murmur runs through the listeners. He looks up and finds Agnes's eyes on him.

"After that, me and the girl became enemies, while she became my brother's friend. She was sad about what we caused to happen. When the war started, I was in Lagos. In university. One day, my uncle called. My brother has disappeared . . . They entered Biafra—him and Nkechi, and all her people. All of them. They escape."

Bube-Orji whistles through his teeth, shaking his head.

"You come to find them?" Agbam says.

Kunle nods. "I followed Red Cross people to come and look for him. But the moment we entered Enugu, I ran away. I followed the address to Nkechi's village, which is also close to my mother's village. My mother is Igbo. But before I can even go far, they catch me—Biafra militia people, they catch me . . . They took me to Fifty-wan Brigade. There were many commanders in one room. But Commander Amadi asked me to join and become Biafra citizen. So, I join. Only that way, I would not go to prison, and, maybe, I will find my brother again." He pauses, swatting mosquitoes from his ears.

"Chai, chai, but it was an accident, what happened," Bube-Orji says. "You should not 'av allowed it to bother you so much. Is not your fault."

Kunle nods. His father has told him this before, and even Nkechi's brother Chinedu, in the days when he first withdrew from everyone. He'd often rejected the idea, holding on instead to the hot-metal conviction that it was all his fault. Mostly, he saw this claim Bube-Orji has just made as the exaggeration of a small truth. Yet, there were times when he compelled himself to believe it. And sometimes he did. But every time there was an incident involving his brother—whether he was being mocked as a cripple in school or complaining about being unable to play soccer or move around like the others—Kunle would again find himself sinking into his guilt.

"So, what is your real name?" Felix asks.

He looks about the faces of his comrades; then, as if to contain within himself a truth that should not be spoken, he whispers, "Kunle. Ade-kun-le Aro-mi-re."

The crickets seem louder now, almost threatening.

"You're a special Biafran, a true brother," Ndidi says suddenly. "It is not your war, but you are fighting it like it is your war—"

"It is his war." This is the first time Agnes has said anything since they left Agwu, though he has been constantly aware of her eyes on him, and in the back of his mind, the image of her naked has remained. "His mother is Igbo. He is our brother."

"Eziokwu!" Bube-Orji shouts.

"He is—he is . . . a true one." Ndidi slaps his leg, swatting a mosquito. "Our hero! He has not suffered any loss like any of us. None of his relatives has been killed, yet he is fighting."

"Yes!" Bube-Orji says. "But-tu, eh, I don't like this 'Peter' again."

"Kpomkwem! Me neither!" Ndidi snaps his fingers several times in quick succession to accentuate his point. "I will call him Kunis."

Kunle did not expect this. For months he's feared they would hate that he was from those fighting them, but instead they embrace him. Steiner coughs, then speaks a smattering of French, at which Agbam laughs, then says, "Commander say your story is the only one that doesn't involve pregnant woman killed."

They all laugh except for Kunle and Agnes.

"Every one of them," Agbam says, "always talk of the pregnant Igbo women murdered and whose belly was cut open by the northerners as the reason for them fighting. Is it true? Commander want to know."

The men look at one another, astonished by the question and afraid that they may have believed a myth all along. Then one of the lieutenants, scratching his head, says, "It is true." His brother, he says, witnessed such a scene in Kaduna in '66.

"Ah," Steiner says, his face obscured by the slowly rising smoke. "Corporal Azu—Azuki?"

"Azuka, saa," says Agnes.

"Why you not tell us—huh, why fighting? . . . You?"

For a moment, she does not speak but stares at the grass between her curved legs, while Kunle finds himself waiting for her story as though for a long-lost lover.

Agnes was a nurse at a hospital in Makurdi who had become close to a fellow nurse who was also a hairdresser. As she is saying that she went to get her hair done at her friend's place one afternoon, something rustles in the bush nearby, cutting her off. Agbam puts out the hurricane lamp, and they are thrown into darkness so thick that Kunle cannot see the eyes of those closest to him. He can only hear their guns clicking into place and the increased beating of his heart. It must be at least ten minutes until Steiner says it was perhaps an animal and signals to Agbam to light the lamp again.

Agnes continues: She had heard of riots in other northern cities, but in Makurdi they had come to feel safe. It had been spared the Araba riots of '66. But that day, something different happened. It was the tenth of July, and Biafran planes attacked the nearby air force base.

"Ah," Felix cries. "Zumbach—pilot Zumbach."

Agnes nods: While at her friend's house, she began hearing screams. Her friend's family were not Igbo but Idoma, neighbors of the Tiv. As the cries of "Nyamiri must leave!" flowed from the angry, violent crowd in the streets, Agnes and her friend panicked. She wanted to return to her house, two kilometers away by foot. But her friend would not let her. While they argued, the mob arrived, armed with sticks and rifles. The friend's husband hid Agnes behind a petrol drum till the marauding crowd left.

Agnes ties her bandanna around her hand. Something in her voice seems to be changing, as if with every word, she is becoming someone else. She raises her hand, gesturing in a way that moves Kunle so much he feels a spasm of grief flow through him.

"E don pass midnight, after police have sweep the streets and sent the crowd away, I finally walk out from where I have been hiding . . . My husband friend escort me. We trek, trek, o . . . ah, everything have changed. Burned vehicles, buildings, scattered everywhere. In fact, it was like Ikem or that other place, Eha—"

"Eha Amufu," Kunle says.

"Yes, yes. After, we reach Wurukum, where more easterners live. Almost all the buildings for this place have burn down. This was when my heart begin to shake . . . my whole body, because I was afraid."

The first thing she remembers of her apartment is seeing the front window destroyed, the white curtain flailing. The front door was open, and outside, on the dirt, all her belongings were scattered about. She saw the bare feet of someone lying half outside the door and half inside. She knew at once that it was her husband, Zobenna: "They have cut off his head. I see blood—blood—blood . . . blood from one person. One person! Kedu ife omere? What crime did he commit? And my sons, James and Chukwudifu. They cut their throat like fowls."

For a while it seems as if the world itself has fallen still, and her story lies like an explosion in their midst. She sits with her mouth bloated with air, fighting the urge to weep. Kunle can see that what has happened to her is not something she can overcome now, if ever. It will always come to her whenever she is alone and sweep her in its sorrowful waters like a migrant river flowing across time.

She begins to say something in Igbo with an urgency that surprises him, pointing into the darkness.

"What is she saying?" he whispers in Felix's ear.

"I will avenge your deaths . . . No matter how long it takes, I will chew the bones of those who took your lives . . . Every one of them will pay with blood." Felix shakes his head, shrugs. "She is telling this to her sons."

HE WAKES FROM the recurring dream of Tunde among the dead, this time seated in his wheelchair. The forest is still dark, and most of his comrades are asleep, except Steiner, who is seated on one of the ammunition boxes, smoking. Kunle sits up, reaches for the letter with urgency, as if it were a thing that could explode in his pocket. He picks up the dim lantern, and he is surprised to find that the message is only a paragraph long and dated September 14, 1967. *Come back home,* his father wrote. He tells Kunle that his mother has developed hypertension and is having strange dreams, and he fears that she might harm herself. Auntie Ifemia, Uncle Idowu's wife, came to stay with them for three weeks because he could no longer leave her by herself while he was at work. Again the firmness of his father's voice shoots through the written words: *Come home, Kunle. I repeat again that you are not the cause of your brother's condition. It was an unfortunate accident. Only God knows why it happened. It is not your fault. I blame only the stupid driver and not you. Kunle, come home! Stop putting your life in danger. Me and your mother are waiting.*

The plea is seared upon his mind: *Come home.* In the dark and in secret, he weeps. For a long time, since the first battles at Eha Amufu, the struggle to stay alive has derailed his original mission to find his brother. But now, in one sweep, it has returned with an all-consuming power. For the rest of the morning, he does not sleep, and he is groggy while they wait in ambush for the federal convoy to pass. Every now and again they hear the voices of the two local sentries on the road, redirecting traffic and pedestrians. He is crouched in position with the others, thinking only of his father's words, of his mother's sickness.

The blast shocks him. It rattles the trees and is instantly answered by the uniform cry of a flock of unseen birds. Steiner, red in the face, runs forward, shouting, "Run-gun! Réveillez-vous! Run-gun!" The commandos charge forward, firing their rifles. At first Kunle does not enter the road but lies under the cover of a tree, his father's plea thrumming like a small heart in his head. But then he sees Agnes crawling to get away from the line of fire and something nudges him forward. He finds that he is rushing after her, in the direction of a banana tree seventy meters away. Between the flagging branches of the withering tree, he glimpses a federal soldier and fires at him. The man spins at the impact, then falls into a mound of raised grass. Kunle makes for the road, where two Panhard armored cars are slaloming towards him. One has been blasted open, its turret hanging partway off, flaming. The other has barely been damaged, its front hood cracked and lightly smoking. A Land Rover has been tossed by the second mine into a ditch, its windscreen shattered, and its body riddled with bullet holes. A federal soldier hangs from its window, blood from a gape in his head slowly pooling into his helmet on the ground. Another Land Rover now diverts into the bush, knocking a commando over. Steiner, aiming with one eye needling into his rifle scope, blasts out the side window. The vehicle blunders into the undergrowth, tugs blindly to one side, and jerks to a stop like an old hog shot through the heart.

15.

They have been at rest for three weeks, and this Sunday, which is the last day before they return to action, they have all come to church with Ndidi, except James and Agnes, both of whom refused Ndidi's pleas—Agnes on the grounds that she no longer believes in a God who allowed such calamity to befall her, and James because, he says, the idea of God is "goddamn bullshit." They have been here for nearly an hour, and now the priest is chanting in a singsong voice, yet Kunle feels a terrible silence around him, as if he were alone. He moves his eyes off the big white candle on the lectern up to the ceiling, as he often does whenever he gets that strange feeling of eyes watching him from above or of a proximal voice only he can hear. Once, as a boy, he'd reported this phenomenon to his mother, but she'd dismissed his observations as mere childish imagination. In the years since, he's come to believe that the voice and eyes belong to Baba Igbala, the Seer. He joins in singing the familiar song the priest is leading, shouting the lines to drown out the thoughts of the Seer. The song reminds him of the last time he visited a Catholic church—for the wedding of Auntie Lucy, his mother's younger sister, in '55. It seems the war has made his mind an impaired eye, able to see things only within a circumscribed space: confined to the present.

An image of Tunde in a white shirt and oversized bow tie at Auntie Lucy's wedding returns, and Kunle finds himself laughing. As they leave the church, Felix asks why he's been laughing.

"Nothing," Kunle says. "Ah, Prof, I just remembered something."

Felix shakes his head, which shines from having been shaved to the skin; many of them have done this to mourn the 120 commandos who died at the garrisoned town of Agbani three weeks ago. Some 150 men, led by the newly promoted Lieutenant Wilson, had been loaned to the commander of the 14th Battalion to help defend Agbani when federal troops launched a surprise attack, wiping out most of them. For two weeks, Steiner and the men of the battalion were despondent, until Colonel Ojukwu sent 1,200 fully trained men so that Steiner could form the Biafran 4th Commando Brigade. Now, one week after the formation of the brigade, they are headed back to the front.

They stop near a line of traders with articles for sale on their heads or slung across their arms. From a man in an old suit and worn tie, Kunle buys a wristwatch with a leather band. Felix buys a bunch of bananas, and Bube-Orji a fistful of kola nuts, which he chews to stave off his constant hunger and to stay awake during shelling. Each of them tears a banana from Felix's bunch. They eat as they go along, watching people on bicycles or walking back from the church. Between mouthfuls, Bube-Orji points out that the black Holden with a Biafran flag and a red pennant flying from its bonnet is filled with military police and reiterates again the violent mythology attached to the MPs: that they hunt down deserters with merciless zeal.

Kunle and his friends enter an open street lined with wooden shacks; in one, two women sit before large pots, frying akara. It surprises Kunle every time he comes into town how little of an impact the war has had here. While many places in Biafra have been destroyed, the only sign of the war in the town of Etiti is the commando brigade headquarters and the swollen population of refugees, most of whom have fled Enugu, and other places that have fallen into federal hands. But in general, anywhere outside the front and military camps often harbors a strangeness to the soldiers each time they enter—as if they've stumbled upon old, faded photographs whose moment they can vaguely recall. It is why they go almost crazy whenever they go into town—eating whatever they can find, chasing whichever woman they see, drinking as much as is available.

Bube-Orji stops talking and points at a mob gathered around an old statue of a bird. Felix, as if on cue, races towards them, flinging his banana peel into the side brush. It is a mob of mostly Biafran Civil Defence operatives, wielding sticks and Dane guns. They surround a man lying in the dirt, shouting, "Sabo! Sabo! Sabo!" Felix breaks into the center of the group, speaking in rapid Igbo, of which Kunle does not understand a word. Felix says something to the accused man, and the latter tries to rise. In sudden rage, Felix kicks him in the spine and places the flat of his boot on the man's back. One of the militiamen takes out money from a goatskin bag that seems to belong to the accused. Felix and Bube-Orji examine the wad of new Nigerian currency notes and a copy of the previous day's Nigerian newspaper, *Daily Times,* with MARCH 1, 1968 boldly inscribed on the top. At first, Felix's face is expressionless. He hands the paper to Bube-Orji and grabs a rifle from the closest militiaman, checks the magazine, and closes the action. A stir runs through the crowd, and the man, sitting up quickly, raises his bound hands, crying, "Officer, Officer . . . please! I am . . . not a saboteur—"

"Everybody moof back!" Felix shouts, gesturing at the crowd. "Moof back!"

The crowd staggers back, people falling into each other. The accused man turns back again, pleading in a louder, more urgent voice. He crawls a few paces, turns again, lifts his earth-stained palms in supplication, bursts into tears.

"Sharrap! Shar-rap and face down!" Felix shouts, cocking the rifle. His arm jerks back as he fires a single shot through the back of the man's head. Blood darts out of the man's head in leaping blobs and spills over the ground. The crowd disperses behind the line, screaming, as more dark red blood oozes out and begins slowly expanding into a pool. The man lies still, the fine pattern of the sole of Felix's boot printed on the back of his worn white shirt.

They return to the camp in silence, except for Felix, who whistles one of his favorite patriotic songs, which casts northerners as crying goats. He seems to be in high spirits, as if redeemed by the singular act of killing one of Biafra's enemies. Bube-Orji walks with his mouth half open, his vitiligo more pronounced, chewing a kola nut. Ndidi fiddles with his rosary, a faraway look on his face. Until now, it had not seemed possible that Kunle could be angry at his comrades. But in this moment he feels revulsion towards Felix for killing the man, and Bube-Orji for firmly supporting the act. There is something in the dead man's apparent helplessness that bothers Kunle. In battle, once the commander orders to charge, the world changes and the frontline soldier is driven by a passion of such intensity that there is no time for rationalization. The enemy who shoots at him and at whom he shoots has no time to explain or to defend himself against any accusations. An overwhelming combination of fear and panic simply drives the soldier into some lower base of being where instinct rather than rationality rules. If there is a single law in the soldier's mind on the battlefield, it is to avoid, as much as possible, a cruel death. But outside the front, this is not so. Felix had had time to talk to the man, yet he'd wreaked the same level of violence.

They are walking on a road lined on either side with palm trees where, once, they'd seen apes. Kunle cannot hold it in any longer. "Why did you kill the man?" he finds himself saying, his heart racing. "Eh, Felix?"

"What?" Felix's expression is something Kunle has not seen before. "Why? Eh . . . you don't know—"

"No!" he cries. "You don't know for sure if he was—"

"Sharrap!" Felix's voice is a violent thing. "Sharrap, Yoruba man!"

Felix charges towards him, but Ndidi nudges Felix with his elbow, and he falls into the brush. Kunle, a hot thing rising in his chest, rushes away towards the barracks, ignoring the shouts from Bube-Orji and Ndidi calling him to stop. He arrives at the Madonna High School library, where Agnes and the new other female officer live, panting. Agnes is sitting on the porch, her hair wet and smelling of pomade. He tells her what happened. She shakes her head and, without looking at him, says, "Him do the right . . . Felix, yes."

Kunle presses the knuckles of one hand against the palm of the other. He wants to know, to understand why she would say this. She smiles, and then her face turns stern.

"This is war," she says. "It is not a time for . . . em . . . for obioma—that is, kindness."

He sits on the porch beside her, stunned by the harshness of her words. There are times when he feels himself existing in a heated world, alone in his head, while others seem calm, unaffected. This is such a time. Is she not bothered by the killing of a man who might be innocent of the crime of which he was accused, who might have been unjustly murdered by Felix? He lets himself calm and watches her hands slowly working the comb through her hair.

"Ehen, let me ask you—will you go and find your brother, Tun . . . Tuli?"

"Tunde," he says, looking at his hands, the tips of his fingers blackened with soot and gunpowder.

"Ehn?"

"Yes . . . I want to go. I really want to go, but what can I do when I find him? I can't jus' take him home."

She brings down the comb, a mass of hair trapped in its teeth, and looks at him.

"I am a soldier here—if . . . I can't jus' leave. If I do, they will court-martial me."

"But you no come from here," she says. "O bu ro agha gi—this is not your war."

"It doesn't matter!" he finds himself saying, louder than he'd wanted to. "It no matter at all—I am a Biafran soldier. I took oath."

Beyond the porch, the quartermaster's lorry from army headquarters wends its way slowly towards the officers' mess. Soon all the soldiers will be summoned to the parade ground for their monthly pay, and Kunle does not know when he can be alone with Agnes again. He wants to take her hand, to kiss her, but seeing that she is still busy, he says instead, "Agi, what of you? Where are your parents and siblings? I mean, are they alive?"

She nods.

"What did they say . . . they allow you join army?"

A smile appears on her face, obscuring the scar for a moment and quickly disappearing. When it's gone, her face wears something closer to scorn.

"Yes, my father—he don't like it at-all, at-all. He is very *very* annoyed. Why me instead of my two brothers?" She coughs. "But . . . mhuu. Darly, I have seen things that is possible only in terrible dreams. See, when . . . when people tell me, 'Agnes, don't do this, don't do that,' I just shake and shake my head."

Again she smiles.

"I listen to them, but I don't hear anything. You get? It is as if they are speaking a different language—a language I cannot understand." She raises the comb towards her hair, brings it down and points it towards herself. "I know what I am doing."

He nods. "I understand."

For a long while they are silent, his eyes on a butterfly hovering over the small patch of dry flowers. He does not see her stretch her hand towards him, but he feels her grip on his wrist.

"But, darly," she says, her voice descending into a whisper, "you are a good man. Reall-really. But . . . truly, this war is not for you."

IT IS STILL somewhat dark when they arrive. The front is a cleared field that winds along a declining macadam road on the outskirts of Abagana. Just before the field is the replica of a billboard near Kunle's house in Akure, with the familiar image of a chubby baby seated by a giant tin of SMA and the slogan WELCOME TO NIGERIA WHERE BABIES ARE HAPPY AND HEALTHY. Past the billboard, they see a distant rising cloud of smoke. The remnants of the 18th Battalion—men disconsolate and worn out, many of them with bandages around their heads or limbs—are retreating along the roadside. Everywhere the scars of fighting lie like leaves on a forest floor. Kunle grips the *Daily Times* newspaper he's been reading so tight his fingers dig holes in it. He is seized by the strange state of being at the front—the state of a sharpened awareness of the surroundings. He can see dragonflies hovering above the brush and, along the stand of distant trees, vultures. The air here has accepted and molded together the smells of men, blood, gunpowder, and burnt things; it is different from the air of anywhere else he's ever known. It is the air of the front.

Steiner gathers them—the full force of the commando brigade—and reads out the mission details, translated by his new second in command, Captain Emeka. For weeks, Steiner says, the federal 2nd Division has been trying to enter the city of Onitsha. The new brigade and the 57th Battalion are to block any possible linkage between the enemy's forces in Abagana and Onitsha. To do this, the wealth of the Biafran Armed Forces has been given to them directly by the head of state: sixteen 81mm mortars, twelve 60mm mortars, three thousand shells, sixteen pairs of binoculars, one bazooka, and 120 hand grenades.

But these supplies do not seem to make a difference, for it quickly becomes clear that they are being shelled with the same cannon fire as in the Milliken Hills battle, the bangs so deafening that Kunle feels painful pressure in his ears at every explosion. Soon the front is filled with clouds of black smoke and shattering noise, the disquieting screams of the dying. Kunle succumbs to the endless numbness of the body, the madness of the mind cycling the edges of life, the rime that settles on the soul after a while and does not thaw until the end of the day.

After five straight hours, it seems that the shelling has ceased. There is so much smoke over the battlefield that it has turned mildly dark. Kunle is eager to rise out of the dugout, to see where Agnes or his comrades might be, but he is lying in a mound of emptied sandbags, the wood of a torn and broken parapet fallen into the trench by his side. He'd moved without knowing it to a position in the direct line of an enfilade, far from his comrades. He is with men from the 57th Battalion, most of them wearing black steel helmets. Earlier, they'd had a machine gun and, a hundred meters to the left, a foxhole with an Ogbunigwe rocket launcher system and crew. Now the foxhole has been destroyed, and the men beside him sit with the machine gun between them like a sleeping child. He sees then, as through a suddenly opened door, two soldiers scrambling up to the surface. A third man makes to follow, but there is a quick sound and the hot draft of shrapnel as it flies past. For a moment the man stands still on the rungs of the ladder, headless, blood springing in different directions from the sudden gash in his neck. Then, slowly, his hands unclasp from the top rung and his body swirls. The soldiers flee from the falling body of the man in a frenzy, tripping upon each other. He falls dead against the trench wall, a curious specter of war.

The new wristwatch has come off its hinges, its surface cracked in multiple places. Kunle cannot tell what time it is. He sits up, a faint ringing still in his head. His eyelids are heavy, covered with wet mud. He hears the voice of Captain Emeka calling for the commandos to return to position, so he pushes the wreckage out of the damaged trench like a man unearthed. He walks between the corpses towards the mud-covered wooden ladder. A man is on the lowest rung, trying to hitch himself up the embankment. The man turns to face him, and Kunle lets out a shriek and steps back. The man's belly has been torn open. A long bloody mass of viscera is bulging through his shirt, entrails sticking out between the buttonholes and staining the ground with dark blood. The man's eyes are filled with wordless suffering. He falls back at Kunle's touch, and lies crouched against the trench wall.

Kunle leaves the position, hastening through the crowd in search of his friends, or even a commando. But there are men from the 18th Battalion huddled together, numb and weary, that it is hard to pass through. A man, shell-shocked, is shaking his head and slapping his ears violently, two men trying to restrain him. At a point 150 meters from where Kunle began, the way is blocked by a broken embankment, from which sandbags have filled the trench. He jumps over these, and almost at once, he meets men with the death's-head insignia of the commandos on their shoulder patches.

He finds his platoon at the edge of a pass, the same place they'd been before the shelling began. Without speaking, Agnes hands him her canteen, and he drinks until the water spills from his mouth to his chest and he lets out a childlike burp. Standing beside her, he can feel the world moving again, like vertigo. Unclear and indistinct thoughts percuss his mind. He reaches for her hand and at once there is a loud shout of "Excuse!" She steps towards him, and corpsmen carrying the wounded zip past in the direction of the first aid post at the rear.

"Jisos!" Agnes cries, turning sharply away. He sees the charred body of a dead man whose head has morphed into something gory, alien, as of eyes and skin melted on a deformed, plastic blob. Kunle is holding her trembling body against his chest, saying, "It's all right, is all right," when he feels a sharp pain in his calf, winces, and quickly grabs her arm.

"Agi! Ndi! Bube!" he cries, clenching his teeth. "I no fit move. Muscle-pull!"

"Ah, come o?" she says. "Fada—come . . . please lift him, he get muscle-pull!"

Ndidi helps her half-carry him. They bring him to a small house hidden behind the artillery batteries to the rear. It is an old colonial building overlooking a garden, a clothesline, and two huts covered in ancient uli motifs. It seems mostly intact, though stripped bare to a bedstand in one of its two bedrooms, a worn-out mattress. An old dresser stands beside it, ransacked. They lay him down on the bed, spasms searing his right leg. Ndidi finds, in the other room, hidden behind a slanted table, an ammunition crate for what seems to be a Kalashnikov rifle.

"I will go and show this to CO," Ndidi says, hefting the crate to his shoulder. "I am coming back, oh?"

"Ngwanu," she says.

"Let me follow him," Bube-Orji says.

Kunle hears the door close, its bolt falling closed behind them, his heartbeat rising. In the black vision of his half-shut eyes, Agnes undresses, the slanting light upon her buttocks. She is now only in her green T-shirt and underpants. Her feet are bare for the first time, out of the rain boots she wears. The red paint on her toenails is now mostly smudges, browned or blackened. He feels her weight on the edge of the bed, near his own reeking feet.

"How are you now?"

"Fine," he says quickly, his heart thumping, for desire, like fire, has erupted in the otherwise quiet region of his being. "The muscle-pull have gone."

"Okay. Thank God."

She seems to rise, but her weight rests deeper into the mattress, so that his left leg falls into its slight depression.

"I want to thank you for—"

"No, Agnes, no . . . no need to thank me."

He opens his eyes, but he can barely see her. Darkness has encroached quickly, eating away every trace of daylight.

"I must-to," she says. "You remind me of him."

"Who?"

After a pause, she says, "My husband." He can hear her exhale. "He was a quiet man. Even, everybody oh—everybody fit dey talk-talk, he will just keep quiet. . . . You resemble him."

He feels a lurch in his heart, and an understanding: this explains the mystery of her choice of him despite his youth and insufficiency. It surprises him that his characteristic reticence, a behavior cultivated out of desperation, has brought him something good in the end. He feels again a rising longing for her body, and the hardening of his organ. He closes his eyes so she will not see it written on his face. He listens to the phantom echo of her bare feet on the floor and feels then the weight of her body as she settles into the bed beside him.

"He was a good man," she says, directly into his ear. "Like you."

Kunle turns and, with a brisk motion, pulls her to him. When he's stripped her completely naked, he stops, as if in terror at the immensity of her body. She draws him close, and when he enters her, he feels a tremor around her waist. She clasps her hands around his back with an urgent, tight-fisted grip, as if afraid that at any moment he will leave, be dead, beheaded, never to return.

Bube-Orji is knocking, but she merely holds him with a grip of gentle violence. Bube-Orji whistles through his teeth and asks if they are there, then goes around the room, knocking on the windows. By the time Bube-Orji's voice recedes, Kunle has fallen against her, panting, sweating, feeling the last bit of semen spouting out of him.

They lie there naked, her head cradled in his arm; he gazes at the ceiling where a bulb should have been, but there is only its wiring, the colored strands hanging down. He wants to speak but cannot find what to say. It is in times like this that he hates what he has become: silent, filled with this unwillingness to say anything unless he is spoken to. A quality that, to his great surprise, is what Agnes likes about him.

She rises and moves to the window, as if called upon by an unseen presence. The darkness lifts off her back, and he can see, by the dim light in the hallway, the two dents where her hip bones meet, the long line running down her back. She looks out, her face angled up for a while, speaking to herself so quietly that the words sound as if they are tumbling out of her soul. He calls to her.

"What?" she says.

He looks at the silhouette of her breasts, the nipples still taut from his fondling.

"I . . . I . . . I am . . . sorry."

"Why?" she says, turning.

"Your husband. Your sons."

After that, he watches her sleep, thinking about how he's stayed away from sex in peacetime and now, on the battlefield of an internecine war, he's had sex for the first time. In peacetime, he'd run from friendships and romance. But the war has opened him up to friendships, to being constantly in the company of others, so much so that he feels the pain of solitude when away from his comrades. The war, it seems, has remade him into the boy he was before the accident. And it has gone further and fangled an unexpected romance out of the ruins of their lives. Agnes now occupies a place so deep and hidden in him that it feels as though she has always been there, her presence only now manifesting itself. He wants not just to fight by her side but to rescue her, if he can, from the war itself.

16.

It is the sixth day of engagement, and as with every battle, the war has carved sinuous tracks through the minds of the fighters. Images bleed together, and moments once filled with the vigor of life now exist only in a red mist, so that the soldier cannot tell one encounter from the other. It feels as though every blast is a menace, every gunshot a destruction. And during the fighting, the soldier lives in a continuous realm of noise, of rumbling and rattling, of cries and screams and clicking of triggers and chamber bolts—in terror. This is why, at the end of each battle, a great silence descends, a terrible, menacing quiet that exists only on the battlefield. It is a biting mystery that the battlefield that breeds the greatest noise also harbors the most complete silence.

It is afternoon, and as they have done for all six days, the federal troops have shelled for five hours without pause. Agnes whispers into his ear that she needs to urinate. He asks her if she can hold it in. She pinches his hand so hard he gasps. "You know that I can't do it here—I'm a woman."

He nods, the others gazing at him now, their faces almost totally covered in mud, so that they look like ghosts.

"Escort me," she says, her voice thicker. "If not, I will go by myself."

"Okay," he says.

He holds her hand, sweat warming his own, and waits, listening for the direction of incoming shells. When he rises with her and she starts to move up the ladder, there is a uniform shout from their friends below. "She wants to urinate!" he cries, and quickly, they run in the direction away from the salient, over burning craters and singed trees, still smoking. He can hardly breathe when they reach the bush near the rear—his voice hoarse from crying to every officer on the way, every MP, that she needs to go. She squats, and, resting both hands against a tree, he hears the slow rolling of the urine upon the leaves and sees it flowing down, slightly shifting a dry leaf, washing away a cluster of velvet mites. He turns to her, and at the sight of her rounded buttocks, he feels suddenly possessed by a desperate longing. He rushes towards her, and their mouths clatter in a rushed, frenzied kiss. She is raw and gasping, trembling at the concussions. He steers her towards the big tree and slides into her from behind. She glances about to see if anyone has followed them and occasionally at his face, as if to ask if he has gone mad. As he reaches the threshold of pleasure, he finds that her moaning voice—shaped by the acoustic beats of the distant concussions—feels like a violent thing. After he has dropped down among the dry leaves, she laughs at the sheer madness of the act.

"We are doing it inside hellfire," she says.

He and Agnes return to the trench to find that Ndidi has suffered a mild shock and has somewhat lost his mind. He was thrown into a daze by a blast, but when he woke up, grabbed by both arms by Felix and Bube-Orji, he first felt his chest for his rosary, then the piece of paper with the cross in his pocket and a small stone he always carried. Objects that would otherwise have been useless acquired significant character to the soldier at the front—sometimes a deeply spiritual one. Ndidi has become so obsessed with keeping his prayer book safe from the rain that he ferreted out nylon bags to wrap it in, tore off every food wrapping, until it was so tightly bound up that it took him minutes to untangle it. After Ekpeyong's death, Ndidi carried a stone he claimed had been on the spot where Ekpeyong was killed. He washed the thumb-sized rock sometimes, and because it could prevent him from sleeping if he rolled over it in his chest pocket, he slept with it in his clenched fist.

Now Ndidi is seated with the stone in his fist and a piece of Bube-Orji's life-saving kola nut in his mouth. Bube-Orji immediately passes lobes of kola nut to everyone in the dugout, chanting his mantra: "Oji bu ndu!" He often insists that they chew kola nuts to keep their minds alive and prevent them from breaking. Kunle chews his bits for over an hour, but when they are finished, his throat is parched. At three P.M., when the shelling stops, an uneasiness sets upon the field. Already, twenty-two commandos have been killed by the day's shelling. A battered command jeep races up the front line with a sergeant shouting, with his hand cupped around his mouth, that the federal infantry is approaching.

There is a scrambling. Steiner, Captain Emeka, and Agbam depart, leaving only the new female officer, Layla, to give orders. Lieutenant Layla, who simply showed up a week before and joined the Special Commando Platoon, has become good friends with Agnes, with whom she shares a room in the library, and two of the nurses who work at the brigade clinic. She is short and slight but possesses a commanding presence. Her green helmet, often strapped beneath her jaw, was stripped from federal soldiers she'd ambushed with her unit, earning her a promotion.

Kunle stays in the dugout beside Agnes and Ndidi, their rifles placed over sandbags. Lieutenant Layla, who is at the end of the perimeter, watching with binoculars, is the first to see the enemy: at least a thousand men scattered between columns of vehicles. At first, it is hard to believe her report. There has been no infantry for days, and now there's a swarm. The commandos break into a wail, and one man, throwing down his rifle, attempts to flee. Layla, taking a single aim with her rifle, shoots the man dead. The field quiets.

The enemy arrives like austere pilgrims: expected yet undesired. And when it is all done, much of the battlefront is alight with fire and smoke. The air is thick with ash and the smell of burnt metal, and the slow moaning of dying men. Over two hundred commandos are wounded or dead, and the battalion size is reduced to a little more than two companies. It had drizzled a bit, and the soldiers are wet and bloodied. Along the fields, wet mud is sloping away into ruts and craters and trenches. For a while, all Kunle can hear is the rumble of enemy vehicles retreating into the distance and a voice shouting over a megaphone, "Surrender, Ajukun sojas! Surrender make Nigeria be one! Surrender!" Slowly, the voice recedes, and near sundown, a signalman raises the Biafran flag from the road, six hundred meters away, and the commandos erupt in frenzied cheers.

IT IS DIFFICULT even for one watching from above to determine how long Kunle sleeps. When he wakes, he is in a room with his friends, including Felix, whom he has resumed speaking to again only recently. It is dark, and they are illuminated by the bright moonlight. He can see Ndidi, teeth clasped around a cartridge round, chambering his rifle. Kunle becomes conscious of clicking sounds near the door. He grabs his rifle and follows the officers and guards out of the damaged house. At once they see, even in the dark, the contrails of a jet.

"Something in their minds, I think," Captain Emeka says.

"Something fishy, sa," Kunle says.

They follow Steiner towards the bush on the left flank, the trees swaying lithely in the night wind. From here they return to the trench lines; there are a few men asleep in them. Three riflemen stand watch behind sandbags, gazing into the unyielding darkness that is no-man's-land. They hear a sound, and there, in its terrible glory, the fighter jet zips northward, trailed by a line, dropping something iridescent white.

"Le pahashut!" Steiner cries.

The parachute is floating in the distance, the dark-shaped figure of a man dangling beneath it. Ndidi raises his rifle, but Steiner stops him—"No, no, no, monsieur—nothing you must do . . . understend? . . . Oui, merci."

They watch the parachute drop like a stone, the white thing fluttering above the parachutist. It lurches to one side now, deforming its shape as if suddenly free of all air. The wind thrusts it up again and it floats freely, then torques, making the noise of a mighty tent uncoupling. It flings itself into the trees and stays there, its dome cast over the trees like the shape of a strange hut.

They watch for close to an hour for any sign of the intruder, but they see nothing of him, only the parachute constantly tumefying and releasing itself, whooshing. Every now and again, Kunle looks towards the damaged house, where Agnes lies asleep in the bed in which they'd first made love, his heart reaching. Neither she nor Lieutenant Layla has come out, and it seems they have not heard the jet. Gazing at Captain Emeka, Steiner says something in French.

"Major wants to know who can stay watch till morning while the rest goes to sleep," Captain Emeka says.

"Me, saa!" Kunle hears himself shout. "I will watch."

Even in the dark, Kunle can tell that Steiner and his friends are surprised. This is one of the rare times when he has ever spoken without being spoken to, and in such a situation. Later, when he is alone, he cannot understand why he volunteered to watch—except that when he'd looked at the house, an image of an intruder breaking in and killing Agnes had filled him with sudden dread. He reckons now that all his old interests, even the desire to return to Akure and escape this war, have been swallowed up by the single desire to be beside her.

After the others leave, he stares into the interminable darkness, and at the distant silhouette of trees, as if the world has been reduced to the perimeters of this single field. For what seems like an hour, he struggles against his dissolving strength, the creeping weakness dimming his vision and filling the trees with stirrings of life. He is in Akure, his back propped against the backyard fence, watching Nkechi fetch water out of the compound well, singing. He gasps and, waking, finds that he's slid from the crest of the boulder down to the brush beneath, his rifle falling away from him. "Oluwa mi oh!" he shouts.

It is still very dark, but the outlines of light have begun limning the edges of the horizon. How long has he been asleep? He reaches into his pocket for his wristwatch but remembers that it is in the house, in his ammunition pouch. By the dim, intersticed light of dawn, he can see that the parachute has moved closer, its cloth still waving in the whispering wind. He looks about as far as he can see, up to the trees spray-painted white to mark the beginning of no-man's-land, but can see nothing. If the enemy soldier has come out of the bush, why has he not heard his feet at least? But what if the parachute is simply hanging there, no longer anchored to a person?

A rooster crows from somewhere distant, and as if on cue, Kunle descends the incline and crashes through fallen trees into no-man's-land. He has almost gone past it when he hears a whooshing sound like the swinging of an iron chain. He sees first the dome-shaped canopy waving restrainedly above the trees. The suspension lines are tangled around a network of branches, from which a man in military uniform hangs, wrung around an iroko tree smeared with blood. The dead man's helmet is caught on the forked black branch beside him, and below, just a few feet from where Kunle stands, there is a concentration of blood and a leg severed from the knee.

Holding his hand to his chest, Kunle lets his breathing calm. He shakes the tree, untangling some of the lines. The chute inflates, drags the body through a network of branches, up between the canopies of two trees. The body swings gently, scattering more blood about the forest floor. He picks up the helmet, which has three lines marked on its front.

He is greeted with raised fists, and as he arrives at the salient in clear morning light, Ndidi and Felix rush towards him and lift him up. It is the first time he has embraced Felix since the killing of the saboteur, but he is too happy to hold on to the grudge. Though tired, he finds himself raising the trophy helmet and laughing, elated from an action that still feels like something an unfamiliar part of him has done.

THE DAY BEGINS as feared: early, just an hour after he finishes his report to Steiner about the trophy helmet of the enemy parachutist. Around ten A.M., Ndidi is carried off the field with a shrapnel wound to the back. James's cursing rings out: "Bloody fuckers! . . . Goddamn you!" The mortar round that nearly killed Ndidi also destroyed the trench emplacement, sank a few sandbags, amputated one man's leg, left another man's nose split open, his pharynx visible through the slit, and killed two others. The commandos huddle behind the breastworks and bunkers, most of them shaking. Throughout the trenches, men are wailing and cursing. Not even Steiner going about shouting the frightening charge "Réveillez-vous!" is able to quiet the weeping men.

Kunle is groggy, his vision hazy. He has been trying to sleep on the other side of the dugout, beside Agnes. He has a headache, and it seems that he has come under a strange, weary sickness that fills him with ague. He blinks, rubbing his eyes. He rises, dashes for the embankment ladder, but Agnes wrestles him down, dragging him by the neck. Bube-Orji joins in, and for a while they talk to him, but he cannot hear what they are saying. He points his finger in a semicircle, for he is surrounded by sinister creatures whose breathing he can hear but whose faces he cannot see. With every concussion, every bang, every eruption of earth fountaining out, the desire to sleep becomes overpowering. Now a shell lands so close it slams the wooden beams against a man a few meters away, and Bube-Orji dives farther under, releasing Kunle. Partially freed, Kunle bites Agnes's hand—which loosens its hold on him—and with a lurch and a swerve, he is up the ladder.

Agnes and Bube-Orji call after him, but he continues. It is a dangerous egress; smoke from the blast blows about him, and the violent whistling of incoming shells surrounds him. The earth concusses again and again, and twice he falls. He crawls but, touching something hot, recoils, gnashing his teeth. He shakes his grazed hand, spits into the reddening edges. A blast shakes the ground, lifts a burst of dust towards him. From somewhere nearby, he hears the sharp and distinct sound of grass rustling, the loud coo of some strange animal— perhaps a fox. He can tell that this peculiar sound has reached only his ears, the way strange voices sometimes do. He falls. There is no fox. Again Bube-Orji's voice rises with fervor, coupled with Agnes's. But both are swallowed by a familiar, distinct voice that sounds as though it comes from the edge of the world and beyond the limits of time: *Turn back!*

He looks behind himself, but there is no one. He lumbers forward, and in a few paces more he is standing outside the ruins of the small house, the bed he longs for within it. From its ruins, smoke is rising. Where might he sleep? He will go mad if he does not rest. He raises his foot to move and feels, in that supple instant, a strong stiffening of his body as if he's been electrocuted and released. He falls.

He lies writhing for a while, turning his head this way and back again, kicking his legs. The blow to his head has encouraged a circuit of paralyzing shocks, which now resolves into numbness. For a moment, he cannot move or speak, just lies among the debris, aware only of a certain vision of bright light pointing towards him. The light becomes now a long, relentless beam into which distant forms are entering and vanishing. He opens his mouth, something like a discrete mass filling his lungs as he struggles to breathe. He feels something cooling a region of his body, as if it is being slowly sunk into a pool of water. A quick, moving darkness rivers through him, attended by the sounds of explosions, the cries of anguished men, and the staccato snarl of machine gun fire. He remains there, quiet, half-concealed by the rubble like a thing hidden from the world, forgotten.

Part 3

The ROAD *to the* COUNTRY

THIS IS THE moment the Seer's been dreaming of all his life, but when it comes—as is common with humans—he almost misses it. The second Kunle leaves the trench, something scuttles in the undergrowth at the foot of the hill. The Seer turns—and there, a brown fox is staring at him with a sparkly, reddish glow in its eyes, as if surprised to find a human sitting here in the dead of the night. The fox stamps on the rock, its feet making a rapping sound, and lets out a howl. It stops, stares at the Seer. Ignored, it curls its tail upwards and plunges back into the bush.

When the Seer returns his gaze to the bowl, the unborn man's eyes are fastened upwards in search of the sound he's heard. It is clear to the Seer, who has been watching him from above, that Kunle has heard the fox too. And in Ifa's mystical miracle, the Seer is sharing the exact same experience with a man from twenty years into the future. The unborn man walks on through the singed field like one deranged. He kicks his legs, gasps as the whistling sound of a shell tears the air. The Seer knows that he has come to bear witness only, not to intervene, but he cannot help it. The shout drops out of him like a coin into an interminable hole: "Turn back!" At once it becomes clear that the unborn man has heard the Seer's cry. For he stops, looks about, and walks on.

Shortly after the man falls, Ifa's bowl is covered in formless darkness. This is to be expected. The Seer has learned that in the intermediate space between life and the afterlife, there is at first nothing. It is from that nothingness that the outer cosmos forms and takes an immaterial shape whose borders and trace lines are hidden from the eye. And now, from the body of the man lying among the debris, a mystic figure rises, ascending out of the wounded city of his being. It is much like the replica of the man but with a spectral form. It stops for a moment some thirty meters up, gazing at itself, and at the body beneath. Then, as if in silent pilgrimage, it moves quickly into that dark road whose esoteric tracks are hidden from the human eye. It is a road known only to the discerning. Thus, even among the most knowledgeable of mystics who know the voice of Orunmila and who carry in them the ancient history of the universe, the road is known only by a single, strange, and unexplainable name: *the road to the country*.

The Seer watches this figure with awe. He recognizes that it is a duplicate, similar to the one he'd seen rise out of his beloved and not the mangled one lying in the rubble. They are so similar except for the soul's litheness of form—for when the unborn man's soul rose, smoke had coiled about it like a sheet of organza in the wind. Now, as it travels the strange road, the Seer can feel the stillness, the tranquility, the absence of pain—the cathartic explosion of chaos into order.

The Seer remembers this road from that unforgettable night when, in great grief, he asked his master to help him do something incredibly rare. His master, acquiescing, led him into a séance. And in the most unforgettable moment of his life, as white smoke thrilled the air and the world of man faded into the shadows of the afterlife, he watched the austere form of his wife, Tayo, slowly rise and morph into a realistic expression of what she had looked like the morning she died. This was his first taste of the ethereal world through Ifa's bowl, and the brief reunion with his beloved was why he had decided never to turn away from it.

The portent has grown now, filling the horizon with oneiric illumination, as if the star itself has been split. Light is flowing out of it in thick rods. His eyes are so fixed on this transformation and occultation of the cosmos that he does not look in the bowl for a while. When he does, all he sees is the reflection of the portent's light. There is no star—only the scar of yellow light curving down towards the edge of the earth.

Though the translucent darkness remains on the surface of Ifa's bowl, the Seer can hear the young sound of a world forming—like something pounding through the core of the earth itself. The unborn man's form appears again. The form seems to have a more heightened sense of perception that forces everything he hears to lodge inside him in infinite threads. It is clear: Kunle is no longer human. He has no body, no organ through which he can sense things. Every movement now uses up the entirety of him, as if he is in totality an instrument of sound, vision, touch, and smell.

The Seer finds himself on the verge of tears. Ifa the invincible, he says, I am your servant forever. Let the soil build its own shores, the sea its own. Let the footsteps of thunder be imprinted only on its own path. On that path, let no one else travel. *Shopona gbe mi lodo ona. Eja ti o soro, fun mi l'ohun ti mo n wa . . . eshu alagbongbon, je ki n'simi.*

17.

It has taken some time, but it occurs to Kunle that he's been existing in the significance of his own presence like a thing without anchor. And now he begins to see things: a refracted light spreading across a distant plain, its reflection brightening up the face of this world. On a track that runs as far as the eye can see, beings are floating in different directions. And from somewhere comes the toll of some unearthly bell, so loud and overwhelming it feels as though he is being plunged into the core of the sound itself. He clamps his hands over his ears and steps away from the place. When he can no longer hear the bell, he looks about, and the horizon spread as far as the eye can see is covered in painterly rows of purplish-blue light, as if it were an imagined world—something in a picture book. Again he wonders, What is this place? He searches for any trace of what this place might be: Where is Agnes, the front, his comrades, the war?

He is covered in dirt, leaves, blood, and mud. There are semen stains beneath the zipper and on the legs of his trousers. His heart leaps: Have his comrades seen them? The stains must have come from one of the daring times these past few days when he made love to Agnes hastily in some patch of the bush in the midst of a shelling. Every time

Kunle touched her, he felt his soul descend a secret stair into a bunker, sheltered from all the torments of war.

He notices now that his right boot has been torn and he can see the top of his foot, the rest of it robed in dust. His trousers are so dirty and caked with flecks of mud he wants to take them off and wash them. He hears a distant cry and turns about, his eyes scanning the undulating stretch of hills as far as they can see. But nothing stirs now or makes a sound. When he moves, his feet produce a sound that echoes and tumbles into some vast, endless void and sets off little muffled detonations of sound all around him. It is clear to him that this place is not of the world that he's come to know all his life. Here, one's footstep echoes and occupies space, and what one sees here becomes a thing that is irrevocably seen and whose form soon changes. Yet he feels whole, alive in some mystic way. He becomes conscious of some change, a growth of the mind, as of a child coming into the recognition of new things. This realization alarms him: he is dead.

In the time it takes for this thought to take shape, he finds that the place has changed and the world that only a moment before was hesitant to come into being has suddenly become fully realized. Figures like him are scattered over the plain—all gazing at themselves first, then at this place. Among these are two Biafran infantrymen standing on a terraced path beside a large pot containing some colorful plant with a strange stem curved in several places. He motions at once towards them, but before he can move his feet, the bell tolls.

The uniforms of the two soldiers are worn and torn. One has the tag LVII still on the shoulder patch, below the rising sun badge. At first the two men do not regard him, immersed in their discussion, and their voices penetrate him and lodge in the core of his being.

". . . I blame him, I blame am oh," the older man, in his late thirties, is saying.

"Me too, I blame him. If he didn't start shooting at his own men, we will have returned and regained our courage," the younger soldier says, gesturing at himself with a sweep of his hand from his chest down to his waist. "Look at me. Jus'—jus' look at me, eh? What will anybody say? That I was killed by my own commander."

"Chai, air raid, ewoh, air raid!"

"My brother, it is sad! Chei!"

Kunle can see the air visibly flowing from the direction he's just left, carrying with it small, shiny transparencies. It is a sight so brilliant and extraordinary he feels his heart lurch. The two men, as if used to the phenomenon, continue their discussion unhindered.

". . . Once I saw he was shooting at your people," the older soldier says, "I run back to front. In fact, I load my Mark IV, run and see just opposite me, near that Onitsha main market, Gwodogwodo men. All of them, dey tall—dey tall, eh. I did not even cock my gun before I hear *gboh!* I feel am immediately, the bullet, for my chest here."

The hole the older soldier has pointed to is large—like something shot through with a 7.62mm cartridge used in a Bren light machine gun. Light stretches, rodlike, through him to the other side, forming a small circle on the ground. Kunle remembers his own moment of death: how he fell, and how slowly black edges grew around the field of his vision. He felt pain in his head, and his mouth saying words he cannot now remember. He felt his body yielding to something, like his entire being was being dragged into some unfamiliar realm. The next thing he knew, he was here.

"For onoda trench I see two snake bat people—one man for chest, onoda for hand. Before dem fit even turn, one of dem don run. Na so rocket clear am . . . clear the man like say na toy!"

"You don't mean it."

"My brother, I see am," answers the younger soldier. "The thing our eyes dey see for this war, eh, only God can say."

But now, with these great sighs, the men fall silent. The younger soldier, still wearing an electrician's helmet, scarred and pocked with bullet holes, turns and, noticing Kunle, taps the older soldier.

"Brothers," Kunle says, "I greet you." Aware of his limpid anonymity, his voice takes on a newer, more forceful cadence.

"Ndewo!" they both say.

"I come from the country. I fight with the commando battalion, Taarti-two Brigade at Abagana."

"O-o ya, you people are the ones there after us?" the older soldier says.

"Yes, yes," says Kunle.

"We were there too, rear flank. We saw your men, the white men, fighting in the open. We saw you people—"

Kunle nods. "Yes. I was killed near the rear. I was—"

"Your head!" the younger soldier says, nodding. "We can see it—shrapnel. Chei!"

Kunle touches his head. The skin feels loose and rough, as if something is glued to it. Towards the side of his head is an object with a sharp edge—the fragment of some hard material lodged in the hole in his head.

He tells them how he slept little the previous night and wanted to close his eyes only momentarily. He made for a house in the rear but ended up here instead.

The men shake their heads.

"It is how we will all die—everyone before the war will end." The younger soldier, shaking his head, sighs. "Chei!"

"Eh . . . sa, where are you people going? W-what will you do . . . I mean . . . now that you are here?" Kunle points. "The people leaving, where . . . those, like that man in that valley now starting to disappear . . . where will he go?"

"Hills of the ancestors!" the men cry in unison in a way that is uncharacteristic of the living, as if something external and austere has spoken through them.

Kunle looks in the direction the two soldiers have pointed, but he cannot see anything, save people crowding various parts of the large, endless fields. The men appear different: both have acquired the clean translucence of young toads, the insides of their bodies and the faint outline of what lies beyond them visible. The men turn from him and follow the path with such speed that, even though his eyes are trained on them, he cannot see where they go.

Kunle remains standing there, confused. He sees that his shirt has been torn, with one of its buttons missing. One of his shoes has been removed and, as he is trying to make sense of that, the other is gone. Something seems to be happening to his back, and putting his hand behind himself, he feels that his shirt has been ripped to the waist. He feels a sensation around the part of his head where the foreign object was lodged, but now he can no longer find it. There is instead a wad of extra flesh or some plaster glued to his skin.

At last, when it seems the unseen hands have left him alone, he goes towards a clear, glistening brook with birds of strange and unusual colors swimming along its shore. He finds a small crowd of people sitting here in a circle, phrases in certain pitches reaching him. One of them, a man whose body from the waist down is gone, bears on his face a glorious sorrow as he speaks. He is finishing to the cheers of the crowd as Kunle nears their circle, and silence falls as an elderly woman whose body is complete makes it to the center and begins speaking in Igbo, which, strangely, Kunle finds he can now fully understand:

"It is true, something cruel and unforgiving has taken over the world. A thing opposed to fear. The Nigerian soldiers came into our town early in the morning, dragging our men out of their houses, shouting, 'One Nigeria! One Nigeria!' I knew that my husband and first son may have been killed and that they were coming for this one who remained with me. But where would we go? Their tanks were already spread like the legs of a spider on every corner of the town, and their riflemen were hiding in our forest. The previous night, they had dragged out the daughter of Emenkwo, the nursing mother, and defiled her through the night. Her body lay on the road to the Ugwu Forest, her pants and brassiere scattered about. Our elders say it is better to look for the black goat before dark, so I rose, took my son to the small hut that used to be the kitchen of my mother, an ancient hut made of mud, sticks for pillars, and thatch for roof. I sat him under a table covered with a mat and left him some roasted yams wrapped in banana leaves and water in a calabash. Then I knocked down the hut with my son in it. I waited under the zinc roof that extended to form a shade over the porch of my own house for them to come.

"Ha, Chukwu-okike! When they came through the long road to the hills, the first thing I saw was the elder, Agbaso, shot through the belly, trembling in a spill of his own blood. The men, in deep green uniforms, swearing, shouting, 'Ajukun soja,' shot the blind son of Nwike, who lived by the three palm trees. How could he have become 'Ojukwu soldier' when he was blind? From there they came to my house. They asked me where are the men in this house? 'You have killed them all,' I said. One of the soldiers' eyes were red like an evil spirit; his lips were chapped, and there was still sleep in the corners of his eyes. He cocked his rifle. 'No, no, no!' another said, restraining him. 'Oga order, no woman kill walahi!' The angry soldier lowered his rifle, stormed through the door into the house. I heard them kick at our things, upturn the spring bed. I heard the rattling of plates and pots and tawa. I heard one of the wooden windows slam against the outer wall. Then they came rushing out, panting. They threw only a momentary glance in the direction of the hut where my last son sat and left. But that night, I was asleep in the bed when the angry soldier returned alone. Before I could see him clearly, he knocked a tooth out of my mouth and shoved his manhood into me—a place where nothing had been in more than ten years. To defile an old woman is a nso-ani, and it was not fit for me to continue to live. So, I begged him to kill me. And when he was done, he sank his knife into my chest, above my left breast—again and again and again, until all I could see was the glorious light of this place."

The woman's words fill Kunle with profound sorrow. While they were at Enugu, Felix and others had spoken about the Asaba massacre committed by the men of the federal 2nd Division. It had helped galvanize some recruits, like some of the men in his company, to join the Biafran army. But now here was a grim witness to the crime.

"My children and I had not eaten for days," another voice begins from the center of the crowd. "We were trapped in a small house in a village that, when we woke the next morning, had become a front line. To the east, a few houses down, were federal men; across the narrower street, our men. They were shouting and screaming. We could see them through the only window in the room. The rest of the house had been destroyed, a great beam fallen right across, blocking off the door to the room. My husband, whose stubbornness was why we had not left for a safer place, was trapped in the sitting room. The first night, we heard him shout, pray, cry from morning till night. There was a great rumble outside, and it seemed like he was in great pain, but I could not get to him. There was nothing in the room where I was save a crate of Coca-Cola we had bought before the war began for my brother's wedding. Me and the children, for three days, peed and shat in the room, drinking bottle after bottle. For those two first days, I heard his voice—Ofodili, my own heartthrob. The man who married me when I was young, who drank the water of my youth in its dewy morning. A strong man—agbara nwoke, an iroko who stood where his mates stood. But there he was, helpless, imprisoned by the walls of the house he'd built with his own bare hands.

"All day I heard him cry. The second night, his voice tempered by fatigue, he asked, 'Ije, have I been good to you?'

"'Yes, Dim. You have been good.'

"For a long time he did not speak.

"'Is this the truth?'

"'Yes, my husband. If I return to this earth, I will marry you again even in my seventh incarnation.'

"For another long while, he did not speak. Then I heard him sob. I called his name again and again, all the names I have known him by, and the ones I spoke into his ears in the blessed nights when he gave me, on our squeaking bed, what no one else could ever give. But to none of this did he answer. I called, till my chi inflicted on me the worst heartbreak of my life. In grief, I thrashed about the floor, in the wild glare of my sons. But my Ofodili was gone. He did not say goodbye to me; he left with only the assurance that he would always remain the love of my being. The morning of the fourth day, through the window, I could see that our men had been vanquished, their bodies lying about in the streets and brush. The soldiers rolling in were the enemy. Perhaps they will help my sons, I thought. They were young—my twin boys not yet six. So, through the window, I squeezed them out. 'Go and tell the men I'm here.' Once they were gone, I pushed my way through the door into the cascading bricks, towards my Ofodili."

KUNLE CAN SEE now that this is a carnival: of testimonies, of the relieving of the burden of the old life, of the reckoning of the dead, of the archiving of the memorable moments of life. There are clusters of these carnivals everywhere in this place—one a thousand meters to the left is full of white people, soldiers from some war in a place called "Vietnam," arriving in their own shattered forms. And farther, people from Asia Minor, but a force compels him to be here, among the people who have come from the same place as him. He can think of nothing else but to remain here, among this teeming crowd, as the next one, a soldier in a federal green uniform pockmarked with bullet holes as if he were a building somewhere in a frontline town, takes the stand. After this man comes another, a twelve-year-old girl, killed by an air raid in Oguta. Also in line is a white woman from Scotland, the wife of a Biafran architect, killed by artillery fired by an advancing federal unit. And for a long time, the voices meld into an amalgam of stories. Kunle is transfixed by the transcendent eloquence with which they describe the events culminating in their deaths. It occurs to him that the only true thing about mankind can be found in the stories it tells, and some of the truest of these stories cannot be told by the living. Only the dead can tell them.

He listens for a while, but because time here travels on the softest of feet, its footsteps unheard and its distance unmeasured, even he cannot tell how much time has passed. And by the time a man who'd been killed by a speeding Biafran military police car begins speaking, Kunle notices that he's been wrapped in a white hospital cloth, and he can feel the sensation of his arm being poked with a needle. He sees, too, that the field beyond is now filled with brilliant, colorful transparencies shining like a sea of confetti.

Turning, he finds that he is in a valley with translucent balloons and strangely shaped pennants floating in the air in different directions.

From the balloons or someplace he cannot see, soft music rises, so enchanting that Kunle's ears feel as though they have found their most secret melody. He wants to cry, to stay here forever.

For a moment he sways helplessly to the music, feeling a kind of freedom he's never known. For there is no sense of time here. Nothing feels exigent. He continues dancing as the sky changes colors—from white to light yellow to purple, then white again, then ocean blue, then red. At one point he stops, his vision obscured by a cloud of steam. He is naked now and hands are running over his body. It seems then as though something external is imposing itself upon the integrity of his being. And for a long time, he is unable to calm himself. For a moment, he stands there, weary of his own feelings. If he cannot return to Biafra, why not the spot where he has just been?

Now, again, is darkness felt, not just seen, as if one were looking through a dark mist. When he opens his eyes, the world is not as it had been only moments before. From some hidden place, mystic light has crouched upon the horizon, and below the place is crowded, filled with voices, lamentations, screams, arguments, as if he were at a motor park in Akure or in Biafra. "Chai, o bu ka'm si je!" . . . "Anne ben ölüyorum!" . . . "Fayah me for chest and I just fall" . . . "You no wake again, abi?" . . . "Anh ta bắn tôi" . . . "I git hit bad, man, en now won't be going back to my mama no more!" . . . "Jesus! Help me! He-lp me!" . . . "Dem too wicked" . . .

Wishing to escape the commotion, he thrusts forward and feels himself moving again, amid an increasing tide of people. The desire to return to the battlefields to find Agnes and his comrades, or to his brother, or home, comes upon him. He asks two women, but they do not know the road. They both wear bloodstained wrappas and are thin and gaunt, their bodies riddled with bullet holes, which now seem like strange parts of their skin. Past them, he asks a man who is gazing at his bare feet.

"Road, where?" the man says, taking his eyes only momentarily from his miraculous legs.

"Etiti. I'm from Fourth Commando unit." Once he's said it, he knows he is wrong, but the man is already pointing somewhere he cannot see. "No, sa, I am sorry, I been mean, Biafra. Are you from Biafra . . . land of living people?"

"Eh, why do you want to return—are you not dead?"

He looks again at himself and mumbles that he does not know. The man steps closer, stands on his toes, and cranes his head towards Kunle's face before retreating again, his eyes widening like those of one who's seen a sight of unspeakable horror.

"Ush! Ush! You . . . you are alive!" The man takes another step back. "You are alive! How come?"

"I—"

"Ohoooo!" The man looks at Kunle's legs, at his chest, then up at his face. "If you are not dead, then you should go. Go there."

"Yes—sa," Kunle says, glancing in the direction the man is pointing.

"Once you start, don't turn. Don't turn at all, are you hearing me? Once you turn, the road don disappear be that."

"Is all right, sa!"

The man has pointed to a path, shiny and purplish, that winds—eternally—through a blooming bush where eddies of flower petals swim lightly in the air. He walks in the direction of the light. An orchestra of colors and wind flows towards him, and then archipelagoes of houses and strange, august plants. He arrives near a familiar field with people carrying bags, all dressed in the same colors, their clothes shining in the elemental light. They all rise at his approach, as if he's royalty. Among them, he recognizes a young woman—Funmilayo, a girl who lived in their street and fell into a well in '59, causing much sorrowful mourning in Akure. She looks just as he remembered, smiling with a bewildered expression on her face.

If he's meeting the long dead, then will he be able to see Mamocha, his grandmother? Will he see Ekpeyong, his beloved friend, or even Captain Irunna? He looks around and cries, "De Young!" into the air a few times. He waits, looking about, but nothing stirs. Instead, it seems as if his effort to summon the dead has altered something in the place, plunging the world into complete stillness.

18.

He passes through the fugitive form of things—structures that must be buildings in this place—like a spectral being flowing through holes, easing out beneath doors. For much of the last few hours he has been thinking about his parents and brother and the fact that he is in a city of the dead. If he cannot find this road, he may not be able to rescue his brother from the war. He thinks with sorrow that Agnes might die without him by her side. Anguished, he resolves again to find a way out. He walks for a while, though it feels like he is passing the same place repeatedly. The world from which he's come feels more distant with each passing moment, and he can hear the rumbling of its wheels as it recedes even farther away. When, at last, he arrives again at the carnival of stories of the Biafran dead, he is relieved. Here, the silence is as it was earlier—as if the lips of everyone but the speaker have been hermetically sealed.

A Biafran lieutenant, commander of a company in the Calabar sector, is speaking now in a voice both somber and loud. He was killed after his unit suffered a surprise attack that blew up their trench and trapped him under the rubble. "The night was dark beyond all imagination," the lieutenant says in impeccable English. "A slight drizzle of rain has been falling, sending flashes of lightning. My boys were screaming, 'No bullet! Bullet don finish!' To my right, left, and even center! Some of them then started screaming, 'They are coming!' To my left, my two-in-c was lamenting in Igbo, 'Arh, Chineke'm, o bu ka'm siri je!' Before I could open my mouth, another of my boys was saying, 'Please, sa, please no kill—no kill—eish!'"

The lieutenant falls silent, shaking his head. Next, he says, he heard a rash of gunfire hitting human flesh, and from somewhere, a voice cried, "Fayah them all! Finish all Ajukun soja!" There was no light, and the lieutenant lay there, seeing the federal soldiers moving about the parapet looking for anyone still alive, shooting at the dead. In the pocket of the officer's trousers, his radio suddenly began crackling with rushed static and wind, and a voice rose from it as if from some far edge of a lost world: *Lieutenant Umeh . . . over? . . . Command HQ orders tactical withdrawal . . . wan-tuu, wan-tuu, can you hear me?* He desperately tried to move his arm, to reach it and throw the thing away, but he could not move. The enemy soldiers began looking for it, and he heard their movements. A torchlight flashed on him, behind its light the faces of four enemy soldiers, foliage covering their helmets. He prayed as one of them aimed a rifle at him. Next he knew, he was here, in this place of bright colors and unearthly music.

The tale is too painful to bear—what a calamity, a waste of lives! Kunle turns away to go on looking for the path the man instructed him to follow, but then he stops. He has heard a familiar voice. He rushes back towards the crowd, panting. He thrusts his head over their shoulders, cries with all his might, but not even the woman right in front of him can hear him. None hear him, and the fellow continues with his narrative. Kunle has no choice now but to listen to the mournful voice of his friend and comrade Bube-Orji.

". . . But-tu, they say make we follow Commander Wilson and go and support the people of Fifty-four Battalion. Their commander is Leftenant Colonel Nsudoh, Calabar man. So, we all follow and go to fight at Afor-Igwe market, just close to Onitsha main town. Some days before vandals throw bomb here, mortar, and it killed plenty Biafra commanders—even air force commander, Colonel Chude-Sokei, die there, and plenty others. Many wound . . . So, we fight. We use a lot of weapon—artillery, bazooka, Bren, Mausa, even Ogbunigwe. We fayah them! We fayah them from morning, before sunrise reach afternoon. But-tu, chai-chai, ammo finish. Inside ammunition box, nothing remain and the one wey remain, fire catch it. You see how bad luck finish us?"

For a while, Bube-Orji does not speak, just shakes his head, and the attendant silence is so complete, it feels as if the world itself were dead.

"So immediately after our bullet finish naw, trouble begin. Mind you—vandals know say our bullet always finish. The night before, after everything calm, they send person who hide somewhere for no-man's-land and hold megaphone to say, 'We go kill all of una like moskito, Ajukun soja! Una bullet go soon finish and we go come kill-kill all of una. Wallahi, we go marry your sisters, and your mothers—by fire by force!' So now, when we no fit shoot again, vandals know we have finished our bullets. They start to pursue us and gbam, our position . . . they don overtake us. Left flank, they have filled, only them. Ha, we hear fayah, fayah. We ran—me and four other commando. We miss road, separate from company, and run for onoda direction, and we didn't know we were in no-man's-land because of the smoke—smoke everywhere, no visibility. They were fayahing us left, right, and center. I pass one store, and bullet smash the glass, the sound nearly cause me headache. But, chai, no ammo. I turn, enter inside one church—it is full of dead bodies. Flies everywhere; the smell so bad. Plenty vultures inside eating some of the bodies, and when they see me, everywhere in the ceiling full of vultures flying inside the church. I run out, very afraid."

Again Bube-Orji falls silent, shaking his head. He looks up at the sky, which has thickened into a glowing orange, as if this world has been lit by a strange, unknown sun.

"I look at my H&K G3, no bullet, only click and click. I hold am tight, running, and I will turn and point as if something was inside. But nothing! Why are we fighting war when we no get weapon? Why? I am asking you—why?" he asks, his face somber.

That morning, they were down to only a few hundred rounds of ammunition for their rifles, ninety-something mortar shells, one bazooka with less than forty rounds, twenty-two hand grenades, and just six machine guns for the entire company. Of this, every soldier took fifteen rounds. While they were trying to escape, the enemy infantry cut down two of the men, shooting out the eye of one of them. Wielding his gun as a club, Bube-Orji hid inside a house largely intact save for shattered louvers. He knew death was upon him, and lying in the empty house, the barrel of his gun facing the door, he prayed and wept. As the footfalls of the federal soldiers approached the house, he felt his body rouse in violent protestation against what it knew was imminent. The door burst open and the last thing he saw was the wind swaying the branches of a mango tree outside, and his eyes focused on a ripe mango on which a charaxe was sucking. He opened his eyes to find himself in this place.

"That is how they kill me," Bube-Orji says with bitter restraint. "The vandals."

IT SHAKES THE foundational harmony of Kunle's spirit to see Bube-Orji here. This was one of the comrades in whom he delighted the most. Bube-Orji had spent these months journeying, like the others, into the very soul of evil, but unlike Felix, who was savagely optimistic, and Ndidi, who has become cynical and pessimistic since the loss of Eha Amufu, Bube-Orji kept a neutral front. Kunle wants to cry for his friend when Bube-Orji exits the platform and is able to communicate outside the circle. Kunle calls out and Bube-Orji rushes forward to him. They embrace, then step back to examine each other.

"Kunis, it's me, oh."

"Oluwa mi oh!"

"I'av been looking for you everywhere . . . I know you will be here."

They embrace again. A shadow darkens Bube-Orji's face, as if it is wrestling with itself for a suitable expression.

"Nwanne, they'av killed me. They'av . . ." Bube-Orji shakes his head, and Kunle can tell that his friend is crying, but there are no tears, only groans of sorrow. "They'av separated me from my lady . . . I neva even born yet. But see naw, they'av killed me."

Kunle turns away from his friend to look about at the landscape, which has changed, even though they have remained on the same spot. They seem to be near bright, strangely colored mountains—glowing like a pink that has been exposed to fierce yellow flames. It occurs to him that the place itself is why he cannot feel emotions. For before he can begin to feel something, he's distracted by something else. And now he sees, with incalculable, almost microscopic focus, a field of shiny trees. It strikes him that he's been looking through the hole in Bube-Orji's head—a clean hole drilled through the front of his head, neatly grazing his brain and skull, then exiting through the back. The hole, Kunle can tell, must be 7.62 millimeters in diameter—the size of an AK-47 cartridge. There are three more on Bube-Orji's torso—one on the left breast below his heart, one on the spine, and the last just beneath the shoulder blade on his right side.

"How long 'av you been here?" Bube-Orji says, with a sullen smile. "In fact, you come here straight, o kwa ya?"

"Yes."

"Oh, okay."

"But"—Kunle focuses again on the hole, shaking slightly—"how long have I been here?"

"You? Six days. Almost a week now."

"Oh—"

"Yes." Bube-Orji faces him. "But, Kunis, you cannot stay for this place."

"Eh?"

Bube-Orji looks him in the face. "You'av not die . . . You are still alive."

He wants to speak, to ask how Bube-Orji knows this, but Bube-Orji's eyes are following a strange object at this moment sailing across the field.

"Yes, you'av not die. You'av stayed here for six days now—going to wan week. The day when we no see you again for battlefield was the same day major withdraw us. The vandals retreat—"

Bube-Orji casts a quick glance at the flying creature, the words dissipating in his mouth, then turns back to Kunle. The federal 2nd Division commander, Murtala Muhammed, had asked his troops to retreat two kilometers and strategize. Seeing no need to pursue them farther, Steiner declared the mission accomplished and handed command back to Major Achuzia, the new commander of the Biafran 54th Battalion. The commandos were about to return to Madonna 1, brigade HQ, but Ndidi insisted that they find Kunle's body, seconded by Agnes. She led them to look for Kunle at the former commando salient, which had become a no-man's-land, with the troops having moved five hundred meters farther away. In the dark dead of the night, they found Kunle near the ruined house, from which smoke was still faintly rising. Touching his hand, she felt life—perhaps some pulse. Bube-Orji and the rest watched her, dazed, recognizing the miracle of the moment, the testament of the bond that had formed between her and Kunle. "He's alive!" she whispered again and again. Then, like a mad person, she hauled he who was thought to be dead up from the rubble. The rest came and lent a hand, nearly a dozen of them.

Kunle remembers this moment clearly now: it was when his shirt had been suddenly ripped open. Bube-Orji continues: Kunle was taken afterwards to the hospital at Iyienu, in a coma. He was alive but had sustained a traumatic blow to the brain when the explosion blasted what remained of the house and shrapnel hit him on the head. This was six days ago, and just the day before, when Bube-Orji, Felix, Ndidi, James, and Agnes had visited Kunle, the doctors said they were thinking of taking him off oxygen so they could release the bed for others who had greater chances of survival.

"You must go back, nwanne . . . because of Agnes," Bube-Orji says, impatiently. "We for don bury you if no be for her."

It seems that they have been standing there for a long time, for more people have started to trickle in, and a brook has opened nearby, its waters shiny and brilliant, sparkling with little pockets of light. Small animals float in it, transparent and delicate, their innards visible.

"Kunis, please go, o? Go—now-now! Enter the . . . the . . . road to the country! No go . . . no go . . . ono . . . da place!" Bube-Orji says this hastily and, looking up from the nascent brook, Kunle sees that Bube-Orji has become naked, his body slowly being covered with earth. A patch of earth appears on his face, then his chest, his arms, and then most of his legs.

"Kkkk-ssh," Bube-Orji says, spitting out a bubble of earth.

Earth has covered Bube-Orji's face so quickly that Kunle can see nothing save the slit of an eye and his mouth.

It is a thing too hard for the mind to contemplate: a body being buried while its soul is upright. It is difficult to watch, and so Kunle turns away, listening to the increasingly muffled words of his friend. Spitting a burst of earth, the grotesque figure of his friend cries, "Go, Kunis, go . . . go! G . . . guuuurrrrrrrrrrr!"

Kunle stands staring for a long time at the spot where his friend stood only a moment before, now empty except for a footprint in the colored earth. About the field are a mass of people, swelling by the minute. Kunle goes on like one commanded, saying the name of the road. At last, he comes upon a detached path that splits in three directions. He stands at this crossroads, weighing his decision like a jury in whose hands lies the fate of all of mankind. With a valiant shout, he drags himself to the darkest road.

THE SEER STANDS outside himself when the unborn man crosses into the dark road. At first it is quiet, like the silence at the front, but soon he hears the voices of multitudes. In Ifa's waters, the man recedes—farther, and farther, and farther, until he is swallowed in fuchsia light. The light slowly dims, and the Seer sees the moment his master has often spoken of: when the soul fuses with the body. The Seer trembles at the sight of the fusion, at the quick, shocked expression that lights up the dead man's face in the moment his soul returns to his body in the hospital bed. When the fusion is complete, the comatose body quivers, and at once the man opens his eyes and gasps.

The unborn man, Kunle, glimpses first a white ceiling patched with waterproof plastic, a yellow stain on the other end of the wood. Somewhere nearby roosters crow, and through the open window, a persistent wind howls. A guttering kerosene lamp by the side of his bed is throwing dark smoke into the air, its glass half-covered in soot. He blinks, makes to speak, but coughs instead, the network of things on the bed rattling with the force of his effort. He becomes aware then of the intravenous drip swinging beside him and of the patient in the bed to his left, watching him. He hears a voice speaking between intermittent gusts of static:

"... so, ladies and gentlemen, we now go from the State House to London, where the ambassador of the Republic of Biafra to Britain, Chief Ignatius Kogbara, is. Sir, welcome to the show—"

"Thank you—my pleasure."

"... even if ... it's not true—and everything ... efforts being made?"

"Well, as I have been saying, we are getting a lot of support. His ... even this morning ... that ... we have to encourage our people to have faith. Before this war started, we were fourteen million people in our republic. Now we are ..."

Kunle must have coughed when the static resumed again, for the young, wounded soldier in the other bed moves, stretches out his hand for the water cup beside his head, and lifts it.

"Sa, water?" the young soldier says, then repeats the question in Igbo.

The voice from the radio declares with forceful clarity: "... *we cannot be conquered—no. I am telling you this—*"

"*But, but, Ambassador—*"

"Biko off the radio," the young soldier says, and the radio is turned off.

Past the young soldier, Kunle sees a valley of light, something moving, like a slow vehicle on a track. He feels something taking shape in his mind, strange calculations, and without much of an effort, a sound escapes his mouth: "Ouh."

"What, sa—I should call nurse?"

Kunle turns towards the young soldier. Again he sees light, flimsy, inordinate refractions from a source unknown. A question forms slowly within him: The people, the great penetrative voices, the steaming pools, the carnival of stories—where are they?

The young soldier is speaking again, gesturing through the smoke of light to the others in the many other beds, on mats, on the floor.

"E'ouh," Kunle cries again.

Kunle's right arm is free, and now he swings it. He gestures as he repeats himself twice, pointing into the rod of light now slowly fading. A patient on the floor whose legs are bound in casts suggests they call the nurse. Another, rising, begins to leave the room with a limp.

"But wetin him dey talk?" the young soldier asks.

Another wounded soldier, tall and lanky, his left arm gone except for a bandaged stump near the shoulder, says, "Shhh," and on cue, Kunle shouts even louder: "E'ouh! E'ouh ah ouhun!"

"Owl," the young soldier says.

"No, no, him say 'hole.' He see hole," the one-armed man retorts.

Kunle glances at the three men and shakes his head. He tilts his head back slowly, feeling a rising sense of distress and confusion.

"Road," the armless man says ecstatically, and Kunle's head snaps back up, his eyes widening, "E'ouh ah ouhun."

"The road," the man says again, "that is it—he is saying 'road' . . . The road to ohun."

The men watch as Kunle speaks again, working his hands between the web of light motes, as if wrestling an invisible thing. Two nurses rush in—one of them a white woman with spotted skin and the other a beautiful Igbo woman he thinks he knows. The Igbo nurse holds him while the white nurse removes something that had clung to his face and mouth, beclouding his vision.

The women seem upbeat, gathering the tubes they've unplugged from him, helping him sit up in the bed. "Can you see?" asks one, and the other says, "He is alive! Can't believe it! God is great!"

Kunle regards them only with muffled disbelief.

The waters change now, and the Seer realizes that a living memory has risen within Kunle. The Seer is looking at the compound in Akure that he'd seen at the beginning of the vision. Kunle is here again as a boy with his brother, Tunde. They are chasing a wounded bird around the yard, Kunle giving commands to his brother: "Don't let it fly! Catch it!"

The Seer is returned to the hospital room, and now he can see that something in the memory has stirred the unborn man, who is suddenly in the grip of rage, banging his hand against the railing of the bed. The nurses, screaming, clasp his hands in a firm grip. He struggles, shouting, "E'ouh u ah ouhun! E'ouh u ah ouhun!"

"Morphine!" one of the nurses shouts, and quickly, they hold him down and the white nurse plunges a syringe into Kunle's arm.

Kunle quivers and clenches his fists. Slowly, his eyes turn as if rolling in their sockets, and he sees again clouds of indescribable colors and hears vain, loud mutterings as of distant voices, speaking through a tube. He feels his vision blurring as he begins to wilt like a plant being slowly pulled off its roothold, to be dragged into a realm beyond.

THE SEER REVELS in what he has just witnessed. The portent has been uncloaked; the dark patch of cloud has disappeared. His mind is full now, however. He has witnessed that which must be the envy of all humanity. For centuries mankind has been asking, What else is there? What lies beyond the walls of this life, in the outer dark? The Seer is shaken, moved. He is beckoned by the unspeakable, allured by the past. He's seen the living dead speak and move about. He's witnessed the thronging at the squares in the golden world, heard testimonies. He's seen the transcendence of time, the splendor of the afterlife, where his wife remains. He understands now why she had not looked sad when he'd seen her during the séance, while he had swallowed despair, his stomach full of its black fruits. "Ololufe mi, I am resting in a quiet place whose light brings itself to me and fills me daily," she'd said. "Do not despair . . . do not despair." Her voice had continued to echo and tumble as her form faded and faded, until she was no longer there.

While the unborn man had stood among the crowds, listening to stories, the Seer had searched faces, looking for his beloved. His master's words come to him now like a presence from the void: "Ifa cares. The vision he gifts you is never for your entertainment but for the sake of repairing a rift in the world—and most times, that rift lies in you, his servant." It is true: Ifa has given him this vision of the unborn man's life as a way to heal him.

The Seer is eager to see what the unborn man will do next. He wishes that Ifa would take him quickly into the farthest reaches of the future, pass over many days, so that while the portent remains he will witness what the end of the war will be for the man and this darkened world.

19.

For the past few days Kunle has been asking how long it's been since he regained consciousness, but no one has been willing to tell him. The sun has broken through days of gray clouds to illuminate Agnes's face. He asks her again and she smiles. Her face is oiled with cream; she has a new hairdo and is wearing bright red lipstick. She cups her hand around her mouth and says into his ear, "Almost two weeks." For days she's been sleeping on a wrappa on the floor beside his bed, being leered at by the sick men. She's told him stories of the things they'd done together, of his home. Slowly, she helped him through the flux and madness of his first few days of consciousness, when all he'd done was chatter, jerk, and hallucinate. Now, on his thirteenth day, he's settled back to his former self.

"So, it is time to go home. You are well now."

"Home?"

She nods. "Commander say you can go home now. To Akure."

They are seated at the back of the hospital, on an old bench. On their right is a banana tree, half of its leaves tattered, sagging down like dead limbs. There's a clothesline, on which hospital clothes swing lightly in the soft wind. He gazes at her, feeling too heavy to speak.

"Tomorrow, they will use hospital car to drive you to Enugu and hand you"—she hesitates, staring into the distance—"I mean, hand you over."

She looks at him, her eyes brimming with tears.

"Commander say this—Stana?"

She nods. A vehicle starts somewhere he cannot see, but soon, just above the low, treeless bush, a Bedford truck appears, driving on the unpaved red road, trailed by a slowly rising cloud of dust.

He recalls the first night they made love, at the small house near the battlefield, their bodies entwined, the darkness like a broken hedge around them. The image comes to him now in vivid colors, as if drawn by a rope through the window of time into this moment: he is gazing into her eyes, sweat gathering on her temples, and at the faint scar on the side of her face. Bube-Orji is knocking on the main door of the house, and quickly, his thrusts intensifying, he reaches the pitch of pleasure.

He takes her hand presently, and at once she says, "Everybody was thinking say you have even died, but—"

"I know so," he says, and with strange zest, he tells her what he saw in the realm beyond.

He can see that his account has astounded her, for she sits with her mouth slightly open, watching a hen and her yellow chicks grazing near a pile of used medical equipment—IV poles, boxes, syringes, old casts made of plaster of paris, empty bottles of iodine and gentian violet, the springs of a broken bed. The bell from a church nearby tolls.

"I died," he says again. "Any of us can die here e-eeytime... aetam—"

"Any-time," she says, looking intently at him.

"This is why I am happy we are going to leave." He squeezes her hand with a fresh flash of joy. He starts to speak, but the hen flaps its wings and dashes forward with a worm clasped in its beak. He stares at her, her face expressionless now.

"We will be able to live in Lagos," he says. "And we will marry and... we... Darly?" He has noticed that her face has darkened, and she lowers her gaze. "Agi... Darly, please, what'z it?"

He can feel his heart starting to pound again. Once he began regaining his memory, the first thing he'd said to her was that she should come with him to Akure. He came to this war to repair a wrong he once did against his brother. Now he wants to do the good that matters most to him: to save her life as she saved his. But Agnes had told him only that she would think about it. And for two days, every time she gave him an account of what had happened in his absence—the sorrowful service at Madonna 1 in memory of Bube-Orji, Sergeant Agbam's injury and return to service, James's mother's visits, during one of which the woman had brought her two brassieres and some tights—he'd break in and plead with her.

"Chai, see, Kunis—you know," she says, scratching her head. "I love you, but I am soldier. I can't leave my comrades."

"No, Agnes, no. You are—you're a woman, for Christ's sake! You should not even be fighting!" He does not mean for his voice to climb so high, but there is a pulse in his brain he still cannot control. Nearly every moment agitates him and sends his voice into small furies.

"I promised my sons, Zobenna, my . . . people."

He sees a tear sliding down the side of her face where a faint outline of facial hair has become visible.

"I can never abandon Biafra—never. Ya bulu onwu, ka'm nwuo!"

She rises, dusts off the back of her trousers, and begins walking. At first, he fears that she is going away, but when she turns in at the hospital door, he touches his chest in relief. It occurs to him that since he cannot dissuade her, there is no point in pressuring her.

He goes back to the nurses' office and tells them he wants to return to camp. The three nurses cannot believe it. He is free, released from the war; free to leave Biafra or go to his brother. But he is resolute. She is at the maternity ward, but at last they go to fetch the matron. While he waits, he gazes at the posters all over the room—one poster announcing the breakout of measles in Biafra and the efficacy of the vaccine, another warning of kwashiorkor, its direness made clear by the harsh image of children with distended bellies and swish-thin arms. The sun shining through the stained windows of the office falls across his body, splitting him in two, half in the shade and half in the glow of the sun, in a way that reminds him of Bube-Orji, half-covered in earth. He puts his hand over his face to shield it from the glare.

"You all right?" the white nurse says, panting and peeling off bloodstained gloves as she enters the office with the nurses in tow.

"Fine," he says, stepping back. "Fine . . . jus' remembered something."

"You see," Nurse Nkechi says. "You are not really well yet, Corporal."

"I belong here. I cannot leave Biafra," he says.

The matron, her lips almost purple from the hot Lipton tea, asks again that he reconsider. "Corporal . . . this . . . I mean, it is a serious matter."

"I am fine, ma," he says.

"What? You are—"

"I want to stay here."

"Corporal Arom-ri? You may be brain damaged, you know?"

For a moment, a gust of fear blows into his mind, swaying branches of thought and unsteadying him. This is his chance—he could go home now, answer his father's call; find Tunde. He glances out the window at a group of wounded soldiers talking near a dry fountain at the center of the courtyard. As if to warn him, a white lorry pulls up beside them, a big red cross painted on its top and on its side the inscription IYIENU MISSION HOSPITAL. Before it has stopped, its back doors are flung open, and two soldiers carry a man out on a litter. The man is convulsing, his movements an extravagant, violent dance, and from his throat comes a thin, grasping cry. The scene shakes Kunle, and for a moment he looks into the questioning eyes of the nurse, his jaw wobbling. Then, nodding, and as if assured by some presence, he says, "I am well, Nurse . . . I want to go back to my comrades."

Agnes is waiting outside the ward when he comes out, pacing. She has dressed in fresh commando camouflage, the red bandanna wrapped around her neck and a familiar green helmet on her head. He nods. She removes the helmet and he remembers why it is familiar: it's the federal paratrooper's helmet, now painted all green. He is remembering things more now, but the most recent memories walk into his mind with sluggish feet.

"You . . . please, darly . . . go home—"

He holds her by the waist and she stills, buries her face in his chest.

"I stay here," he says, breathing heavily. "With you."

She does not speak, though he sees that tears have gathered in the corners of her eyes.

Once they settle into the back of the Volvo Steiner had sent to pick them up, she says, in a voice on the edge of breaking, "You are a good man, Kunle."

They travel a long distance in the dim, cloudy light of day, through multiple claps of thunder. It begins raining. The smell of the soft earth stirs in him a feeling of nostalgia. He and Agnes sit separately, as if afraid to be close. He rests his head on the worn back of the seat, his eyes half-closed. Every time he looks up, he sees her watching him, her eyes holding a weightless smile.

"Darly," she says suddenly, reaching for his hand.

"Yes?"

"Something has been bothering my mind since that day when you tell me about this place . . . em . . . that look like heaven."

"Ehen, what?"

"What happened, what you saw . . . Don't tell anybody. Especially for camp, please."

He sits up. "Why?"

She stares at him for a while, then shakes her head.

"I don't know. My spirit jus' tell me that you should keep it secret inside this war. Until after it finish. Jus' say you were in coma and did not know anything until you wake. I know your friends—Felix, Ndidi, James, and even late Bube—they like you very much. Many times, they came here direct from front, without eating or sleeping. They will lie down on the grass outside the hospital and sleep there instead of going back to camp . . . They really love you. It is like you come here to Biafra to find one brother, but now you have many."

"Yes," he mumbles, moved by what she's said.

"I don't doubt that they love you, but don't tell anyone till war finish—i nu go?"

He nods a few times, places his hand on his brow, and nods again. Although he cannot tell why she has thought this, it feels wise that he should keep the experience to himself.

As he starts to fall asleep, seeing colors merging with the rain threading down in the bright yellow glare of the headlights, she takes his hand again and draws her mouth to his ear. "Please don't ever leave me again—are you hearing me?"

In the darkness, he can see that her eyes are clouded with tears.

"Yes."

"It can't happen to me again. Ozo emela—God forbid!"

He hears the snap of her fingers over her head.

"If you must die again, we must die together . . . Are you hearing me?"

He nods, then, opening his eyes, says, "Yes."

EACH DAY FOR the next one week, he thinks of this warning and why Agnes said these things to him. He is reflecting on them while sitting on the porch of the dining hall, watching the barracks' entertainer, an old man playing the flute. While in the realm of the living dead, he found its most distinct difference to be the ubiquitous presence of music. And since his return, he has become attuned to music, which has helped in his recovery. Agnes had begged that they bring the flutist to play in the mornings, and it is because of him that this man now pays regular visits to the camp.

Kunle says nothing when the man finishes, does not clap. Instead, he begins picking his teeth with his worn-down chewing stick. He spits the last crumb of stick into the dirt as one of the new white men who'd arrived at the camp during his absence stops to speak with the flutist. The white man is dressed in a bush shirt and brown shorts, his breast pocket lined with two Parker pens and the outline of a cigarette pack. A camera hangs on his chest. Kunle stares at him with resigned curiosity, wanting to know if the man is a priest, one of the Irish or Swedish missionaries now increasingly present in Biafra.

"Oga, please, who is that man?" Kunle asks one of the wounded soldiers.

"Freddie," the man says, wiping his brow with the back of his hand and flinging the sweat into the dirt. "Freddie Forsyth. Him na journalist for BBC. He come here all the time. Sometimes sef, he follow Commander Stana and others to front."

Kunle thanks the man and walks back to the dormitory room that serves as the commando clinic. His headaches have started again. Just yesterday morning, Agnes had put the back of her hand on the front of his head, pulled gently at the lower lids of his eyes and said, "You have fever—maybe from malaria." Now he feels the same way again. He lies on the bed, wondering what has happened in the four weeks he's been away. Something about the white journalist reminds him of home, of his parents. In the first days after he regained consciousness, he'd fought to remember things, the anguished hand of memory quickly closing the doors before he'd entered them. But now that his mind has repaired, his parents have started to linger in his thoughts. Last night, restless, he dug up his father's mud-stained letter and read it again. And this morning, he thinks about his parents' deteriorating health. He finds himself wondering with slight, irreverent fear about what would have happened to them if he'd died.

By nightfall, convinced that he's made a mistake by choosing to remain in Biafra, he descends into misery. He eats little the following morning, sitting up only enough to answer the cognitive test questions posed to him by the doctor who certifies his daily progress. Today he answers the questions as weakly as he can, twice misidentifying the image of a giraffe. The doctor, a young Igbo man who introduced himself as "Dr. Okey," looks stunned. He raises his glasses and enters something in his blue ledger book, whispers into the ear of the nurse. She taps her thermometer, and the mercury floats upwards. Kunle feels the cold tip under his armpit. Good, the nurse mutters, as she notes the number on the thermometer in her ledger book. Wiping his upper arm with wet cotton, she injects something into it with a syringe, saying, "This will help you rest well and gather yourself."

Later, he is sitting by himself, watching the red sun slide down through the window, when shouts erupt around the school premises. From the room next door he can hear a radio, and the familiar voice of Okokon Ndem.

"Shon, sa!" a recuperating corporal tells him. "Ah, big-big news for battlefield today, oh. Mhhm—that Onitsha sector. Vandals hear weeh for there!"

"Na we do am?" Kunle says, worried at the thought that there has been another engagement with the federal 2nd Division.

"No, sa. Na strike force—Taarti-nine strike force do am."

The commander of the 39th Battalion had been tipped off that almost half of the federal 2nd Division was heading towards Abagana with all their ordnance, including several Panhard armored vehicles, Ferrets, Alvis Saladins, trucks loaded with food, uniforms, and fuel, and trailers carrying ammunition. Major Uchendu and his troops ambushed them and fired two rockets at them.

"Dey kill all—all the vandals. Dey hear weeh. Ogbunigwe firebomb their tanker and *gbom!* Okokon Ndem say almost six thousan' of their men die. Six thousandn'! Plenty-plenty vehicle. Armor tank-oh, trailer-oh, gwongworo-oh even, sef, that their plenty Ferret. Total, dem say ninety-six vehicles."

Kunle watches the yellow bulb in the ceiling come on, then die, then come on again, making a guttering sound like the fluorescent bulb at the Opi Health Center, unable to explain the peace he feels at the news. That Biafran troops can inflict such damage on the federal army surprises Kunle. They have been fighting now for almost a year, a defensive war of underdogs. Not only does the federal side possess superior equipment, they employ hundreds of mercenaries from the USSR and Niger, who march in front of their infantry and cast terror into the hearts of the Biafran soldiers. But now it seems that if Biafra can mount more successful ambushes, they can win the war. And if that happens and he and Agnes survive, then he can gain both things at once: Agnes, to whom he owes his life, and his family, to whom he owes so much.

For most of the next few days, he weighs these thoughts, oscillating between the two poles, sleeping little, staring at lights for so long that he feels pressure build again behind his eyes. At last, he resolves that even if he continues to stay in Biafra, he must find his brother first and make sure that Tunde is safe.

20.

HE MEANT ONLY to tell Dr. Okey that he wants to visit his brother, but the doctor—moved by Kunle's near-death experience—urges him to leave Biafra entirely. To convince him, Dr. Okey shares secret intelligence he's received from a contact at Biafra's seat of government in Umuahia showing that Biafra is in trouble: the country is failing on the diplomatic front, and state funds for foreign arms procurement are increasingly short, and so Biafra has virtually no chance of winning the war. Also, Kunle reasons, Agnes has been gone on missions with the Special Commandos for many days, and it is easier to make such decisions when he is not looking at her face. So, he agrees with the doctor's plan to telephone the staff at Iyienu Mission Hospital, most of whom he knows, and inform them that Kunle has changed his mind and now wants to leave Biafra.

Now, two days later, Dr. Okey has returned, and once they are out of earshot of most of the camp, Dr. Okey tells him that the matron is happy to help him leave Biafra. "But," the doctor cautions, "Biafra is under heavy blockade . . . sea . . . land. It will be difficult, but they say . . . they say if you can go with yua brother, they will send you and yua brother to Calabar, and hand you over to ICRC there. Maybe they can take you through ferry to Onitsha, then Asaba . . . then, you enter Nigeria."

For a while after the doctor pedals away on his bicycle, Kunle fights the urge to weep. He has tried to leave for almost a year, and now, only a few days before he is to return to active duty, he has brokered a certain plan to go home. He walks to the caravan RV that's the officers' mess to submit the doctor's recommendation that he visit the Iyienu hospital. The new officer who signs his pass, Taffy Williams, is one of the changes to the commando unit. Tall, lean, and with a dreary face marked by too many light wrinkles, he is now the second in command of the new division. He is reticent, often smoking a cigar and gazing at maps and battlefield plans. Though he is white, he speaks English with a strange African accent, owing to his origin as a South African.

Major Williams hands him the pass and says, "Only two days, eh?"

"Roger, sa!" Kunle shouts and salutes.

He takes a bath at the back of the hostel, washing himself with a small bar of Imperial Leather soap Agnes gave him. During his first few months at the front, he rarely washed. But at the hospital, he was washed every morning, sometimes by Agnes who soaped him as though he was a baby. He has returned with a sharp sensitivity to the smell his friends carried on them when they visited—often of mud, smoke, gunpowder, urine, and filth.

He has just finished dressing in his new uniform, one whose sleeves have, beneath the rising sun badge, the new insignia of the commandos: skulls and crossbones against a black background. Now, he is walking towards the barracks gate when he hears a whistle, followed by a shout of "Kunis," as Bube-Orji often called him. He turns and finds Felix, who has returned from the front to recover from malaria, approaching. Felix's uniform is grayed with sweat, his skin greasy and smelly. Felix is anxious and talkative—he's been listening to the radio continuously, and the news is discouraging. The air raids have increased with so much rapidity that more than five hundred Biafrans were being killed or injured daily. They are bombing markets, refugee centers, even hospitals! His sister, he says with muffled rage, escaped such a raid by a whisker. Kunle tries to tell him he has to run, but he cannot break into Felix's anxious speech, so he walks instead, and Felix follows. When they reach the barracks' exit checkpoint, Felix puts his hand on Kunle's shoulder and says, "Ehen, Kunis, you know . . . you are my best friend—eh?"

"Yes," Kunle says.

"Egwagieziokwu, something is in my mind . . . you know . . . about Agnes. Look—it is not good in this situation to be in this kind of relationship." Felix shakes his head. "War is going on, Kunis."

Kunle finds himself nodding repeatedly, unable to look his friend in the eye.

"I like her, Kunis . . . she is like my sister. And I know—as you know—that she likes you . . . Ah, she likes you very much."

"But why does she like me?" Kunle says, anxious only to hear what Felix would say.

"You don't know?" Felix widens his eyes. "Raveli-vous, Kunis! Simple: because you are mysterious. You don't talk. Listen, human beings like mystery. No pleasure in something we already know. Yes. Even poems—what do you think is a great poem or even art? It is one that you cannot easily interpret. It is . . . it is both clear and at the same time mysterious—you get me? We like that."

A private walking past carrying a broken desk on his head shouts a greeting, and they respond.

"Look at me, look at Inamin, Fada, even Bube—she has seen us completely. But you—she is discovering you."

Kunle nods.

"Anyway, all I am saying is, there is a war. This relationship can cause you serious problem . . . I am not saying you should leave her, though that may be better. Our people say, A person who is crying can still see. So, you can continue, but be very, very careful and don't allow yourself to make any foolish decisions, inu go?"

Kunle nods and shakes his friend's hand. He rides on the back of the bicycle of one of the civilian volunteers who serves the commandos, conscious as he leaves the barracks of his thoughts darkening with the fumes of Felix's words. It is true that the relationship is precarious given the situation, but they have gone too far and planted their roots too deep into each other's souls to part ways now. Yet, since his return, he and Agnes have had sex only once—the night they arrived at the camp. Since then, she has been increasingly absent, occupied at the front. And in the few times he's seen her, he has concealed his plans from her. But the night before the last time she left, four days ago, he feared that she was growing suspicious. After supper with his friends and listening to Felix's radio, he snuck into the library and, finding her alone and naked from the waist up, had tried to kiss her. She'd stepped back from him and said she knew he wanted to leave.

"Why do you say this?" he asked, struck by her words.

"My spirit—I feel am for my spirit."

He looked at her, pressing his knuckles together until they cracked.

"But," she said, sitting up and drawing up her brassiere—one of the two James's mother had brought her—"Darly, don't stay because of me. Mba—if your heart don't want you to stay, no stay."

He wanted to speak, to deny his intent, but she was staring directly at him the way she did when she suspected a lie, her eyes fixed in a continuous gaze made menacing by the cuticle-shaped scar on the side of her head.

"Well," he said, his voice weakening. "I was not leaving, just to find my brother. I . . . want to see him and make sure that something bad have not happened to him. That is it . . . I am not leaving you."

She said nothing more.

Now the bicycle man drops him off at a town a few kilometers from the commando barracks. He boards a minibus that bears a legend he's seen on other vehicles, painted on both sides in large letters: FREE BIAFRA. As he takes a seat in the back of the bus, he keeps thinking about the look on Agnes's face—of suspicion and betrayal. Has he done something wrong? Is he—by wanting to redeem himself in the eyes of his parents and his brother—committing a bigger immoral act by breaking his promise to her? As if in response, he recalls the moment in the golden place when Bube-Orji admitted, *We for don bury you if no be for her.*

His gaze is fixed on a woman seated on the other side of the bus who is dressed in a white T-shirt with the image of a man on it and the inscription CALL TO GLORY. The woman has a grimy iron pail of giant snails writhing in a shiny congregation that has filled the bus with the animal smell. He is seated by two men both in Red Cross caps and bell-bottom pants, one of them reading a copy of *Drum*. The last copy of the magazine he'd seen was one Dr. Okey was reading, and on whose cover was the face of the black American activist Martin Luther King, above his head the inscription MURDERED. It had occurred in the early morning of April 4, and just one week from then, the doctor had explained, on April 12, King was to visit Biafra and put an international face to the struggle of a people whose flag was the Pan-Africanist Marcus Garvey flag. Recognizing the skull and bones on the sleeve of Kunle's shirt, the two men salute him, saying, "Good morning, Commando."

For a while, his mind is under the spell of the music on the radio, and he is in a trance when a violent lurch of the bus jolts him. The bang is so loud he thinks at first that he might be dead. But opening his eyes he catches sight of a bomber flying off low among the distant trees and he hears shrieks, screams, and the long tolling of metal against hard surfaces. The bus is swerving between trees, slamming up a mound of soil and brush, people jouncing in their seats, hands upraised, heads shaking, voices screaming, "Driver! Driver! Stop! Chineke!" There is a mixture of speed and the chaos of objects flying around—glass, grass, tree branches, luggage, people.

At first, there is a weak, sharp pain in his head—the sensation he remembers having felt when he went into the coma. On his thighs, green leaves and small, foliated twigs are scattered, and beside his leg is a severed tree branch. The man who was at the end of his seat now lies against the battered door, his arm shiny with pebbles of blood. The other man has been cut on the face and is mournfully calling, "Alfred, Alfred." All over the bus, people sit or recline in different positions of pain or death. A man hangs partway out the window, impaled through the belly by a spike of glass crowned with a wreath of blood and flesh, his legs still shaking with death spasms. The driver is slumped against the wheel, as if in rueful sleep. Two passengers lean against him from the other side as the slow throttling of the engine continues, broken intermittently by the low, ebbing voice of some foreign musician on the radio.

Kunle struggles for a while, and when he finally manages to get out of the bus it is almost eleven—nearly an hour since the accident. His left shin is bleeding. They'd been traveling for only twenty-five minutes. Eight of the passengers and the driver are dead, five others injured. Those who survived have all climbed out. A wounded man lies with half his face shaded by a wild guava tree, blood wrapped around his neck like a damp cloth, wailing and speaking to himself: "Is it a crime to be Igbo? . . . Why oh why are they killing us like this?" For a long while the man laments and bleeds, and every time Kunle raises his eyes to look, the mat of blood on which the man is lying has widened. Kunle rips a strip off his undershirt and sits on the dirt dabbing his bleeding shin with the torn piece and listening to the fellow.

When it seems he's stanched the blood, he throws the drenched rag in the dirt. He puts his hand on his chest. He thought shortly after his return to consciousness that his brief foray into death would inoculate him against the bone-shattering terror of dying that he felt on the battlefield, but now he finds himself more afraid than ever before. He worries more about the fate of those whose bodies cannot be found and buried, and who roam the otherworld instead of heading to the resting place of the ancestors. How tragic would it have been if he'd died a second time, here in the forest? There is a sound and, glancing in the direction of the wounded man, he finds one of the snails climbing up the man's body unbothered, its bloodstained tentacles darting about as it goes. He had not noticed that the man had fallen silent.

Kunle rises, squirming, blowing loose air from his mouth as if to remedy the pain in his body. Through the strange parting in the bush created by the bus's violent passage he sees the crater, still smoking in the distance, so large and deep it is a miracle the driver had diverted in time to escape it. The Biafran army is not as strong as the federal army, fighting only out of the primal will to survive. So why had the federal troops progressed to attacking civilians?

He crushes a handful of wild thyme leaves together and squeezes their juice onto his wound. He gnashes his teeth—"Oluwa mi oh!"

His shin no longer bleeding, he goes back to the bus, up to the driver's seat, to see if he might find any water. Its wreckage is a fearful sight: there are flies everywhere, clothes, personal effects, basins, a red feathered hat, bloodied papers, glass fragments, mangled bodies. And all over the bus, snails are crawling, some with broken shells. A crowd is cheering as a man's voice emerges on the radio: "*. . . starring Dean Martin! Kim Novak! Cliff Osmond! Ray Walston . . .*" Kunle pries the front door open and steps back and lets the driver fall out, his nearly severed head tilting backwards.

"*. . . an unforgettable story!*" the radio shouts. "*A drama of our times. Come on, head out to a theater or a drive-in theater and enjoy . . .*"

He turns in the direction of the road, shaking the last of the drops of water from the driver's plastic bottle into his mouth, then pitches it into the bush. He walks awhile and, thinking that the road might lead back to the commando camp in Etiti, he veers onto its shoulder to be partly concealed by foliage. His shirt is torn open at the back, and wind pours through the tear. He's been walking for almost an hour when he sees a convoy of Biafran soldiers traveling behind a bunch of tall elephant grass and wild creepers. At first it looks like a federal unit, for there is a Saladin, its gun almost fully concealed by a stitched garment of foliage. Behind it is a truck loaded with soldiers, followed by men carrying on their heads shovels, axes, rifles bound together by hempen ropes, bazookas, crates of ammunition, Ojukwu buckets, and Ogbunigwe artillery barrages; one of them is carrying a loud transistor radio. They are marching mostly silently, most of them barefoot, trailed by a bearded, lanky man in a worn black suit, brandishing a tattered Bible above his head, preaching about victory over the enemy.

Kunle walks as fast as he can in the opposite direction. He is sweating, his head ringing, when he sees a roadblock, a Volkswagen stopped in front of it. He turns, the pain in his back and shin stitching at him again, but he hears the shout to stop.

"You there—hands up! Hands up!" The clatter of footfalls and the sound of a rifle being cocked follow. "You move, I shoot!"

Kunle turns, trembling. They come forward, constables in dark blue uniforms, their green helmets shining in the sun. Behind them are two others in green fatigues and red berets, a rising sun patch on their shoulders and above it, on their collars, the red insignia of MPs.

Only forty meters from Kunle, the first man shouts, "Officer, any weapons?"

"No!" Kunle cries.

The man edges forward again, still pointing his rifle at him, while the other MP pats him down, running his hands along Kunle's back, then his thighs.

"Officer, sorry, sa!" the first MP says, saluting. "This is our command duty."

Kunle nods. "I understand."

"Pass, sa?"

Kunle pats his shirt pockets, his trouser pockets—where is it? He turns back to the road, then looks at the constable. He must have dropped it while climbing out of the bus.

"Constable, I had an accident . . . coming from commando division HQ, going to Iyienu Hospital." He hitches up his left trouser leg to show his shin, the dark red encrustations of blood tracing down to his foot. "Air raid . . . almost kill us."

The constable nods gently—he understands. But they cannot let him through without a pass. He must return to Etiti, get a new pass. They are under strict orders because of desertions.

He walks on the straight road the constables had suggested, striding close to the bush, until he arrives at a bend that opens into a street with old barns and huts with uli paintings on them. The deserted village is filled with green flies and a terrible odor. Since returning, he's found that there is a stench everywhere in Biafra, not just at the front. As he walks between the buildings, he begins to see bodies in various states of decomposition, torsos rotten to the bones and innards hollowed out. Now he finds that he's stepped on the flattened corpse of what seems like a man, covered in shreds of clothes like a drawing on the dirt. The dead man's paper-thin jaw is flattened on the ground as if caught in an obtuse smile, his hands folded backwards, bound together. From his waist downwards, his body is shaded in the dark remnants of his black, decaying trousers, and at the end of his legs where his feet might have been, gray twine half-sutured into the ground is bound to his ankles. Kunle, gasping, steps away from the body, looks about, struggling to calm his heart's furious beating. He wades between damaged coconut trees. He picks a rotting coconut from the ground, the water in it sour, yet filling. He breaks the rest of it against a stone and, standing, devours its decaying meat until only its hard shell is left.

Belching, his stomach roiling, he passes a spent mortar shell hanging between the branches of a cashew tree. Behind the tree, a middle-aged woman is sitting on a bench, her neck long and slender, her skin greasy with dirt. She is naked to the waist, her bare breasts hanging off her chest in depressed lumps. She lifts herself as if to run at the sight of him, but he stops, raises his hands, and cries, "Agbana oso!" She is apparently one of a gathering of about twenty refugees in the distance, most of them women with shaved heads and children, seated under a camouflaged tent of stick pillars and thatched roofs. They watch him pass with fear in their eyes, though they can see that he, a limping soldier of Biafra, would not harm them.

Brick houses line the next few blocks, and soon a small hotel with the words NEW BIAFRA HOTEL on it sits by the side of a long red-clay road, a graffitied image of Colonel Ojukwu on the blue painted wall. On the spur of a small hill, he finds a group of people gathered under a tarpaulin covered with very thick foliage. There is a troupe of musicians, their bodies tattooed with uli symbols, their clothing patterned with Jorge prints. A woman and a man dressed in Igbo clothing are dancing in front of the other people, most of them seated. At first, Kunle watches the goings-on with incredulity. What he is witnessing is a traditional wedding amid a brutal war.

Once past here, he comes upon a roundabout with a statue of a bird. He remembers that this is the square where Felix had executed the saboteur, and it strikes him that he is close to the commando barracks.

21.

He's burdened by his failure to leave Biafra, but he knows he will not get another chance before he heads back to the front. So, when the Special Commandos return the following day, he rushes straight to the school's defunct library, where he knows Agnes will be. He sits in front of her without saying a word, offering no answer to the many questions she asks. Is his head aching? Is he having dreams of the afterlife again? Has he been taking the drugs from Dr. Okey? He fixes his eyes instead on the things she has arranged on the bed, among them the wages she gathered from the quartermaster, which she is preparing to send to her parents. Ants walk across the stash of Biafran ten-pound notes, the image of a palm tree framed by the rising sun visible on the topmost bill. What is more unbearable than a thing from which there is no redemption? What is more violent to the soul than the impossibility of making right that which one has broken?

She can see that he is troubled, and when she puts her hand on his back, he breaks down and tells her the lie he has concocted: he'd tried to return to the hospital at Iyienu to see the matron and rest for a few days, but had almost been killed in the process.

She does not speak at first but stares at him, closely, as if probing his intent with her eyes. She draws the curtains so that the room darkens, the only light a reflection from under the door. He can barely see beyond her silhouette. Why has she said nothing? Does she doubt him?

"Agi?" he calls, his voice shaky.

He makes to touch her, but she steps back briskly. She raises the curtain again, and light fills the room. She sits in the chair on the other side of the room, books balanced on the shelves behind her. He tries to follow her.

"No—no—no. Don't come, okay? Don't come." She shakes her head. "Kunli, tell me all truth. You wan run out, o kwa ya? The accident stop you . . . tell me the truth."

He feels the shudder of her words, drops his eyes instead to the plaster around his shin. Panting, he kneels first, stands again before speaking. "Yes."

She shakes her head. "You for never know your child."

A quiet laugh escapes her mouth, and, like a small spirit, it enters him, travels to his heart, and drops like a spent mortar shell into his gut. He stands quickly, as if compelled.

"What . . . you say?"

Again she smiles.

"You are pregna—" he starts.

"Shhh." She rushes forward and slaps his arm. "Nobody . . . I mean, no-bo-dy must know. Are you hearing me?"

"I . . . it was . . . it's jus'—"

"Answer, Kunli, answer me. Nobody must hear, o?"

He nods.

"Two months, maybe," she whispers, rising. She makes to speak but instead squints as she tries to stifle a sneeze.

"Sorry—sorry," she says as he rubs his arm, on which she's sprayed the sneeze.

"Is okay," he says.

She wipes her nose with a handkerchief.

For the rest of that night, he does not see her. He spends it with his friends, who take turns telling stories of their missions, of the increasing difficulty of the war, and of their recent forays into civilian areas.

But his mind lies in the thing Agnes has revealed, surprised at the effect the news has had on him, how it has wiped from his thoughts the sadness of his failed attempt to go home. Unspeaking, he tries to grapple with its incomprehensible immensity: that he could, at his age and these circumstances, come to father a child. He came here seeking his brother, restitution, and now the war has brought him something he was not expecting. But what is he to do with this news? How could Agnes, a corporal at the front, have a child?

In the morning, feeling groggy, having risen early, before he is to join the commandos for the first time since his return, he goes to the library to see her. After a few knocks, he waits, unsettled, until Lieutenant Layla comes to the door and tells him that Agnes does not want to see him. He salutes, steps off the porch—what has he done? He stoops, picks up a stick, drops it again. Does she not realize that he would not have attempted to leave had he known that she was pregnant?

He is not himself, but moments later he is awaiting Major Steiner's arrival in the salute position, trying to focus. Steiner comes out of the RV smoking, wearing only a pair of trousers and a chain with the medal Colonel Ojukwu had given him over his hairy chest. It is the first time Kunle has seen the commander without a shirt. A tattoo of a snake curls on his left arm. Steiner stares him down from head to foot.

"Mon corporel Kunis?"

"Yes, sa!"

"I understend you ready."

"Yes, Major!"

"Hmmm, uh. Okay, I give you mission first . . . first before you join again, okay?"

"Yes, sa!"

THE COMMANDO SUPPLY van is waiting, but Kunle feels one more frenzied urge to knock on the library's door. He rushes to the library and leans in, listening for any sign of Agnes, but hears nothing save the hand of a clock.

He returns to the van and sits in the backseat, by the escort rifleman. In the front seat is a military police constable and the driver. He's seen the van a few times and once helped unload it, but now he is to lead this mission to the Biafran Annabelle airport at Uli to procure supplies for the division. The task is meant to prepare him for a return to active service, but he would prefer to go straight back to the front rather than travel in a car on the dangerous Biafran roads, especially the road leading to one of the war's biggest targets, the airstrip at Uli. Since the accident two days before, he's come to believe what Felix has always said: that civilian dwellings in Biafra are more dangerous than the fronts. What if he is attacked again? What would happen to Agnes, to his child? How would they survive if he died? Again the feeling rises within him of being trapped in a place from which there is no escape.

He stays awake through the journey, his new semiautomatic rifle pointing out the window. Because of the constable, they pass easily, but sometimes he has to hand over the pass Steiner gave him and say, "Corporal Nwaigbo, Fourth Commando Brigade, Pilgrimage to Annabelle" before the military policemen or Biafran Freedom Fighters militiamen lift the barricade, usually a wooden log balanced on oil drums. They have gone through a third one when the sight of women traveling along the road, some with children strapped to their backs, baskets and basins on their heads, stirs in Kunle the latent ache to know more about what Agnes has told him.

He has just seen the old sign that says ULI: 15 KM when a siren begins blaring. There is a loud bang and the van shakes. The enemy bomber is climbing into the upper pit of the horizon, black smoke rising from where it has lifted its bloodied talons. The driver thrusts the wagon onto a dense mat of brush on the roadside and parks the van. They hear cries from the surrounding habitations, one of which is a former school with a long row of low-roofed buildings, now turned into a prison. He can see the big green signboard that reads BIAFRAN CENTRAL PRISON, ACHINA in front of it. One looking at him from above can see that he is beside himself with fear.

Suspecting the bombers might still be in the area, they wait in the cover of bush till the sun has fully set, to move again. With his arm stretched over the seat back, the driver stirs the van into reverse and guides it out of the bush, back to the road. They pass a mostly empty village, where Kunle is surprised to see small yellow lights from candles, lanterns, cooking fires. Somewhere close by, a red knob of light hangs from some pylon like a bloody eye gazing upon the land. A dog follows the van, barking. It disappears as they slalom down a path pitted with holes, the van wading so close to the bush that creepers and grass rage against it and fill the air with the smell of cut grass.

Moments later, they come upon men waving white flags, their faces obscured in the darkness: they have arrived at the new airfield, its construction not yet finished. They park the van in a bunker. Inside wait two lorries, a mammy wagon, and a military jeep, all with their passengers: drivers, soldiers, women, and even some children—who, in the dim light, appear like the images he'd seen on the posters in the hospital. The airstrip is a long macadam strip with blocks of white markings stretching as far as he can see in the dark. At some distance to the left, nearly obscured by the bush, is what looks like the splayed-open wings of a wrecked airplane. On either side of the runway are oil drums, perhaps a dozen on each side, with men standing by.

He sees a small red light attached to the front side of a thing in the air that is approaching the airfield. A whistle blares and fluttering yellow flames reveal the drums and the hands and faces of the men who lit them. Through the sudden chorus of light a plane appears, its propellers rotating under its wings, the two earphone-wearing foreigners in the cockpit illuminated. It is all too quick—the plane lands, flares rippling through the open air closer around it, bursting into yellow fire somewhere in the distance. The lights go out in quick succession and the plane comes speeding forward on the blind tarmac towards the bunker.

Cheers erupt, and from everywhere rise cries of "Loaders! Loaders!" Kunle and the men in the bunker rush to the door of the plane, but a guard shouts for them to move back. "Make way, Foreign Minister, Chief Jaja Wachuku, wan pass! Shift! Moof!"

Three men, one of them in a dashiki and the other two in bell-bottom trousers and T-shirts, step out, sweating, and rush off towards the bunker. Sacks and crates are flung out of the plane. The whistling man calls for more hands. Kunle finds himself drawn into the mild heat of the plane beside a sweating white man and two Biafrans, the air thick with the smell of dried stockfish, salt, milk, and sweat. As they work, they hear the distant din of the enemy MiG, hovering closer now, undaunted by the anti-aircraft fire threatening it from the bush. The flashes of tracers light up the inside of the plane in eager splashes of color and, in turn, he sees hands silvered or yellowed or faces whitened, then thrown back into silhouette. Out the window, he glimpses threads of broken red flares shooting into the dark sky and dying out like a throng of small eyes winking.

Afterwards, he sits exhausted, not by the weight of the work he's done, but by the speed with which he's done it and the terrible anxiety that possessed him throughout. He is drinking from a canteen in the van when the calls begin again. Another plane appears, and the violent drama in the night sky is repeated—the bursts lighting up the sky, creating miniature and fleeting versions of the otherworld's firmament. There is a moment in which it feels—even to an eye watching from above—that the plane will be hit. And in that moment, held precariously like a thing on the palm of a child, Kunle's heart pounds. But this and two more planes all land in the same dangerous panic. He helps load children who've come from the kwashiorkor hospital in Ihiala onto a plane heading for Gabon, his hands trembling as he carries their skeletal, malnourished bodies. One of the children, naked and not older than six, has a belly so tumefied and veiny it seems on the edge of ripping open. By midnight, they have evacuated scores of children and packed the van full with twelve crates of ammunition, a cluster of Czech automatic rifles and Thompson submachine guns, two German Panzerfaust bazookas and a box of explosives, a box for Taffy Williams containing jewelry for his girlfriend, cartons of Black Galleon cigarettes, packs of ampicillin and gentian violet, two walkie-talkies, cartons of BEREC radio batteries, rolls of Izal toilet paper—nearly everything on Kunle's list. They drive back out for a while, then stop under the cover of a tree outside a village to sleep.

THEY HAVE BEEN driving for an hour, headlights off in the predawn dark, but now it is almost first light. Kunle wakes from a dream of the otherworld to a sharp cry and sees the right-side door of the van open and the constable and the private springing into the bush. He hears a gunshot and a cry, and jumps out of the van. A tall man in a loose shirt and trousers lies dead in the grass. By him, kneeling and wailing, a young boy, not more than ten or eleven years old, is sobbing and speaking Igbo in a breaking voice, waving the small cloth sack in his hand.

"What—what, here?" Kunle says, panting.

The constable, smoke still rising from the barrel of his rifle, looks dazed. "We thought he was a saboteur, sa," he says, pointing at the dead man. "I shoot am, sa . . . I no know say na salt him go take from Afia attack. I no know oh."

The sobbing boy is stamping about in deranged confusion, tugging at his lifeless father's arm; rushing towards Kunle, he cries, "Save him, he can . . . please, Officer." The boy returns again in mad haste to listen to the dead man's chest, pleading, "Daadi! Daadio, biko, biko tee ta! Tee ta!"

When his dead father does not budge, the boy falls against Kunle's knees, tugging at his trousers. "My daadi, my daadi, Commander . . . They kill . . . oh, my daadi."

The boy continues to sob, constantly shaking the bloodstained cloth, from which small grains of salt fall, as if to say again to that unseen jury of all of mankind that it was for this sackful of salt that his father was killed. Kunle and the men sit numbly like handcuffed men, speaking from time to time to counsel the boy. At the hospital, Kunle had heard about the scarcity in the shrinking country caused by the land blockade imposed by the Nigerian government and the loss of agricultural lands as the battlefield expands. Biafra is being starved, and one of the scarcest of commodities is now salt. Kunle has not paid keen attention to this, as the food supply at the commando headquarters is still undiminished.

At the nearby crossroads, a Caritas wagon draws up slowly from the side road, its back caked in dirt. In its truck bed, covered with a white tarpaulin, sit a bevy of foreign and African nuns dressed in white cassocks. The boy calms a bit, looking at the nuns. Then he picks up again, choking through his wails. The word "daadi" rises in Kunle's mind with disquieting force, as if the boy is warning him about his own impending fatherhood. The boy's misery fills him with such sorrow that he feels slow pressure building behind his eyes.

22.

He spent much of the morning with the orphaned boy, and became so tired that he slept most of the day. He wakes discombobulated, unsure at first of where he is or what time it is, the shrilling wail of the orphan boy still in his head. His hands and cheeks are marked with the embossed words on the hardback cover of the *Encyclopaedia Britannica* he'd used as a pillow. He's been sleeping on the floor of a library room adjacent to the one in which Agnes and Layla sleep on a bamboo bed. He blinks, shades his eyes, and there is Agnes, already fully geared up, sporting new rain boots, wearing the green helmet, her red bandanna tied around her left wrist.

"What is time?" he says.

She has been pouting, but now the pressure of a smile builds over her face.

"You get watch naw—look."

He feels his breast pockets for the watch. It is nearly four p.m. He makes to sit up, but winces from the wound on his left shin.

In her silence, he wonders if she still harbors ill will against him. In the war, lives are often so frail, often kilting on the edge of demise, so grudges and all the pettiness of life have difficulty staking a hold. What is exigent now is for him to prevent her from coming on the next special commando mission, which Felix has said will be extremely dangerous. He can hear the soft voice of Lieutenant Layla, so he whispers that they should speak outside. They walk behind the library, ducking under the clothesline on which her inner shirts hang, and continue towards the foot of the nearby outcropping. He is winded, trying to keep up with her.

"Shhh," she says, nodding upwards to direct his eyes, and he sees a faint rainbow spread arcwise across the sky, disappearing into the outcroppings in the distance.

"The world," she says quickly, "can be beautiful if we let it be."

He nods and for a while does not speak, for he remembers a similar moment of reflection when she taught him about other nuances of life. It was a few days after he regained consciousness when she took him to the field outside the wards and said that the war had changed them so much that they appreciated life more now. She pointed into the air and asked what he saw, and he noticed then that if one looked closely enough, one would see that the air was always full of insects.

Now he turns to her, holds her by the waist.

"Darly," he says.

"Eh—?"

"Please, don't come to front again—please. You are pregnant—two months pregnant."

"Wetin be that?" She steps back from him. "What do you mean—"

"You'a sure—"

"Wait—wait, let me finish."

"No, Agi, it's no—"

"Kunle—Kunle—"

"No . . . I am—"

He thinks that she will speak on, that their words will keep wrestling like lizards, tumbling over each other, but she falls silent. An idea comes into his head: since she is a nurse, why not persuade her to return to Iyienu or some other hospital and contribute to the war effort by helping wounded soldiers?

"You will be doing more if you go," he says. "Listen, when our men are injured, you help save them. You bring them back! You—"

He becomes aware that he is starting to raise his voice, so he stops, wilts. She was shaking her head as he spoke, and now tears are running down her face.

"Wait—wait—"

"No!" she says.

"Darly, listen—"

"I am sta-*ying*!" Her voice wobbles as if trying to reel itself back from the precipice. "Am staying, are you hearing me?"

Before he can grab her hand, she has headed back to her room.

He puts on the white shirt Agnes washed for him that morning, still smelling of the sun. He goes out into the main hall of the library, where the guards are seated on chairs and mattresses, talking in loud voices with Captain Emeka. The orphaned boy, whom he'd left there before going to sleep that morning, is not there. Where is he?

"The mess," Felix says. "They like him. In fact, Major Goosens—the fat one—Belgian. Him, he say he will adopt the boy."

"Yes," Captain Emeka says. "He even name him already—their people name: Ador, or something like that."

"Eh-eh?" Ndidi says.

"Yes, broh! Some funny name lak dat, you na'amin?" James says. He squints, adds, "Fucking whites."

"Ha, Inamin have come again," Felix says. "What did they do again? He helps orphan Biafran child, and you—"

"Bullshit, Prof!" James says, shaking his head at Felix. "I call fucking bullshit to that, broh. They always look for ways to hurt us black folks—finally, I'm telling you. Open your eyes, broh. We niggas, broh, you na'amin?"

Ndidi, clapping, nods. "Tell him! Tell him. You are a true son of God, my brother. I know, this people are helping us, but their brothers are still killing us. Is it not because of Wilson and Britain that we are losing this war? Is it not?"

"Yes," Felix says, his voice falling, "but also, look everywhere. The only reason we are alive and still fighting is because of white people. Look at the fathers—Caritas, Irish Council of Priests, Holy Ghost Fathers, and all the people coming in to give food. How many foreign pilots have died trying to help our people? Eh? More than fifty! At least fifty. And who is killing us? Our own people—our brothers."

James waves. "Prof . . . Prof, we niggas, broh—that's it."

Kunle does not speak, merely stands by the wall until Captain Emeka leaves. Since returning to the barracks, he has fastened himself to Agnes, becoming increasingly distant from his comrades, and Captain Emeka has moved in to fill that gap. Kunle sits on the raffia-plaited chair still warm from the weight of Captain Emeka's behind and whispers that he wants to say something.

"Oho! Welcome back from . . . em, paradise!" Felix says, winking.

"Paradise of pussy!" James says.

Kunle finds himself laughing too. "But, look—it is serious. I wouldn't have said it, but I don't know what to do . . . so I need your help."

"Ngwanu, tell us," Felix says, his eyes narrowing.

Kunle swallows. "Prof, the walls have ears."

"Okwu!" Ndidi says and crosses himself. "Make we go field, eh?"

They go out, all of them, through the cluster of soldiers, past the heavily camouflaged ordnance store, which had once been a classroom, images of various historical figures still on the walls. Soldiers have congregated in groups everywhere and are talking or playing games—ludo, cards. At the parade field, half of which is covered with drying uniforms and other clothing and filled with grasshoppers, Kunle stops, clears his throat, and blurts out, "Agi is pregnant."

"Ehh?" they all shout at once. For a moment, a range of expressions pass across their faces.

Felix says, "But—but, eh, are you sure?"

Kunle nods.

"Goddammit, broh!" James says.

"It is not a joke," Kunle says, trying to make his voice sound bitter. "It is serious—"

"Yes! Serious thing but we must be happy first," Felix says. "We cannot believe—even though we suspect you have touched her—that it really happened. With her condition, nobody would have believed she can . . . I mean . . . it can happen."

"It can, broh! I'd have it anywhere!" James is laughing, stamping his feet. "Oh, miss my babes!"

"But when you almost die, everybody saw she likes you," Ndidi says. His face darkens, and he looks at Kunle. "She really really like you."

Ndidi's words run warmly down Kunle's spine. In the beginning, he'd seen it himself. They'd all wanted her, but none of them had been able to approach the black gate of her heart and seek entry, for they could see that it was shut to the world with a great barrier. But without his asking, she'd let him in.

"It is allowed, mon Corporel," James says now. "Even us, maybe we are guilty the two times we went out."

They all laugh except for Ndidi; he had not joined Felix, James, and a few officers of the Special Commando Platoon when they went to a modern bar in Etiti town decorated with disco balls. They picked up girls craving relationships with the commandos to get money and better food. Both men took the girls to an abandoned house only half a kilometer from Madonna High School and had sex with them.

"You know," Felix says with a look of utmost seriousness, "Bube-Orji mention it—he mention it. Before he died, he said he hope Agnes is not pregnant because of what he is seeing on her face. Chai, ebube nwannem, I miss him!"

Without meaning to, Kunle finds himself looking up into the sky, where he sometimes imagines the otherworld to be.

"This is why I call all of you here," Kunle says. "I don't want her to continue fighting in this condition—"

"Mbanu! Tufia." Ndidi snaps his fingers over his head and fingers the foot of his rosary. "She must never."

"Yes-yes, so . . ." Kunle coughs. He can see her outside the mess in the distance, talking with Layla.

"You know, in military law—in British military law, which we follow—you are not allowed to sleep with a soldier or officer," Felix says, gazing about. "Yes, it is prohibited, especially now where you impregnate her."

"Goddammit!" James whispers.

"What do I do? I don't—" Kunle stops, for he can hear the beating of wings, as if some bird were hovering over his head. He looks up the way he had months ago when he heard a similar sound, that of an invisible fox, or the strange mutters of a measured but familiar voice saying strange things and making prayers to "Ifa."

"What happen?" Felix asks him. "What are you looking at?"

"Nothing," he says quickly. "Okay, what do I do now?"

They all sigh and shake their heads. It is a matter that needs thinking, and so they think—Felix rubbing his beard. If Kunle reports it to Steiner, and Steiner punishes the couple, then his friends will feel they have implicated him. If Steiner is merciful—as they hope he will be—and if they can convince him that Agnes will continue to contribute to the war efforts as a military nurse, then perhaps he will let her go. Then again, she might be angry with him for this betrayal. How can he bridge these gaps? Would saving her life be worth risking her wrath? It is Ndidi whose voice prevails: it would be worth saving her, he says, not just because they will be saving Agnes, but also the child if she is willing to keep it, which she seems to want to. If not, she would not have told him about it. They pat Kunle on the back and resolve to go inform Steiner immediately.

They find Steiner sitting with other mercenaries at the caravan, his new Belgian binoculars around his neck and his camouflage trousers hitched up just below the knees. After Felix, with his hand cupped beside his head, his body stiffened at attention, says they want to pass a confidential message to him, Steiner removes his cigarette and smiles at his friends, saying, "C'est confidentiel, mes frères!"

They all laugh except for another white officer, Captain Armand, who wears a sling around his neck to protect his bandaged left wrist. Captain Agbam wants to translate, but Steiner raises his hand. "No, they understand. They under-stand, oui?"

"Mon Major," Felix says and salutes again when they are out of earshot. "It is for Corporal Kunis."

Kunle, saluting, coughs lightly. He looks at his friends and is possessed with a sudden conviction now, in the colonel's presence, that they have made a bad call.

"Corporel?"

"Commander, sa! Agnes and I—"

"Oui—yes, Corporel Azuki?" Steiner says and cups his fingers.

They do not expect this reaction, and they all laugh.

"But, problem, sa . . . She preg-nant."

Steiner's mouth opens to speak, then clamps down on the edge of the nearly finished cigarette. He drops it on the ground and moves his white shoe over it, making fine concentric circles on the dirt littered with dry blades of dead grass.

"Problem, Corporel. Problem."

"Yes, sa!"

Steiner's face has slowly darkened.

"When do this, you?"

"Excuse me, sa?"

"When—" Steiner gestures with his two hands, two people mating, and the others laugh.

"Oh, sa, at least three times. During Abagana when I go with her inside the bush, then it happen."

Steiner keeps his gaze on him, then moves it to the others. Some of them said there was a secret relationship between Steiner and Layla, that they had slept together, but these were rumors. Steiner seems to care little about frivolities, wanting only that things be clean and that they win battles. And it is this seriousness of focus that makes Kunle even more afraid.

Steiner, speaking slowly, tells them about a certain Obumneme, an officer he'd taken a liking to who left camp without permission and was found by the military police.

"Now, mon General Madighabe . . . He say court-martial. Et see?"

"Yes, sa!" they shout.

"Problem. But okay, you good officer. You wounded . . . come back und fighting for mon legionnaires. And you not Igbo—you should not be Biafra soldier." He places his hand on Kunle's shoulder. "I will help you—mhmm. We release her, okay—but after new mission. Oui?"

Kunle feels a sudden warmth in his chest, and the shout leaps out of him, "Yes, sa! Thank you sa!"

"Et tu—et tu. Must come new mission, Corporel Azuki must come."

Steiner brushes off a leaf-green grasshopper clinging to the back of his shirt and steps away in the direction of the reddening sun.

"Réveillez-vous!" he says from a distance, turning back. "Must go soon!"

They all stand at attention as Steiner leaves, and when he has gone out of earshot, they embrace each other and congratulate Kunle. He shakes their hands, embraces his friends, but with half of him relieved and the other half worried about how Agnes will take it.

Ndidi, scratching his sideburns, says, "Biko nu, onye ka commander na-akpo Madighabe?"

"Speak English, oh!" James says.

"Yes, it means: Who is commander calling Madighabe?" Ndidi says.

"It is obvious." Felix is grinning. "It is GOC, Brigadier General Madiebo."

They laugh, Kunle amazed at how sometimes, suddenly, small things jump into their darkness and light it up like this—with glowing fire. In all his years, the past year has been the hardest, each day full of its own bouquet of terror, yet, in ways that constantly surprised him, it was also the year he'd laughed the most.

"Commander sef-eh? How can he finish the name like that? How can Ma-di-e-bo become Man-di-gba-be?" Ndidi shakes his head.

When they reach the library, they see that a third open-roofed Land Rover has entered the school grounds, driving slowly. It wears a death's-head fixture—a cranium and two femurs velcroed to the grille. On the bonnet, a death's-head pennant hangs, waving in the wind. One watching from above can see from the way he fixes his eyes on the pennant that he is bothered by this ritual of excavating the bodies of the dead. But he cannot find a way to say this to his friends, who have never been where he's been, and with whom he does not want to share his experience, because of his promise to Agnes. So, he asks only a question of them: Whose idea was it to put this symbol everywhere?

"Eh, Kunis—you no like am?"

"No," he says to Felix.

"Thank you, Kunis, thank you!" They are back sitting on the porch outside because it's too hot and stuffy inside. Ndidi points upwards. "I have been saying it: maybe God is punishing us for all this. Kunis, it's Stana who order them to dig up burial ground. One cemetery near Etiti hiah. They carry bones and skulls—dead people."

"It is not true, kai, Fada. That is—"

"Did they not dig dead bodies, yes or no? Our European commander, did he not dig up actual skeletons from graves and attach them to all the cars?"

"Hmm but . . . hmm," Felix says reluctantly.

"All of the heavy casualty we suffering sef, who knows what caused it? Eh, who knows? And maybe, it is also because of these people we don't know where they are from fighting for us."

"Egwagieziokwu, every military use it. Even British, the vandals sef, if you look well, they have used it. Simple. Even the vandals: Look at their Third Marine Commando. Even their commander, General Adekunle, is his name not 'Black Scorpion'? All am saying is, Rolf Staina is a good man. Look at him, he is the only mercenary fighting for free. Why? He love Biafra so much he even took Biafra citizenship!" Felix glances about, mostly at Ndidi, who is licking his lips. "Only Staina—only him! So, biko nu, if he want to fight for us and die, we should appreciate it. We should—"

Two recruits, in shirts dyed green with uneven spots of white on them, brandishing trumpets, pass by them, stopping momentarily to salute. "Ndewo," they all reply, waving.

"We must appreciate them," Felix says again. "Look at even this mission we are going for—which commander is doing this? Even Onwuatuegwu, or Achuzia—are they taking this kind of risk? Even sef—let's say major is taking money from us. Can it buy life?"

"He is right," Kunle finds himself saying, and the others, as if surprised that he's spoken, look at him.

"Thank you, Kunis!" Felix, rising, dusts the small grains of sand from his palms, then crouches again. "Look at Norbiato. See how he die—like chicken. Their country is good. They don't have to be here . . . Even the Caritas priests, Joint Church Aid, all from abroad. Without them, most Biafrans would have died by now."

THE ANXIETY IN the camp about the mission is so strong that in the morning, Kunle resolves that if he is to die on this mission, which Major Steiner has said will happen "soon," then he should at least send a letter and a photo to his parents. He runs to the officers' mess to ask Steiner for permission, but Steiner has gone to Umuahia, Biafra's capital city, to see the head of state. Captain Emeka issues the pass—for only a few hours, so that Kunle can take photos with Agnes in Etiti town and he can send a letter home just in case anything happens. With the pass in his pocket, Kunle watches impatiently as Agnes applies cream to her face, looking in a shard of mirror. For the first time she puts on earrings, and her face beams so much that he is surprised that he, Kunle, could bring joy to such a person as her.

For the first time in a long while, he is alone with her as they walk the road out of the camp, towards the village two kilometers away. She is dressed in her green T-shirt, her hair loosened, covered with a red headscarf. She does not ask him what the photos are for. For much of the way, his sweating palm twined in hers, he wishes he could tell her what he's planned: that they rob a house on the way, get new clothes, and make their way out of the Biafran-controlled area to where they might find a federal garrison, claiming to be husband and wife. They would then go home to Akure, and she could return to her family after the war. This idea has taken shape in him while he waited for her, but out here in the open, with military lorries driving past every now and again, he realizes it would be impossible. For a long stretch they walk, birds chirping and unseen animals yelping.

"Kunis," she says as they approach a group of people standing outside a small Volkswagen, stuffed with belongings, goods bound to its roof.

"Yes, Darly."

She looks at him, the scar on the side of her face appearing larger than it has ever seemed, adding, in some mysterious way, to her good looks.

"Now that this have happened, you have to come and see my people."

"Yes," he says urgently. "Yes, maybe after we go-come. After mission . . . I will bring my brother and we will go and see them."

She nods, looks up, the sun in her eyes. "It is tradition, and—"

"Officer! Officers, please help us!"

Some eighty meters away, three men covered in mud are trying to haul a small Volkswagen Beetle out of a wet rut. One of the men, in a raffia hat and trousers cinched with a hempen rope, approaches them.

"We are going to Umunede, and our car just die," the man says.

Kunle hands Agnes his pouch and canteen. He finds a spot at the back of the car between four men, all gaunt, one of them a boy no more than fifteen, with one eye swollen. They push, the wheels spinning, drilling into the dirt and spraying wet mud at them. It seems his arms will snap, but suddenly, the car races up the incline, its engine erupting. The driver hits the throttle, and the men are engulfed in black smoke. They hurry their thanks and soon are gone.

At the photo studio, Agnes stands beside him with their hands twined. The photographer, moving about and instructing them about how to pose against the white background, flashes a few wild lights with his Polaroid camera. Afterwards, they both stare at the single photograph, the only one they can afford. They hoped it would cost no more than five Biafran pounds, but the photographer would take nothing less than ten pounds. There he is, his face changed more than anything he can imagine of himself. He has a wound under the right side of his jaw, like a deep scratch, and he has become darker than ever. His face is bonier than the fleshy face he'd had back in Lagos, roughened with pimples, and there is a slight depression on the side of his head where the shrapnel hit him. Agnes's face is whitened by the photographer's makeup powder, and full of peace. A glint of light is caught in her eyes.

She puts the photo in her pocket, and through the journey, he wishes they had been able to get more copies. As they walk back, he feels more than at any time he can recall a sense of elation. He tells her the story of Ofodili from the otherworld. When he is done, there are tears in her eyes. He kisses the tears, their warm salt in his mouth.

"Agi, I will always love you," he says, standing in front of her, the sun behind his head.

She wants to speak but turns away instead. A group of men in white coveralls with Red Cross badges on their sleeves pass them, ferrying sacks of powdered milk and supplies on bicycles towards some refugee camp. They greet the men with "Nnoo!" and once they are beyond earshot, she says, "If you love me . . . then don't leave me. Don't leave. Don't die again—you hear?"

He nods. The sinking sun's golden hue rests on her face, and he thinks that she is the most attractive she has ever been. When he sees an abandoned building on the roadside, he pulls her off the road. The house must have been hit by a bomb. Its floor is littered with rubble, shattered glass, clothes crusted with blood, bird feathers and shit, and there are footprints on the dusty concrete floor. She laughs at the urgency of his desire and how he is able to arouse her. With her hands against the wall, he slides into her with rushed gentleness. The sound of his frequent thrusts—wet and plodding—come to him like footsteps in sludge. Once they are spent, his mood is quickly replaced with the realization that he has arranged for her to leave and will now be the cause of their eventual separation in this dreary and battered country.

23.

HE HAS BEEN away from the front for so long and now, as the convoy of three Land Rovers pulls up at an outpost of the commando brigade in a forested village, Kunle feels a heaviness upon him. It is almost daylight; uniformed men join them, and in a loud, drenching rain, they ride, covering their rifles and shells with tarps to shield them from the rain. The rain occludes everything, whistling and carrying with it tattered thoughts of the past few weeks—the deadly accident as Kunle was trying to make his way back to the Iyienu hospital, the photograph session with Agnes. After a while, the vehicles stop on the shore of a brown river.

The bridge was blown up months before, the sentry says, by retreating Biafran troops. What remains of it lies half-submerged, its deck stretched in tendrils of concrete-coated iron rods and guardrails hanging above the water. They will have to cross the river with their supplies, then continue the journey on foot through the forest. They step out into the water, Steiner cursing in French and shivering in his raincoat beside Lieutenant Layla. They walk first along a clay-red path into a thick forest, their boots catching in the sludge of matted roots and leaves. Then they stumble through a dense savanna, long, prickly stems of elephant grass flogging their skin. Felix and another corporal are slashed on the face, a line of loose, watery blood running through Felix's beard. Kunle feels a snapping in his heart at the sight of the wound, worrying for Felix until Agnes has stanched the bleeding and cleaned the wounded eye with antiseptic spirits and cotton wool.

They have waded through the lush green territory for five hours, barely resting. By four P.M. the rain has stopped, but the trees, blackened from the rain, continue to drip on them, and a persistent growl of water remains underground, like some great vehicle tunneling beneath the forest floor. They come upon sites where it seems there had been fighting, bodies of the dead sown among the thickets and foliage like strange plants. A broken jeep sits at the end of a small clearing, wild grass sprouting from its interior, its body covered with moss. A few meters from that is the concave form of an empty mortar shell with wild mushrooms in it. Twisted and rusting iron and steel hang from trees. After a few paces more, they find a field covered with bones and complete skeletons, all lying in poses aping the living—knees high, arms curved over the chest, one seated at the foot of a tree, what remains of it packed into the rag that had been its uniform, its full set of bared teeth grinning. Another lies on a blackened, fallen trunk, water dripping from the eyeless sockets as if it were weeping. A high wind blows towards the north, bending the foliage and filling the dead with brief, sudden cameos of life. It is a sight too hard to bear, and longing to know how Agnes is processing it, he lifts his eyes and is gazing at Agnes when the signalman announces that they have entered enemy territory.

Twice they hear jets flying overhead in the distance, on their way back to the airstrip, as night falls, and each time the commandos all crouch and remain still. It is nearly midnight when, looking at a map, Steiner says they can complete the journey the following morning—the airport is only fourteen kilometers away now. They stop at the edge of the jungle, and two privates disguise themselves as old civilians and walk into an abandoned village.

For a while, the privates do not return, and the rest of the troops wait, most of them seated on the roots of a great tree, Agnes and Layla on ammunition boxes. The moon is full, but the trees' canopies have edged it out, leaving them in darkness. Everything, in this time of waiting, assumes a quality of considerable dread. Kunle feels restless, for it seems as if the fate of the entire group lies in these two men. No one knows what might happen—they could be attacked, bombed. The unpredictability of things—this is what threatens the soldier the most in a war and the thing to be most feared. His friends wear the same intense demeanor of apprehension. Ndidi is fiddling with his rosary, and Felix is reading from his jotter in the colored light of the moon, a pencil clasped between his teeth. Agbam and Steiner are crouched on the root of a tree farther into the bush; the red glow of their cigarettes, close together, resembles the eyes of a beast.

Agnes looks sullen and detached. The previous day, as they made love in the abandoned building, Kunle's joy and pleasure was so profound and feverish he felt a rupturing within. She whispered afterwards that she had fallen in love with him. And a profound silence fell, so that he shuddered when she whispered, "But, if . . . if we die, we must die together—eh?"

"Please stop talking like this, eh," he said, sighing. "We will not die."

"Chukwu ga zoba anyi," she said after a long pause. "But, if we die, we die together."

Standing here now, he thinks he could try to send her to find Tunde and the two could leave Biafra together. But would she agree to go? The only viable way to get her to leave seems to be through an official order from Steiner—an option that would anger her and make her feel that he'd betrayed her wishes and exposed the pregnancy.

Something moves in the near distance, four meters away. In a moment they can make out the racing silhouettes of the two privates by the fractured light of the moon. The privates found the village deserted, and the remains of a partly damaged cathedral looks to be the most secure place to rest for the night.

THEY LEAVE AT dawn, hastening through the dark, and soon Steiner points to the airport mast, now within sight. They have been traveling through a thick, wet jungle since four-thirty, but now they can see three kilometers of tall vegetation, burned, blackened, and dry, dead bamboo stalks sticking out among heaps of ash and coal-black debris. The federal troops, to better protect the airport, have cleared out the bush so they can see as far as possible.

Turning from Steiner, Sergeant Agbam announces that according to Biafran intelligence, four hundred men are guarding two Ilyushin planes and four MiG jet bombers at the airport. There are also Ferrets there, and one artillery gun. But the team of thirty commandos has come prepared.

Again, Kunle feels a coldness within. He watches Agnes chamber cartridges into her Thompson rifle. He knows hopelessly little about pregnancies, or how safe the child might be, and he has fears about the child surviving what is coming. One watching him from above can see his struggles etched on his face. He moves up beside her and whispers, "I am going to be beside you. Please, Agi . . . please." He touches her neck; her body is warm. "I love you, Agi."

Steiner, having finished his speech, begins chanting, "Réveillez-vous!" The soldiers and officers cheer loudly. They rub soot on their helmets, field caps, faces, so that they all appear like a band of ancient marauders. They crawl the rest of the way, their hands scabbing, the burnt shoots reduced to brittle grass, gasping and coughing, sweating. They all look like animals: eyes red, face painted with soot, ash on their lips. Kunle's heart is pounding when the major signals for them to stop. They've crawled for nearly two kilometers and are now within sight of the airport. From beyond the scorched plain, they can see the tower, a line of tarmac, and the outline of a building.

They lie there—the world coming to a pause. A vulture makes to perch on Agnes's back, but she shakes her head and it flees in the direction of the airport.

"Shake head when they come!" Steiner says. "Shake head. They no think we dead bodies."

For nearly an hour they struggle against the hungry birds, constantly moving their heads, trying not to stir too much. A vulture loiters for a while on the still body of one of the second lieutenants, walking up and down his back. He strikes it with his rifle, and the bird tumbles into the ash. Soon after, men in green overalls with tools appear in the distance. They remove the tarps concealing the planes, open the cockpits, and begin fueling and loading rockets under the wings of the bombers. This is what has been killing Biafrans, what is deciding this war, and what, once, almost killed Kunle. On the radio, a foreign observer put the number of dead so far at four hundred thousand, with seventy percent civilians. Kunle feels a panting wish to destroy all the planes. Hastily, he rechambers the magazine of his Bren light machine gun.

The bugle sounds again, and hundreds of federal soldiers in identical lizard-green uniforms line up before the big Nigerian flag. In this moment, planned for months, Kunle finds himself possessed by a strange, wild spirit. He does not know when he rises or takes the first shot, only that he is suddenly firing into the horde of confused men near the tower. He can see, directly, the men falling, bombs exploding behind them in the distance. When his rounds are spent, he races through the line for the ammunition box. Behind him, he hears a great blast. One of the Ilyushin jets is aflame, a wing adrift in the air.

He feels the thud of bullets in the grass a few meters from him. Someone cries, "Layla!," and twisting, he finds the lieutenant kneeling, a hand on her belly. She sways on her knees, shaking her head, bending low and then rising again as if engaged in some strange prayer. He has not had many encounters with her beyond seeing her seated with Agnes or Steiner, always smiling, her lips always painted red. She is struggling now to talk, bright red blood oozing from her mouth. Kunle looks up and finds the sniper on a small hill some forty meters away. In that moment, the grass beside him shakes, and some dust flies into his eyes. He falls back, the plopping sound of bullets hitting the ground beside him. He pulls himself up, but the sniper is no longer on the hill.

Troubled by the wind, ash rises from the incinerated brush and dead grass into his throat. He claws back to the line and sees a group of commandos farther out, closer to the airport tarmac. Agnes is among them, two commandos beside her, firing away. Beyond her, in the hangar, the second Ilyushin explodes, crackling, wild billows of red and tangerine flames reaching into the clouds. He races to catch up with Agnes, and finds in the distance towards the far left side three federal soldiers fleeing towards the tower. He aims and all three fall into trembling piles, smoke rising from their backs. He is about to shoot at another when someone shouts, "Ferret!" and then "Fall back!" He throws himself flat, pulls Agnes down with him. He hauls her up and they race back.

Later, he finds the night inalterably dark, and the world empty—as of something whose core has fallen out. The commanders are mostly silent, and despite traveling this time in Biafran territory, it feels as though danger is still present. But he cannot think of anything else than Agnes, whose face is pressed to his chest, weeping, her tears soaking through his uniform. Her voice is quivering with repeated cursing and calling the names of her dead.

Part 4

The ERUPTION of the STAR

It had not occurred to the Seer till now that he is witnessing not only the yet unlived life of a man soon to be born in Akure, but also the lives of the others caught in the net of the vision: Agnes, Felix, and the rest of the soldiers. Perhaps Agnes is now, at this moment, a toddler sleeping beside her mother. But he can see her fully formed body, her intimate parts in the full glare of his eyes.

Something cries out from the stand of trees to the east. The seer glances in the direction from where the sound came and sees only its white wings flapping in the dark. Did he make a wrong choice in coming to this hill? Twice there have been interruptions: first a fox and now this white owl. He was supposed to go far from human habitation, to avoid such interruptions. That is also why he chose to do this at midnight, when most creatures are asleep. But he cannot prevent a fox from coming to the hill, or this evil owl, beating its wings so loudly that the unborn man, Kunle, can hear it two decades into yet uncreated time.

The Seer raises his hands. "Ifa, please shield your bowl. Prevent osho people, awon aje, and all kinds of evil spirits from it tonight. Let nothing—nothing prevent this vision. Ifa and Orunmila: the fruit that issues out of stones, the thunder that strikes in water, hear me. Mo juba re!"

The star is slowly being veiled, darkness gathering around the edges of its colorful light. The vision, he can see, is starting to come to an end. He must be discerning and persistent enough to forge through the mass of darkness into the single path of light till the end. He is Ifa's messenger and must endure to witness all that Ifa desires of him, for they are things which once encountered are irrevocably seen.

24.

ONE WATCHING FROM above can tell that Kunle has changed. There is now a cut on the left side of his lower lip, an inward scar where a ricocheting bullet grazed his mouth. There is also a hardness on his face wrought by the war—wrinkles line his forehead and the sides of his face. It is not age but the encrustations of all the extreme emotions that his face records in a single day, or even a moment. And in the past seven days, his face has experienced more shifts than most people might register in an entire lifetime. Weeks after the Enugu airport attack, Steiner turned the entire commando brigade into a special forces group that went on dangerous ambushes and suicidal reconnaissance missions. He created new groups led by every one of his six other European commanders who went on expeditions into enemy territories at high costs, with one of them returning wounded from each of his five missions. For nearly two months, Steiner rested his Special Commando Platoon, which he called "the guards." Then, nine days ago, Steiner returned from a visit to Colonel Ojukwu's bunker in Umuahia with bottles of French gin, a carton of St. Moritz, and a promise to Colonel Ojukwu that his men would raid enemy positions in Calabar, a city that's been in federal hands since '67, and destroy enemy armor being readied for assault on Aba. Despite being warned by the Biafran

Intercept Unit that there are federal signal posts and Soviet-trained snipers on every corner, Steiner pressed forward.

Kunle and the others have now been in the forest for seven days, ambushing enemy formations, going behind enemy lines. There has come upon him a certain weariness, a total closure of his being, as though it is his soul itself that has taken ill. Just the night before, they leapt into an enemy trench with clubs and knives and emerged blinded with the blood of dead federal soldiers. Kunle retreated with a line of blackened entrails stuck to the front of his shirt and a patina of bloodied flesh on the end of his truncheon. He wept afterwards—ashamed, scared, and shocked by what he had done, become, witnessed, and how he'd survived it.

They are walking under the cover of darkness and treading a forest path when rain begins falling. At first, they scud through the howl of black wind rifling through the trees. Thunder blasts, and lightning washes their faces as if some unseen camera has taken a photo. All at once, they come under sniper fire. Agbam's knapsack is struck and ripped off his shoulder, tumbling into the wet bush. James fires his submachine gun from a left position—but what? The forest is impenetrably dark and it is impossible to know from where the sniper is shooting. A branch snaps, from somewhere behind him a violent yelp rises, and now, just a few meters to his left, Kunle hears a sound like a stone hitting a padded bag, and Ndidi falls backwards with a cry. Kunle ducks behind the closest tree and shouts, "Fada!"

A hailstorm of bullets follows. Reddish-yellow sparks alight on every spot in the dark—on trees, on Ndidi's dropped rifle, on the body of a dead comrade, in the brush. For a while the forest is alive with the ceaseless cry of steel, like a living, sinister creature. Then the firing stops, just as quickly as it began, and for a while, no one moves. The brush smells of burned wood, of singed grass, and the smoke is blue in the dark. It is Kunle who rises first, before Steiner, and rushes in the direction of the awful sound. There he finds Ndidi seated with half of his back against the root of a tree, gazing at his hands and his shirt as if in wonder. His uniform is soaked with dark blood, and his face has turned the color of shaded violet.

"Ndi? Fada?"

Ndidi merely blinks and nods, and clenches his teeth. Kunle lifts him and carries Ndidi's body towards the other commandos. More men surround them. They kneel over the body in the dark, for no one can put on a light. Ndidi, in Kunle's arms, is bleeding out—Kunle's thigh is soaked, his hands sticky, and even the air smells of blood.

"Wh . . . wu . . . ta!" Ndidi manages, and tracing his trembling mouth, Felix pours from a bloodied canteen. The water spills, seems to gag the man, and washes him.

Ndidi goes into a fit—his hands sweep again and again, clench powerfully, and try to reach for something in the air, then his neck. Even in the dark, Kunle can see Ndidi's eyes changing as he kicks and trembles. He witnesses the very moment Ndidi falls quiet—only the sound of his intestines, of something digesting or passing out, can be heard.

For long minutes, Kunle cannot take his eyes off Ndidi's lifeless body. There is something about it that holds his gaze. Is it Ndidi's half-open eyes staring upwards at Felix? Or the bloodied cross lying on the side of his neck? Or the shirt with the pope's face, now darkened with arterial blood? Kunle can think only of that evening, days after Agnes had left and he'd begun experiencing the natural sorrow of love. His comrades, wanting to cheer him up, began telling him about their own encounters with women, except for Ndidi, who kept completely silent.

James, intending to tease Ndidi, asked why he never spoke about women—was it because he wanted to be a reverend father? They all laughed, but Ndidi cleared his throat and said, simply, "It is because I'm impotent." The words forced a silence among the group, and Ndidi went on: "I was born in '35 in Lomara, where my mother hails from. She went to visit her parents, and as fate would have it, while she was there, lightning struck the house. Suddenly, only seven months pregnant, she put to bed . . . I was so small, like the size of a rat, they could carry me on one hand. In those days, in our village, no real hospital, they said I will not survive. But somehow, I am here today." Ndidi would discover that he had a severe case of undescended testicles. He could not produce semen and could not impregnate a woman.

He had not known this until last year, when he'd challenged his parents about trying so hard to get him to be a Catholic priest and be celibate when he did not want to. In tears, his mother had told him.

Presently Kunle turns away from the body, fighting the urge to cry. He looks instead at Major Steiner, who is visibly angry. He has lost three of his special forces men in just ten minutes. He curses in German and French and gives orders in English.

"Commandant say we can't sleep in this jungle," Sergeant Agbam says. "He orders that we move now!"

Strung together in osiers of grief, the men do not move.

Felix says, "We can't leave him—"

"Nonsense!" Steiner cries. "Réveillez-vous, monsieur! Then carry him! Carry him!"

There are only six of them, but it's enough. They carry the body and make their way out of the forest as quickly as they can.

KUNLE CAME TO Ndidi's burial with suppressed eagerness, and now the rites are almost finished, and they are headed to the burial ground for the interment. He joins the procession trailing the casket in the sun. Afterwards, Major Steiner and Captain Emeka give speeches extolling Ndidi's bravery. Felix reads a line from Shakespeare: *Sweet are the uses of adversity, which, like the toad, ugly and venomous, wears yet a precious jewel in his head; and this our life, exempt from public haunt, finds tongues in trees, books in the running brooks, sermons in stones, and good in everything*—a line Kunle has heard him quote before but cannot recall on what occasion. But here, at the funeral, the words acquire the force of a clenched fist. Yet Kunle still feels a deep and profound sorrow. Once, there were many of them from the training camp—including Ekpeyong, Bube-Orji, and, of course, Ndidi. He has tasted death, and Agnes—it almost hurts him to think—would have been killed had she not worn the federal trooper's helmet during one of the aerial attacks, when shrapnel lodged on the back of the helmet, which stopped its progress. There seems to be one destination for all who come into this sad fraternity: death. It does not matter what time of day or how long it takes; it is always waiting. If outside the war a young man is constantly looking towards the future, here, the future is a fearful being with black eyes and on whose face no one can look.

Kunle's hands quiver when he throws his fistful of earth into the grave. This is the first time in his life he has attended a funeral. Ndidi is lucky: his is the only proper burial for a soldier Kunle has seen in this war, and this is partly because Agulu, the new base of the 4th Commando Brigade, is only thirty-five kilometers from his hometown. Kunle turns back quickly and salutes Steiner and the other senior officers, who have begun walking straight towards their open-roofed Land Rover, the black pennant waving in the wind. Kunle thinks that he, too, should be on his way—ideally to find Agnes—but he has the rosary and prayer booklet Ndidi often carried in his trouser pocket.

Now that the ceremony has ended, he goes up to the man dressed in an oversized black T-shirt on which is the image of some mountain in America, with the inscription ASPEN. The man has his walking stick in one hand and in the other, a framed black-and-white photo of Ndidi in a suit and bow tie, his hair well-groomed and parted down the center. Once Kunle introduces himself, he regrets at once that he's been the one delegated to do this. He holds the small bag containing Ndidi's possessions out to the man and says, "Your son's things, sa."

The old man's eyes light up. "Oh . . . oh, you are his comrade, o kwa ya?"

"Yes, sa. He was my good friend."

"Eoow! Chai, looku-at, eh . . . just looku-at." The old man takes the bag and Kunle's hand and locks him in a deep embrace. "Thank you, my son. Thank you."

"Is okay, sa."

The resemblance between father and son is strong. The way the man curls his hands in the air, gesticulating, the way he shakes his head and folds his mouth into a pout—these are all Ndidi. The old man thanks Kunle, prays for him, and goes away hugging the rosary and the book, shouting, "Eoow! Eoow!"

It is, at last, time—the moment that, as if on an old, lost path, he's been making his way towards these past few weeks—to find Agnes and his brother. He rushes past a Bank of Biafra branch and a post office, outside of which a long line of refugees stand with bowls and cups, waiting for their daily ration from a Caritas organization. He should not be in such a hurry, because Steiner—perhaps drunk or crazy, or because of Ndidi's death—has given him a rare three-day pass. But he cannot help it. He passes the magistrate court where, weeks before, the case of Felix's extrajudicial killing of the saboteur in Etiti had been concluded with a verdict that it was a rightful killing, carried out by an officer of law and order. Kunle gets to the motor park half an hour later, and boards an old, broken-down car. Its driver, an elderly man dressed in a worn shirt and thin slippers, is running about shouting, "Biafra One! Lohum, Umuahia, Uzuakoli."

The car is a worn metal frame devoid of almost any leather covering, its floor so rusted he can see the ground beneath. He has a headache—they have started to come frequently again, since the morning, two weeks after Agnes left, when he hit his head on a tree branch during a stroll with one of the European commanders, Major Marc Goosens, and the orphan boy Goosens had adopted. His old head wound had bruised and bled. A month later, he became sick with malaria, feverish, having mild hallucinations that the walls of the library were filled with dead people. The clinic at Madonna was out of chloroquine and Largactil tablets for days. A Super Constellation plane on a humanitarian flight carrying medical supplies and food had been shot down by federal forces at Uli on July 1, killing all occupants, and it had scared the other relief mission pilots. Kunle had thought he was dying until, days later, another plane bringing medicine had finally arrived.

He reaches into the front pocket of his khaki drill shirt, fishes for the small bag of Largactil tablets, the bag's insides white with the pills' detritus. He brought no water with him. The car is jerking as they dip in and out of potholes and skirt bomb craters and cross rickety wooden pontoons over shell craters. He puts two tablets in his mouth, the chalk loosening quickly over his tongue and filling his mouth with its bitter taste.

He has not slept well in days—he struggles to keep his eyes open as the car moves through a small village and a crowd springs out of the bushes and mobs it, begging for food. He gives them two packets of Biafran "dry pack"—small balls of fried cassava seasoned with salt and pepper and bound in small knots of three or four in small nylon bags. Since the commandos came to Agulu, the local women have been bringing them this, and it has increasingly become a practice across the territories of the nation where the forces still hold sway. He thrusts them into the hands he can reach and then pulls away.

At last, the sight of the hospital moves him to tears. He's longed for this opportunity for two months. As weeks passed without a word from Agnes, pain and discomfort crept into his entire body like tropical weevils—burrowing into his throat, into some bone of his lower back, and into the side of his head where the shrapnel had injured him. Sometimes, he'd walk about with the feeling that his body had been diminished, like a frayed old garment, unable to resolve within himself the decision he'd made to send her away from the front. He reflected about the day after the Enugu airport assault when, once they returned to the Madonna barracks, Steiner had the general commanding officer of the Biafran army himself issue her the letter of relief from duty to work at the Queen Elizabeth Hospital in Umuahia as an army nurse. The previous evening had been the happiest of the war—the news of the raid had been announced all over Biafra, so they met a crowd upon their return to Etiti. In the darkness, the celebration lit by torches and lanterns and the headlights of motor vehicles, the residents waved posters, palm branches, cocoyam leaves, and Biafran flags, singing, *"Odogwu Steiner, Beke Biafra."* Agnes burst into tears as she spoke on the telephone with Colonel Ojukwu, who declared that night that Steiner had been promoted to colonel and all of the Special Commando Platoon corporals—Agnes, Felix, Ndidi, James, and Kunle—to sergeants. The following day, she received the order, surprised that she was going somewhere without them. Kunle saw a shadow of suspicion in her eyes as she got in the car with Agbam, who held Kunle's letter to her in his pocket, to be given once she settled into the hospital. In it he'd bared his heart: he'd gotten her to leave because he wanted no harm to come to her or the child in her womb.

The hospital's roof is painted with a big red cross, as is the ground in front, as well as the gate. It is a colonial building, with columned walls and carefully laid brick siding, with ixora flowers and wild rosemary lining the gravel path into the archway entrance, on which is the inscription QUEEN ELIZABETH HOSPITAL. People are seated everywhere—under tents, on open land, under the pavilion by the main ward. A white ambulance pickup with its lights on and its siren bleeping is leaving the premises as Kunle enters. A few meters from the main door, around the sprouts of ixora, wounded soldiers lie or sit on mats in clusters.

He stands in the long line that stretches through the open door. Over the heads of the people, he can see ceiling fans swirling, and somewhere inside, a voice is wailing with terrible anguish. The air is suffused with the antiseptic smell of Izal. When his turn comes, he presents the pass.

> *Lt C-in-C, Biafra 4th Commando Div, Agulu*
> *Lt K. P. Nwaigbo to visit Lt Agnes Azuka rtd*
> *At queen's hosp Umuahia. Official & personal*
> *Visit encouraged. Please grant access.*

"Wait here, sa," a lady in a blue pinafore says after gazing at the paper. She leaves the cashier cubicle and heads into the interior.

Something about this place—maybe its smell, its curtains and cubicles—reminds him of the clinic at Opi. He is wondering what his life would have been like if he hadn't left Opi when the lady reappears and says, "Officer, is it Nurse Agnes that you are looking for?"

"Yes, my sister."

"Oh, she take voluntary leave. She suppose to come back, but we don't know when."

"Okay—" He cannot find what to say. He scratches the side of his face and folds his pass back into his pocket.

He gazes at the poster behind the nurse. Beside the image of a pregnant woman, a bottle of medicine, and a huge red cross, the inscription urges, BIAFRAN MOTHERS, PROTECT YOUR CHILDREN! THE FUTURE OF BIAFRA IS IN YOUR HANDS!

"How long ago, and where did she go to?"

"Ah, it have been long o. Maybe one month now." She turns to a lady who is arranging coins in a plastic casing. "Julie—akwa one month?" The other lady nods.

"One month," the nurse tells him. "Since one month."

"Okay, thank you," he says and steps away.

In Biafra, like a world removed from the known world, one discovers new vistas of emotions, new faculties one did not know were there before. This feeling of being drained and abandoned, which comes upon Kunle so quickly that it invades his senses completely, is one such experience. Out in the open, he wonders what to do next. Nothing has prepared him for the possibility of not finding Agnes here. Not only had he not heard from her at all since she left, but she'd also not responded to him in early July, when he wrote her about his illness. And when he called the hospital, a nurse had said only that she was "not able to answer this call." Was she still angry with him? What had he done wrong? Should he have allowed her to keep fighting even with the child in her womb? Running through bushes, slamming her body into the ground at a moment's notice, sleeping crouched in trenches? Why would she not speak to him?

He walks a bit, the dark weight of his anguish bearing down on him so that he has to stop, put a hand to his chest, and exhale. Across a small, empty pool at the other entrance to the hospital, a woman is crying while two other women kneel beside her to offer comfort. He nods through the salutes of the guards at the gate—"Lieutenant, nnoo!" "Commando, shun, sa!"—and heads into the city. He veers into a busy junction, around which are old, empty sheds and office buildings. He waits on the side of the road as the female traffic warden waves at the right lane of traffic to move forward, then signals for him to cross. Here, a Texaco petrol station, now abandoned, with one of its pumps torn out, sits like the relic of a bygone era. He crosses the darkened dirt between the damaged buildings, walking over a wooden bridge to the other side of the street, where there is still a functioning Kingsway store, its roof covered with so much foliage that only a part of the name is visible. A man in a tucked-in shirt stands near a light pole with a megaphone, shouting about the kingdom of God and salvation in Christ. The man holds up a tattered Bible whose black cover is pockmarked with white spots, as if it's suffering from some strange disease. On the pole is a sign Kunle has seen elsewhere around the city, sometimes painted on the side of buildings: PARK UNDER TREES AWAY FROM BUILDINGS, BY ORDER. The sign and the rows of cars covered with foliage in the parking lot offer sad evidence that despite the destruction of many of the bombers in the Nigerian fleet, the air raids over Biafra's civilian population have merely intensified.

He leaves the store with a small box of McVitie's, a blue Biro, a foolscap sheet, and an envelope, having paid two pounds, six shillings for them, and walks up the road to a clearing with small stacks of bricks where a building has been destroyed. He sits on a pile of bricks, eating the biscuits and writing a letter to Agnes. He details the death of Ndidi and his own rising disenchantment with the antics of the foreign commanders, especially Major Taffy Williams, who left Biafra and returned, and even of Steiner's rising ego. He wants to know how the pregnancy is coming: How many months is it now? Is she sick?

He gazes at his wristwatch, which has cracked in many places; he can barely make out the time. It seems it is a quarter to four. He has to find out how to reach Agnes somehow before returning—he has two more days.

He walks back quickly and finds that a military lorry from some battlefront is parked outside the other entrance to the hospital—the one near the emergency ward—and from it wounded men are being carried out on stretchers. A white man in a doctor's coat stands there directing the unloading, a stethoscope around his neck. Only after the last man has been brought into the hospital—a man whose leg is completely gone—do they let him go in.

"Yes, Officer—you again?" the nurse says upon seeing Kunle at the counter.

"Yes, Nurse," he says. There are now three women in the cubicle, one of them a middle-aged white woman in white coat. "I jus' want to know, did Nurse Agnes tell anybody where she was going?"

"Abiriba," the lady says. "That's her hometown. Her people are living there."

"Okay, in case she returns, eh, biko . . . give her this for me."

The nurse takes the letter from him and he turns and steps out, walks a few paces, and stops. At first, his heart seizes in fear that he has heard again the strange voice only he can hear—austere, yet familiar. He turns, blinking as one of the wounded soldiers makes his way forward, limping. The fellow is dirty, dressed in a tattered brown uniform through which his chest and shoulders can be seen. His feet are bare, his toenails dark with grime. There is a patch of dirt on the back of his head from lying on the ground and the smell about him is the odor of the battlefront: mud, urine, blood, gunpowder, sweat. The man walks with the help of a walking stick with a recurved handle. There is a plaster on the side of his face, and he's grown a beard so long he looks twice his age. Yet Kunle can still make out the fair complexion for which the neighbors had once referred to him and his siblings as "yellow." It is Nkechi's brother Chinedu.

"Oluwa mi oh! Nedu?"

"In flesh, in blood," Chinedu says, and the other soldiers seated on the raffia mat in the hospital's front yard laugh.

They hug. Kunle's breathing is rushed, and his chest boils with the words he wants to say. He is smiling, beaming, and it is clear even to the eyes watching that he is filled with joy. He was derailed from his first mission, to rescue his brother, but the war has since given him other things he had not requested. And now, after an excruciating year has passed and just when he has stopped looking, they have come back to him.

25.

AT FIRST THEY do not speak. Kunle and Chinedu take turns gazing at each other and turning away. It is too much to believe, to understand—this great transformation of life. It was not long ago when this man here who spoke Yoruba without an accent often sat on Kunle's front porch, singing the songs of Haruna Ishola. Now here is the same Chinedu—a veteran of war, a sergeant, dressed in a tattered uniform. Chinedu's Biafran drill uniform is so worn that Kunle can see through it, and there are holes at the knees of his trousers. Even Chinedu's full-faced grin, revealing his gapped teeth, which he shares with his sisters—Nkechi, Helen, and Ngozika—and their mother, has changed somewhat. Chinedu kneads his chapped fingers together again and says, between deep sighs, "Wonders shall never end!"

"How, how can we be here?"

"That's why I say wonders shall never end." Chinedu shakes his head. "It is as if I am dreaming. Let us go and sit down—where should we sit?"

They settle on a bench beneath a camouflaged tent outside the hospital, near where the generator is hidden under a shade cloth.

"Goodness me!" Chinedu says, mimicking his father. "What an adventure, Kunle."

Kunle nods. "I have suffered, Nedu. I am telling you. You know me naw, I don't usually complain. But—what of my brother? How—"

"Yes, oh yes. It is suffering—just look at me." Chinedu sweeps a hand over himself, from his chest to his feet. As if he's not heard the question Kunle asked him, Chinedu begins telling about how he joined the Biafran army. He was reluctant at first because his brother, Nnamdi, had joined. But he's been fighting in the 52nd Brigade, under the command of Colonel Ugokwe, without break since March. He was home only the week before. His brigade is stationed on the Owerri road, blocking any federal attempts to advance from Port Harcourt. Increasingly frustrated at the unsurmountable defensive tactics of the Biafran 52nd, federal troops had set up snipers everywhere. A sniper shot a bullet through Chinedu's left thigh the day he returned.

Chinedu speaks of his wound with great bitterness, for he is eager to return to battle. He is in the middle of his narration when a uniformed man starts the generator, and at once, a bright yellow bulb illuminates them. Kunle sees that Chinedu's mouth is still moving.

"I can't hear—can't hear you!" he shouts.

They sit a few meters from Chinedu's wounded friends, where the din of the generator is quieter. The wounded men are in the middle of excited chatter with a nurse who is holding up an X-ray sheet and gazing into it with the focused light of a battery torch. She says something in Igbo to a man whose left leg is in a cast up to the knee. Kunle does not need Chinedu to translate, for he can understand most of what the men say now, but Chinedu, nodding towards the fellow, says, "Lucky man. He thought they were going to amputate him."

Kunle nods. Again he tries to contain his urgent curiosity about his brother. He does not want to interrupt Chinedu, who is filled with words—of the difficult battles, air raids, the famine in Biafra, the silence of the United States, and the support of Britain and other countries for the Nigerian side. There is a hardness in Chinedu's voice, in his violent gestures, that scares Kunle—a hardness that has never been there before.

"For this war to end," Chinedu says, "we must win it. We must be allowed to have our country."

Chinedu has raised his voice, so Kunle nods quickly to relieve his agitation. Why has he not mentioned Tunde or responded to his question? Is Tunde dead? Oh—God! What will happen to his parents if this great evil has occurred? Words dance in Kunle's head with troubled feet and he wants to let them out, but he is afraid of the things that lay yet hidden. Did he know, Chinedu says suddenly, about the Seer on Ijoka Road back in Akure?

"Yes, Baba Igbala," Kunle says urgently. "The man came to our house the day I was born."

"Yes . . . mhuu . . . your mother told Mama. You see—that man, if only they allowed him, maybe none of this would have happened. I heard that he had visions of the war, that he saw everything. Every—single—thing. I don't even know who told me, but they said he knew."

Kunle nods. "My father told me the Seer saw it and told newspaper people, but nobody believed it."

Since he's been here, nurses and other staff members have been coming up to the wounded men to bring them things or take them into the hospital to dress their wounds. Now the young British doctor he saw directing the unloading is having one of the men with bandages covering his belly stand so he can administer an injection into the man's bare buttock. As the doctor puts away the syringe, one of the men says in Igbo, "Dr. Phillips, I will surely get you an Igbo wife once the war ends!"

Kunle laughs with the men, all except Chinedu, whose face does not stir.

"Your brother," Chinedu says, his voice hurried, "he is in our house."

Kunle bends forward, then sits up again, as if struggling against a force pushing at him from behind. The thing of which he'd wanted to talk all evening has come, and it seems now that he is unprepared for it. The generator stops, and from somewhere, a voice shouts, "No fuel! No fuel o!" In the darkness, the world again seems to return to what has so far characterized Biafra: lightless nights.

"He speaks Igbo now," Chinedu says. "Almost fluently."

Chinedu laughs. When he was a child, his soft, rich laughter had endeared many of the adults of the neighborhood to him. In the months after the accident, he was one of only a few who tried to remain friends with Kunle. Then at age twelve, Chinedu was off to boarding school at Igbobi Boys High in Lagos; he came home infrequently, and when he did, he was caught up in books.

"They are taking care of him. They are trying, but you know his condition."

"Yes," Kunle says, as if compelled. He can feel his breathing steady.

"Things are hard. Lagos is squeezing us from everywhere. This is a war of genocide . . . What have we done to deserve all these, eh? Just, what? . . . You and I, we grew up together, on the same street even—in fact, your mother is Igbo." Chinedu squirms again as he repositions the wounded leg closer to his body. "Why? Eh, why all these?"

Kunle has no answer but to nod. "What about your sister?"

To this, Chinedu is quiet and instead casts his eyes on the ground. When he begins speaking again, his voice is lower, measured: Early in the year, Nkechi joined an army food drive group that sent food to soldiers at the front. This group often went on Ofia attacks, traveling into federal territory to get food that was scarce or unavailable in Biafra. The leader was a sixty-six-year-old woman who had been part of the Women's War in 1929. Everyone had begged Nkechi not to do it, but she'd continued. They made daring trips, and in March, while supplying the Biafran 58th Brigade at Akwete with food—dried stockfish, rice, milk, beans—the women, about six of them, ran into a column of enemy soldiers in two jeeps. The soldiers shot the older women and were attempting to capture the four younger women when a single Biafran rifleman on recce in the area engaged them in a firefight, killing three of the federal soldiers from a well-disguised ambush position. In obvious terror of the lone Biafran soldier, the federal commander ordered some of the men to drive away with the captured women, and at this, Nkechi fled into the bush towards the Biafran corporal, who'd been shot in the shoulder. For a whole day, four Nigerian soldiers pursued them. Nkechi and the rifleman hid under thick bushes, making no noise, eating crackers and pieces of crayfish. Unable to travel faster due to the injury, they spent two days in the bush. On one of those nights, delirious with pain and lack of sleep, they had sex, and he slept for the first time. The following day, they arrived at a village within Biafran territory, Nkechi famished and exhausted, the corporal nearly dead.

Chinedu falls silent, kneading his hands together and cracking his knuckles, his breathing heavy, as though he's just finished a race. Kunle feels the pain behind the words seep through the air, into him. He is surprised when Chinedu continues, his voice harder: "Last week when I went home, nobody told me before—nobody. I was surprised to find Nkechi's belly so big. Nobody—nobody told me they brought him to see our parents. Last month, June, when she found out, he paid her dowry."

It is the last they can say—what can be said after this? A single act, like a shot from a sling, has traveled through their lives, through many years, and has now taken everything away from them. That one act had forced Nkechi, on whom he'd pinned his young heart, to get attached to his brother, and forced his brother, in turn, to come here. The single act has caused him to follow his brother into the most dangerous place in the world. And for what purpose? Why? Nkechi has married another man and is pregnant with the man's child. And what is the fate of his crippled brother? Confined to a wheelchair in a war-torn country, with a people who are not his family, his life condemned to the fate of a ragtag army whose defeat at the hands of a superior enemy is only a matter of time. Again—why? The answer, he sees, is him: he is the cause of all this. All that night he weeps on the ground where he and Chinedu lie down to sleep, hugging himself and watching his shadow on the wall of the hospital, his weeping shadow.

HE DOES NOT wake Chinedu in the morning when he leaves. Despite going to sleep late—just before midnight—it is the most restfully he has slept in a long time. His body has gotten so used to little sleep, to bites of rest, that he no longer feels groggy after only two hours of sleep. His body has also become used to pain, to his body tearing open everywhere—his head, back, hand, legs—or getting burned. Right now, his back and legs are aching from his journey's strain. But there are marks of pain everywhere on him now. The shrapnel that put him in a coma reshaped the side of his head, and his hand is now scarred, too. The war forces the body to become accustomed to bruises, and even then such a body is the lucky one.

He breaks off a stick from a low-hanging branch of a guava tree, cleans his teeth with it, and sets out. The moon is bright and round in the far side of the sky, and the morning is thick with dew. He has been walking for over three hours when he sees a signboard just across the road, but a thronging crowd prevents him from reading it. "E be ka anyi no?" he asks an elderly man beside him who smells of gentian violet. At first the man does not understand his bad Igbo, but when he repeats the question in English, the man nods and says, "We are in Lohum. Ehen . . . all this place is Lohum." It is the name of the town Chinedu had inscribed on a piece of paper that he would get to before Nkpa, the Agbanis' hometown.

A hand tugs at his shirt, and he looks down to see a young woman so starved that the bones of her chest are visible, carrying a child on her shoulder. From his pouch, he gives her the last of the biscuits. At once before him is a multitude of hands. A young woman thrusts her child forward, a girl of four or five with plaited hair, the flesh of her face half-eaten by disease, so that her teeth are without cover. At the sight, most of the people disperse. He searches his pouch, but there is nothing left.

He cannot tell why—perhaps because of the sight of so many suffering people—but Chinedu's words fly back into his head: "I am worried about our army, about the blockade—in fact, the time it is taking to finish this . . . Listen, Kunle, the tragedy is not that we are in a war; it is that it has no end. If a people in the face of great adversity know that it will pass, then they can bear it. In fact, they can bear anything! . . . They will believe that the famine that has come upon this land will be gone by the end of the season. The sickness? Once the dry season comes, the warm weather will drive it out of the land. But the end of this war, no one can see. They said it would not even start at all, but look now: it is the biggest armed conflict in the history of Africa. They said it would last only a short time, but it has gone on for more than a year. Every month, federal troops threaten a 'final offensive' that never succeeds... If one day a strategic city falls, by nightfall Biafra recaptures another. The cycle continues without end. This is the tragedy!"

Across the street he finds a man on an old two-seater bicycle who is certain that he knows the address and can take him there for five Biafran shillings. The man shows Kunle the bullet scar in his left hand and says he fought with the Special Task Force Brigade. They ride on crowded roads, through towns untouched by the war. Young boys line the road near a junction selling bush meat—pangolins, wild hares, rabbits, apes, snakes—and behind them a two-story building has the inscription WIN THE WAR HOTEL painted on its façade. There is an anti-aircraft battery on top of the next building, heavily camouflaged with foliage, its barrel pointing to the empty sky. At every checkpoint, Kunle presents his pass, until the paper softens and tears in the folded middle—a reminder that it is now almost noon of the second day of his three-day leave and he must hasten to his brother.

The sun is heavy, blazing down through the hot air. For a while, they ride in silence, past children playing football on a small grassless field, past a camouflaged church from which the sound of drumming and singing can be heard. Then, pointing, the cyclist veers onto a jagged red-earth path and heads up an incline flanked by banana trees. And as if in a valiant dream Kunle sees, beyond the low bush, a pregnant woman talking to a man seated in front of her. In the same moment, she shifts, and the face of the man appears: the image of both his parents molded into one. He pays the cyclist and hurries up the path like a long-absent prisoner who, arriving at the door of his house, becomes suddenly overwhelmed by the battered image of himself. He clasps his hand to his chest, crying, "Oluwa mi oh! Oluwa mi oh!"

It is Nkechi who sees him first, and with a shudder, she goes still, water sliding from the bowl in her hands. Ngozika, her younger sister, shouts his name from the foot of a tree nearby and runs towards him. He waits for her, a tide of blood rushing through his body, then walks a few paces and lifts Ngozika into an embrace. More than a year ago, he set out on the journey to Biafra, thinking it would be a short road to his brother, but the road has been long, muddy, and rough. And now, after many detours and roadblocks, through a thousand collisions of life, he is gazing down at his brother.

26.

The air is still—the sky is gray, and dark clouds fill much of the horizon. Right after Kunle arrived, thunder struck and a whoosh of violent wind coughed up a few drops of rain, awakening the smell of raw earth. Nkechi and her sister rushed to unclip the clothes on the laundry lines. The rain had forced them into the small living room, Kunle finds that he cannot look his brother in the eye. There is something about the face that he cannot in this moment fully grasp: its veritable nudity and innocence; how the face bears upon it the mark of both familiarity and distance. A person's face is never the same at any moment, especially one he has not seen for so long and now is with him. It is also too hard to watch the continuous stream of Tunde's tears. He gazes instead at Ngozika. Not having interacted much with the girl in years, Kunle feels conscious of her much older body, her fruiting adulthood evident in the two small knots of breasts poking through her blouse.

Nkechi maintains a looming presence—coming in and leaving, her gait often quick yet measured, as if she were conscious of some invisible nakedness that strips her of the courage to be in his presence. She brings a jug of water, then a loose oha soup with pieces of stockfish scattered in it. He eats quickly, with all his fingers, listening to Ngozika, who talks at length about the air raids, the bunker near the village square, and the *stand-still, stand-still* drill. Voices drone in and out from the other compounds, and from the backyard, where a lone hooch with a long hallway sits, the voices of children and women constantly reach them.

"They are orphans and widows," Nkechi says, as if to answer the curiosity in his gaze. "Mmhuu . . . Auntie Helen brought them from Church Aid—you know Church Aid?"

He nods. This is Nkechi, always closing her sentences with a question, as if always anxious that someone will not follow her line of thought. She sits down at last beside her mother on an old sofa whose side coverings have ripped open, exposing the inner wooden structures.

"Mmhuu, they are really helping. Ah, they are! If not for them, if not for airlift into Annabelle in Uli, and the one in Uga, we would have all been dead by now."

"Eziokwu, Nnem," their mother says. Of all of them, she is the most recognizable. It seems that despite the intense ravages of dire suffering, she has remained, even now, dressed as she always was: in a familiar calico scarf. She lets out a sigh. "Agha a joka. O joka."

"Many of them come from the shelter in Mbaitoli," Nkechi says, her voice strangely childlike. "They have recovered from kwashiorkor. If you see these children before, eh, mmhuu. Oburo zi akuko—jus' let Auntie Helen come and tell you everything. She will sometimes see many of the children after they have this kwashiorkor, their belly big like pregnant woman, almost about to burst. Their head will now be so small—"

"Like atu," Ngozika says, stiffening beside him.

"Ehen, nne, like toothpick or even broom sef. Sometimes she say she will see death coming for them, and she would know. She will give them glucose, spoon after spoon if there is no supply—you know when they were shooting all the plane, bombing, and bombing them and every oyibo people were afraid to come and help?"

"Yes," he says and, raising his eyes, looks in her face. "I have been to Uli."

"Mmhuu? Oh, chai. We call it Annabelle . . . Auntie Helen will see the children, when they are about to die, because the hunger have finished their voice, they cannot talk again, most of them cannot even cry again—only making sound like they have cough inside-inside their throat—"

"Eoow!" Their mother begins sobbing.

He feels again a cold, piercing shiver of sadness. He glances at his brother, but Tunde's head is turned upwards, resting against the back of his wheelchair, his hands folded together as if in some silent prayer, the way Ndidi had often clasped his hands.

"Please don't mind Mommy—just listen," Nkechi says, her voice shaking. "Auntie and the other nurses tell the children to wake, and to prevent them from sleeping, they make them sing—many songs."

"Yes, I have seen—like the song the orphan children sing all the time," says Ngozika.

"Mmhuu," Nkechi says, nodding at her sister.

"*Obi kerenke,*" Ngozika sings, the expression of sorrow still on her face, but her voice—a moderated version of her sister's—is unruffled by the sadness.

"*Gowan-Gowan,*" Ngozika begins, choosing a new song, "*onye eze rere ere, onye ausa otaa granot.*" And when she is done, they are all looking away—out the window, up at the ceiling, towards the floor—as if something has fled out of their midst, unseen.

"Egbonmi," Tunde says suddenly, like one out of a trance state. "It means: Gowan, man who teeth have rotten. Hausa man who only eat groundnuts."

"I . . . it is . . . that—" Because Kunle cannot stitch the words together, he turns away to gaze at the low fence out the window, on which a yellow lizard sits, nodding.

"Maybe he hear Igbo now," Nkechi says, slapping her hands together. "Kunis, you hear Igbo?"

He nods. "A little."

"Chai—mmhuu, lemme finish my story. So, Auntie must not let the children stop singing so they don't sleep before ration arrive—you know, protein? So, she ask them to sing, sing, sing . . . with the last energy inside their body. But still, in the night . . . every night when she wake up . . . she see their eyes half open, red around inside it." Nkechi is looking directly at him. "They have died."

AT LAST, THEY are alone—he and his brother. The air in the garden has cooled even more, for another brief rain has fallen, wetting everything, and leaving dark spots of cloud in the sky. It reminds Kunle of the day Ndidi died, of the lightning in the bush. Tunde's presence consumes him—it is like a beam of light from which he cannot turn or hide his shame. He holds one of Nkechi's wrappas around his body and sits on a stool in the open, facing his brother. It is here, under a lone ogbono tree, that Tunde wants to speak—away from the family with whom he spent the past year. This need for a secret place reminds Kunle of a time even after the accident when they often sat together, spinning tales or defacing walls. Sometimes it had stopped when Tunde, forgetting he had been crippled, would try to rise and, in a rage, burst into tears. After a while, Kunle, more afraid of Tunde sliding into these moods than anything else, had stayed away, and slowly, Nkechi had filled that space for the young boy.

It took an effort to wheel Tunde to this spot. The wheels of the chair have become stiff. Now Tunde says, in a low, quick voice, "Egbonmi, you look different."

Kunle nods. "And you too, Aburo."

"Well," Tunde sighs. "This war changes us as much as we remain the same. It changes us, Egbonmi."

Tunde wipes his eyes with the back of his hand.

"Jowo ma su ekun," Kunle says, the words cluttering in his mouth, for it is the first time he has spoken Yoruba in at least a year, and he sees that it must be so for his brother too, for a shadow passes over Tunde's face.

Tunde looks about quickly, bows his head, and says, "Egbonmi, no o, no. Don't speak our language here."

"Why?" Kunle is troubled by the look in his brother's eyes.

"Ah, Egbonmi? We are killing them. Don't you see everywhere? . . . What the rest of Nigeria is doing is too bad, too bad. Kai. Kai. Have you seen the air raids? Every day, every single day they bomb everywhere. Nowhere is safe—church o, school o, market, even hospital. Nobody is safe. Even Europeans, Nigerian army shoot them anyhow and kill them if they see them. It doesn't matter whether they are Red Cross or Church Aid, or whether they wear priest garment. They just finish them. And many of those who are killing them are our people—Yoruba people!"

He can see that Tunde has changed in every measurable way. Almost eighteen now, he has traces of a beard on his face, and a moustache over his mouth. He appears to Kunle somewhat bigger, much taller, as if he has outgrown his wheelchair, and he has to curve his legs unto the footplate or suspend them in the air as he is wheeled. The leather seat is worn, patched up with thread and padded with layers of old clothes, and the wheels squeak noisily. It is the changes in his personality, though, that are more pronounced: he is eager, anxious like one who is trapped in a place from which there is no escape.

Though Tunde speaks with such energy of spirit, there is often agitation in his voice, and his words are girded with fear. He looks about himself constantly, even up at the tree near the house, suspicious of everything, afraid to be accused of being a saboteur. Even within this family, these people they've known since they were children, Tunde cannot relax. Nkechi's father, who has unfailing faith in the Biafran project, forced his two sons, Nnamdi and Chinedu, to join the army. There were times when the father, in anger at the depleting fortunes of Biafra on the battlefield, insulted Tunde, even once calling him an "enemy in our midst." Though the man would later apologize and call Tunde his son, there is still a tension, and Tunde lives in constant fear of Mr. Agbani as much as of the air raids and the war. He is worried about rumors, that the federal troops are planning a final offensive to take Umuahia once the Aba offensive is completed. Tunde fidgets as he speaks of these things, and then, leaning close, whispers, "Brother Kunle. I don't know why, but I am very afraid. Help me . . . Take me home."

Kunle sits in silence, holding his brother's hand, feeling in him something he's never felt before. The world he has been searching for no longer seems hidden; only now it has an unfamiliar shape. Nkechi comes out of the house with a handful of shimmering ube on a metal tray. He observes that she is thin, the shapely buttocks that were one of her defining features now almost flat. In their place is a pregnant belly, which bulges over her knotted wrappa. So changed is she that he wonders what would have happened if the accident had not come between them. What would have happened if she had not moved away from him, towards his brother.

She thrusts the tray towards him, genuflecting as he takes two pieces of the fruit, and Tunde, with a smile, follows and puts an ube in his mouth, chewing quickly.

"You know ube?" she asks Kunle.

"Yes, yes, shebi . . . I mean, we have it in Akure naw."

She smiles, nods. "Mmhuu, you are welcome again—how long will you stay?"

"Tomorrow . . . early in the morning," he says, almost with resignation. He'd hoped to find Agnes, but he knows that he could not have left yesterday. He needs to spend more than a few hours with his brother. "I . . . I have to report back to camp."

She nods rapidly, then faces Tunde as if to speak, but instead raises her hand to her mouth and nods again. Tears cloud her eyes as she walks back. Kunle restrains himself from turning to watch her leave, worried about his brother.

"How many months is she?"

He sees the wetness in Tunde's eyes, and Kunle worries that he should not have asked. It is the war, the brutal blacksmith, that has molded his brother with the anvil of cruel fate.

"Four months—or maybe close to five . . . It is not my child."

"I know," he says, his heart sinking suddenly at the thought that flashes in his mind: Agnes's pregnancy must be around the same age. "Nedu told me."

Tunde nods and, working his hand to his chest, spits out a seed of the bush pear.

"The husband . . . Egbonmi, he does not like me. If she was for . . . if she was for me before, now she has another man!" Tunde seems to tear out of himself, to raise his voice as if this anger has never been vented before and was so pent up it flows with a kind of dark élan. "So, you see . . . why am I here now?"

"Are they taking care of you—are you people eating well?"

After some hesitation, Tunde says, "Yes, yes." His eyes again lift towards the sky. "You know, their father is working for gov'ment and Helen is a nurse. So, they bring food here. That is why we have those children and women, as Nkechi told you. But, Egbonmi, the suffering is still too much. Sometimes, we eat only once per day. Even something as cheap as salt—no salt anywhere in Biafra. Imagine—jus' imagine: common salt! Egbonmi, the suffering is too much!"

From the hooch in the back, the sounds of children crying rise in the cooling air. Kunle sits unsteadily; he is wondering what it is that is making the children cry when Tunde speaks again, his voice lower and a certain shadow over his face now.

"Egbonmi, so tell me—was it Maami who asked you to come here?"

"No," he says, catching himself before replying in Yoruba. Then he tells Tunde the whole story, starting from the night Uncle Idowu came to him in Lagos.

Tunde is silent afterwards—whatever he is thinking seems deep, and it is clear to Kunle that those things are breaking him. Kunle turns away, his eyes following a butterfly floating gaily in the air. The vegetation here is dense, a rich tropical forest that surrounds the eastern part of the village in endless terrains of palm, acacia, and udara trees for what must be several kilometers. They seem to be at the uttermost tip of the village, near the ancient ikoro drum, sheltered under a tent roofed with corrugated iron sheets.

When Tunde speaks, his voice, tearful, feels like a weapon striking against the air: "Look at what I have done to you, to everyone, just because of an accident—an ordinary accident! Why—"

"No, no—" Kunle says, his voice flying beyond his aim.

"I can't, I can—"

"Lai-lai," Kunle says, his voice agitated, wanting to resort to the language of familiarity, with which he was used to speaking with his brother, to find solace in the common tongue.

"Egbonmi, it was not your fault . . . it was—"

"No, Tunde, no! It's not—"

"Am sorry, Egbonmi."

Again, at the time when it matters the most, he is unable to speak. He is unable to stop his brother from rising out of the chair and falling to the ground, kneeling.

"Please forgive me . . . Because of me, because I have been angry, you have risked your life—"

"No, Aburo, no—"

"You have to for—"

"It's okay . . . no—"

"Please, let us go home, Egbonmi. I want to go home, please help me."

"We will—"

"Please. Even though you said Paami sent you a letter in September, I have not heard from Paami or Maami since September, when I called Pastor and Maami go and answered the call. She was so relieved to hear that I am safe . . . but was sick out of fear that you have died. That was when I first knew you were here. Many times, Mama has tried to commit suicide and even said they would go and see Igbala if no other way, to find out what happened to you. But since that time, no way to reach them. No one can post letter anywhere outside Biafra. Post office is now dead. Every day I know what I did is wrong . . . ple—"

"No! No, Tun—"

"Please take me home. Don't go back and fight again, my brother. It is too dangerous, please. Let's jus' go home, or jus' stay here—please, hide here."

Kunle turns around, glances at the trees, at the Agbanis' house, at the sky. It strikes him that after running for ages, he has finally reached the finish line. He could stop now, for this, Tunde, had been the destination. He could stay here and take his brother home if things were still the same. But things started changing, he reckons, long ago. Time and war, like discrete geological forces, have widened his internal geography. Now there is Agnes and the unborn child. But if he stays here, he will need to hide from Biafran military police and conscriptors till the end of the war. And there are also the commandos; for a senior noncommissioned officer, it would not take long for them to find him. How would he find Agnes then? What would become of her and the child?

It is not something he likes to do, but he brings out the pack of cigarettes and lighter Steiner gave him, lights one, and takes a drag. Then a realization comes to him: men are deserting every day. He heard from a lieutenant in the 70th Brigade who came to visit the barracks about how his entire company had deserted. The lieutenant had gone with his orderly to the ordnance supply point at the battalion's tactical headquarters and had returned under shelling to find all of the trenches, including that of his sergeant major, empty.

Kunle crushes the cigarette under his worn boot and gazes into the dark, up at a distant tree where bats are nesting. Then he turns to his brother, on whose face a heavy shadow now sits.

"Don't worry, Aburo," he says. "We will go home."

He assures Tunde that they will go home but says that he has to return to base first; he cannot desert now. From the base, he will try to reach the nurse at Iyienu who'd promised to help him before, and once he has a plan, he will come back to fetch Tunde.

He is still speaking when Ngozika rushes out to announce that her father, Mr. Agbani, has arrived home. Kunle rises to wheel his brother into the house to see the father, but Tunde pulls him down to the level of his mouth and whispers in his ear with urgent finality, "I will kill myself if you die here because of me. You hear, so please, go home!"

27.

AT THE PARADE ground Colonel Steiner, who has shaved his head and has a plaster below his right eye, which is bloodshot, announces that army headquarters has ordered the commandos to defend the city of Aba at all costs. Thus, the division, which he had divided into four brigades in April, must unify into a singular force. Steiner addresses them in the halting English he now speaks, his voice heavier, tinged with inflections of rage. He smokes; half of his face is shadowed by his new green beret, which bears the insignia of a dragon brandishing a sword.

Kunle listens to Steiner's speech with strange indifference. Since returning from Nkpa, two weeks ago, he has found that even the sight of Felix and the other comrades feels like a burden. He no longer wants to be here. He has resolved that unless Umuahia falls, Tunde and Agnes will be safe. The hospital where she works—if she has returned there—is funded by the UN and staffed chiefly by British people and bears the name of their queen; it cannot be attacked.

Steiner, having finished his speech, signals his new special band to begin playing "March of the Foreign Legion." Kunle feigns that he needs to relieve himself, placing a theatrical hand on his belly. He slips out to the little headquarters of the Marine Commando Brigade and settles into the armchair he has come to believe has the most comfortable cushion in all of Biafra. Soon he's dreaming of returning to the otherworld, the sound of light audible, everything glowing brightly. He hears "Kunis" and, blinking, sees Felix's face staring into his. He sits up. "Prof, what happen?"

"Come, come—I am . . ." Felix says.

They go to the back of an abandoned classroom where a pile of trash sits, green flies droning over it. Felix stamps his feet and says almost with a shout, "Kunis, it's over! Is over!"

"What?"

"Everything, Kunis, everything! I have finished with them, these nincompoops!" Panting, his old friend dusts his palms in demonstration. "That is it for me—finished."

"Eh?" Kunle says. He can smell his friend's stale breath. This is one of the things the war has done to them. Even though they have been at the camp these past few days, they have gotten so used to going without washing their mouths or their bodies. No one has cared to use the Macleans toothpaste set up on top of the drum outside the bath tents.

"You did not hear? Just now, GOC—GOC himself!—General Madiebo kneel down and beg Staina and his hooligans!"

They both glance around again, and, seeing no one near, Kunle drops his voice: "Why?"

"They want us to go to start now. Vandals are coming to attack Aba with heavy equipment. Tortoise Division have finished with us, so it is General Adekunle and his gang again—Third Marine Division. Army headquarters want us to defend today immediately, but Taffy has refuse to fight. He refused! Can you imagine? . . . Egwagieziokwu, eh, Staina is a liar!" Felix wipes his brow with the back of his hand, the sweat dripping down his hairy arm.

Kunle licks his lips. He is trying to make sense of what his friend is complaining about: Steiner and the mercenaries have disobeyed an order from army headquarters to counterattack. Felix is now convinced that they are sabotaging the war effort. Ever since Ndidi's death and James's bladder wound—which landed him in a hospital bed in Orlu—Felix has been mercurial and sad, and the scar beneath his left eye from the Enugu raid has given his face a permanently angry look. He now listens to his new Grundig transistor radio with religious devotion. Two weeks after Kunle returned from Nkpa, Felix was glued to the radio, listening to the news about fresh peace talks—this time hosted by Emperor Haile Selassie in Addis Ababa. When the talks failed, everyone noticed the ghastly inflection in Okokon Ndem's voice as he tried to embellish the catastrophic news to the advantage of Biafra: *"According to honorable Pius Okigbo, the vandals, afraid now at the fire and brimstone our able forces—unparalleled in the history of war—will unleash . . ."* Yet the men in the room murmured in anger. After fourteen months of fighting, the floating rafts of Ndem's praise singing has become worn at the edges. They know the news means a return to the increasingly deadly battlefield to defend Owerri.

At one point these men liked the war. They'd fallen in love with the veiled princess only to find, one year in, that there is no beauty in her. Nothing worthy of poetry or comfort—only hunger, danger, sorrow, and violent death. And now they want none of her. But they have to fight. A soldier cannot flee in the face of battle, else the nearest officer to him is obligated to shoot him, as he's witnessed Lieutenant Layla do. Even when one is wounded, he is treated quickly and returned to the front. And if one injures himself and the military doctors at Agbogwugwu army headquarters determine the wound to be self-inflicted, the soldier is court-martialed. Four privates who, before the final battle at Ezillo bridge, had stabbed one another in the belly had been shot in no-man's-land.

Felix has been one of the few soldiers who still carry within themselves the full, undying spirit of the Biafran resistance, which holds that surrendering means the genocide of the easterners. He now spars with anyone who shows less enthusiasm for the cause, even his friends. Now no one challenges him for fear of being seen as a saboteur. Winning each argument only seems to reinforce Felix's confidence, to push back the enemy threatening to breach the gate of his own psyche. Successes further inflate this confidence—whether they are of the commando unit or any Biafran unit, or even diplomatic. But failures hurt him deeply. When he heard that Cardinal Rex Lawson, whose song

"Hail Biafra" Radio Biafra played daily, had defected to Nigeria, he was deeply affected. And now he's begun to complain about the mercenaries because of what he sees as their increasingly fraying allegiance to the Biafran cause.

"Just look," Felix says presently, pointing into the distance at the Italian commander of the marine commandos, Captain Armand, who is standing with the foreign journalist Freddie and Major Taffy's German girlfriend, examining an artillery cannon captured from federal troops. "We are here not doing anything—just look, look, vandals are coming, near, almost inside Aba, but look at what our commanders are doing."

The heat is stifling, and Felix removes his shirt. His torso seems smaller and thinner. He shakes his head. "Egwagieziokwu, I can't be here, playing when my country is burning. Look . . . just look, eh—where is Bube? Where is De Young? Where is Fada, Inamin? . . . Even Agi?"

At this, Kunle feels a bite in his heart.

"Who knows what have happened to her? Look, Kunis, we can't be playing when our friends are dead. So, I am going to join Twelve Division."

"Ah, Prof, no-oh," Kunle says urgently—for it strikes him that Felix might mean this and leave. "No, no . . . Prof—"

"I am going to onoda unit, real Biafran army . . . Ndi was right. Staina and his mercenaries have tried, but they are not one of us. They are foreigners."

From somewhere far away an explosion causes a slight tremor in the ground. They duck under the tree a foot away, and they gaze up at the skies between the branches but see nothing. There have been multiple air raids in the eight days since they returned from the initial failed attempt to stop the enemy advance into Owerri, leaving it to the 12th Division to complete the job. A frond snaps off the palm tree a foot away and falls.

"Yes, Staina helped us," Felix says, his eyes on the branch. "He is . . . his heart is for Biafra. Major George from Italy—okay, he died for us. He fought for free. But what of the others? Look at Marc, Armand, Taffy? Even Roy. All they do is talk with journalist—*Daily Sketch, Daily Mirror,* daily this, daily that! Even Steiner, for how many days did he carry about copies of that *New York Times* paper about our last ambush written by Garrison? He cares more about his photo in a foreign newspaper drinking tea than for us to win this war!"

Kunle does not know what to say, but he has to say something. "I understand what you are saying, nwanne. But . . . you can't desert your post like that. HQ will query you. Just talk to Emeka . . . Please, biko . . . let him talk to colonel."

Felix's face seems to come alive. He shuts his eyes briefly and, opening them again, says, "I am going. Will you follow me or not?"

Kunle feels something small and sharp leap into his throat, and he flinches. One listening to his thoughts can hear that he wants to tell Felix that he wishes to leave not merely a unit but the war itself. Besides, other units are less equipped and would only drag him deeper into the war. But he does not speak. Instead, he fixes his gaze on a crumpled, oil-stained newspaper page flattening itself against the grass, listens to the wind riffling the paper. For a moment Felix's belly makes noises. Felix breaks open a kola nut and puts a lobe in his mouth.

"Sooo, you are not coming?"

Again Kunle looks up—"I . . . Felix . . . there is—"

"Oh, I see." Felix turns away, a bitter look in his eyes. "I see—I am now alone."

Felix does not speak again, does not answer Kunle's frenzied pleas to wait, to listen. What is left afterwards are the deep imprints of Felix's rain boots in the soft earth, and the red worms writhing in their wake. For a long moment, Kunle stands there with the words he could not say lodged in him: that he has also been looking for a way to leave, to rescue his brother, to find his woman and the child growing within her, to return home. There is another bang, and he shudders, as if something with wings has leapt out of him and fled. When it stills, he suddenly feels alone, bereft of the world.

It is a feeling so strong it stays with him all day. In war, every soldier comes to understand that faced with the possibility of cruel and sudden death, what they fear most is being alone. They did not come into this world on their own; they belonged to other people and sought companionship, even in its most cradle form, in the face of the gravest dangers.

He did not think that Felix would leave, but now, as the 4th Commando Division gathers, there is no sight of him. Kunle is shaken as he sits with the orphan boy, Adot, and his Belgian mercenary father, Marc Goosens, in a Land Rover with a red-and-green French Foreign Legion flag glued to the bonnet. Bound to the grille is a fresh eyeless skull and two crossed femurs. As they ride into the night in a convoy of three vehicles, two trucks and a wagon carrying the field hospital tent and the medical staff, a British photographer's camera flashes in the dark from the open-roofed Land Rover. A speaker attached to one of the wagons blares "March of the Foreign Legion," the foreign, orchestral voices mixing with the earthly music of night insects. When the procession enters Aba, the city appears like a long line of red lights in the ocher dark. People are lined on the roadsides, clapping and singing. The commandos greet them with honks and cheers, all except Kunle. He is gripped by the realization that for the first time in this war, he is now alone—with men he does not know.

In the morning, Kunle arrives at the commando division's new tactical headquarters at Aba's Ministry of Justice building and walks to the north side of the compound, where his men are gathered around a dry fountain with a statue of a blindfolded figure holding a scale. At the sight of the statue, Kunle kilts as though a blow has been struck into his side. *Agnes,* he gasps, *please, come to me.* In the distance, smoke is rising into the sky and a crowd of birds are circling above it. He wonders what she might be doing now: Is she sleeping? Has she gone back to the hospital? How is she faring?

Kunle hears voices and, turning, sees the men under his command gathering around him, asking if he is okay. He nods, spits into the red dirt, and cries, "At-ten-shun!" The men stamp their feet. He observes them, most of them new and young. As Chinedu had pointed out, since early in the year, army headquarters has begun allowing everyone who wants to join the army to do so, even conscripting boys in their teens and men of advanced age. These new soldiers wear the new duck-hunter camouflage Colonel Steiner now prefers; those still in plain olive-green camouflages are the more experienced soldiers.

"Bia, Private," Kunle says, pointing to a recruit who has sleep in his eyes and a white smudge at the corner of his mouth. The private looks like a boy, no older than fourteen. His Mark IV rifle, with its numbered wooden butt, is taller than he is.

"Yes, sa!" The boy stands still, his arms straight by his sides, his chest pushed forward, blinking rapidly.

"How old are you?"

"Eh, sa?"

"You no hear English?"

"Am sorry, sa! I hear small-small."

"I said, afa ole ka'ibu?"

"Emm-emmu, twenty, sa."

He gazes at the boy, and for a reason he does not know, something ignites in him. He slaps the boy. The boy falls, rises quickly, and stands again at attention.

"Now I ask you again, Private, how old are you?"

"Am sorry—very sorry, Commander. I am fifteen years, sa. I was born fifty-tiree, sa."

Blood is reddening the boy's teeth and dripping down his jaw. The boy's face trembles and twitches as he struggles against tears.

"Dismiss, Private," Kunle says. "Go and wash your face."

"Yes, sa! Thank, sa!"

The rest of the men are afraid now—of him, of his anger. He brings out a pack, lights a cigarette. "At ease!" he cries, and then he asks them the question he'd wanted to ask. "Who is from Abiriba here?"

None of them, but one of them knows another commando in one of Taffy's four companies, now many kilometers away in the direction of Port Harcourt, who is from there. Kunle returns to the camouflaged command tent in shame: Why had he done what he'd done? Was it fury, shock, loneliness, fear? Was it about his promise to remove his brother from this ruined country? Was it about Agnes and his lack of contact with her? Was it about Felix? Was it his curiosity about the child, *his child,* of which he knows nothing? He cannot tell; he knows only that some presence has overlaid his present life and wrapped him in a thick cloth he can't tear himself from.

He goes out to the main market, where a crowd has gathered to watch Steiner's parade. Many of the paradegoers are gaunt, in tattered clothing. The women's heads are shaved; often a woman will be carrying a child on her back and a load on her head. Earlier, while on reconnaissance in the area with his platoon, Kunle understood that the federal army desperately wanted to capture the city, for they bombed it so badly from the air that it now lies in ruins. They'd passed mostly shelled buildings, charred trees, roads blocked by craters and rubble—in one of them, half of a lorry was sunk into the ground. Beside the crater were the ruins of a cathedral whose bell tower still stands, birds lined up on its roof. Somewhere in the auditorium, a white marble sculpture of the Madonna remains upright, seated with her son on her lap, one of his legs torn off. He could tell that there had been many dead in the church, for the sky was filled with vultures, floating like black kites, the air festering with the fumes of rotten corpses.

He has been standing here for a while, watching the platoon band set up, and it has become obvious to him that Felix did not come to Aba with the commandos. He reckons that this is what has been bothering him all day. When he could not rescue himself or his brother from the war, he stayed back for his comrades and Agnes. Now all his friends and Agnes are gone. The sun has spun on its centrifuge too quickly and turned its dark side, and so, in daylight, on the eve of possibly the biggest battle yet of this internecine war, he is alone.

One watching from above can see that Kunle's mind is battered as Steiner speaks his halting English into the megaphone. The bugle sounds, and Steiner's band of twenty recruits, dressed in fresh duck-hunter camouflage and green berets stamp about blowing trumpets, flutes, striking a bass drum, led by two flag bearers, one of them carrying the black flag of the 4th Commando Division and the other, the Biafran flag. Steiner shoots his pistol, and the band begins singing "March of the Foreign Legion" to the raucous cheering of the crowd.

Above the cheers of the crowd, Kunle hears the boom of distant artillery and cannon fire. Since they arrived in Aba the previous day, they have been hearing artillery—evidence that the Biafran units fighting to halt the federal advance into Aba are slowly withering. It is closer now, for he can feel the reverberations under his feet—perhaps no more than twenty kilometers away? At the sight of such a large crowd, he is afraid. What if there is a bomber now? Will the single anti-aircraft gun protect them? What if a mole alerts the federal bombers to the presence of the crowd? Why, he wonders, is this parade being done in broad daylight? He coughs, and his new batman, the boy he'd slapped, steps closer and answers, "Yes, sa."

"I didn't say anything," he shouts.

In the boy's eyes, Kunle sees a quick, vanishing image of his own brother's—a helpless gaze nestled within a cold iris, like a hidden poison. He'd checked the date on the operational signal: August 22. It has been over three weeks since he was with Tunde, and yet he can still see his brother's red-rimmed eyes as if it were only yesterday, and his brother's persistent voice has continued to plead with him in his head, *Please, go home!*

Another bang rattles the ground. A feeling flames in him as if his heart has drunk from a dark brook. He turns with sudden energy and thrusts his rifle and bandolier into the boy's hands, saying, "Hold it for me, am coming." He goes first in the direction of the shed where the Igbo commanders are. Then, as if pushed from behind, Kunle makes his way towards a narrow path partly blocked by the spilled rubble of what may have been a bank. Again he peers around to check whether anyone has seen him, for the MPs, in red berets, hang at the perimeters of towns and villages where a Biafran unit is garrisoned. He jumps into the building, his heart thudding, gasping, one hand on his chest, the other against the wall.

For a long while, he stays here, dizzy. His throat is parched, and when he spits, there is a tinge of red in the sputum, which leaves a gray shape on the dusty floor. Something lifts its head from the rubble and rushes up a flight of stairs filled with pebbles, glass shards, cushion foam, and the broken parts of chairs, all covered in white dust. The lizard struts up a raft of fractured bricks and wood up the splinter of a wall still standing, almost shaped like the map of an incipient nation; on the bulky fragment, the familiar framed portrait of Colonel Ojukwu hangs, its glass shattered.

He rushes forward, thinking that if only he can remember the way to the creek where the Special Commandos attacked a few weeks ago, he'd be fine—but how would he get there? To his left, a small room—a toilet, damaged, the smell stale and fetid, the latrine filled with bricks and clothes and bits of the roofing sheets. A broken mirror hangs on the blue wall, and in it he sees himself for the first time since the photo he took with Agnes: darker than he recalls being, his face scarred, the side of his head with the shrapnel scar slightly bald, a tooth missing from when the militiaman had struck him, his hair tangled and uncombed, last cut by James with scissors many weeks ago. As if the image of the madman in the mirror has scared him, he heads for the hallway and climbs through a shell hole in the wall.

He bursts out at the rear of the market, wading between empty sheds and blackened tables stacked one upon another. The flies are loud here, gathering around fragments of spoiled meat, vegetables, rotten and deformed. The smell is like a force that propels him so that he veers into a street whose buildings are still mostly intact. He hears a patter of feet and youthful laughter and turns to find three boys in tattered clothes running after him, shouting, "Commando! Commando!"

"Unu gaba!" he shouts at them, pointing towards the market. The boys laugh harder. One of them has on his head a damaged helmet and another, the shell of a fragmentation bomb. He reaches for a stick, stumbles, falls, and at once the children are out of sight.

He rushes towards a house on whose front is a Peugeot 404 being loaded up. A woman is sitting in the passenger seat with a child suckling at her breast. He stops a distance from her and asks which road he can take to Umuahia. He follows her directions, walking quickly towards a dirt road narrowed by a deep gulley in whose pit he can see the remains of many vehicles. He runs into the bush, rips his uniform shirt and rain boots off, Ndidi's paper cross falling out.

When he is on the road again, his faded green T-shirt sticking to his damp back, he can barely hear the music from the market. At last, he comes upon a group of refugees—about ten people and a few children—with just one bicycle between them. For a few meters he ambles behind the group. He has started to feel at ease when he sees first the Biafran flag, then a long truck blocking the road. He jumps back into the bush. Rising, he goes on in the opposite direction, the voice in his head angry and resolute: he will not return, no matter what. If caught, he will say he was captured by federal forces and was trying to make his way back to his men.

He crosses an abandoned railway whose wooden tracks have been removed. A lone boxcar marked ROYAL NIGER COMPANY sits tipped over the side of the rail, overgrown with weeds. The road on the other side of the rail track is littered with cartridge casings and mortar shells, and the burnt carcasses of vehicles. One of them, a silver van, half-burned and overturned, has on its side a familiar legend inscribed in black ink: FREE BIAFRA. Scattered all over the bush are decaying bodies of soldiers, stripped naked or in rotting camouflage, flowers springing from the bodies and mushrooms fruiting between the bones. There are destroyed trenches, almost—it seems—recent, the blackened and decaying dead seated or sprawled in them, maggots writhing in the shell-sized hole in the back of a corpse prostrated against the parapet. A flyer is stuck to the back of the corpse, copies everywhere in the bush. It is a leaflet warning of a "final offensive" and asking Biafran troops to surrender and civilians to go to the nearest town under federal control. Kunle saw one on his way back from Nkpa: the bomber, instead of dropping a bucket explosive, had filled the sky with the leaflets, which fell upon rooftops, trees, strewing the road. He'd grabbed one and read it. On the other side of what looks like a four-man command trench, he spies long, dark ropes—now curling, now twisting. He walks up to the edge and sees that the tails belong to a band of rats eating through a raffia basket of what had been food. Hastening backwards, he steps on a bloodstained bandage caught in the thickets, its end waving like a pennant flag, and green flies explode out of the thicket. He flees.

He stops when it becomes clear that he is again on occupied land, outside a compound of mud huts, fenced with thatch, and a barn, now empty, littered with dead tubers. One of the huts is damaged, its red-clay walls split up into rubble. In the backyard are bits of things: an overturned pot, a bench lying on its side against a dark ogirisi tree, pieces of chewed stick, and fragments of shrapnel, mortar shells, spent cartridges, bloodied rags, and bandages blackened with old blood. He pushes open the door slowly, cranes his head into the damp room. It is empty save for a few books on the floor, swollen and wrinkled, their pages stuck together. He hugs his torso through his thin T-shirt once he enters the room and quickly sits on the floor. He is relieved. It is risky, yes, but if he does not take the risk, he will die here—in a ruined country, for a war that is not his own. Even Felix has taken the risk—left without a discharge paper. No pass.

The words sound so loudly in his head that he looks about. Something has moved on the other side of the house; when he lifts his head, it becomes obvious that it is a door carefully plastered with mud, as if it were part of the wall. Before he can stir, an elderly man appears, pointing a Dane gun at him. He raises his hands: "Biafra army—Biafra army, sa! Pl . . . eas-se, sa, don't kill me."

He sobs, for it feels to him in that moment that he cannot run, that there is no immediate desire to do anything, and if this man so chooses, Kunle will be dead—killed by an old man in a damaged house far from the battlefront.

THE SEER HAS come to be invested in the unborn man's story, and now he watches with his heart at a stop as the old man cocks the weapon. Tensed and shaking, Kunle raises his hands in surrender, weeping and pleading until the old man lowers the rifle. For a moment, the old man stares at him; then, gesturing, he leads Kunle into the other room and shuts the disguised door. The room is stacked with wood and sandbags. A clothesline runs from one wall to the other. The floor is unpaved, a part of it dark from water spilled from the clay pot near the wall. In the corner, a bamboo bed has been balanced upon a makeshift stand of bricks and logs. On the bamboo bed lies the man's wife, half-blackened by burn wounds, her mouth fluted and rimmed by an ugly scar. On a stool by the woman's bed is a near-empty bottle of calamine lotion, the bottle defaced by its syrup. The room is stuffy, and a revolting smell as of spoiled food hangs in the air. But the Seer can see that the unborn man is beginning to relax, for he asks the old man where this place is. "Owerrinta," the old man says, the gun still in his hand. "Owerrinta village."

Gazing into the lamplight, Kunle reckons that the village must not be far from Aba. If he can head southward, he might be able to get to Ikot Ekpene, or at least the Port Harcourt highway. He rises and begins to leave, but the woman cries, "No go! No go!" Kunle stares at the door for a while, but slowly, he steps back and sits in the lone sofa in the room. He is tired, having had little sleep for days. He will rest a day or two, and then resume his search for his brother.

The Seer sighs in relief as the unborn man sits down—safe. The Seer closes his eyes and resolves to take a break. He has seen much, and there is more yet to come. He reckons that some of what he has seen so far—the unborn man's reunion with his brother, the wounds from the many struggles of the past—all bear resemblance to his own wet history. When he was at boarding school, his father had, in a drunken bout, almost killed his mother. And the rift between his parents—which culminated in his mother leaving without him or his sister and never returning—shaped his life. Even after these many years, the Seer still dreams of a reunion with his mother. He once jumped on a bus towards Ijebu Ode, where his mother had moved, like a man intoxicated, but he got off halfway, as if only realizing then that he had no address for where she might be.

He has started to wonder what impact this vision will have on his life. Will he be able to live, knowing that someday in the future, there will be this war and this great suffering brought upon millions of people? And these things will be of consequence only if he is unable to render his vision to those for whom Ifa intends it. Will he suffer the pain of carrying this inside him for the rest of his life?

He tells himself that he should not think this. His master often said it was not a seer's burden to worry about what Ifa chooses to do with the vision lest he take things into his own hands and, by so doing, fall into discordance with Ifa.

The Seer starts to sing Ifa's praises but stops himself so the unborn man will not hear it. He looks up as he ties the ropes of his kembe around his waist, into a knot. The star is for a moment occluded by a dark passing cloud—a floating mass of gray. Once the cloud passes, the star creates the illusion of expanded presence, as if it is trying to draw in others and encircle itself with them. The Seer understands this moment—the birth of the child is imminent. He hurries towards the bowl, and as he sits on his raffia mat, he hears the unborn man's voice.

28.

KUNLE HAS BEEN gazing into the oil lantern for long, and one watching from above can tell that he is uneasy. He senses something coming—a thing whose footfall he hears but whose face he cannot yet see. This feeling started in earnest three days ago, when he stepped out of the house for the second time in the more than two months since he started living with the elderly couple. He's spent much of the time plotting to leave, but too afraid to do so. There are military police everywhere in the surrounding towns, and a Biafran defensive position somewhere to the east. Instead, he passes the time looking after the woman when the old man left to get supplies and reading books—mostly the Jehovah's Witnesses' *Watchtower* magazines the old man occasionally brought him. The woman was wounded during an air raid at a market that also killed her only daughter. The woman had burn scars all over her back, and often sat naked, her blackened body bathed in calamine lotion.

Three nights ago, Kunle walked out of the house, down an empty street. He was afraid he could be spotted, but he longed badly to see the world beyond the half-ruined house. The night was lit by the moon. With Agnes's words about noticing the small things in his head, he stood watching the fireflies dazzling among the brush, serenaded by the deafening whine of crickets and the croaking of toads. Raising his eyes, he saw in the distance a man wrapped in white cloth sitting on a hill. His eyes were fixed on this spectacle, for it bore a wavy resemblance to a vision his mind could not place, until something stirred in the grass behind him. When he returned his eyes to the sight, there was nothing save the dark silhouette of trees. He closed and opened his eyes, but still there was no hill, no man in a white cloak.

For three days now Kunle has been thinking about the uncanny resemblance between this vision and the one he had on Milliken Hills, and the old man and his wife have been asking what is wrong. But Kunle has come to hold on to Agnes's advice to keep such experiences to himself. And this night, after the meal of yam porridge made bland by lack of salt, the old man asks again if Kunle is okay. He shakes his head, his eyes focused on the pebble of yellow flame fluttering in the kerosene lantern. They have used up almost all the fuel, and now the glow is squint-eyed. The old man groans, stifles a belch.

"I hope you are not going outside again."

Kunle looks up at the old man, his wife beside him. "No, sa."

They eat in silence like hermits shut out from the world. Afterwards, he helps the old man lay his wife to bed, clean the wounds, and apply more lotion. Her body is discolored—yellowish in some spots, purple in others, but mostly blackened. Every region of her body is a well of pain. Soon she is snoring, and the old man, rubbing his balding head, tells now of the rumor of the enemy approaching the village, the reason he has not gone out to try to find more kerosene. Kunle listens keenly, as the old man has become, in these two months, his only link to the world. Just weeks after he arrived, the old man told him that indeed Aba had fallen. Kunle wept that night—for the commandos, for Steiner, for Biafra. At other times, he has learned from the man's news the state of the famine, of the scarcity of salt and food, of the lack of petrol due to the federal capture of the oil field at Egbema.

He is thinking about the figure on the hill while half-listening to the old man, when they hear the banging of the door of the room on the other side of the disguised wall. The old man puts out the lantern, grabs his Dane gun and stands behind the door, shaking. They can hear men in the other room arguing in Igbo that this was where "the man" had been seen. The old man looks up at him, and Kunle understands that he has done wrong. Someone in the village saw him and suspected him to be a young man hiding from conscriptors or a deserter. The old man and he know that the men on the other side will hear any sound they make. So, for a while they gaze at each other. Then the wife, waking, says something, and the old man, pointing to the wall stacked with sandbags, cries, "Run!" He picks up his shoes, and at once it seems as if there are no barriers, no door, no sandbags.

Kunle rises from the wreckage of the disguised window, pain in his back, his calves, his head, and blood from some gash sliding down the back of his shirt. He is in the empty street, his shadow galloping ahead of him, merging into the still outlines of the trees. He makes for the deep forest, blood soaking his back, his vision dimming and his limbs strained. After a while he slows to a walk, the moon big above the farmland. His image is framed in the moonlight, carrying his destiny like a hunch on his bent back. Thoughts float about in his head like foreign things: he should head in the direction of Ikot Ekpene, where there is a federal garrison; he should go in search of Agnes; he should find Tunde. At last, he falls between the ridges of two mounds of soil, his eyes hazy, his heart thumping.

When he wakes, the sun is shining and the day is hot. He reckons that it is at least midafternoon. He rushes to sit up, looks about for anyone, but sees nothing save a worn scarecrow and birds swimming above it. He is on a farm, among yam and cassava ridges, the young plants growing in long rows in both directions. On his leg is a praying mantis and, just a few meters away, there's a line of soldier ants. He remembers Bube-Orji's incident, and from a place he cannot understand, he smiles. He digs with a stick for yams but finds, in mound after mound, only small heads of yams with long tendrils. He bites into the raw yam seedlings, swallows, and spits them out.

For half an hour he wades through the thick nearby forest, thirsty and hungry, spitting green saliva still thick with the sharp tang of unripe yam. Sometimes, a wave of anguish rushes into him in the form of fears about the fate of the old man and his wife, or about the whereabouts of Agnes. Because the two times he tried to leave Biafra he got lost, he resolves this time that, despite the dangers, he will stay as close as he can to the roads. But without a map or a sense of direction, the sun shaded by the trees' canopies, he finds that the road is no longer in sight and that he is lost deep in the forest. He picks a snail off a tree, but the dried thing fragments in his hand and there is nothing of it he can eat. He comes upon a palm tree, under which is a scattering of palm fruits. He gorges on them till his belly is filled with the tangy taste of raw oil, and his fingers are red.

It is dark when he arrives at a deserted road outside a village. The road is damaged and littered with what must be the aftermath of an air raid. There is a strong smell of burning, of ash in the air. Amid the clothes, car tires, door of some house, smashed plastic buckets lying about, is a Renault, stopped dead just before a deep crack in the macadam. Its doors are flung open and a man is seated by the open door, one leg hanging out. Something is leaking out of the boot of the car, the quick sound of the dripping liquid filling the night. A gust of wind from some trail to the east comes, sweeping loose ash off the macadam as it passes.

He sleeps in the shell of an Isuzu station wagon parked farther away, closer to the bush. Its tires and front seats are gone, leaving only the worn backseat, the windows smashed in. There is a strange smell of something decayed in it, but it is filtered by the air pouring through the empty window frames. There are belongings under the steering wheel—Jorge wrappas, what seems like a pile of books, sticks, empty cases of cigarettes. He rests in the blue light of the moon. When he opens his eyes again, fireflies are blinking above the roof of the car. He watches them, seeing Agnes's hands cupping them with unusual dexterity that one night in the hospital's courtyard.

In the morning light he finds that blood is all over the floorboard of the wagon, mixed with feathers, rags, dirt, and what looks like human teeth. He picks up an operational signal from under the seat. The edges of the paper are smeared with blood and dirt, but the message is still legible:

OP IMM. 1/7/1968
TO: 2/Lt Moses Nwanya
FROM: Comd 69 Btn, S Bde
SUBJECT: Urgent Rfcm Request

2-in-c on notice. En shelling Osu road. Tps in serious need of rfcm. cas very high. En cas, zero. Please treat as urgent.

Signd: I. N Ebbe
Comd 69 Btn, S Bde

He puts it in his pocket. What happened to the signalman, and why was he here? Kunle looks at the bullet holes in the side of the wagon. There are bloody palmprints all over the interior and on the lone tree outside. He takes one of the *Leopard* bulletins from the pile near the wheel and walks through thick jungle for hours. The dusty haze of the harmattan season hangs over everything, making it hard to see beyond a few meters. And as the sun rises, he begins hearing cars streaming down some road. Like a deranged man, panting, he reaches the road. There is at once a field of grass, an old post office. Men naked to the waist, their hands tied behind their backs, are being shepherded into the post office, on whose façade is painted the Biafran insignia of the rising sun. Two others are doing frog hops along a thin wall, their balls dangling between their legs. He hears a sound from his left and turns: it is a convoy of two military policemen on Honda motorcycles. He jumps back into the forest, dropping the bulletin.

He arrives at a bridge under which a mud-colored river is rippling down steep declines, flowing snakelike through the forest. After he has drunk his fill and is drenched in water, he finds that the bridge leads to a road, one so quiet that all he can hear is the sound of birds calling. The disquiet he feels inflames his blood. Only last week, for the first time in more than two months, the old man asked him about the war: Had he been afraid in battle? And he said yes, but that when he was in battle, he tried to not think about his fear. One cannot dread something about which they don't think. You think about being separated from your family, from your body, from your dreams—that's what terrifies a person. If one focuses instead on the enemy, on his movement and armor, then fear remains only as a shadow rather than a concrete thing.

Kunle stops at a field newly burned, ashes rising from the singed trees and plants, and wonders what can come from this direction or that. Is he in the path of some advancing or retreating troops? As quietly as he can, he retraces his steps, heading towards a different bank of the river—perhaps it would be safer to cross than to take the road. He finds this shore filled with spent cartridges, empty mortar shells, the rusting casing of an Ogbunigwe rocket launcher. Farther down are dead Biafran soldiers, their bodies half-covered by the shore sand. One of them is lying facedown, his body from the waist downwards hidden by the sand.

The smell of the corpses weaves a lump in Kunle's stomach, and he spits repeatedly. He walks with his eyes up, for he's come to find that he must avoid looking at the faces of the dead. If he sees only their bodies, they remain just corpses and rotting flesh, but if he looks in their faces, they become people—*dead* people. He wades between limbless bodies, mangled and shapeless, lying in the gutted earth like piles of old clothes. He steps on a hand with only a shoulder still attached lying in a big halo of dark blood, still wearing its sleeve. He looks down: beside it is a leg lying isolated, still clad in a boot. He shouts, "Oluwa mi oh!" and hastens forward. In the water, there are broken trees, a federal tank floating, uniforms, tree branches, papers, guns, and bodies lying on the surface of the water, arms spread-eagled.

Kunle stops, clutches his chest to stem the tremor in his heart, for it is clear to him now that these are casualties of some recent battle and that he has entered an active area of war. Stepping back a few paces, he runs, in a crouched position, over the bridge to the road.

Something flies past him and thumps into the water. He ducks, falls to the ground, shaking, for a bullet has nearly hit him—only an inch of a shift to the left and he would have been dead. He lies in the rut, a coating of mud on his face, raising his hand and shouting, "No gun! No gun!"

There is a flurry of voices. Men emerge out of the forest, covered in foliage, their faces painted with green leaves, their uniforms worn and ripped, their feet bare. He sees from the bright sun badge on the sleeve of one of them that they are Biafran soldiers.

"Fourth Commando Brigade!" he shouts. "Lieutenant!"

"Stand up and come forward, hands raised!" one of them shouts.

He rises, staggering on his tired legs.

"No! No, come this way. Don't move . . . turn left and come." When he turns, he realizes that the red dirt is uneven where he almost stepped. His heart flies—he came within inches of a mine. "Yes . . . yes, this way—quickly," the officer says, rushing forward to help him up. "They are coming!"

29.

IT IS A story as old as time itself, told across cultures and among all people: a man is thrust into something beyond him and that is not his own, and somehow, by a stroke of luck, he succeeds in it. Here, Kunle—about to be decorated—is standing beside Lieutenant Colonel Joseph Okeke, his brigade commander of the past six months. A tall man who reminds Kunle of Ekpeyong, Okeke has broad shoulders, is older than he by at least two decades, and such a commanding presence that he fits the nickname his troops have given him: "Papa Joe." They are in the center of a room that was once a shoe factory, across a table from commanders of other Biafran army units and the general commander of the Biafran army, General Madiebo.

For nearly three months, Lieutenant Colonel Okeke begins, his 61st Brigade has held their frontline position near the Awka-Onitsha road, in fortified trenches on both sides of the road. For months, federal troops tried to dislodge them with artillery, and the twelve-mile front line became a wasteland filled with shell carcasses and unburied dead. Every attempt at ground assault was repelled by his gallant men, using Biafran-made Ogbunigwe dust mines. Determined to break the gridlock, the federal troops planted a sniper. The sniper, shooting at anything that stirred, rendered mobility impossible even at night.

Lieutenant Peter Nwaigbo here, Lieutenant Colonel Okeke says, gesturing at Kunle, who is now his two-in-c, was commanding this area. Nwaigbo was with his officers in a command foxhole when the sniper shot dead his two-in-c and shot out the left eye of another officer. All day, they heard the violent pop of bullets stuttering across the surface, hitting the dead, meeting used shell casings, nudging sandbags, and raising a continuous cloud of dust. For two days, Nwaigbo and his officers, hungry and sleepless, the dead and dying huddled among them, remained in the foxhole. Then, around two o'clock on the third morning, Nwaigbo raised up an umbrella. When nothing happened for about ten minutes, he and his batman took their rifles and fragmentation bombs and dragged themselves through the debris field, avoiding the paths of their own mines, crawling between the rotting bodies of dead comrades. Two hundred meters into no-man's-land, they saw three men—two of them federal soldiers holding a torch, the third, a white man. The white man climbed a ladder up a tall palm tree, and Nwaigbo lobbed a grenade there. The explosion splintered the tree, killing the sniper, for Nwaigbo could hear a voice shouting, "They don kill Ifanofish! They don kill Ifanofish!"

As all the officers dress Kunle in the garb of a captain, with three stars on his epaulette, and cheer for Captain Peter Nwaigbo, he feels a sense of vertigo—as if he were again having an out-of-body experience. Ojukwu had handed him a medal at the Biafran leader's secret bunker at Amorka only a few nights ago. All of these should make him happy, stir in him some pride. But he feels only a clinging emptiness. He sits beside his commander and tries to focus on the important address about the Biafran army's plan to retake the city of Aba while his mind wavers from thoughts of Agnes to Tunde, to his parents, to the Seer, to Felix. But now he must look closely at the map spread over the rickety table and take notes as General Madiebo issues direct orders to the brigade.

General Madiebo raises his staff and says, "Let us finalize, it is nearly half five o'clock." Without his elegant peaked cap with the red stripe and red emblem bearing the Biafran coat of arms, the general looks different from the man Kunle saw a few times at the Enugu sector nearly two years ago, when Madiebo was the brigadier commanding the 51st Brigade. His face is sun-beaten, a scar across his forehead.

"So, gentlemen, phase number one: Sixty-wan Brigade—"

The other commanders all nod.

"You are to sever all links between Aba and to the south," General Madiebo continues. "Send First Battalion—let them move quickly, eh? Send infantry from Obokwe to Ala-Orji, then link up old PH road. Once you are settled there, send op signal—understand?"

Kunle and Lieutenant Colonel Okeke shout, "Roger, sa!"

"Once they are settled, immediately—and I repeat, immediately—send Second Brigade to the north area, clear Ohabiam. Enemy has no armored vehicle there, only riflemen . . ."

Again Kunle finds his mind floating; this time, it is tethered to Agnes's face as she poses in front of the camera.

". . . then, phase two begins promptly," the general says. "Move your men close to Aba River bridgehead as soon possible, then send more men to clear them all the way to Azumini."

"Roger, sa!" they all shout, and then they all rise swiftly and salute.

General Madiebo wipes a smeared white handkerchief down his neck, gazes up at the ceiling fan, swirling slowly because many of the Biafran power plants have been blown up and the electricity is operating on half current. He gazes at the walls, camouflaged and heavily sandbagged outside, takes up his peaked cap, and they all rattle to their feet to salute.

Kunle follows his commander out of the room, carrying the notes the latter has taken. It is hot, the sun shining at its fiercest. They both unbutton the top of their shirts, the commander making a whooshing sound and shaking his head. Their command car, an old, beat-up Peugeot 404 with two bullet holes in its right rear door, is being refueled by the lieutenant colonel's batman and driver. The driver is siphoning TEL fuel out of a jerrican with his mouth, then plugging the pipe into the fuel tank. In the sun, the car's faded silver paint has turned into a rusty brown. Its headlights are reduced to cracked glass and a bulb perched on the tip of a bunch of naked wires. The floor is coated with dry mud, which has entered the car through holes in the floor from rain-filled potholes. Since he joined the 61st Brigade, 12th Division, Kunle has been surprised at how different these soldiers are from Steiner's commandos. The men are clothed in worn-out uniforms, mostly stripped from captured enemy soldiers or the corpses of fellow Biafran soldiers. Nearly all go about barefoot. Carrying on their clothes trench mud, urine, blood, sweat, and all sorts of dirt, the men smell terrible. Kunle once delayed an offensive march with his company when they happened upon a river; he forced all the men to wash before they could continue. His men were allocated only five rounds of ammunition for every battle, hoping to capture more from enemy soldiers. Yet they've fought, in these months of relentless engagements, with a courage and determination that matched and sometimes surpassed that of the commandos.

As they ride, Lieutenant Colonel Okeke keeps talking to himself, shaking his head. The lieutenant colonel's breath stinks—a mix of phlegm and food. He says something now, then makes the sign of the cross. Kunle can see that the lieutenant colonel is afraid.

"Ehen, lest I forget, Captain Nwaigbo," Lieutenant Colonel Okeke says, turning to him.

"Yes, sa!"

"You can go see your wife and child, o, before offensive start."

"Oh-o, thank you, sa! Daalu," he says, clasping his hands together and bowing in his seat.

Lieutenant Colonel Okeke smiles. "Quickly . . . we have forty-eight hours before H-hour. Go."

They are back in Ala-Orji, fifteen kilometers from Aba, which is occupied by federal troops. Kunle must be careful to find his route in the shrunken mass of land that is now Biafra. In haste, he finds the middle-aged man who serves as liaison for the brigade. The man takes him on his Enfield motorcycle on what feels like a secret road, sandwiched between thick farmlands. For long they are slowed by a gaunt, shirtless man drenched in sweat, pushing a wheelbarrow whose wheels are almost flat, squeaky. In it is the body of a woman, a big chunk of her belly gone, the bedsheet with which she was covered pressed into the hole. Her head bobs from side to side, as if in vehement disagreement, as the man moves her over potholes and broken asphalt. Perhaps her soul is beckoning from the otherworld to this man who loved her to bury her and let her rest. At last, they pass the man, who wears a bitter, horrified rage on his face, and soon they are at a place in the bush where old, rickety cars and lorries are parked.

As he sits in one of the cars, Kunle wonders what might happen this time. His last attempt to leave Biafra scared him so much that he banished all thoughts of fleeing from his mind. The men who caught him asked him his name, and he said Peter Nwaigbo in an accent that drew their suspicion. They asked him to say, "This is harmattan season" in Igbo, and when he could not say it, they thought him to be a spy or saboteur. They'd begun tying his hands when he pleaded that he was a Biafran soldier. He showed them his scars and described the battle of Enugu in detail. They then took him to Lieutenant Colonel Okeke, who, his face darkening, said, "You are a soldier indeed, so now confess to me what happened." In fear, he said only that he had woken up in a federal-controlled village, away from his men, and been taken in by a loyal Biafran family behind enemy lines while waiting to link back up with his men. The commander telephoned the 4th Commando Division and got Emeka, now a major, on the phone. Kunle listened with his heart waging a slow, considered battle as Emeka's voice returned: "The officer was a highly respected officer in Steiner's elite guards. We believe his account to be true." Saved from court-martial, Kunle stood there, gripped by an urge to weep. For he had not been close with Emeka, and suspected that it must have been Felix, having returned to the commandos, who'd prevailed on Emeka to save his life. Later, after the lieutenant colonel requested that Kunle join the 61st Brigade at the rank of lieutenant, Kunle asked why they had not telephoned Steiner instead. The lieutenant colonel and his orderly looked at him with surprise. Had he not heard that Steiner and most of his mercenaries had been deported out of Biafra in handcuffs?

Other reasons have come to deter him from deserting, one being the increasing brutality of the Nigerian troops. At Emekuku, once they broke into the town, they shot everyone—women, children, soldiers, nurses, doctors. Scarier was what was done to the foreigners—Irish priests and nurses, Red Cross volunteers. The federal troops had begun to treat any foreigners they found in Biafra as mercenaries and simply execute them.

The car has entered Owerri, Biafra's new capital city since the fall of Umuahia. He thinks at once that this is not where Agnes would be. There are no houses left, only the ruins of the old ones, destroyed in many months of fighting and occupation by federal forces, and new buildings that have just been constructed. Everywhere there are men in Biafran army uniforms standing or sitting in clusters—some in a bomb ditch, filling up sandbags. There is no sign of a hospital. He turns from the window—in the past few weeks, he's been thinking that she will have had the child by now, that his responsibilities have changed. They are no more to his brother or his parents, but to his woman and their innocent child. If she is not here, she could be anywhere in the small patch of land that is now Biafra—consisting of only two cities: Owerri and Orlu, a few small towns, and many villages and refugee camps. As if on cue, a man drives up, calling for passengers to Orlu, where Kunle has heard the Queen Elizabeth Hospital has relocated after the fall of Umuahia.

In the beaten-down car to Orlu, Kunle is squeezed between two women, one of whom has a suckling child. The child and its mother both appear healthy, if slightly thin. He cannot recall who said it, but someone joked that Biafra is the only country in the world with no fat people. Weeks before he left the old man's house, he saw for the second time a child with kwashiorkor. The old man had found the child's mother outside in the open. The child was thin, wasted to the bones, with a stomach so round and distended Kunle could see the skin on the side beginning to rip. Her eyes were pale yellow, exuding a slow, watery pus that clotted the lids. The child's hair was bristled like a very sick old woman's and reddish. The old man roasted watermelon seeds for the child to eat. Later that evening, they fed the child a wild rat the old man had caught in a trap. The following day, Kunle was left with the little girl, who went into a deep sleep. When she woke, she was so revitalized that she could now move and stretch her dark, wrinkled arms. Some life had come into her eyes, and they looked so different from when she'd arrived the previous day, too weak to cry, a terrible groaning escaping her bone-strewn chest as she'd muttered continuously, "Aguu, aguu, aguu . . ."

Kunle finds the hospital at Orlu, a makeshift place that was once a seminary, now marked with the familiar Red Cross on its roof and walls. Outside, there's a crowd of wounded soldiers and civilians maimed by air raids. On a stretch of mats lay pale-faced naked children, dressed in thin garments of flesh, as if they were creatures in the otherworld. Kunle can nearly see their innards. Between the legs of one of the children hangs a limp, haggard shred of cloth that must have once been pants worn around the waist. Around the crowd, four men hold long sticks with palm-husk candles at their tips, waving them intermittently at the army of vultures that hang on the trees, on the roofs, on the hoods of the parked vehicles.

He joins the crowd trying to enter the facility, but a guard with a long switch refuses to let him in. "Busy! Busy!" the man keeps shouting, scrunching up his nose.

Kunle waits outside under a tree, near a woman whose neck is so badly swollen with a debilitating goiter that he wonders how she is still alive. The woman's intermittent groans strike him like lashes as he watches the door, desperate to see a staff member emerge whom he can ask about Agnes. He is sweating, fanning himself with his pass, when the white doctor he saw at Umuahia comes out, peeling a pair of bloodied gloves from his hands. Immediately the crowd of people begin mobbing the doctor. Kunle joins them, following the doctor as he walks briskly towards a car at the outpost. "Doctor, I just want to know where Nurse Agnes is!" he shouts at the last moment. The doctor stops, craning his neck above the flurry of bodies around him.

"Nurse Agnes Ezka?" the white doctor says.

"Yes, sa! I am her husband."

The doctor signals that the crowd allow Kunle to come forward.

"I am a captain . . . Sixty-wan Brigade in Aba sector, sa. Where is she?"

"Not here, sir, I'm afraid . . . She had her daughter, as you know—in December." The doctor scratches the side of his face, then the arm below his shirt, which is hitched to his elbows. "Is she your child?"

"Yes, yes." He hesitates. "My child—my daughter."

"Oh, congrats, sir. She is well. Nurse Ezka was supposed to return here after maternity, in May, I think. But you know the situation of things . . . we got evacuated in February, you see. She hasn't come here since then. Probably, she does not know we are continuing our service here. I'm afraid that's probably the reason."

"I—"

"I'm afraid I need to get going, Officer. Too much here, you see?"

He nods. "Thank you, Doctor!"

"Good luck and goodbye."

BECAUSE THE 61ST Brigade's men are unpaid, he has no money. Whatever the Bank of Biafra paid the brigade was donated to a local branch of the Biafran "Land Army"—a group of dedicated farmers founded by a proclamation from Ojukwu earlier that year to cultivate every field and prevent the mass starvation of the besieged Biafran enclave—to procure food for the brigade. So, Kunle has made this trip to Orlu by commandeering seats or being given passage out of respect for or fear of the pistol hanging under his belt and the three stars on each shoulder. Now, with the sun setting, he does not know where to sleep. He passes a warehouse turned into a Red Cross feeding station. Two trucks with red crosses painted on them are parked outside, unloading dry-milk rations and stockfish for the sick and hungry villagers in the long queue.

He feels suddenly possessed of a desire so strong he steps backwards, colliding with an elderly woman being helped by another woman towards the line. Mustering an apology, he walks quickly away, determined to do something at all costs. There is a child whom he must live to see. There are his parents, from whom not even Tunde has heard in a long time. Why is there such a tight lid on life, on this world, on everything? He kicks a broken plastic kettle by the side of the street, and the muddy water in it splashes on his trousers.

He turns a corner and stops by a small shelter, in which he can see men dressed in magistrate's robes arguing a case and a man in handcuffs in front of a lone bench. Kunle and the others had been surprised how, despite the war, the court in Etiti had carried on with Felix's trial for killing the saboteur. A few meters from the court, a legless man sitting in the tray of a bleached wheelbarrow raises a placard with inscriptions on it, shouting, "Help! Please help in the name of Ahiara! Ahiara says all Biafrans must be their brother's keeper. Help!" On the shoulder of the bush sits the reddish, rusting shell of an armored vehicle.

Kunle stops under a coconut tree and, thumping at his chest, says, "Look at me, as dirty as a pig. What kind of life is this? I must do something. Let me . . . die, even!" He stumbles, blinded by his own tears, and rises with a fresh pounding in his heart. He will not fight in the Aba offensive—no. There is no longer any purpose to this war, no chance that the enemy will leave or be conquered. And the Biafrans, deeply wronged, will keep fighting without weapons, against an enemy who becomes angrier and deadlier by the day. But most terrifying of all is the coming offensive: How will his ill-equipped division stack up against the twenty-seven Soviet tanks, twelve British Ferrets, and 106mm artillery with hundreds of thousands of rounds the federal army has just obtained, according to Biafran intelligence? Even worse, Nigeria has employed hundreds of mercenaries, many of whom are World War II veterans from the victorious USSR. And worse still, how will they fight when there is no food in Biafra?

His past attempts measled with failures, he wants to be cautious, but the pull on him is one he can no longer bear. He shouts into the air, "No matter the cost, I will never return to front! Never!" He wipes his brow, for he has broken out in copious sweat. He stops by a house from which he can hear a man talking about the size of the cow he bought for his son's wedding; elsewhere inside, a woman is calling a person named Isaac—"Aaasic! Aaaasic oooo!" Before he knows it, he is in the house, pointing his pistol at the three middle-aged men and two women, shouting, "Everyone, down!" At once, all of them are lying prostrate on the ground, their trembling hands over their heads. Not having seen his uniform, the three stars on his sleeve above the rising sun badge and the inscription XII indicating the Biafran 12th Division, one of the men keeps mumbling, "Faa abia go! Faa abia go!" They give him all he asks for, shouting, "One Nigeria!" and pleading for their lives. With his trouser pockets swelling with roasted yam and fried meat and carrying a demijohn filled with water, a T-shirt and a pair of trousers hung over his shoulder, he opens the front door and runs into the bush.

Hidden by creepers and wild brush, he eats the meat. It has been more than a month since he has eaten anything beyond stockfish, snails, termites, grasshoppers, garri, wild fruits, yams, wild leaves, and powdered milk. So desperate have the food shortages become that during the many-weeks-long lull in fighting brought by the heavy rains of April and May, his men began to fraternize with the federal troops. He was asleep near the half-empty trench when he was awoken by men speaking Yoruba. He reached for his rifle, but his men laughed at him. Eight federal soldiers had come with gifts—corned beef, cigarettes, "33" lager beer, and sardines. The men of the two sides knew one another's names. He was confused—should he detain these enemy soldiers who, unarmed, had breached his line? Should he have his men all court-martialed? Then it struck him that in his hand was a bottle of beer, half of which he'd gulped without a moment's thought, and a pack of St. Moritz in his shirt pocket. He himself was already guilty of fraternizing with the enemy whose food was in his belly. So, he merely regarded the federal soldiers with bemused curiosity, wondering how they'd felt when they'd engaged his comrades in deadly battles. Had they harbored hatred in their hearts, or were they fighting merely because they'd been commanded to do so? One afternoon, as his men played a board game with the federal men, he asked them this question. One of them, not knowing that Kunle was Yoruba, said to his friends, "What kind of question is this?" Then, turning back to Kunle, he answered simply, "Me, am not fighting for money o. Jus' make Nigeria be one. Simpu!" The others affirmed this idea with nods. Later, he heard that such a thing was happening everywhere on the southern front, even among the commandos in the unit headed by Taffy Williams, the only mercenary still left in Biafra.

He removes his uniform and puts on the T-shirt and trousers. Where should he leave his uniform? Because there are too many soldiers in rags—like most of his men—he wants them to be found. But with the thought that they might be found by some MP, he throws them upon a tall branch, and they hang, the trouser legs swinging softly like the legs of the paratrooper at Abagana. The medal in the pocket of his shirt, given to him for killing the sniper, he puts in the pocket of his new trousers. Slants of light breaking through the trees' canopies reveal that the sun has begun to lessen in intensity. He has to move quickly, as he has not brought a torch with which to travel through the forest in the dark. Two men in his division, during the rainy season, died of snake bites.

He comes upon a place, quiet and deserted but with a stench so strong he holds his shirt to his nose as he walks. Littered on the dirt everywhere are hessian mats, broken plates, yellowed newspapers, baskets, cartridge casings, a damaged bicycle. A line of soldier ants run along a rut in the red-clay earth, to the root of a large tree, and he walks with his eyes scrutinizing every path, afraid to step on them. Soon he comes upon a strange cluster of plants, dark, large-capped mushrooms, gently stirring in the wind. He makes to wade through them but, hearing a sound, stops. He sees it: a small, wrinkled head turns towards him, its white eyes blinking. He throws himself against a tree in flight. Uttering quick, sonorous calls, the black wings explode into a half dozen vultures leaping into the woods. A lone black feather lands on the ground, around bird dung, dead grass, pieces of cloth. On the spot is a human body still wearing a darkened tunic, half the flesh stripped away and writhing with maggots. One arm is curled above the head, and on the shoulder patch is the dark zigzag insignia of the Biafran S Brigade below the Biafran rising sun badge, still visible. The rest of the uniform is discolored and stained with dark blood, feathers, and dirt.

When it starts to rain, he takes shelter under a cluster of big trees with large canopies. He sits there, hugging his knees, the pistol in his hand with only four rounds in it. As it turns dark, he begins to reckon with what he's done. What would happen tomorrow if, by some miracle, he reached Ikot Ekpene—the closest garrison of a federal unit he knows of? Would they believe his story? What if they suspect that he is a spy of Biafra and shoot him straightaway? How would he prove, beyond speaking Yoruba, that he is Yoruba? He stops, steps back, and stops again. And as if a petulant voice has been trailing him, the last question comes to him again with savage urgency. "Ah, mo gbe!" he cries in response, linking his fingers over his head. Then, as if his comrades or Agnes, who wouldn't understand what he has just said, were here, he repeats himself in English: "I am finished!"

He makes a mad dash in the direction of where he'd hung his uniform, but after half an hour it becomes clear to him that he won't find it. From somewhere beyond the trees, he hears a familiar voice shouting, "Help in the name of Ahiara! All Biafrans must be their brother's keeper. Help in the name of Ahiara . . ." It is at once clear that this is the same beggar he saw earlier and that he has returned to where he left, near Orlu. He sinks to the ground and, raising his hands, says, "Oh God . . . whoever is up there . . . Baba Igbala, please help me! I . . . I want to go home!" Never in his life has he been this confused, this shattered. Not even in the plain of the dead did this happen. That road—what was it called? Even that had not been too difficult to find. If only he'd spoken to the Seer, he'd know what to do now: whether he should head on into the unknown or return and go on fighting.

He moves away from the voice, in the opposite direction, until, soaked and shivering, torn inside, he finds an abandoned shed.

HE WAKES IN the dead of the night to someone singing outside the shed and holds the pistol in firing position. He's heard the song a few times, and it sounds as if it's sung by the spirit of one of his dead comrades:

Onye akpakwala nwa agu aka n'odu,
Ma odi ndu
Ma onwuru anwu
Onye akpakwala nwa agu aka n'odu.

A man with tendriled hair, an old bicycle wheel looped around his left arm, naked from the waist down, appears at the threshold of the open shed, then steps back as if he's seen an invisible barrier.

"Oh," the man says, laughing. "Onye agha ji egbe."

Again the man laughs, swaggering. "I fayah—boom, boom, boom, boom! Fa-yaaah! Fa—yaaaaah! Fa—aaaa!"

Kunle puts down the pistol, relieved—a madman. It is possible the man had been a soldier and the war had caused this. A week or so after Ndidi died, a lance corporal had gone mad at the front. The man had begun complaining that he heard voices in his head and of constant headaches. Steiner had at first declined to release a soldier with no obvious wound from the army. But while resting outside a town, the man rose and began commanding unseen troops, asking them to stand at ease or to fire. Steiner gave the order for him to be taken to Madonna 2 hospital and discharged.

"Gaba!" Kunle says, waving away the madman. "A sim gi gaba! Gerrout!"

The man laughs, stops, an air of terrible seriousness creeping upon his face. Then, his hands still poised in the shape of a rifle and making gunfire sounds, he goes away.

Kunle tries to go back to sleep, but he cannot manage it. Too much has been awakened by the playful acting of the stray madman, too much that cannot be lightly dismissed from his mind. Once he hears the first rooster, he sets out on his way.

Part 5

The EXPLOSION *of the* STAR

THE UNBORN MAN has summoned him again in a time of trouble, and the Seer is moved beyond what he can bear. He watches as Kunle runs, panting and weeping, through the thick bush of thorny plants and elephant grass. The sun is rising and Kunle is drenched in sweat, but even he—the Seer, watching from above—can see that in Kunle stands a mighty will, determined to end this once and for all. And with a man so determined, nothing—not time, not the woods—can overcome him.

It has taken Kunle nearly two full days of walking, but now the Seer can see that Kunle has entered the landscape of his desire: a mangrove forest. It is a dense wooded area floating in water, which, in the sun, looks green and is filled with pins of light. He finds a man with pants hitched to the knee and naked to the waist, fishing with his son. Kunle asks where the nearest federal camp is, and swiftly they mention the name of a village outside Ikot Ekpene. Kunle, pointing the pistol to the fisherman's chest, struggles through his order: "T . . . t-take . . . me to federal barrack!" Quickly, the man and boy settle in their canoe, Kunle at the back, pointing the gun at them. The canoe travels beneath slanting tree branches, pushing between clusters of dead plants poisoned by years of oil spills, their dry stalks like thin bones floating along the river, their roots black. They pass through stretches where the water has a rainbow sheen and its slick, oily surface shimmers, the air thick with the smell of petrol. Overhead, white herons rise and scatter with a cackling sound, and some unseen creature races over the surface of the water, threading a straight line, then vanishing. For a moment, Kunle feels as if he is back in the otherworld, and he breaks into a quiet wail.

At last, the canoe stops at the shore, facing a field burned and dead—a wasteland, as of a world singed and vandalized. For several kilometers it stretches, its sand thick with mire and bearing a sea of dead stumps and litter, including many oil drums sunk in the slough, dozens of herons seated on them. The fisherman points towards the shore, from where Kunle can hear the voices of people speaking in Yoruba. "They are over there, Officer . . . four hundred meters." Kunle gets out of the boat, wet and groggy, his brother's voice in his head: *Please, go home!*

It is difficult to watch, but the Seer steels himself as the unborn man steps out of the bush, into a clearing, with his hands raised, weeping and shouting: "Kunle l'oruko mi! Emi o'n she omo Biafra!" Rifles are pointed at him, and in the commotion, he lies flattened in the muddy grass, shaking, shouting even louder in Yoruba that his name is Kunle, and that he is not a Biafran.

Soldiers in leaf-green uniforms bind his hands behind his back, and drag him into a room, where an Ibibio man telegraphs a mole in the Biafran army headquarters to confirm his identity. He sits against the wall, longing for water, for food. He is left alone, and soon the Seer, watching, can see that it is night. In the morning, asleep, Kunle jolts awake to a touch. He is lucky that the man addressing him says that his identity has been confirmed. A dozen men question him in the open yard about fighting against his own people. One of them smacks him on the face and shouts, "Nazi Sally!"

For much of the day he sits in the open, handcuffed, except when he eats or relieves himself in the bush. He can hardly imagine the abundance of the federal troops—everywhere, even in the smallest quarter of the camp, are vehicles. Tanks, command vehicles, petrol tankers, personnel carriers, wagons—and near the perimeter wall, the remains of a Biafran Red Devil tank gathering dust. The officers are well-groomed, perfumed, in polished shoes. The previous evening, a Panhard drove into the camp, still covered in dry palm fronds and other foliage, with its cannon prominent. He sat staring at it. It looked so formidable that he wondered how in the world he and his comrades had been able to withstand even one Panhard assault.

Rain beats down on him, and all through the night mosquitoes afflict him while he is sleeping in the open yard. The next morning, a man emerges from the backseat of a green Opel Kadett, raises his sunglasses, and cries, "Ah—tani mo n'ri yi?"

Kunle, looks up as if transported out of his body.

"Adekunle Aromire?"

"Mobolaji Igbafe."

It is indeed Mobolaji—one of Kunle's primary school classmates; his parents had moved the family to Lagos after form five. Mobolaji confirms to the others that Kunle is who he said he was. Kunle is then put in a storage room, where he is watched by two soldiers, who attend to him without mockery. Two days later, Mobolaji returns. Kunle was lucky, he says, over beer. These men are fatigued, angry that Ojukwu's "bush rebels" are prolonging the war.

"You see that man there?" Mobolaji points out the window at a scrawny figure laughing and speaking with others, all in peaked caps. "That is the famous General Adekunle—Black Scorpion . . . your namesake. Even him . . . every single one of us wants to finish this thing and go back to Lagos."

The storage room is hot and stuffy, the air thick and dry. The windows are open, but with half the room filled with crates of ammunition and provisions piled to the roof, not much air circulates. Mobolaji tries to cool himself with a leather fan, pausing only when caught in the thick of speech. Kunle tells Mobolaji how he joined and about Tunde, whom Mobolaji remembers.

"Ah, I will try and see if we can get your brother. Third Marine don't operate in that area right now, but I will try."

"Thank you," Kunle says.

"Do you know," Mobolaji says after a long silence, "that someone in Akure saw all this before? Do you know that?"

"Yes." Kunle nods.

"Baba Igbala, the prophet. In fact—" Mobolaji reaches into the inner pocket of his uniform.

The Seer stiffens, for he fears that he is about to witness his own future rebellion against Ifa. Mobolaji unwraps the yellowed page from an old newspaper; the paper has been softened by rain, but the photo of the Seer is still visible on the front page of the *Daily Times,* along with the header: "PROPHET PREDICTS NIGERIA WILL DISSOLVE INTO WAR IN SEVEN YEARS."

"I have been carrying this since I came here. Everyone who sees it is shocked, but look—Baba Igbala saw it."

Kunle confirms that it is from October 16, 1960, fifteen days after independence. Kunle reads the article, surprised that there is no mention of him. Nor has the Seer spoken about what would cause the war, only warning, "I advise Nigerians to learn to live with others who are different from you, from other ethnic groups. This country belongs to everybody."

"He warned us," Mobolaji says, "and as I hear, even gave up his ability to see visions to reveal this. They say he can now rarely see anything because he disobeyed Ifa by giving that vision not to the owner but to everyone." For a moment, Mobalaji does not speak but gazes instead at the yellowing paper, at the young yet familiar face of the Seer. He folds the paper slowly and, with eyes reddening, says, "He warned us . . . why didn't we listen?"

THE SEER CLOSES his eyes and rises, steps away from the bowl. It is confirmed: a time will come when he will break Ifa's command and lose his gift. But he reckons that this, too, is Ifa's will. True, the mysteries are beyond the understanding of a simple man like him, but he cannot help but wonder: When the time arrives, many years from now, and these things come true, what will his role have been in the life of this unborn man, this Kunle Aromire? Will he have been for Kunle a source of confusion and caution? A mystic presence? Or some kind of guide? It seems to him, as he stares into the night, that the answer may involve all of these roles, but mostly the last one. Perhaps this is why Ifa will allow, some twenty years from now, Kunle to see him seated here on this hill that night outside the old people's house. And the same reason why Ifa will break the cosmic boundary between the present and the future, so that Kunle will hear him shout, "Turn back" in that memorable moment before falling dead. And, in times of trouble, for Kunle to call on him. The Seer reckons that Ifa has shown him this vision because Ifa has twinned their fates, and neither's life would be complete without the presence of the other. As these thoughts take shape in him, he feels sympathy for the unborn man.

He sees in the sky a sudden bright light—the star is at its glowing maximum. It is the moment, he can tell, before the great mystery of life happens and a thing is fashioned out of the intrepid darkness of oblivion, into existence. There is in this light eternal a great brightness—an indication that its journey is nearly complete, and the star will soon explode. He can imagine the unborn child's mother on the cusp of delivery, surrounded by people, asking her to push. Beyond the brightness, he can see nothing.

Past this point, his master had often said, one must assume that the vision is ending. It is for the individual seer to know when to remove the amulet from Ifa's bowl and end it. But he does not want to. He closes his eyes and mouths incantations for Ifa to allow him to see all that Ifa wills for him to see.

When the Seer opens his eyes, he becomes certain at once that he's fallen asleep. He gasps: For how long? He glances in the bowl and is overwhelmed by the light, which, to his freshly opened eyes, now feels too bright. At last, what he sees surprises him—it is the unborn man, Kunle, standing before his mother. The Seer steps back from the bowl as if some strange alteration has happened in the scheme of things. Then, gathering himself, he inches closer again, with a burning anxiety to witness that from which he cannot turn away.

30.

THERE IS SOMETHING on the horizon, in the slow drive towards Akure, that moves Kunle. But for a man with a life like his, one whose present moment carries in it the old sickly heart of the past, it is hard to come to a full understanding of things when they first occur. Nevertheless, he can tell, sitting in the car beside Uncle Idowu, that it must have something to do with the fears that will not leave him. And one of those fears comes from something someone he cannot recall had told him: that the end of a thing often bears a resemblance—no matter how vague—to its beginning. And now, as he hugs his mother, both of them sobbing, he can see the resemblance to when, upon Uncle Idowu's prompting, he came home two and a half years ago. It is this fear, that the end may be near, that worries him.

His father, older, with a walking stick, is in tears too. His voice is husky, as if trapped within his throat as he asks: "Did you receive that letter from the reverend sister?"

Kunle nods. He had it until the very moment he was moved from the Eastern Region to, first, a prison in Enugu, then to the Lagos prison, where he stayed for nearly six months, until two days ago, when the prison erupted in shouts of celebration upon the news that the war was coming to an end. It seemed like a strange, awkward dream to him. But soon his new comrades—two men from the S Brigade who'd been in prison since the fall of Enugu—began leaving the cell. Then his name was called and he was told that Uncle Idowu had come for him. They gave him back the clothes he'd been wearing when he was arrested. At once he looked for the letter and his wristwatch, but they were gone.

His family leaves him to himself, and in the bathroom he at first just stands there, overwhelmed by this new world. From the sitting room, he can hear his parents and his uncle's joyful chatting, and then his mother comes to the door, asking, "Is everything okay?"

She speaks English to him now too.

"Yes, ma!" he shouts, and finds that he has responded too loudly, in the voice of one answering orders.

When the water touches his body, he is surprised at its pleasantness. In his two years at the front, he bathed only a few times—most of those during the many weeks at Nkalagu after the fall of Enugu. In these past months, he often remembered himself, Felix, and Bube-Orji bathing in the open at the nearby stream like children. Uncle Idowu wants to leave, so Kunle comes to bid him farewell and thanks him.

"Is okay . . . just rest, eh?"

Kunle nods.

"I will come back this weekend. Don't forget all I said in the car—put the past behind. We will speak to the registrar of your school—maybe they will take you back. She o ti gbo?"

Again he nods.

Later his parents leave him to himself, in his old room, cleaned up for his arrival, bearing all the marks of the world long gone. Uncle Idowu had retrieved his books and belongings from his apartment in Lagos, and now they sit in one corner of the room—the physical manifestation of the many things that now lie asleep in the decaying palace of his dreams. He looks through the window—at the neighbor's yard, an unfamiliar girl grinding pepper on a flat stone. He becomes conscious again of something rising inside him like a fever. He knows at once that it is Agnes. It was she who, through the months of his imprisonment, laid siege to his mind. It was Agnes he saw during the nights when he studied the rectangular reflection of light on the wall of his cell. It was Agnes who sometimes spoke to him as if in a close whisper, so that he often rose from fitful dreams screaming. He hopes with helpless desperation to find her. In her absence, he became aware of her more fully—as if her portrait were being painted while she was with him, and now, in her absence, it has fully formed. And all these months he has often remembered the incredible litheness of her body, how soft she felt despite the stern composition costumed upon her by the army uniform, and the lines of her clavicles when she unbuttoned the top of her uniform. And daily in prison he paraded the image of her in the shrunken van of his thought.

He knows that he will not live on if he does not find out where she is, what has happened to her. So, in the morning, before anyone can wake, he is at the Seer's house. He hears a noise, turns swiftly, but there is no one save a rooster picking at the foot of an old cocoa tree he does not remember. It has taken years, but he is no longer in doubt that before he was born, Baba Igbala, the Seer, had entered the secret chambers of his future and has since walked through his life like an invisible presence. It is a conviction he has come to hold from the months that have turned his life around. He is convinced the man may well hold the knowledge of what he now seeks: the whereabouts of Agnes and his child. And so, after all these years and on just his second day home, he has returned to the Seer's house.

He waits for nearly an hour; he is glancing at his new wristwatch when he hears a cough. He turns and, coming towards him in a steady, rhythmic limp, as if counting his steps, is the Seer. The man is much older than Kunle expected him to be. The Seer stops at the sight of him, steps forward, and examines Kunle's face with his hand cupped over his eyes. Kunle swallows: Has the Seer seen this moment? Did the Seer know that he was coming?

"You?" the Seer says in Yoruba.

"It is me, Baba. E ro ra, sa."

The Seer looks up at the sky, then closely at Kunle's appearance. "Ah, Ifa, Historian of the Unconscious! Many times have passed, but I remember this moment." The Seer, in a movement that feels choreographed—as if an unseen audience were watching—places his right hand on Kunle's forehead. For a while the old Seer feels the scar on the side of his head with his fingers. Kunle gazes into his face, noting the gray hair in his nose, the constant blinking of his eyes.

"Shrapnel . . . shrapnel caused this," the old man says, switching to English in between fits of coughing. "Be-before you die . . . in Abagana. Oh, what a glorious moment to witness your travels in the plains of the dead."

The Seer again lifts his eyes to the sky, and now the familiar words emerge from the old man's mouth as Kunle first heard them fourteen years ago when, on his way to school, a voice as clear as day said, "Ifa, Historian of the Unconscious, Chronicler of Hidden Stories, help me."

The Seer stops chanting, and tears slide down his jaw. "I remember when you returned through that portal, that dark, unknowable road."

Kunle's heartbeat is quickening. There is no doubt that this man has seen what he's claimed to have seen. It is a thing too heavy, too difficult for a mind to contemplate, but he is convinced. This man has lived his life with him, hovering like a spirit whom he could hear but rarely see. What, he wonders, would have happened had his parents granted this man an audience? Would it all have been prevented? If people had heard the true and full story of the war—told by both the living on earth and the dead in the otherworld—before it occurred, would it have been stopped? It is a biting question that must be asked, but there are other pressing questions now, and he finds himself saying, "E joor, e ma binu si mi, Baba."

"Why do you apologize?"

"That . . . I . . . I did not come here before."

The Seer shakes his head and grins, his lower teeth sharp-tipped and dark. "You did nothing wrong, my son. It would not have made any difference. An animal that has crept on four legs all its life does not seek wings at old age . . . Ifa sees what has happened, what cannot be changed. If it could be prevented, then I would have seen that too."

"I have heard, sa."

"Life is like earth, soil—you never know what you will dig up. Only Ifa and Orunmila can see, can know. Let me tell you, fifty or even twenty years from now, the children of those men dead in the fields who may not know or witness what you and your friends have been through might again resort to this. Ears that have been severed from a head do not heed warning signs. It can happen again . . . To stop it from happening, no one can."

The old man, swatting flies from his face and shaking his head, begins walking away.

"Baba," Kunle calls, his heart pounding again. "Please, did you see her . . . Agnes . . . in your vision? Can you tell me if she is safe?"

The Seer once more shakes his head and does not speak for a moment. Kunle can tell that he knows her too. Without turning, the Seer says, "As you must have heard by now—from your friend who captured you—I gave it all up long ago . . . Ifa took it away for disobedience. I am no longer a seer; I am Igbala. Only Igbala. I can't see more than fifty meters away, let alone the future."

Kunle nods. He remembers that Mobolaji said so. "I am sorry, sa."

The Seer laughs quietly. "You did no wrong, my son. It is as it is meant to be . . . Ifa is a custodian of words yet unwritten, of things that have not yet begun their process of actuality. The process has begun—and must be finished." The Seer falls silent, gazing at the patterns of his bare feet and Kunle's shoes on the dirt as if reading something in them. He shakes his head again, leans into his walking stick, and says, "I cannot say more. Go and look for her."

IT IS A charge from which he cannot turn away, one that ignites in him a furious fire. But he knows that his parents, who have suffered much, will not hear of it. So, he stays within himself for two days, trying hard to contain the force that will not leave him and the images that haunt him. On the morning of the second day, as he gazes at steam rising from his cup of Ovaltine, with his parents seated on either side of the dining table, he finds himself saying it: he has to go back to Biafra. Swiftly, his mother throws herself on the floor, her buba coming loose, weeping and lamenting in a strange voice—as if, sometime in the past two and a half years, a hole had been drilled into her throat.

"Omo mi, haaa? After how long, you . . . haaa? Is this how much you hate us—me and your father?"

His father clears his throat only to make his presence known, or perhaps to make his wife see that he is intervening. But he says nothing.

Knowing they will not say more, Kunle leaves the room. He has returned a stranger whom his parents can no longer look in the eye. They speak to him with the utmost carefulness, as if at any moment this child who disappeared for years might be angered to new flight.

Disarmed by his parents' treatment, he keeps to himself. On the third day, he walks out the door into the bright late afternoon light to stare out over the moss-green fence at the Agbanis' old house. In the backyard, a laundry line has been set up. On it hangs clothes belonging to a woman—blouses, a white shimmy, two headscarves pegged together. Last year, the new neighbors came one night and settled into the house, his mother said when he asked who was there. She ran over to meet them, hoping they had been in contact with the Agbanis, but the man who bought the house had not. Who had sold them the house? The man, a policeman, would not say. Only that it belonged to him now.

Kunle wants to tell his parents about the meeting with the Agbanis in Nkpa, how he found Tunde and the family safe. But he can say nothing because he does not know what has happened to them in the many months since.

"You should rest," his mother says.

Kunle nods. He lies in his bed gazing at the bulb, the yellow light diffused by the sun. In it he sees an image of Agnes in motion, her eyes tearing up as she sat in the car beside Sergeant Agbam, the last time he saw her.

He's started to fall asleep, but he rushes to sit up when his father, radio in hand, comes into his room shouting, "Ope oh! Eledumare eshe un oh!" Kunle grabs the radio, signals to his father to let him hear the fast-clicking voice. *"The world knows how hard we strove to avoid the civil war. Our objectives in fighting the war to crush Ojukwu's rebellion . . . We desired to preserve the territorial integrity and unity of Nigeria. For as one country . . ."* Kunle is desperate to hear more, but there is only static and an incoherent jumble of voices. He steps out of the room and another voice comes on, the static retreating: *". . . that the military leader welcomed the decision of the rebel forces to surrender and will address the nation shortly . . ."*

Gently, he sinks down to the floor, sobbing. He can feel sorrow and joy knotted together, both emotions curled within him like caged snakes. When he gathers himself, he throws the wardrobe open, picks out clothing—old now, a trouser and a shirt. His father, watching him, asks what he is doing.

"I am going there," he says. "The war is over! It is no longer dangerous."

He stands up, his voice floating away from him. There is something disrespectful in speaking English to his parents, but he cannot bring himself to do otherwise.

His mother, summoned by his helpless father, appears, her hands gray with dishwater.

"Look at your father. Look at him, eh? Look."

Kunle glances at the lean man who sits on the edge of his bed, his hands, covered in gray hair, clasped together, trembling.

"Ehen, you see?" his mother says. "He is a shadow of himself. Was this how you left him? Ehh, Kunle? Look at how thin he has become . . . how old he is looking." She sighs, touches her finger to her tongue. "And even you—look at how you have been seeing ghosts, screaming every night."

He's embarrassed, for what she has said is true. Only hours before, he tumbled out of a midday nap searching for his rifle, shouting, "Take position!" He realized where he was only when she rushed in, calling his name. He had to steady himself, letting the past settle like sediment upon the floor of the present. He looked out of the window and saw what had caused him such a reaction: a party in the Agbanis' old house.

"And now you say you want to go back?"

She starts to weep again.

"It's okay, Mama Kunle, it's okay." His father shakes his head again. "O ti to."

Kunle has not wanted to speak of it, but seeing their troubles and fearing that there will be no way for him to leave without sharing it, he tells them about Agnes, about the child.

His mother, wiping her eyes, tries to smile. "So . . . we have a grandchild? O, o, Olodumare."

They are won over—if he has a wife and a child, and the war has now ended, then he may go and bring them. But first, they beg him, he must find Tunde and bring him back, dead or alive. This, his father stresses, was, after all, the reason he left in the first place.

He nods. He wants to say that he will do as they have asked, but something in their pleas breaks him. He sinks down to his knees, wraps his arms around his mother's legs, wailing, trying as much as he can to muster the words that linger in his mind: that he is sorry for it all.

31.

As the bus picks its way out of the park, Kunle feels a sudden sense that for the past several months he's been hovering and now he is finally entering himself. The bus moves between hordes of hawkers; one man dangles magazines and newspapers, all declaring the surrender of "the rebels." It has been two full days since the announcement on January 15, yet in all the papers, it is still front-page news. Most have the image of the Biafran vice president, General Philip Effiong, shaking hands with a federal officer, and General Madiebo in the frame. Since the announcement, Kunle has been wondering what the federal army did differently to end the war. There were many times when the federal forces thought the war would end, but it continued. They thought the fall of Enugu would end it, yet it only created a stronger Biafran army. Likewise, the loss of Umuahia only led to Owerri being recaptured. For more than two years, Kunle saw daily the intransigence of the war surprise the armies on both sides, and now it is all over.

The trip takes longer than it used to, the River Niger Bridge having been blown up by the Biafran forces only weeks after Kunle arrived in Biafra. At last, after eleven hours of travel, Biafra suddenly emerges beyond the bus window, as if from ashes. On the side of the road, a pylon, broken near its bottom, bends prostrate, its wires sagging down. Beside it is a big signboard with the inscription THIS IS THE EAST CENTRAL STATE OF NIGERIA. At the sight of the sign, one of the women breaks into a wail.

As they drive through the center of Obollo-Eke, he sees that the wreckage has been mostly cleared, and the town is filled with people. Occasional burnt and rusting carcasses of vehicles lying by the road's shoulders and damaged observation posts are the only signs of the bloody battles that took place here in '67. Near Milliken Hills, two men bear a coffin, trailed by a group of sullen faces. And everywhere, federal checkpoints.

"All of you, down! Come down!" shouts one of the two soldiers manning one of the checkpoints near the hill. Everyone rushes out with their hands raised, chanting, "One Nigeria!" One of the soldiers pats him down slowly, gazing at his eyes, until he notices the scar on Kunle's head.

"Mister-man, who are you? Where are you coming from?"

"Adekunle Aromire, sa! I come from Akure, sa."

The soldier turns to the bus driver. "Na true him talk?"

"We take im for Akure motor park this morning, sa."

"How come you wound for head like this?" the soldier says.

"Accident, sa . . . last year. I come because my brother is here. I want to bring am back. His wife is Igbo . . ."

The soldier waves him on. He returns to the bus, his heart rocking with so much fervor, he has to place his hand on his chest.

"You are lucky, brother," the man behind him says. "Many of them—they have been here for more than two years. They are not okay again. They can kill anybody for no reason."

He nods.

"You are lucky," the man repeats.

They enter Enugu—entire streets lie in ruins. Weeds have grown everywhere, lianas climbing up the walls of houses and fences, snaking through ceilings and stretching out like strange flags. The bus is held up in the heavy traffic of lorries and rickety vehicles, all loaded to the brim. The driver continues through Zik Avenue, where Kunle went with Felix. On the street where the press was, nothing remains save the shells of destroyed buildings.

The sun is starting to set. It's nearly six P.M. by his new watch when he steps out of the bus at Umuahia. He stops in front of a two-story store he recognizes from when he first came in search of Agnes, a Nigerian flag on a pole in front of it. The inscription on its lintel is still as he remembered it: LIVE & LET LIVE VOLKSWAGEN HOUSE UMUAHIA. But there, hanging beneath the lintel, is a banner with another inscription: MILITARY ZONE, KEEP OFF! The streets' boundaries are blurred by extensive rubble, whole sections blending into each other.

Where can he get a bus to Nkpa? Nothing seems the same as it was last time—everywhere people, gaunt, broken, and tattered, beaten by the crude anvils of suffering, are walking or towing rusting bicycles, or riding in ramshackle cars so full they can barely move, or carrying whatever remains of their possessions on their heads—basins, baskets, clay pots, mattresses, bags. Something from some deep sunken hole in his memory rushes up at him: *This war changes us as much as we remain the same.* But he cannot recall who said it. Near the market, he stops at a checkpoint at whose side a dozen Biafran soldiers, dressed in filthy rags, sit on the red clay, their hands tied behind their backs. Flies hover over them, perch on their unkempt hair and on their weather-beaten faces. Their uniforms are so worn it is hard to see which unit they were in.

Kunle comes upon a house whose front side has been destroyed, and from it men with noses covered with handkerchiefs and masks are pulling out bodies. In a wheelbarrow are already dug-out bodies, clothes tattered and moth-eaten, faces thinned to skulls. Kunle seeks directions to the motor park from the men and they tell him to head straight as carefully as he can to the next street, then turn left and move carefully through the rubble for some four hundred meters. He thanks them in Igbo and, bowing, walks on with eager wariness, wondering how all the toil, all the blood, all the courage has in the end come to a waste. Is Felix alive? Is Major Emeka? What of Lieutenant Colonel Okeke? And—Agnes: Where are she and the child?

Has something happened to her? Did she return after all to the hospital? Has she, in all this time, tried to reach him? Has she forgiven him?

He is now near a field filled with mounds, many with palm fronds twisted into the shape of crosses. In a far corner of the field, a few men are lowering bodies covered in hay sacks into the ground. Strangely, he is reminded of his medal—handed to him by Colonel Okeke in a bunker at Amorka, a few meters from the Uli airport. He'd buried it somewhere, together with his service pistol, just before reaching the federal troops. He wonders if he might be able to trace it, to keep it as a memorial. He does not realize he has been saying this aloud to himself until he comes upon a couple seated near a torn-down store, their load beside them. They are both gaunt, their faces and necks covered with thin, wrinkled layers of flesh. They are standing on the edge of the forest from which they have just emerged after weeks of hiding. Once Kunle makes to speak to them, the woman jumps up and straps him in a hug, shouting, "Agha ebi go! Agha ebi go!" He can feel her bony arms tightened around his neck, the quivering of her body as she sobs. Yes, he says, the war has ended. He is close to Nkpa, they tell him; Abiriba is farther away. In fact, they are heading to Nkpa to see their daughter and grandchildren.

The man pauses, clasping his hands together. "We don't know whether or not they are even alive. Only Olisabinigwe knows."

"We will pass Nkpa on the way," the woman tells him, retying the knot around her headscarf. "We pray that you will find your own too."

"Amen," he says, louder than he intended. "Imela nu."

"Ndewo," the man calls. "Ya ga zie!"

"Happy survival!" the woman says.

He squeezes into a car with five others, but the ride is quick, and in less than an hour he is at Nkpa. Even though it is nearly dark, he recognizes the place. There is an old ikoro drum seated on some ancient trunk, and on the edges of the sandy field, a long line of palm trees. He quickens his stride, and even in the near darkness, he is relieved to see that there has been minimal damage here. The village is quiet—

birds calling in the nearby bushes, the restless chirping of crickets. From some hut beyond the sandy road, someone is blowing into a harmonica as a group of people sing, "*We are serving the God of miracles I know, yes I know. I am serving the God of miracles, Hallelujah . . .*" Kunle stands for a moment, listening to the familiar song, which, almost daily, he sang in prison. The conditions in the cells in which the Biafran POWs were held was such that they would have been less endurable than the most violent front, if not for the succor religion provided. On his second day, he was given a Gideons Bible, and through the months of maltreatment by the guards, of strenuous drills, illnesses, hunger, struggles with rats, he read the Bible so many times that he can quote whole passages by heart, the way Felix could Shakespeare's plays. He took solace in singing and praying. Now he crosses himself, saying, "God, please let him be alive. You say if I ask anything in your holy name, you will give it. Please, help!"

He is surprised to find now that he has arrived at the Agbanis' house and is standing under the same ogbono tree under which he sat with Tunde the last time. The beating of his heart reaches a fury. There are no lights in the house, though the front door is open. He hesitates, and then he hears his brother laughing.

HE CANNOT QUIET his brother, so he lets Tunde sob like a boy. The war, though just two and a half years long, has weighed on Tunde like a lifetime. It has created an accelerated world where things change within a short space of time. A man who was seen yesterday, face smoothed by the sparkle of youth, can today become a one-eyed man whose face is delved with a thousand wrinkles, and missing a limb. Here is Tunde, who has grown a beard all over his face; who speaks Igbo with a lilting dialect. Here is Tunde, who has been with a woman. Kunle has been here for less than a day, and already he has come to discover a brother he never knew before, but who is in every way familiar.

This second night, they sit talking in the mud hut that had belonged to Nkechi's great-uncle, the only member of the family who died during the war. In his case, the trouble had been complications of prostate illness because the hospitals had been too crowded, and no doctor had been available for the chronic ailment of an octogenarian.

He listens as Tunde talks about the last days of the war as experienced here in Nkpa. There was fighting in Uzuakoli, where Biafran propaganda had branded the town "Nigeria's Waterloo." For days they heard nonstop federal artillery, and a bomb, perhaps from an aircraft, destroyed a house near the village lake. But that was it. The fighting did not come closer to Nkpa. What they had to suffer through had been hunger and starvation, and occasionally air raids. Nkechi's two brothers survived, Chinedu having fought in the entire thirty months of the war. The other, Nnamdi, was the orderly of one of the cabinet members of General Ojukwu, never going to the front lines. Their father suffered a stroke in November and now mostly lies in bed perpetually listening to the radio, his mouth twisted leftwards, his eyes able to open only up to a slit. The other person who did not survive is one of the reasons Tunde is cheerful: the soldier who impregnated Nkechi. He was killed near Port Harcourt in September. Not long after, Nkechi promised to marry Tunde if he would adopt the child. He agreed and renamed the boy.

"Adekunle is his name," Tunde says, his voice shaking again.

Kunle sits up. "But why?"

Tunde laughs, quietly. "Well, Egbonmi, I was very afraid that they have killed you."

Kunle gazes unsteadily at the empty bowls of vegetable soup and foofoo Nkechi has brought them, arranged on a wooden stool, conscious of Tunde's eyes fixed on him by the light of the kerosene lamp.

"Since you came, I have been thinking," Tunde says.

Kunle pulls himself upright again on the cane chair, in which he has kept sliding down.

"I . . . know, you help me because . . ."

Tunde's wheelchair is worn out and squeaks at every turn, and he's had to stuff old clothes into the seat to cushion the spring. With the blockade of Biafra, no new machines could be imported, and even that which was needed for basic survival was in very short supply. Nkechi comes to the door, her feet clumsy. She, too, has changed. She wears men's clothing, a black shirt and black trousers whose drawstring hangs between her legs. She seems to have acquired a sort of restlessness, as if in perpetual haste—coming in now, vanishing the very next second; asking a question, then quickly dismissing it. This time, she is carrying the little boy, dressed only in a brown cloth napkin wrapped around his waist, against her bosom.

Kunle feels a shudder as she hands him the boy, who, kicking against his arm, breaks into a cry, thrusting his arms wildly for his mother.

"He-he . . . he—"

"Little Kunle is hungry," she says, lowering her voice.

Kunle turns away, nodding. One watching from above can see that, like tidal water breaking into a culvert, Agnes has rushed into his thoughts again, throwing him off-balance.

"Have you finished?" she says, looking at Tunde.

"Yes, darly."

"Mmhuu."

She stacks the plates. Then she leaves, closing the door so gently that Kunle has to look to be sure she is no longer there.

"I know what you are saying," Kunle says. 'Don't worry, Aburo—it is all well now. We just have to—"

"But, Egbonmi, I worry," Tunde says urgently. "You almost died because of me."

Kunle slaps his wrist, hoping to kill the mosquito he felt on it. He folds his hands across his chest.

"You almost died," Tunde says again, gesturing. "Look at everything that happen, eh? I . . . should not have been angry with you all those years, eh, I should not. E wo ibi to gbe wa de."

When Kunle visited the first time, and also this time, he heard Tunde speaking Igbo. Now he almost laughs at his brother's wobbly, badly accented Yoruba.

"You are my brother," he says, his voice lurching from him. "I wanted to bring you back home . . . I didn't know it would take two and a half years."

"And we are"—Tunde bursts into tears—"going home finally."

Kunle feels a cold sensation, as of a wet shawl being placed around his shoulders, as he watches his brother cry. Yet, in some strange way, he now feels most alive, eager—like a thing sprinkled with salt. He rises and puts his hand on Tunde's quivering shoulder, gently rubbing it.

"Is all right. Everything is okay . . . now. I will go and bring my own wife and child, and when I come back—maybe tomorrow or next, we will all go home."

Tunde, still crying, takes Kunle's hand in his firm grip. "Tha-tha-thank you—thank you."

IN THE MORNING, when he stands at the front of the compound, facing Nkechi's mother, Nkechi, and Ngozika, Kunle feels again a crushing desire to weep. In their faces, on their bodies, the scar of the devastation is so visibly written. Yet he cannot shake the thought that they have been some of the luckiest people in all of Biafra. He had not seen it in the night because she'd worn a headscarf, but this morning Nkechi's appearance had shocked him. Her hair was tangled into small knots like the uncombed hair of a boy, and the side of her head was gray from the chalk she rubbed on it to disguise herself as an elderly woman who would be less prone to rape by the advancing federal army. Her smooth skin, which used to be unblemished, was full of pimples and spots. On her is writ the terrible insignia of the war: the altering of every attractive feature in her body.

He has been hugging everyone, and now he embraces her and feels at once a loosening—as if a decades-long understanding has been suddenly struck. He can tell that there is no longer a teenage animus nor childhood affection between them. And it strikes him that one of the wounds of his life—his loss of Nkechi's friendship—has been resolved. He understands that they'd both tied their hands to that one moment of life that changed everything: the accident. And as long as they were bound to it, they could not be friends. Now it seems that they are free and that something has fangled out of the dead body of their old relationship, like mushrooms growing from the rotting corpses of youthful men. She is now his brother's wife, and thus a member of his family.

He leaves them with the baby crying behind him, feeling a strange freedom—as if something that had been bound to one of his vital organs has, after all these years, been let loose.

32.

He did not expect to be so lucky, having found, upon getting here, that Abiriba consists of seven villages and he had never known which one Agnes came from. But the driver at the park in Lohum, excited to receive twice the usual fee for the ride, in new Nigerian notes, says he knows the Azuka family. Kunle sits in the Oldsmobile whose back window has been torn out, covered instead with a translucent plastic bag that flaps continuously, finding it hard to believe that he may have located Agnes without any trouble. What if there is more than one Azuka family—and, ah, what if it was the name of her dead husband? But he does not ask, and soon the driver stops near a white marble cathedral, and says, "If you go down that paved road, just keep going, going, going, you will see a signboard, then Agbala market. That is Amogudu. Stop there."

"Thanks, sa."

"Yes-yes—just go in, walk straight, and you will see their compound. Twenty minutes and you should be there. If not that I must go to Igbere now with this people, I would have taken you inside."

"Daalu," Kunle says.

"Ndewo," the man says. "Happy survival!"

"Happy survival!"

With the sun slowly peeking out of the harmattan fog, he walks for twenty minutes before meeting a group of refugees outside a town that has clearly drunk some of the last and ugliest waters of the war, among them a man on crutches. In a low, treeless field nearby, long lines of trenches wind for as long as the eye can see; all over the field there are black-mouthed holes, as if there had been a thousand hearths there. Everywhere the decaying bodies of the dead are strewn about, some lying partially exposed from shallow graves. Kunle spits till he feels his throat ache. Federal troops are here in abundance, a roofless Land Rover every few kilometers. Kunle slings the polythene bag Tunde gave him over his shoulder and raises both hands as he passes a federal checkpoint. He comes upon a market, mostly deserted, feeling as though he's become privy to some knowledge about Agnes that he will not admit. He stops at a shed into which two men are loading white sacks filled with some kind of powder or grain. The white dust is in their hair, on their eyelids, beards, and clothes. He asks if they know the Azuka family.

One of the dust-smeared faces scrunches, the man's hand on his jaw as he contemplates the request. "Azuka . . . Azu-ka."

"Eee," Kunle says, "they lived in Makurdi—in north before the war."

"Oo-oo ya o! You mean Mbadiwe Azuka?"

Kunle does recognize the first name, but the look on the man's face—of recognition or remembrance—is unmistakable.

"I—"

"Azuka naw—the one who had two boys and two girls. The first daughter naw, nke nurse."

"Yes, yes-sa! Nurse! . . . She is nurse."

"I jus' return yesterday from Owerri. But their house—their house is close here." He points in the direction of a bush, from over which Kunle can make out the outline of houses. "Go past the market, up the small hill, you will see a blacksmith shop. Back of that shop, their house is like this. On yua left . . . Yes, yes—on the left naw. Just when, at the back of the blacksmith shop—that is Azuka compound naw."

"Thank you, sa. Daalu."

Kunle does not walk for long—just past the empty blacksmith's shed, he finds the house. Most of the buildings in this area are intact, but in the next street, all that remains are bombed-out structures and craters. The Azuka house is brown brick with old colonial wooden windows, their frames painted blue. There is a dry banana tree on the side. In the front yard, a pigeon is picking something out of the ground littered with chewing sticks and a desiccated corncob. On the other side, an old car without wheels sits on borrowed legs of wood, a red-headed lizard sunning itself on the hood. There was a legend on its sides, among which were the words "Biafra," "survive," and "future," all blurred out with charcoal. Behind the car, on a clothesline bound between two trees, two wrappas are swinging lightly in the wind beside a man's shirt and two pairs of shorts.

He is looking at the clothesline when a man appears from behind the house, shirtless, the edges of his fingers stained with palm oil.

"Yes, gentleman?" the man says.

Kunle puts his bag on the ground, between his legs.

"Is this Mbadiwe Azuka's compound?"

"Yes," the man says, his face folding into a look of perplexity. "Sorry, who are you?"

Again Kunle feels himself constricting within, tightening around the edges. It has been nearly two years with no word nor sight, and now he sees her face clearly, as if thrown back into a lost time, in the house at Abagana, her eyes staring deep into his own as he made love to her.

"I am," he says, letting the air out of his mouth, "I am Captain Kunle. I am . . . I am looking for Agnes Azuka."

"Oh, Chineke! Oh, yes . . . I recognize you now." The man shakes his hand. "You are the one in that photo she showed us."

Kunle nods.

The man is shorter than Agnes. Yet he possesses the same dimples in his cheeks. The man seems to want to speak, but something holds him back. He throws his gaze instead to the floor, shakes his head.

"Sa—is there anything?" Kunle says urgently.

"No, no, yua welcome." The man throws his hands wide apart as if to sweep the entire place, says, "This . . . this . . . our home. Yua welcome."

THE INSIDE OF the house very much surprises Kunle. It is full—in every sense of the word. The war clearly placed its violent pressure on this place, as a house that once contained a few people now harbors twice that many. Where there must have once been four sofas there are eight, of various colors, moved in by relatives relocating from everywhere. He entered the house half-trembling, but at the sight of the wall covered with framed photos, and the way every corner is stacked with things—clothes, bags, a dusty violin, a carved bronze head of some deity, almanacs—his heart calms. There is a Singer sewing machine with a foot pedal, a piece of Akwa Jorge held above its throat plate, half of it hanging in front of the cabinet. On one side there is an oil drum without a lid, full of clothes.

Something moves, and looking up, he sees that it is a gecko—it is hanging near one of the wall photos, which, he can see now, is unmistakably of Agnes as a young woman, with long cornrows sticking out like a crown on her head; there is another of her wearing a white nursing frock, with her neatly permed hair under a nurse's cap. He looks out the window, where the heat rising off the land appears like a mirage. The man returns to the room carrying kola nuts in a calabash and tells him to sit.

"My brother, please—oo, where is your sister and her child?"

The man merely continues to move forward, towards the small stool at the side of the couch on which Kunle is sitting.

"He who brings kola nut brings life," the man says, raising the lobe of a nut with his now-clean hands. "May this meeting, on this day, with my brother here, bring us . . . life. And . . . peace. Isee!"

"Isee," Kunle says, his tone tentative.

The man offers him a kola nut with a bowed head, and he takes it and dips it in the osee-orji. The pepper stings his mouth at first, for it has been so long since he's had such a thing. At Madonna 1 in Etiti, there was an old man who would bring Bube-Orji kola nuts with this paste, which Felix christened "the weed of Igbo people."

The kola nut calms his stomach.

"You came jus' after my father and senior brother left for the farm," the man says quietly. "It is six kilometers from here . . . It could have been better if they join us, for us to discuss this together."

Kunle glances again at the portrait of Agnes as a nurse.

"Is she here?" he says.

"E bia go." Again the man breathes deeply. "You have come when you have come. Our elders say: the foot of a great guest who has crossed a river to arrive must be cleaned at once before we entertain him."

The man shakes his head and Kunle, with a lurch in his stomach, feels an urge to cry. Something has been broken in the world!

A sudden shout of jubilation arises from the next compound, and the man runs outside. Kunle sits there and closes his eyes. He sees Agnes's eyes the day before the Enugu raid, and hears her voice as if she were speaking to him now, by his side: *Please don't ever leave me again—are you hearing me?* There is a noise, and her brother is seated again, awash in the light pouring into the room through the jalousies. The people in the next house have found their son who had been fighting since '68. And on the face of Agnes's brother Agunna, a rich, mature hope has sprung. The cease-fire was announced on January 12, but the federal army's General Gowon did not ask his men to lay down their arms till the fifteenth, three days later. Since that was only a few days ago, not many soldiers have returned home.

"As you can see, is not only us that is waiting—it's not." Agunna again shakes his head, folds his arms across his chest. "My spirit tell me nothing happened to her. My God is still alive. Nothing . . . nothing happened to her. So, I know she will come back alive."

His temper beginning to rise, Kunle asks what happened, and after a pause, Agunna narrates in detail. Agnes had been here since November '68, a month before she delivered her child. In the months after the battle near Abiriba, in which the Biafran forces retreated hastily, she mostly went underground, hiding in a dug-out hole at the back of the compound during the day. A federal unit was garrisoned nearby, its soldiers routinely dragging women out of their houses and raping them. She wanted to send letters to the 4th Commando headquarters, but even if she passed one through her brothers, there was the risk of it being found, and sending a message to an enemy soldier could get one killed. So, she refrained from contacting him. She was set to return to Queen Elizabeth Hospital Umuahia, but after Umuahia fell, she couldn't. She had started to think of stealing out to a Biafran-held territory to help at a hospital when, on the morning of October 2, a plane strafed the market where their mother had gone to shop. When the remains of her mother were brought in a rag—a piece of her foot, recognized only because it was still wearing the peacock-print sandal Agnes had brought her from Jos, Agnes broke loose. A few days later she vanished, leaving her ten-month-old daughter behind. Two weeks later, two telegrams arrived. The first said she'd rejoined the commandos and was ready to die for Biafra.

Agunna sits forward, folds his hands over his knees. When he starts again, his voice is lower, his breathing heavier: "In the second one, she complained that you'd left and abandoned the war . . . after you'd promised her that you wouldn't. She was angry with you," Agunna says, shaking his head. "Very very angry."

Agunna rises to go in search of the telegrams and returns with a half-knitted baby sweater with a wooden needle entwined in it.

"I didn't see the telegrams . . . it is no longer on the table in her room. Maybe Papa have taken it—I don't even know why I bring this. It is jus' . . . jus' that . . . this is what she was doing when we hear the news about Mama. She didn't even complete the clothes she was sewing for Taata, she jus' go."

Kunle holds up the baby sweater, the sharp-ended wooden needle wrapped in woolly thread, feeling as if he might cry. Quickly, to calm himself, he asks, "Where is the child?"

Agunna gives him a wild stare.

"She is not here. My other sister took her to her husband place in the town after us. She stay there since Agnes went to front. But . . . if you want to see Taata, I can send message and they will bring her come."

"When can they bring her?"

"Mhmm . . . even tomorrow is possible."

The long arm on his wristwatch is moving from the 8 to the 9. He shuts his eyes and shakes his head again. "I want to take her with me until Agi comes back—"

"Ehh . . . ah, no, my brother, no. Mba nu—o buro ka'a esi eme ya. That is not our custom. It is best to wait for my sister—a child belongs first to the mother before the father, especially a girl child. What if my sister returns and can't find her child? She is too small." Agunna coughs and begins chewing a kola nut. "Sorry—even if my sister is here, custom demands that you do the right thing first."

Agunna, chewing, keeps his eyes squarely on Kunle, and now it is he who is uncomfortable. He looks out the window, and what Agunna did not say sounds in Kunle's ears: he has to pay for her head. Without that, he cannot lay any claim to the child. It would insult the family and Agnes herself.

He turns from her brother, his thoughts shifting: perhaps, if he brings the dowry, whatever anger Agnes might have against him, whatever resentment for breaking his promise and leaving, that might sate it. He has returned, after all, not just to find her, but also to marry her.

"E kwe go'm," he says, and Agunna, surprised by his Igbo, smiles.

"O ga dili gi nma, nwannem."

In silence, Kunle watches as Agunna writes down the items for the dowry on the back of an old telegram:

① 1 bottle of schnapps
② 2 tubers of yam or 1 goat
③ 1 roll of akwa jorge
④ fresh seeds of kola nuts

There could be more, but this is an extraordinary time, Agunna says. And if he cannot procure most of these, then at least one or two of the items and the money equivalent of the rest would suffice. They rise together and, shaking hands, bid each other "Happy survival."

33.

AGAIN HE HEARS her voice so close that he sits up, sweating. It has been coming and going for months, and all night he's struggled to sleep in the damaged building he found for the night. The building's front door has been purloined and its windows shattered. The old vinyl carpet, with a floral design, has been torn, and when he tries to peel some of it off, he finds underneath it condensation damp and red worms writhing. There is a shell-sized hole in the roof, and he can see the stars. He should have accepted her brother's offer to sleep on the couch. He slaps his ear to swat away a buzzing mosquito and feels again the dawning of fear. "Darly, where are you?" he says. An engine revs up from somewhere in the vicinity and a vehicle's rods of light climb up the ceiling, graze the wall, and vanish.

Later, even though the sun has risen, the harmattan fog, like gray, immobile smoke, lies in the air, the sun swimming above it like something wrapped in a wet, transparent bag. Near the house are three men repairing a bicycle; beside them, on the shaved earth, is a coffin. Again his heart pounds—all day yesterday he'd seen many coffins and graves. Bodies were being discovered on the battlefields, in garrisoned towns, ruined houses, pools, forests, wells. Some, no one would ever find—

the body in the pool in the forest near Opi, the battle dead lying for too long in abandoned battlefields. Where would they find bodies like Lieutenant Layla's or those of the soldiers killed in the ambushes? Days after he returned to consciousness, he asked Agnes if Bube-Orji's body had ever been found. No, she said, and he wondered who had been burying him while upright in the realm beyond. As he hails a car, he prays again, quickly, that if anything has happened, he should at least be able to see her body.

The car that has brought him to Umuahia stops at the front of what he recognizes to have been Biafra's State House, where once he and the Special Commando Platoon had visited the head of state in his bunker. But this time, a crowd has gathered, watching from across the street, some people shaking their heads as a corpse is being loaded into the back of a military wagon. Armed federal soldiers stand nearby, directing cars away from the scene. He passes with his hands raised, and like the others, once he is near the soldiers, he shouts, "One Nigeria!" Kunle rushes to a man with a burn scar around his neck and on his chest who bears a big basin of his belongings on his head; he is describing what happened. An unsurrendered Biafran soldier was found hiding out in the building on the other side of the road and was shot. "I think say war don end, eh?" the man says, shaking his head. "Why are they still killing people?"

Kunle feels moved by this sight. This is what they feared, the reason Felix and his comrades were prepared to fight to the death. Because of what would happen if they lost. In prison, he heard from a Biafran prisoner about one Biafran unit's bitter defense of the Aba River mouth, how they had to withdraw because of an ammunition shortage. An order for retreat had come, but the entire company, including their commander, refused. They stood there, hurling stones at the approaching enemy tanks, being cut down one after the other. The prisoner, himself in that company, and lucky to have been wounded and captured, told the story with incredulity, shaking his head and saying again and again, "We had brave men . . . brave men."

Kunle takes a few paces, stops. Who is the Biafran soldier that has been killed—who? He hastens back to the spot, wading his way through the crowd to the man with the burn scars, who has begun walking away. "Sa, sa . . . please . . . the person they kill—"

"Ehe, what?"

"Is it man or woman?"

"What?" The man mops sweat from his face, blinking. "Man naw. Na sojaman."

He nods, his heart rate calming.

"Our soja."

A few blocks from the State House, he finds a wagon going to Enugu. Two Biafran soldiers in their olive uniforms, barefoot, their torn clothes covered in mud, sit in front of him in the back of the wagon. The driver rolls the end of the tarp halfway down on the exit side that serves as a kind of door, so they can see the road. A woman who has been brought there on the back of a thin young man cries, suddenly, "Happy survival and Happy New Year!" The others follow. He joins in. But the two soldiers do not speak. One of them, with a chevron on his sleeves, who looks no more than sixteen or seventeen, tries to say the words, but his mouth yields only a bubble of saliva, which dissipates against his lower lip. Kunle wonders what the young warrior is thinking. Perhaps: Have we survived? What is the world that they have left us in? Where do we go from here? And the other, with a bandaged head spotted with blood, sits with his face down, staring at the floor as if ashamed of being here—is he wondering that even if the federal troops, because of the increasing presence of foreign observers, do not commit mass-scale slaughter now, he still might not survive? Does he realize that a new war, a different war, has only just begun—one against the unknown, an enemy more dangerous because no negotiation with them is possible?

Kunle turns away. He might himself be able to win this new war if he is able to locate Felix's house successfully—and if Felix is alive. Now that there is no longer a Biafran army, no barracks, this is his best hope; or else he, too, has to wait until she can return by herself. But how can he wait, and for how long, when he has promised to return in a day or two and take Tunde home?

At a checkpoint just outside Emene, the driver lifts the tarp. A federal officer wearing a black steel helmet climbs in, and the wagon erupts in shouts of "One Nigeria!" The officer points at the Biafran soldier with the bandage on his head, says, "You no talk 'Wom Naigeriah,' Ajukun soda?"

"I talk am. One Nigeria," the Biafran soldier says. "I talk am."

"Na lie, walahi!" The officer slaps the Biafran soldier across the face. "Idiot! Shege banza! Shebi una eye don opem, kwo? Carry gun kwom fight again naw."

The officer lingers, standing halfway in the wagon. "Idiots," he swears again, his breath redolent of alcohol. "Biafra kaput, una hear? Una banana republic, kaput!" He bends his face low so that he is nose to nose with the rival soldier. "You hear me? Kaput! Finish!"

"Yes, sa!" they all bellow.

"Only wom Naigeriah," the officer shouts. "Wom Naigeriah forever!"

Once the officer has left, the passengers turn to the beaten Biafran soldier. Someone gives him a handkerchief to dab at his bloody mouth. An elderly woman at the far end of the row in which he is sitting rises, says in a voice that is not more than a whisper, "We will never forget what you have done for us."

Her words land, as the wagon slaloms slowly towards the highway. Her Igbo is of a stock strange yet familiar—like the kind spoken by the old couple Kunle stayed with.

"Mba nu! How can we? They can kill me—"

"They can beat me, but both of you are warriors. Unu bu odogwu: Ebubedike, Akwakwuru." Her voice dips, softened by an inflection of agony so piercing Kunle turns away. "They did not win this war. We . . . are not . . . we are no conquered."

The boy soldier bursts into a wail. He places his hand over his face, and between his fingers, tears drip onto his thigh.

"What she is saying is true," the elderly man seated by the woman says. "Our people say a person cannot plant yam and harvest cocoyam—"

"Oho-nu!" a man in a worn suit and tie says "See them—they are going up and down bragging that they won. Mmhmm . . . We Biafrans, we fought a war of self-defense, and they don't know that in such a war, what one wins is not victory but justice."

"Yes!" a few shout.

"They planted war and death in our midst," the man continues, "how can they now harvest peace?"

"Oma nme!" the elderly woman says with such vehemence that her wrappa comes loose at the waist. She raises her fist and shouts, "Hail Biafra!"

"Hail Biafra!" they all reply.

Kunle wipes his nose with the back of his hand. There is a feeling again of shame, of what he's done. Perhaps if he'd stayed, if he'd held still against the ground shifting beneath him, they could have won. Perhaps if the many thousands of people like him who ran away had stayed, they would have stood a chance. Oh, perhaps, perhaps! Perhaps he would not at this time be looking for Agnes, for they would have survived together!

"Cry no more, warriors of Biafra." The woman, encouraged, speaks in a vehement voice. "We are not conquered"—again she shakes her head—"mba nu. Don't even think you are humiliated. We will rise again. We will return. Biafra is not dead, umunnem! Biafra will live!"

"Yes!"

"Isee!"

"Biafra is not dead. No! A dream like that, of a people wanting freedom from oppression, cannot be killed with bullets and bombs." As the wagon arrives at a town where one of the passengers wants to get off, the woman speaks with the urgency of finality: "Biafra lives in all of us. It will never, *never* die."

AS HE'D HOPED, he finds the Immaculate High School easily, but it has been turned into a barracks by federal forces. The buildings have been damaged, only the two-story administrative building left almost intact. The statue of the schoolboy remains, with shrapnel chips in its arm and, in its chest, a hole the size of a fingernail; one of its legs is missing. War the brutal blacksmith, he thinks. Not even statues have been spared. Outside the school, a blue-and-white UN jeep is parked. He walks cautiously, past signboards announcing the willingness of the Nigerian government to help the Igbos and images of Ukpabi Asika, the man who is the new administrator of the Eastern Region. A man Felix hated and often called "the god of saboteurs."

Felix's house looks almost as Kunle remembered it, in a street where half the buildings have been destroyed. The family is seated inside the compound—the father and mother eating on a bench on the porch, and Felix's sister braiding the hair of another woman. Their shadows are spread out like wet coats upon the grass in the open yard. He struggles to believe what he sees—Felix's pretty sister, then buxom, now so thin and wiry, her beauty so effaced that looking at her feels like an act of transgression.

He can feel, as he stands, his legs trembling in anticipation of what they will say when he asks of his friend. But, in response, Felix's sister cranes her head and calls out, "Broh-da?" Felix had returned from the war two nights before but is at the latrine, she tells him. Kunle nods, and though there is a settling in his gut, he refuses to sit down, writhing from side to side as if something inside him has been set on fire. Again and again, he wipes the sweat from his brow, writhes, and wipes the sweat again.

Her voice startles him: Would he like some food? They still have some foofoo and onugbu soup.

"No, no—thank you. No."

"My son told me what all of you did for us," the father, who is wearing an Okoko hat, its tail twisted to the side, says suddenly. "I cannot—"

"Oo-oo ya o! Ji-sos Christ! Who is this?"

Kunle turns. Before him is Felix, in a white shirt and shorts that give him the appearance of a child in oversized clothing. They both tremble at the fervor of the embrace. His face is overgrown with beard, and his complexion has darkened. Yet there is richness to his presence, a webby familiarity that at first lifts the weight of Kunle's disquiet and fills him with the same measure of nostalgia he often felt during those long months of prison.

Later, once they're sitting down outside, on two wooden stools a few meters from the house, and Felix has completed his account of how the war had progressed in the last year, during part of which Kunle was in prison, Kunle asks if he knows where Agnes might be. At first, Felix sits silently, twisting a leaf with the scrutiny he once devoted to scribbling in his jotter. Then, as if he's received a signal to speak, he clears his throat, moves his neck from side to side until it makes a sound.

"As I have told you," Felix says, "egwagieziokwu, I was very very angry because of your betrayal of all of us. Of your friends. Of Biafra—of our people! But, when she came back in October, I forgave you."

The arms of Felix's shirt are hitched to the elbows in the manner of commandos, and on his hand is a concentration of darkened skin— the burn wound, he told Kunle, that he suffered when a federal mine set a Land Rover he was traveling in on fire.

"Agi was the same, nwanne—her old self. Brigadier Conrad Nwawo, who took over from Staina, put her in our unit, outside Umuahia. We fought. We did all we could—as you know—no ammo." Felix lets out a tense, bitter laugh. "No ammo—anywhere! HQ, GOC, His Excellency—nobody was able to do anything."

He can sense in his friend a hesitation, a holding back—for certain words, once spoken, can change a world beyond all reckoning. Felix stamps his feet, and repositions himself like a man with a cough trapped in his throat: hidden but malignant.

"It is . . . you see, nwanne . . . many times . . . Sometimes, her uniform was stained with milk, and she would say her child was calling for her. Together with Emeka, we tell her to go back. Even Taffy, the only one of the white people who remained with us. But she refuse . . . She refuse totally. She followed us everywhere, including that time that Twelve Division was compromised by sabos and we were ordered to destroy them. She arrested many of them, killed at least three. Egwagieziokwu, she was brave." Felix shook his head. "One of the bravest soldiers Biafra had. The long and short—look, Kunis, we . . . see . . . we tried our best."

He has focused on Felix with all his strength so far, listening for every dip in his friend's voice, every drag in tone—anything that might suggest the outcome he most fears. Somewhere in the next compound, a shout of rejoicing rings out. Someone—someone lost, it seems—has returned home. He sees that Felix does not look up, and he knows then what happened.

When Felix's voice breaks in again, Kunle feels a shudder. "As you just tell me of your experience for Awka sector, European snipers were also in our sector—everywhere. So, December twentieth . . . no, no . . . excuse me, twenty-fest. I remember—it was twenty-fest! Around five evening-time, near Ugba junction. Federal army sniper fayah her in the chest. She fell, crawl, crawl, crawl for her gun. She tried to stand . . . then . . . another, *kpa!* I hear the sound like this."

Felix raises his head, drops the leaf, its pieces floating in the evening air.

"They were coming, no other way . . . left, right, center, everywhere. They were surrounding us. We fall back . . . We o—we . . . we . . . we leave her body there."

IT SEEMS AS he walks that most of the people are gazing at him. The streets are flowing with people and crowded with vehicles—wagons, semis, cars, lorries, bicycles. It seems, too, that the world is toppling over, keeling. He's known this feeling, encountered it many times before, and thought himself an expert manager of this kind of grief. But now he finds that he knows nothing. In this new world that has been fashioned from the old one, he is only a child.

Felix had urged him to stay awhile: "You can't go out like that after receiving a news like this." But Kunle insisted that he had to give the news to her family as soon as possible, after which he must take his brother and wife back with him to Akure. He'd promised his parents, and they must be getting anxious. And what was more, they must send for his daughter as soon as possible. It is the last of her left for him to have. To this, Felix nodded that he understood.

So Felix led him to a new store near the street and bought one of the items on the list—a bottle of schnapps. Then Felix took him to the new market that had just restarted weeks before, congested with traffic, much of the rubble cleared from this square, appearing like markets before the war. Cars squabbled between clotted traffic, goods spread on tables or on the ground—pamphlets, magazines, books laid out along the edge of the street. Here they bought yams, fresh seeds of kola nuts, and a roll of cloth. It would suffice, Felix said. This was not an ordinary time. "I will see you again soon," Kunle said, and after hugging his friend again, he made for the motor park.

Kunle arrives at the Azuka house as the sun is setting, a bit relieved. He cried in the car—quickly, his eyes doing the short work of the strong release, and it eased him so that he feels more awake. Only now he is more conscious of the growing feeling, of a part of him having been damaged. The three men are there this time with Agnes's sister, a woman who sounds so much like her at first, in the half-light, he wonders if it could be her. To them he gives the account as Felix had told it to him.

The sun goes down while he speaks, casting the gathering in glossy darkness. And Agunna brought a candle on a used tin and placed it on the center table. Once he finishes, it seems that a greater darkness descends on the room. They sit in silence with only Agnes's sister sobbing softly, shaking her head repeatedly and snapping her fingers. But of the men, none makes a sound for a long spell.

Eventually, her father removes his cap and glasses and puts them on the table, and for a time, the three men gaze at the old man. Then, slowly, the man rises and, by the fluttering light of the half candle, unhooks one of her photos from the wall. He places it on the table and, in a voice hushed and low, says, "This is my daughter."

Her father coughs, tries to speak, but his voice is muffled. He lets two lines of tears run down his face and fall to the floor. "This . . . is my . . . is my daughter—ada mu. Do you know her?"

"Yes, I know her," Kunle says.

"As our custom demands, I ask you, her brothers and sister, witnesses, do you know this man?"

"Yes, Papa," they say.

"Is he . . . the one our daughter wants to marry?"

"Yes, Papa. It is he."

He faces Kunle again, his voice trembling, "Do you . . . consent . . . to marry my daughter, the f-f-est . . . fest daughter of her father?"

"Yes, sa."

"We accept your dowry. You are now my son-in-law, ogom. Tomorrow, we will complete the traditional ceremony." The hand with which the father rubs his eyes is wet and shimmering. "Now let me go and lie beside my daughter. It is a grave night."

After the old man leaves, Kunle remains as if fixed to his seat. Will he please stay the night? Agunna asks, standing. It has been a long day for him too.

"I want to see her—my daughter," Kunle says instead.

"Ah, Ogom, but she is asleep."

"Please let me lie beside her too." He places his hand on his head, at the site of the ache he is feeling now, and, lowering his voice, says, "My daughter."

One brother looks to the other, then at their sister and, nodding, says, "Okay, bia-ba." They come to the door, one of the two in the hallway, and at the door, Agunna hands him the candle. Its wax drops on his finger and stings.

"Good night, Ogom," Agunna whispers. He steps away, then turns quickly. "Be careful, she already knows who you are. She is very clever."

He goes into the room, as carefully and noiselessly as he can. His eyes catch, on the high table near the door, the knitting. He takes it, sets the candle beside it, and stands for a while gazing at the pattern, the wooden needle sticking out from the fibers where a second arm had just started to be knitted—an arm that would have been just as long as the other, and that the child would have worn. It is the last thing she had done—*been doing*—before the news of her mother came. He can almost imagine her losing her grip on the knitting in the instant she heard, her eyes closing, the blood rage seizing her. If only she'd finished the knitting, if only someone—her father, their daughter, her brother—had stopped her from going!

Somewhere in the distance, a car honks, and he fears that it might wake the child. But she does not stir, and soon there is only the sound of the night insects again. He sets the candle down beside the girl, and it lights up her face. It is peaceful, quiet, and her mother's. She is curved into herself on the bed, a thumb in her mouth. For a long time, he watches her sleep, unable to decide what to do. He thinks of lying beside her, this thing whose face is much like Agnes's, but he has begun to cry again and worries that he will wake her. He throws himself back and blows out the candle. In the dark, against his wish, he pictures Agnes standing at the carnival of stories in that luxuriant world, encircled by listeners.

How long he'd been sleeping, he cannot tell. But waking, he lets out a scared gasp, thinking the noise is the rattling of the enemy in the bush. He scrambles in the darkness for his rifle, his heart beating wildly. Something falls, making a hollow sound as it rolls away. He blinks—what has he knocked over? He turns and sees a figure kneeling on the bed on all fours, a pair of eyes staring at him in the semidarkness. And before he can speak again, the child's voice breaks through the night, frightened yet assured:

"Daadi?"

THE SEER'S HEART is heavy as he watches the man holding the child, his body rocking with quiet sobs. The child's face is spotlit in the vision, as if all of the world has been reduced to just this face on which is writ the naked eloquence of loss. The unborn man is speaking, summoning his beloved out of the impossible darkness of death. He is telling her not to linger much in the plains, to tell *their* story in the carnival of stories and, once she is done, to head straight to the hills of the ancestors for her rest. Please, do not linger, he begs, as we do not know when we can retrieve your body. He is saying this in a voice too loud for the night, the child watching with silent fear as he calls her name again and again: "Agi, Agi, Agi."

Now the waters go dark, a blackness like that during the moment when the unborn man was being transmitted into the afterlife. The Seer looks up and sees that the star has broken out of its space and is slowly sinking downward, a sign that the child is about to be born. He must end the vision, for one cannot look into the future of a person who has been born. Ifa forbids it. He begins his incantation, his voice as low as he can keep it. But it is necessary to take permission from Ifa to end the vision. So his voice wends snakelike through the path of mystical melody, until he crests the summit of his intercession.

He dips his shaking hands into the water, and in that moment an electric shock grips him as if he would faint. A cascade of images erupt in the screen of Ifa's water. He hears the howling of voices, the soft, drawn-out whispers of unseen people, the rattling of metallic objects, and indistinct sounds that will not cease. His fingers reach for the amulet, and with one quick pull, he draws it out of the water.

THE UNCREATED WORLD has vanished, and Igbala is spotlit in naked darkness as thick as that which covered the water when the unborn man entered the road at the junction between the living and the dead: the road to the country. Above, the star has traveled farther into the ethers, drawing a darkness about it, shrinking as it sails into that early beginning of life. Igbala feels himself strained and tired. He has sat here for what must be at least eight hours, and now he can hear the distant crowing of roosters.

He reaches for the demijohn, raises it to his mouth, and gulps what remains in it. His stomach growls, and he feels in his head a wrangling ache. He lifts the bowl slowly, making sure the water does not spill. Slowly he steps to the edge of the rock and hurls the water into the grass beneath. "The water of life has no recourse to the undesired," he chants. "The shadows of things will not bow before that which does not solicit it . . . *Labolabo* is the cry of the toad in pain, but *lankelanke* is its entreaty to the joy desired . . . Ifa, let the things that you have revealed to me be fulfilled in their time. Let the message you send me to deliver be gladly received."

Igbala sets down the bowl, raises the amulet to the sky, sings the song of enchantments, shaking his head, gnashing his teeth. He raises his fist in the air and cries, "Asheee!"

He climbs down the hill in a rush, leaving the bowl behind, the amulet in his pocket. The sky is lighting up in the slow retreat of night. There are early signs of life, of the fact that this is now March 19, 1947—a new day, one so removed from the future he's dwelt in all night that walking in this time feels unreal. He has arrived at the primary school at the edge of town. He gazes closely at the Union Jack flying outside the school. Beside it sits the new building of a post office recently commissioned by Nigeria's governor-general, Arthur Richards. He walks for a long time along a narrow path, images of Biafra traveling around his mind, until he sees that the star has stopped, resting above a house just outside Oke Aro Road.

The star leads him into a bushy path filled on both sides with things that people have dumped there—a broken bucket, a damaged cyclostyle machine, a clump of corn husks decaying against a rack of putrefying waste. Over these, a clothesline stretches, with a lone wrappa made of rayon on it, waving in the predawn breeze. Against the mud wall, a broken cupboard sits. Something rustles inside it as he approaches, and like a stone, a rat drops out of it and flees into the bush.

He recognizes this brown stucco house, its glazed windows, its surroundings. There, across that road, is where the accident will happen. That house, right now still unroofed, is where Nkechi and her family will move into—seven years from now. He is transfixed for a moment by the awe-inspiring evidence of the vision, this mystical creation of Ifa's eyes, so that when he hears the sudden cry of the baby, he feels a shudder.

He touches the door, then steps back, for he knows how it will turn out. Yet, he wills that this part of the vision will not be as he had seen it.

"Yes?" a sleepy voice calls. It speaks with another, more solemnly, then shouts again: "Ta ni nko ileku ni igba yi?"

"Emi ni," he says, his breathing heavy. "Emi, Igbala, Ojise Ifa."

"Ah," another voice says. He hears more footsteps approach the door and, again, the wail of a little child.

The door opens, and he sees before him faces he can recognize, but now much younger than they will become. First is the father, clean-shaven. He wears a white singlet and a pair of glasses.

"E ku aro, sa," the father greets him. "She ko si?"

"Let him enter first before you ask him these questions," the woman, who is older, says in a strange Yoruba dialect.

Igbala shakes his head. He knows he will be better served if he enters, but he feels apprehension.

"I have a message from Ifa," he says. "I must know if you are willing to receive it or not before I enter your house."

"Message—for me?" the man says, looking back at the older woman.

"Yes." He tries to steady his voice. "It is about your newborn son."

The man glances again at the older woman, then at Igbala. The man blinks, begins to speak, but stops as a woman, looking feeble, approaches, covered from bosom to knee in a piece of wrappa.

"I can hear your voices—who is this?" the younger woman says.

"Igbala, the prophet," the father says, his voice drained.

The younger woman puts her hand to her mouth. The man pulls her back gently, towards a bench on which a small black goat sleeps. Igbala coughs. He can feel the strain in the mother's voice as she whispers to her husband. He waits. The man steps towards the door.

"We don't want whatever you have seen," the man says. "We are Christians . . . We don't believe anyone can see the future, and not the future of our beloved son, who was born not more than two hours ago."

"Wait, what I have seen is grave . . . What Ifa has shown me is—"

"Grave?" the man asks, then looks at his wife's face.

Igbala nods. "Your son is a special child . . . this is why I have seen his star and was led here. There is something that will happen to him that will be rare. There will be—" He catches himself, steps back. "It is grave, but I must share it in full."

They fall quiet, and it seems that the family contemplates his words. Then the woman who has given birth, wincing as she holds the door, says, "We don't want to hear your vision. Please take your divinations elsewhere—we don't use idols and pagan gods in our home."

With a gentle but concerted push, she closes the door. Igbala turns around, facing the horizon towards the east where there is a yellow streak of dawn light, a shadow of the sun in its early emergence. But the star is gone. It occurs to him that this is the first fulfillment of what is to come, and that it has happened exactly as Ifa had revealed it. He has seen much, witnessed the destruction of a nation of people: How will he keep this in? For how long can he carry this burden alone?

He looks up—the horizon has returned to itself, adorned in bright lights as though the long night that came before was itself a dream. The world, asleep before, is now awake, teeming with earthly susurrations and voices, the machinery of life spinning its wheels. Like a merciless stream, life will flow on, carrying in it the yowling joy of birthing, the sorrowful howling of dying. There will be laughter and tears, remembrance and forgetting, pride and shame, silence and noise. Lost in the thrill of it, most people will not look beneath its surface. Even the curious who do look will not see the grave thing that has descended among them, biding its time. Every day the fearful stream will continue its interminable flow, bearing within it the terrible secret vision, so that when the day to be feared arrives it will be as though a thing unwelcome has entered the midst of an unsuspecting gathering—unseen. And, as such, it will be too late to stop it.

Acknowledgments

The Road to the Country is a novel I have always wanted to write and knew I someday would, but the task at first was daunting. A few people helped me, especially my father, Nosike Obioma, who took me to interview Biafran and federal veterans he knew. The structure of the novel was made possible only after a conversation with my mother, Blessing Obioma, who first shared with me the Igbo proverb "The story of a war can only be fully and truly told by both the living and the dead." Thanks to the veterans who shared their stories directly with me. They include Biafran veterans Sergeant Isaiah Nwankwo, Sergeant K Opara, Corporal Isaac Iwuoji, and Private Gabriel Chukwu. Thanks also to Sergeant John Ilesanmi of the Nigerian First Division. Special thanks to Dr. John Phillips, who served the people of Biafra and gladly shared his files and memories with me. And all the doctors and medics who helped, especially members of the ICRC and Joint Church Aid.

I'm grateful to the following for feedback and early advice: Bill Clegg, my agent, and the TCA team! My editor, David Ebershoff, who turned this book around and made it what it has become. And Ailah Ahmed, for her wonderful guidance yet again. Copy editor Bonnie

Thompson for her indispensable eye for detail. Fiammetta Rocco, Linda Jaivin, and Chinaza Joseph for reading. Thanks to the International Committee of the Red Cross, The Hague, for their generosity. And thanks to Merve Emre and Wesleyan University for the space and time to finish the book. Special thanks to Carrie Neill, Brooke Laura, Evan Camfield, David Bruson, Anna Weber, Kalu Osiri, Morenike Williams, Larry Arnn, Manasseh Awuni, Ifunanya Maduka, Judith Mbibo, Ozi Menakaya, Kwame Dawes, Christos Konstantakopoulos, Caroline Von Kuhn, Katerina Papanikolopoulos, and the Oxbelly team.

Though I read so many books, I'm indebted to the authors of several books that were useful in creating the historical background, especially with the "real life" characters in the book: Alexander Madiebo, *The Nigerian Revolution and the Biafran War* (1980); Rolf Steiner, *The Last Adventurer* (1978); Ignatius Ebbe, *Broken Back Axle* (2010); Frederick Forsyth, *The Making of an African Legend: The Biafra Story* (1977); Joe Achuzia, *Biafran Requiem* (1986); Elizabeth Bird and Rosina Umelo, *Surviving Biafra: A Nigerian Wife's Story* (2018); Ken Saro-Wiwa, *Sozaboy: A Novel in Rotten English* (1994); Obi Nwakanma, *Christopher Okigbo 1930–67: Thirsting for Sunlight* (2010); Eddie Iroh, *Toads of War* (1979); Kalu Okpi, *Biafra Testament* (1982).

Finally, thank you to my family, who brought so much joy and peace while I embarked on this journey.

About the Author

CHIGOZIE OBIOMA was born in Akure, Nigeria. His two previous novels, *The Fishermen* and *An Orchestra of Minorities,* were both finalists for the Booker Prize. His novels have won the FT/OppenheimerFunds Emerging Voices Award for Fiction, an NAACP Image Award, and the *Los Angeles Times* Award for First Fiction, and have been nominated for many others. Together, they have been translated into thirty languages. He was named one of *Foreign Policy*'s 100 Leading Global Thinkers. A professor of creative writing at the University of Nebraska–Lincoln, he divides his time between the United States and Nigeria.

About the Type

This book was set in Sabon, a typeface designed by the well-known German typographer Jan Tschichold (1902–74). Sabon's design is based upon the original letter forms of sixteenth-century French type designer Claude Garamond and was created specifically to be used for three sources: foundry type for hand composition, Linotype, and Monotype. Tschichold named his typeface for the famous Frankfurt typefounder Jacques Sabon (c. 1520–80).